Salty are the Tears

Salty are the Tears

Tower of Tears

Tears for Fears

Salty are the Tears

Dawn M. Chretien

Writers Club Press
San Jose New York Lincoln Shanghai

Salty are the Tears

Published by Writers Club Press
an imprint of iUniverse.com, Inc.

For information address:
iUniverse.com, Inc.
620 North 48th Street
Suite 201
Lincoln, NE 68504-3467
www.iuniverse.com

ISBN: 0-595-00560-8

Printed in the United States of America

Epigraph

There is so much good in the worst of us,
And so much bad in the best of us,
That it hardly becomes any of us
To talk about the rest of us.
—**Good and Bad,** attributed to Edward Wallis Hoch (1849–1925) but disclaimed by him; and to many others.

I want to dedicate my first published novel to the most important person in my life, my son Colton, who survived. Patiently he played next to me, without complaint, through the years it took to complete this work. I love you son, with all of my heart. It is you who keeps me going. Secondly, I'd like to thank my Mom and Dad for giving me my first computer, and with it, the opportunity to write. I love you both, with all of my heart. I'd also thank the many unique and interesting people I've been fortunate to happen chance and meet while traveling along the different paths my life has taken. It is all of you who have fueled my imagination and kept me writing. Without you, I could not have written a word.

List of Abbreviations

Abbreviations and Acronyms

AFB: Air Force Base
APB: All points bulletin
ATF: The Bureau of Alcohol Tobacco and Firearms
CEO: Chief Executive Officer
CO: Commanding Officer
CIA: Central Intelligence Agency
CPU: Central Processing Unit
DDO: Office of Signals Intelligence Operations
ER: Emergency Room
FORTE: Surveillance satellite
G Group: SIGNIT analysis group (international communications to and from the US)
GS: Ground Squirrel (fictional code name)
ICU: Intensive Care Unit
IED: Improvised Explosive Device
KH SERIES: Keyhole satellite systems
MMA: Montana Militia of America (fictional name)
MILSTAR: Communications relay satellite
NASA: National Aeronautics and Space Administration
NCIC: National Crime Information Center
NRO: National Reconnaissance Office
NSA: National Security Agency
NSC: National Security Council
PD: Police Department
RR: Rest and Relaxation

SIGNET:	Signals Intelligence
SVR:	Sluzba Vneshngo Razvedky (Russian foreign intelligence agency)
USAF:	United States Air Force

Prologue

September 4

"It must be done. The only way we can guarantee our anonymity. No evil can be passed on from this point. The buck stops here." The man turned to the window from his executive chair and puffed on his cigar. "This land will remain as it always has, ours and under our control."

September 5

His right hand, thin and gray, lay limply in his lap like a stroke victim's, while the other hand hid his eyes from the visions shadow dancing across his mind. His head bobbed forward, making spittle form at the corners of his tightly drawn mouth. He looked as if he dozed off into an unexpected nap.

He bit down on his tongue intentionally, clenching his teeth, grinding them in a calming rhythm back and forth. He squeezed back the pain he felt consuming his entire body from the oncoming clouds of swirling demons laughing at him inches from his face, making his eyes glaze with fear. His head felt like a watermelon ready to burst, so full of noises screaming back at him that he knew an explosion was near that would take his sanity.

They were unrelenting, surrounding his head, roaring back at him like a cage full of lions in fury, yelling appalling things that he could not bear to hear. They were pushing him beyond his limits. The demons were back, and it scared the living hell out of him.

He needed to beat them. He mastered them before, he prayed he could do it again. They were gaining on him, he felt it. Time was missing again and he could not account for his actions. The metallic taste burned his mouth like acid, reminding him of other times it lingered on his breath after days slipped away from his memory. A foreboding crawled over him like a thick web. He slowly sank to the floor, losing consciousness as the fiends chasing him drained his will away.

September 6

The knock on the door came at exactly the same time every Thursday. At one o'clock the doctor opened the door and escorted her patient into her private office. The man wore a long black coat with the collar pulled up and a dark scarf around his neck. The hat on his head was pulled low over his forehead. Behind the dark glasses, he kept his eyes a secret.

Frank Morrow had been her patient for over a year, and he was still a mystery. She felt she was closer to unraveling his past that he had no conscious memory of, a past that so far, started unraveling slowly a horrifying life of torture, abuse, and in the end, murder.

September 6

"Lucas, I have some guns in the back I just took possession of today. Add them to our stock." The heavy man wiped the sweat from his forehead. He watched his partner walk to the back. An evil grin covered his ugly face. He continued arranging his latest jewelry they collected from the unfortunates who pawned their goods today. He locked the display case and smiled.

Chapter 1

Friday, September 6 at 8:00 P.M.
Montana State University Fieldhouse
Bozeman, Montana

The crowd resonated throughout the domed Fieldhouse like rolling thunder in a lightning storm. Their mood generated electricity, infectious. The back up band for the world famous Eagles, Runnin Ragged, appeared on stage.

The heat intensified inside, just as the inferno blazing inside of him, threatened to explode. A bead of sweat formed on his dark brow, then dropped slowly onto his beaked nose, lingering there long enough that he could smell the odor that he knew well.

His parched tongue caught the drop as it rolled down. Salty. He loved salty things, olives, pretzels, Margaritas, and yes, thick rich blood.

Shaking his head wildly, and cracking it towards the ceiling, his eyes popped open. The springs behind them snapped. His head felt trapped in a vise, deliberately squeezing his skull. The lights flashing overhead blinded him, sending his mind flashing back towards provoked madness.

A man, standing in the crowded auditorium at stage center, slowly lifted up his right arm, pointing at the band as the chorus repeated again. Sliding the sleeve of his jacket slightly back with his left hand, he poked a silver barreled handgun a fraction of an inch outside the cuff. He fired twice in quick succession at his target dancing in front of his eyes, singing her heart and soul out, inflaming the crowd.

The chorus repeated for the last time. "Bitten by your bug, I'm falling for your love, It's taking me flying, but now I'm crying. Can't you see?

I'm dying for your love." Her voice faltered, and the music died. The pulsing heart of his prey spurted crimson.

The ca-boom, ca-boom of the gun blasts rang in his ears, creating an uproar within the crowd. A memory flashed across his mind of the bells, bells that rang early every morning before sunrise. Squeezing his eyes tightly, he struggled to destroy the next glimpses he knew would arrive inside his mind's eye.

The auditorium fell in utter silence as Jennica's body flew through the air, then crashed to earth like an angel with broken wings, an angel on her way straight to hell.

Falling off the stage and into the crowd, she gracefully took flight as easily as she sang her gripping love songs. She landed in the arms of two cowboys who caught her between them like a football pass before she hit the cold ground. They stared at her, still mesmerized by her bewitching voice and now, at the blood soaking her white vest. Both men peered into her pale face. They followed the trail of crimson as it rolled down their dusters and onto their polished boots.

Screams gathered, gaining momentum throughout the house, as the realization overpowered the crowd. Witnesses to a senseless and gruesome shooting. The horror-stricken faces on the two cowboys holding Jennica mirrored the crowds. Chaos consumed the entire Fieldhouse like a firestorm.

The five band members on stage rushed forward. Looking down over the edge, fear filled their hearts at the sight of Jennica lying there, her life draining away. Panic rose as they watched. Surreal. A slow motion horror movie. A nightmare alive in the eyes of the audience forever.

Two security guards ran forward from the back of the stage talking frantically into their radios. A petite blonde from the band named Diana, identically dressed like the woman laying in her own blood, turned her head and fainted before the words forming on her lips escaped.

The guard in charge spoke into his radio as he felt for her pulse. "Stryker, Point, send more ambulances and get every available patrol here, now. It's turned into a nightmare." He directed the other guards to make way for the ambulance crew standing-by at the back of the building. The guards battled the crowd, keeping the area clear for the ambulance. A delay in the departure of the ambulance to the hospital risked the life they desperately wanted to save.

Replacing his radio, the senior guard examined Diana. Her body felt like a block of ice and her lips turned blue. Recognizing the signs of shock, he reacted instinctively. "Quick, grab something to keep her warm. Take off your jacket," he said, instructing the other security guard to help.

The second security guard started to follow his orders, grabbing his sleeve, when the senior guard holding the young woman bellowed back at him.

"There." He motioned above him to a black curtain hanging down beside them. "Rip that down. She's in shock and needs to get warm now." The first guard yelled even louder back at the second guard. The roar of the panicked crowd fleeing to every exit sign made hearing almost impossible.

The second guard yanked at it until it came sailing down. It landed on top of the senior guard holding Diana. Wrapping the curtain tightly around her, he pulled her in close. He continued to hold her while monitoring her vital signs, waiting anxiously for the ambulance to make its way from the back entrance of the building.

Looking out at the mass of people jammed up front, screaming at the top of their lungs, he realized the situation had spun out of control. Hordes of people trampled one another as they made their quick exit. It was an unexpected chain of events on an ordinary Friday night.

He shook his head, took in a deep breath, and hoped the fans wouldn't charge any closer. The rest of the security guards on duty fought the crowds who rushed forward to get out of the Fieldhouse as the chaos continued. It was impossible to keep the fleeing fans at bay with Diana in his arms, while they waited for the medics to first attend the critically shot Jennica.

A man cloaked in a heavy gray duster tripped as he ran for the back doors with the mob. His mind chased him like the north winds, stalking him from every angle with no escape route. Voices screamed at him from within in an indiscernible language he didn't understand. They sounded alien to him, shrieking, then clashing together like giant cymbals with the other noises, filling his ears, exploding in his head, causing excruciating pain. He distinguished one sentence from the screeching, "Run you fool."

He ran harder as the voices carried their message to him. Run faster. He sucked in a deep breath, his lungs filling with oxygen, giving him one last chance to push harder for the finish line.

He turned around to catch a glimpse of where he had come. Feeling a great sense of loss creep into his conscious, it ate at him, until he felt a chill run through his body so cold, it felt like he entered a walk-in freezer with no way out. It shut his mind down and left his teeth chattering uncontrollably.

People were everywhere, scurrying in all directions like ants on an ant hill. Stopping dead in his tracks to take a second look, he turned back, but the crowd behind him didn't stop. They dashed past him, pushing him down to the floor.

Groaning, they kept coming at him. A rush of frantic people who desperately wanted out before other shots fired around them.

An MSU Policeman watched the man as he fell. The swarm kept coming, trampling him further into the floor. Dashing to him, he helped him to his feet.

"You all right, sir? Can you walk?" he said, looking up and down at the man and scrutinizing him for injuries. He seemed dazed, but unharmed.

The man wore a tall tan hat with a wide brim, pulled down over his head, shadowing his eyes from the partial lights. Eyes appearing like two tiny slits in a full rounded face. The man returned a nod, and smiled appreciatively, signaling he was okay.

The disguised man quickly turned, hurrying and blending with the frightened exodus of fans.

Squinting up ahead, everything looked hazy. Patting his pocket and feeling nothing, he realized he misplaced his eyeglasses. He felt curiously strange. Searching his mind for an explanation, none came. He continued to stumble forward with the crowd.

Sirens echoed, becoming louder as they approached the opened back door that anticipated the arrival of the extra ambulances and police. It had been eight minutes since the shot and most of the county's law enforcement officers had responded. The officers controlled the crowd, clearing a path to Ms. Jennica James.

The two cowboys holding her in their arms gently placed her back up on the wooden floor of the stage. The band gathered around her, anxiously waiting for help.

Josh Tate, the drummer, dropped to his knees beside Jennica as Scott, Josh's brother, followed his lead, drawn to the scarlet color of the blood pooling beside her body and trickling down her white vest. Their rage infested eyes poised a silent question to one another across the short span of her bloody chest.

Scott shook his head, shrugging his shoulders, trying to deny the mounting questions screaming through his mind, filling him with morbid fear. Scott bent closer to Jennica's face, placing his cheek next to her ash gray one, touching it softly, then kissing it. His body started to shake violently over her, as overwhelming grief consumed him, rendering him useless to help.

"Is she breathing?" Josh stared at his brother, watching him. "Here, move away, let me check." Josh tossed his hat out of his way, brushing back his sandy blonde hair from his eyes and wiping the sweat from his forehead.

Josh knelt closer, listening for breathing or air touching his cheek. He looked down at her chest, seeing no movement. His own heart beat wildly under his jacket, sounding like a huge drum roll. He reached two fingers to her throat feeling down her neck for a pulse and found none. He felt tears escaping his eyes. "Come on, Jennica, don't leave me. Don't leave us. God, no. Please don't take her. We need to start CPR right now."

Ripping open her leather vest, he heard the metal buttons flying everywhere, hitting the floor in a loud chorus like rain pelting off a tin roof. He found her breastbone and started giving chest compressions as the rest of the band looked on like frozen caricatures of themselves.

Scott stroked her bare arm stretched alongside her body, the sweat dripping from his forehead. The bright lights overhead blazed down upon them, making the scene glow with fear.

Josh moved quickly to Jennica's head, pushing Scott out of his way with one powerful arm. "Please, get out of the way or get down here and help me." Josh screamed at him, anger directed towards him as he stared directly into his brother's eyes. For the first time in his life, Josh saw fear flashing behind them.

Scott couldn't move, paralyzed by the horror. He started shaking his head. "I can't. I don't know how. I'm sorry, Josh. I'm so sorry Jennica." He crawled away, gulping down the vomit forcing its way up his throat.

"Where are the EMTs? They should have been here by now. God, we can't just stand here. Go and try to get them up here. She's dying. Can't you all see? Jennica is dying," Josh said.

His voice shrieked into the open space of the stage at the band. It echoed back into his ears. "No, she can't die." Josh said.

Taylor Young and Perry White, the last two members of the band still standing in panic over Jennica, finally took control and ran towards the back of the stage at Olympic speed. They made up the time they had lost being immobilized by their own fears.

They reached the emergency personnel making their way through the crowds. Armed police escorted the entourage. Both men waved their arms wildly for them to follow, yelling, "She's bleeding to death, hurry this way."

Perry and Taylor ran, leading the medics and police who pulled and pushed away the curious bystanders and the horrified fans that stood in shock and blocked a clear path to Jennica.

Four medics started checking Jennica's vitals, stabilizing her body, then they placed her on a board for transport.

Two additional medics relieved the security guard who cradled Diana in his arms. Helping them as they took a quick blood pressure and pulse, he picked her up and placed her on a stretcher. She was out cold, and pale as white tissue paper.

Kate, the band's manager, and Martin, the youngest member of the band who ran the sound and lighting systems, finally made it to the back of the Fieldhouse by the stage. They both hurried together through the mauling crowds to reach Jennica and the rest of their band on stage that resembled a composition of horror.

Martin took the lead and held Kate's hand firmly. He pulled her up the steps to the stage as he kept their way cleared. A young police officer grabbed his arm and held them back before reaching the top.

"No, Officer. Please let us go. We're part of the band. We need to be with them. They need us right now. Can't you see? Jennica needs us. We're family." Kate pulled away, ready to lash out if he stood in her way for another minute longer. Tears started filling her eyes as she looked back into the young officer's solid green ones, reading concern in them for her. She breathed in deeply, trying to get a grip on her emotions that were wildly swirling in a vacuum of dread.

"I'm sorry, Ma'am, but I have to keep you here. Orders. You can't do anything up there now. Let the emergency crews do their job. It's the only chance she has." He spoke calmly, trying to ease the tension between them. He held them on the stairs.

Kate and Martin watched as Taylor and Perry helped the paramedics secure her on the transport cart. The seconds ticked by as they worked over her.

Policemen kept the stage open and clear of curious spectators while others on the bloody stage started securing the scene with yellow tape to preserve it.

The policeman forced Kate and Martin into looking at the scene from a distance by shadows and outlines. From what they could see, the scene frightened them to the core.

Kate's eyes filled, then they burst with a floodgate of tears. Suffering in her own agony at having to stay away and watch from the side lines. She felt as helpless as an abandoned child at Christmas time.

"My God, what happened here tonight?" Kate screamed into the dark dome above. Martin pulled her closer into him, shielding her from the torment he witnessed flickering behind her eyes. The words fell from his mouth, heavy and in a drone. "It's going to be okay. It has to be."

Chapter 2

Friday, the 6th day of September, 8:00 P.M
Law & Justice Building, Detectives Division
Bozeman, Montana

"Della, get your buns of steel over here and sit down for a minute. We need to talk." Dylan lifted his head of dark hair from his paperwork long enough to catch Della's perfect silhouette staring out the window, then stretching the length of her body towards the ceiling like a cat rising slowly from a long nap.

She heard Dylan, ignoring his enduring comment knowing that's all it was. Della felt restless. She let her eyes wander slowly over every inch of the barbed wire fortress that contained the jail next door.

"Dell?" Dylan said.

Della turned slightly towards him bending at her trim hips. "Did I hear you say talk?" She easily touched the toes of her black boots, hearing the sarcasm in her voice. She held her stretch, hiding her questioning face behind her long mahogany hair. She held her stretch for a second more, then reached between her legs further before coming back up. Her silky hair partially covered her face as she cocked one of her dark eyebrows towards him, gazing with her violet eyes glowing. Standing like a graceful panther ready to pounce, she waited, knowing his next words.

"That's what I just said." He smiled at her waiting for another one of her catty remarks.

"Do you think that's possible?" She flipped her hair back out of her eyes, quickly checking his face for a sign that he understood her meaning. She knew it was hopeless, but she was willing to keep trying. She turned back slightly towards the window, watching a family appear from the dark parking lot and into the bright lights at the entrance to the Gallatin County Detention Center. Visiting hour at the jail. What a place for a family reunion.

"Yes, we do need to talk. Business." He emphasized business clearly before continuing. "The report I have here on my desk that you just finished, isn't complete. Or at least by my account, it doesn't match mine. We were both there. We have to agree."

"Think there's a chance we ever will?"

"Come on. Stick to the subject, please." He realized his voice hit a plea at the end in hope tonight she'd leave him be. He flew the papers down across his desk with a flick of his powerful wrist. "If you don't help me with this, I'll keep you here all night and you'll miss your workout. You wouldn't want that to happen, would you?"

"I'd love to spend the night with you. There are other ways of working out, you know."

"I'm serious. You know that's impossible."

"Impossible? I'm serious too. Nothing's impossible. You're the one making it that way. I wish you'd give us a chance. But since I know you better than you know yourself, you'd just stick to the damn report anyway."

"That's right. So, let's get on with it." Dylan caught the disappointment in her face before she turned away from him and back to the window.

The jail stuck out like a giant cinder block caged into submission. It moved Della's bleak mood straight into a depression. She tried fighting it, but after listening to Dylan's words playing back in her mind over and over again like a broken record, she found herself in uncontrollable misery. She needed to get away for a while. Time away from him. Then maybe, she could get on with her life.

Della felt overwhelmed by the work piling up around her, computing in her head the time it would take to get ahead. She figured conservatively that eight hours might just do it. She had been training with Detective

Drake for six months. She felt her spirit of hope draining. Dylan would never take her seriously.

She felt an uneasiness inside that made her jumpy and excited over the smallest things. She knew those feelings had accompanied her everywhere she went for the past couple of weeks. It was a nagging worry she couldn't pinpoint. She kept thinking she might get in touch with her feelings, but just about the time she thought she was, they eluded her. Voices spoke to her low, too low for her to hear. She tried to fine tune them. Letting her mind wander again, she wanted to solve the mystery.

She decided Dylan wasn't the only object of her misery, but it could be just the changes with the Bozeman PD moving in with them at the Law and Justice Center. She felt like a rat trapped in an overcrowded maze mixed with too many politicians and lawyers to make her feel comfortable. They were learning to live together like one big happy family. It all sucked big time.

She rubbed her arms up and down, trying to relieve the goose bumps attacking her smooth skin, sending a rush up the length of her slim body. She let out a little sigh as it finished running the course of her body. Della almost forgot Dylan for a moment. She turned, catching him staring at her with his omniscient eyes.

"Are you all right?" Dylan raised his eyebrows in a comical show.

His green eye color transformed into different shades with his mood swings, just as a Moonstone ring did, changing colors with the person's mood. Now the color reminded her of the Granny Smith apple she just finished from her late dinner. Della laughed at the thought, as she pulled up a chair across from Dylan, wondering what he really thought behind those killer eyes.

"What's up?" Dylan said. "You're distracted more than usual tonight. And I think if I recall yesterday, you cruised off and took a trip somewhere without ever leaving your desk. Care to let me in on it?"

"No. I don't think you want to know." She let out an indignant sigh, grabbing a pencil off the table. She rolled it back and forth between her palms, picking up speed and enjoying the warmth that came with it between her cold hands.

Dylan grabbed the pencil from her rotating hand, snapping it in two. He chucked it over his head and across the room like a discarded cigarette. It pinged on the metal desk as it hit, rolling off, and landed on the linoleum floor behind them.

Della jerked her head up in surprise, meeting his eyes that melted hers with just one look.

"Stop fidgeting. Get a pen and correct this report." He slid it over to her. "Besides this, we have this." Dylan lifted a manila file folder bulging with papers up from his desk. "Half of this is yours. If you don't get serious, I'm going to leave you to do it all. I'm tired. Tonight I'd like to be in my bed before sunrise." Dylan pushed by ordering her around like one of the flunkies, but he enjoyed getting a rise out of her.

Dylan stood, circling Della sitting at the table. He walked over to the window looking out into the night hoping to find what had held her attention for so long. Nothing he could spot caught his attention. He utilized his investigative eye, scanning a few cars parked askew in the gravel parking lot around the front of the Law and Justice Center and a couple closer to the jail. It appeared to him that only employees' cars from the Detention Center and a few county vehicles were left at this hour. The parking lot was crowded when they arrived at five. He decided Della's mind must be as overworked as his.

He flipped the blinds shut, turning towards her. "There. Now maybe you'll stop daydreaming and get some work done. You've become quite a slacker lately." He waited for her pesky reply but none came. He realized she had finally started writing. He walked over, brushing the light switch with his back. The small room turned pitch black like the outside of the building. He knew it would be a minute before either of them could see again.

Della screamed.

Dylan stifled a laugh.

"The lights. What happened?" Della said. A snicker came from across the room. "What are you doing? I thought you wanted this paperwork done. Turn the lights on. Come on. I can't see. Besides, I don't trust you."

"What? You don't trust me? But I'm your partner." He slipped off his loafers, tiptoeing towards her.

"That's right, and you're despicable."

"Tell me what's eating your brain and I'll reciprocate by turning the lights back on before anything bad happens to you." He roared with a demonic grunt, slithering behind one of the partitions separating the desks in the room.

"No, it's personal. If I could tell you, I would. The truth? There is nothing to tell. So drop it, okay?"

"So, are you turning into one of those air heads?" Dylan said. "I don't think so. And I'm not buying your 'nothing to tell'. You'd be better off spilling your guts right now before I have to start requisitioning blonde hair dye so you'll have an excuse to act this way." He kept his tone lively, hoping to not spoil it. He wanted to extract a confession, something he prided himself in being good at.

"You can just kiss my ass, Dylan. Now, will you just turn the lights on and get back to your precious report."

Dylan sneaked back to the table, dropping to his belly, crawling closer until he was a foot from her feet under the table. He reached out, grabbing her by the ankles and pulled her off the chair in one quick yank. He heard a thud.

"Why you dirty son of a bitch," Della said.

He grinned in the darkness as he raced back to turn on the lights. He flicked the switch eyeing Della sprawled out on the floor rubbing her beautiful derriere, glaring at him with a crimson face. She extended her long arm out towards him, giving him the finger. The only sign language she knew he understood.

"Della, be nice. I was just trying to teach you something about covering your ass at all times." Dylan walked smugly back to the table where Della still lounged, trying to compose herself from his surprise attack. He rescued his half of the papers off the table and returned to his desk, busying himself with the stack. He kept one eye pinned to her in case she sought immediate retribution.

They both passed faces of hate and discontent back and forth to each other without saying another word for the next fifteen minutes.

8:00 P.M. Gallatin County 911 Dispatch Center, Law & Justice Center

Grace Weber, the Gallatin County 911 dispatcher, sat reading a training manual on self-defense, scratching the top of her wiry red hair, turning the pages slowly. She wished for her shift to end painlessly after pulling too many long hours here and at her second job at a group home for troubled teens. Her eyes sagged further into her cheeks with every word she managed to read. Making a living in this town wasn't easy, and one day it would catch up to her.

The Friday evening shift crept slowly on in silence, with two calls made by citizens witnessing a minor traffic accident on Main Street. The black and white clock glared at her, 20:13, reminding her to take a short break. The other dispatcher had to leave because of an emergency and a replacement was on the way.

Grace stood up, stretching her tired legs, walking to the coffee pot on the counter. She picked the glass pot up, swirling the black liquid around and around and observing it as it passed in front of her red lined eyes. It looked better than usual. The coffee made by the deputies usually made her gag. They referred to the black oil slicks floating in their cups as their one and only true savior, declaring it the miracle holding them together. Daring herself to take a chance and drink it for the caffeine it offered, she took a white Styrofoam cup from the shelf and poured herself some. Swallowing the first taste gently, she tested the waters before diving into the murk. She wondered how anybody could call this building drug free after drinking a cup of the stuff. A grimace passed across her pale face as she swallowed another shot.

Grace turned back towards the clock. Time stood still this evening, just as her life seemed to do. A glance at her wristwatch confirmed that it was the correct time, that the office clock didn't lie, like everybody else in her life did. Dealing with troubled teenagers robbed what little brain power she had on reserve for the evening.

Grace plopped back into her stiff seat in front of the switchboard. It began lighting up like Rockefeller Center on New Year's Eve, one call, two, then three. Recognizing trouble, adrenaline started pumping her into an alert mode. This looked to be bigger than big, unusual even for a Friday night. Where was April? Responding to all the lines flashing back at her would be a challenge. Hastily placing the headset back on her head, Grace answered the first line. All the while, praying her back-up dispatcher would arrive instantaneously.

"Code 3, a 187 at the Fieldhouse."

"10–4," the microphone cackled after her response. After pressing the red switches activating the emergency crews throughout Gallatin County to the calls, she sucked in a deep breath to try and slow her increasing heart rate that soared out of control. A last swallow of the bitter coffee reminded her of its importance. It would be her last luxury of the evening.

Detectives Division, L&J, 8:15 P.M.

Dylan and Della heard both their radios break in together, creating a stereo effect jarring them out of their private thoughts and back to their jobs.

"187, MSU Fieldhouse. Code 3, 10–49 out." The transmission was clear and to the point.

Dylan and Della quickly stood, reading each other's thoughts without a word spoken between them. That was their unique bond. They picked up on each other's emotional needs, helping each other through the waves of life in good times and bad. He thought of it as being like the innate ability of twins. To split them up, would be devastating. They had been close friends for ten years, and they both knew when one needed the other. The telephone lines buzzed between them when counties separated them. Now that they were partners, even though he protested the partnership for personal reasons, the bond did work for them like a rabbit's foot most of the time. Both were in sync with each other as they responded to the information of the attempted murder at the MSU Fieldhouse.

"Let's roll." Dylan said, turning for the door and responding back into his radio.

"I'm right behind you." Della turned, following him out of the office down the long hall past the dispatch center. She jogged alongside him, trying to keep pace with his long strides in double time.

They both rushed out of the building as if their bodies had been injected with jet fuel, propelling them down the side security door, down the steps, and barely touching the ground when they hit the parking lot and raced to their car. Piling into their unmarked vehicle and engaging buttons and seat belts, they listened to the siren as it shattered the quiet of the evening. It abruptly melded with a chorus of sirens before reaching the Brick Breeden Fieldhouse on the Montana State University Campus.

The sirens of the night, loud and commanding in their screaming chorus of alarm, disturbed the other half of the sleepy college town of Bozeman. They had missed the most memorable concert of the decade. Shock waves raced through the town.

Chapter 3

Friday, the 6th day of September, 8:25 P.M.
Shooting scene
Montana State University Brick Breeden Fieldhouse,
Bozeman, Montana

Dirt rose in the air, swirling like a twister around the police cars as they wove a path to the inside of the back doors of the arena, skidding to a stop. Dylan bailed out at the same moment the wheels slowed, slamming the door behind him before the dust could settle. He propelled himself forward through the crowd, rushing towards them like a defensive lineman pushing past the blocks thrown out in front of him and his goal, Jennica James. Della chased after him, trailing him about a yard.

Dylan retrieved his badge from his pocket, hooking it onto his belt so the other officers could identify him and let him pass immediately. He reached the stairs to the stage, climbing two at a time.

Della pumped her smaller legs harder, keeping up, catching Dylan at the top of the platform.

They walked up as the Emergency Medical Technicians carefully slid the victim into the back of the ambulance backed up to the front of the stage. Four individuals dressed in fluorescent orange suits emblazoned with the EMT logo jumped into the ambulance, continuing CPR as another attendant started to close the van doors.

"Let's roll if we want to see her arrive alive," the lead EMT yelled to the driver.

The idling engine shook itself into gear and rolled away from the stage with the sirens screaming to clear the way. Everyone looked on, posed as if in a still life photo. They followed the van in sequence, all heads turning as it pulled out of the building and rounded the corner out of sight.

The police officers taped off the scene of the shooting, trying to keep it from being disturbed by the crowd more than it already had been. They anxiously waited for more officers to arrive to help them keep the mob under control. Two.police officers stood to the back of the yellow tape, scribbling notes, as they asked questions to the people that had been close to the stage during the time of the shooting.

Dylan walked up to the small group gathered around the departing ambulance. He reached for his badge from his belt, holding it out in front of him like a shield of armor. Della stopped and stood next to Dylan. She took out her badge and flashed it in front of the crowd as Dylan did, while he addressed the crowd.

"Excuse us, I'm Detective Drake, and this is my partner Detective Bishop. We need to talk to each of you standing here. I suggest that all of you get comfortable and take a seat over there where the officers are placing chairs for you. It may be awhile before we can speak with each one of you. I know you just witnessed a horrible incident, but we need your help in finding out what happened here." His arm motioned back across the floor to where the pool of blood lingered as officers secured the scene.

"While you're fresh, I need you to think about what you can recall in the few minutes before the shot. Try and recall anything at all that may have seemed out of place to you. Sit back and use all your senses. What was going on? What did you see, hear, smell, feel? Who would like to go first?"

Loud footsteps clicking their way across the stage stopped behind the detectives. Dylan and Della turned in unison.

"We're part of the band. I'm Kate, the band's manager. We'd like to get to the hospital right away."

"I understand. Were you all on stage when this happened?" Dylan said.

"No. Martin and I were off stage, making sure the crew running the light and sound equipment were on top of it. The rest of the band was up on stage playing the first song." Kate pointed to the other band members grouped closely together, hugging each other.

"Diana's missing. Where is she?" Kate said.

"They loaded her into another ambulance and took her to the emergency room. She fell apart when this happened." Another band member walked over to Kate and Martin, placing his arm around both of them.

"All right, you can leave for the hospital. It's going to be a long night. I'll be over there to ask you some questions when we are done here talking with these witnesses," Dylan said.

He pointed at a man wearing a cowboy duster with fancy boots and gestured for him to step forward. "Where were you when this happened?"

"I stood in front, right about there." He pointed over Dylan's head to the front of the stage.

Della reached in her jacket for her notebook and started writing notes as the man spoke.

"What is your name?" Dylan said.

"Dave. Dave Wall."

"Come on over and show me exactly where you were standing." Dylan walked over and Dave followed him to the front of the stage. Another cowboy followed. Della took up the rear.

"This is Lance, he was standing beside me," Dave said.

"Lance. Your last name?"

"Burnett."

"Okay." Dylan hesitated for a minute as Della finished writing down the complete names. "You two were standing where?"

They both jumped down off the stage to the dirt floor.

Dylan looked down at the floor. "Whoa. Stop. There's blood there. Don't move." He jumped off the stage to the ground, squatting down, getting a closer look at the blood spots covering the area. "Della, get the crew before this is covered up over here."

"Sure. She reached down for her radio and spoke into it. "We need the forensic technician, stage center," Della said. "She's on her way."

"Okay. Let's step back a bit. Now tell me what happened."

The two cowboys told their story, not revealing much. They were both standing there in the front row when Jennica started singing. Before the last few words of her song, she jolted backwards a few steps, then fell forward. She fell off the stage and into the men's arms. Della took down their addresses, along with contact numbers while Dylan finished asking a few more questions before letting them leave.

Dylan and Della continued the investigation by talking with the rest of the people lined up in metal chairs across the stage. From a distance it looked more like an audition taking place on the stage rather than a shooting investigation. They took down everyone's name, telephone number, and address after listening to each person's version of the same story.

The night progressed with the same version of the story. No one noticed anybody pointing a gun. No one even heard the gun over the blaring music. They all just watched her as she fell through the air like an acrobat without a net. Later, they saw the blood spurting from her chest, clueing them in, that they were a witness to a gruesome shooting.

Saturday, the 7th day of September, 12:01 A.M.

The crowd thinned leaving just law enforcement personnel to sort out the details of the crime. They gathered like soldiers at reveille, sharing the information they collected. The midnight hour came and went as they compared notes, theories, and cold coffee. The officers, one by one, split from the group to head back to the Law and Justice Center to fill out their official reports while they were still fresh in their exhausted minds. Crisp mountain air splashed their faces as they left, filling their drained bodies with a welcomed burst of energy. Working another shift straight through became their reward tonight. They all had one desire driving them to the finish line on this one;to find the person responsible for the senseless shooting before the evidence trickled away. The next twenty-four hours would be crucial to turning up any evidence that would lead to the apprehension of the suspect.

Dylan and Della left for the hospital to check on the victim and the rest of the band. They were beginning to feel like the band's name, "Runnin' Ragged".

They arrived just before two o'clock and heard the victim still held onto life. It had been touch and go all night, and they still hadn't stabilized her. The surgeons operating on her didn't think she would last through to daybreak. Too many things were stacking against her as the hours ticked by.

The surgical team had removed a bullet from her chest. It caused extensive damage to the deep tissue and part of one lung. It went in, missing the apex of her heart by a fraction of an inch. They removed a second bullet buried in her right clavicle.

The band members filled the small waiting room off to the side of the larger one, reserved for family members in critical cases.

Kate stared at the wall. Mindlessly counting the number of patterns in the Southwestern motif bordering the mint green walls. She desperately searched for an answer to the nightmare. Realizing it really did happen, she didn't know where to turn. She needed to try to deal with it, even though she felt more like a character in a bad murder mystery.

Kate stood up to find the drinking fountain and to shake out the cobwebs forming between her ears. She needed something she could feel, cold, slick, and wet. Her body felt numb from head to toe, and her nose was becoming immune to the clinical potpourri drifting around the tiny space after hours of waiting.

She reached out, touching Martin on the shoulder as she slowly walked by, searching his eyes and body for a response. All she recognized with her burning eyes was the band sinking slowly away from her like quicksand. That wasn't part of the contract. No one could prepare themselves for that. It was way out there, beyond their normal everyday existence. She kept telling herself it had to be all right. Jennica would be fine. They worked too hard for that gig. Being the back up band for the Eagles was only the beginning. She vowed it would not be the end. Runnin' Ragged, on the threshold of their dreams, would not be destroyed so easily. She wandered in search of water like a thirsty soul lost in a mirage in the middle of a hot and nasty desert.

Chapter 4

Saturday, the 7th day of September, 2:00 A.M.
Gallatin General Hospital, Bozeman, Montana

Dylan and Della walked over to the first person they saw in the reception area of the emergency room. A woman stood hunched over a clipboard, writing furiously. The telephone rang. She scanned the area. Seeing no one else around to answer it, she picked it up and mumbled to herself. "Emergency. Yes, yes, I haven't heard anything yet. I don't know. The trauma team is still working."

She slammed the phone back into the receiver with a defiance caught in her eyes as she stared up with raised eyebrows at the detectives.

"Evening, nurse," Dylan said.

"It's two in the morning," she said matter-of-factly.

Dylan looked at his watch and smiled. "You're right. Excuse me. Good morning then."

"There has been absolutely nothing good about it," she said.

"You're probably right again. We're detectives." He reached down, pulling his badge from his belt and put it closer to her face while he continued. "We're following up on a shooting. The victim is Jennica James. We need an office we could use for a couple of hours. Can you find us one?" He looked into her glassy green eyes, feeling the frost forming on his face. He never met a nurse he didn't like, but she wasn't winning any contests with him so far.

"Right over there." She pointed directly across from where they were standing at the counter. "Have at it." She grabbed her paperwork and hurried through the silver double doors leading away from the emergency room.

"Miss personality," Della said, looking into Dylan's eyes.

"And then some. I thought I actually heard a snarl escaping her lips." Dylan made a hideous face back at her, making her giggle.

"I'm surprised. All that damn charm you usually possess didn't have any affect on her." Della laughed loudly again.

"What do you mean, usually?" he said. "I am always in possession of my world class charm."

"You really think so, don't you?"

"That's right, but sometimes you can't melt a glacier when it's been too long in the making." He walked into the office sitting down in the office chair. He leaned way back, then spun it around in a circle in the middle of the floor. "Nice. I always wondered what it would be like to sit on genuine furniture for a change. Why does this county owned joint have better stuff than our facility? I think my chair at the L & J is a relic, the same as the building."

"Quit complaining, Detective Drake. Taxpayers can't buy you everything to make you happy, now can they? Besides, in the food chain, doctors rate better than detectives," Della said. She sat down in an overstuffed mauve chair pulling it up on the other side of the desk facing Dylan.

Dylan picked up a photo on the desk. An enormous gray cat sat staring back at him with elliptic amber eyes. Dylan cackled as he set the photo back in its original position. He began reading the plaques on the wall facing the desk. One read, Dr. Caitlin Greene, MD, MS, graduate from the University of Washington Medical School. He turned towards Della.

"Look here. A lady doctor," Dylan said. "Do you suppose that was her out there a minute ago? I mean, it would fit. She has a picture of a cat on her desk. I bet she probably has a broom tucked away somewhere in here too. Most people display a picture of their husband or boyfriend, or at the very least, their family," he said.

"Maybe she doesn't have any of those things. What's wrong with displaying a photo of your pet? Maybe that's her only love. I have pictures of my dog all over my cubicle. He is the best male companion I could ask for."

"Really?" Dylan studied her for a moment as she grinned back at him, flashing her perfect teeth. "Well, you at least have dear old Dad up there on your wall with Kiki also."

"That's just to scare the hell out of the recruits." She laughed at herself. "I love to make them squirm when they find out the Chief of the Bozeman PD is my father. Now quit speculating on this woman's life and let's get back to the job at hand." Della reached over picking up the photo. "Big kitty," she said.

"Okay. Daylight is almost upon us. Get out your list and we'll make a new one." Dylan reached in his shirt pocket laying his notebook down on the desk.

Della reached in her jacket, pulling out her hot pink note pad.

They concocted a plan. Together they would interview each band member individually, getting their reactions, and then compare notes. They agreed that putting their heads together would work better on a case like this.

"Let's call Josh Tate first. He looks terrible, but he looks as if he can handle talking right now. Oh yeah, you better get the tape recorder from the car," Dylan said, looking over at Della. She nodded and walked out the door. Several minutes later she walked back in with Josh Tate following her.

"You can take a seat in this chair here, Josh." Della pointed at the chair she had sat in earlier. "We will be taping this interview." She reached over pushing the record button. A red light went on as she spoke into it, "Detective Drake, Detective Bishop interviewing Josh Tate, September 7, at 02:20."

Josh took the seat offered. He put his hands in his lap and clasped them together and slowly started rubbing them back and forth.

Della grabbed the matching chair sitting on the same side of the desk next to Josh, pulling it around to the side of the desk by Dylan. She liked observing every part of the person she interviewed. Body language said a lot.

"You cold Josh?" Dylan said.

"Yes. I can't get warm."

"Do you want a blanket?"

"No, I'm fine. I don't think anything will help me get warm."

"Why is that?" Della said.

"Until Jennica's out of danger I won't feel warm."

"I see. Tell me everything you can about Jennica. Just talk. It might help you feel better." Dylan looked directly into Josh's baby blue eyes.

He saw a young man broken in two. His shoulders slumped forward. His chin rested on his chest and he stared at the floor. When he lifted his head to talk, his eyes wore a thin glaze of red. He felt empathy looking across at him.

His face was smooth and glowing from youth, yet his good looks started showing an inkling of fine lines around his mouth and eyes. His heart shaped face had a hint of a shadow around his strong jaw line. It formed perfect angles with his long thin nose, alluding to a rugged side to the shroud of innocence held in his baby face.

He reached up, running his hand through the front of his straw blonde hair. He wore it sculpted up and back away from his face. He crossed his leg over his other knee, grabbing the side of his brown cowboy boot as he cleared his throat to speak.

"I love her." He looked down at his boots. His foot started moving, first slowly, then faster and faster as he choked back the first word of his next sentence. "Jennica and I grew up in Bozeman. I went through school with her. She didn't notice me until fifth grade. She picked me first for a game during gym class. I've been close to her ever since."

"How close?" Dylan said.

"What? What do you mean? Do you need to know if I slept with her? I said, I love her and I do. I've loved her for eleven years. We're best friends."

"Friends?"

"Yes, I said best friends. I would do anything for her. I would take her place right now if I could." He looked down again toward his boots, making his feet still.

"Do you know anyone who wanted to hurt her?"

He shook his head. "No."

"Think back. Do you remember anything out of place in the past week or so that didn't seem right? Did she act funny, or seem out of sorts about anything or anyone? Did she receive any threats of any kind, maybe a fan who started pestering her?"

"No. I didn't notice anything like that. She would have told us if someone scared her. We practiced longer and harder than usual because of this concert tonight. Appearing in our hometown in front of our families and friends gave us a thrill that filled us with a lot of crazy energy. The Eagles are one of the hottest bands to come to Bozeman. To be part of it has kept us all acting a little crazier than normal, I guess. Jennica held us together with her great sense of humor and friendship. She patched the band up after all our insecurities surfaced about the whole deal."

"What happened? You said patched us up. What do you mean?"

"Well, you know. The typical little fights between us over stupid stuff right before a big concert. It always happens. Someone goes and gets drunk and can't practice. Someone doesn't like it and belts them for being so stupid. Things like that." Josh put his foot down and started tapping his toe rhythmically.

"That happened, exactly?"

"No, not exactly. I just meant it in general."

"Tell me what happened exactly, then."

"Why? What has all this got to do with someone shooting down Jennica in cold blood at our debut concert? None of us could have done it."

"You sure?"

"Of course I'm sure. Everyone loved her in the band. She's the heart holding us together. It's insane to think any of us would want to kill her."

"Is it?" Dylan said. "It seems one person almost accomplished just that, and that person is whom I'm going to find if I have to back track to her birth to do so. That's why we're here right now, to gather all the background information about her to help us find some sort of motive for this. People like you, who are closest to her, can help fill us in on all those details."

"I understand. I'll do anything to help. I just know no one in the band did it." Josh stood. "Sorry, but I have to stretch." He looked out the narrow window at the side of the closed door. "Father Murphy," he said with a bit of excitement back in his voice. He looked back at the two detectives. "Could I go talk with Father Murphy? He's a close friend of our families, Jennica's and mine. I really need to talk with him for a moment before he goes to Jennica. I'm glad he made it." He looked back through the window, turning his head back around to look at them, waiting for an answer.

"Sure, go ahead. We'll have to ask you more questions at a later date." Dylan smiled up at him as Josh opened the door and left.

"Poor guy. I can see he really has it bad for her," Della said. She stood up and wandered over to the window and gazed at him. "Next?" she said.

Looking down at his list, Dylan underlined Kate. "Kate Wood." He stood up and walked out the door. He found her half asleep, waiting on a sofa. He asked her to follow him.

Strolling back together, Kate noticed Father Murphy. She raced over to him taking his hand in hers. Dylan stepped up behind her, stopping to listen to their conversation.

"Father, is everything all right?" She raised her eyebrows to him. "I mean, she didn't?"

"No, I just arrived, Kate. You must remain calm. The doctors tell me she's stabilizing. She's strong willed. You should know that. She'll make it through this. I'm going in to her right now."

Father Murphy dressed casually in all black. He looked upbeat and fairly young for a Catholic Priest. Dylan guessed he was fifty. A little white collar surrounded his neck, displaying his religious calling. He wore copper wire-rimmed spectacles. The glasses sat on his long aquiline nose, sliding down a bit as he spoke quietly with the band members. He pushed them back up with his forefinger, a slight irritation evident in his face.

He tried smiling pleasantly at them between his words of encouragement. His voice, calm and deep, came across smoothly like a television anchorman's. Curly light brown hair enriched his youthful looking face.

"I know she'll make it through this now that you're here," Kate said. "I'll let you go. She needs you now more than ever."

Father Murphy gave Kate and Josh a nod as he ambled down the short corridor.

He turned back to them, reaching the set of double doors leading to where Jennica laid fighting for her life. He bent his head at the door and crossed himself before entering.

Dylan reached out gently, putting his hand around Kate Wood's elbow. He led her back to the office. Kate smiled at him, letting him lead the way.

They entered the room. Della sat with her head cupped in her hands at the desk, rubbing her spent eyes. She jerked her head up. A startled expression consumed her face. Dylan closed the door behind them.

"Have a seat Kate."

Dylan let go of her arm as she sat. He moved to the other chair beside the desk.

Della switched on the tape recorder, repeating the day, time, and interview with Kate Wood.

"Kate, can you tell me about yourself? What you do in the band? How you became the Runnin' Ragged's band manager? How long you have been with them?" Dylan said.

"I joined the band three years ago. I responded to an ad in the Billings Gazette. They wanted a manager for their country rock band. They needed a manager with experience to work hard and develop their raw talent into a professional band that would one day become a household name. That's what I've done. They're finally becoming known, not just in Montana. Their new album is out, and it's been playing all over the United States and parts of Europe."

"I moved to Billings from Los Angeles to get out of the rat race. Jennica interviewed me. Impressed by my qualifications, they hired me right then. I needed the job, so I took the salary they offered. It was far below what I usually haul in."

"How did you get along with Jennica? Did you hit it off right away? Work well together? Have any difficulties?" Della said.

"I love Jennica. She's a wonderful friend. I—"

An intercom blaring inside the room interrupted the conversation, repeating the words 'Code blue' twice. Dylan stood up, watching the two nurses leave their desks at a dead run.

Kate jumped up, reaching for the doorknob. Dylan reached for her hand and Kate stared into his eyes.

"Stop the tape. We'll finish doing these interviews tomorrow after we all get some rest. Let's call it a day. Della, we'll go home and get some sleep for a few hours." Dylan turned the door knob, letting Kate slip out of the room.

"Thank you," she quietly whispered to them as she left. Hurrying towards the doors that the doctors and nurses sprinted towards, she knew they were going where Jennica lay, giving up the one thread of life she had held onto all night.

Chapter 5

Saturday, the 7th day of September, 0500 Zulu (5:00 A.M. EST)
G Group Processing Center
National Security Agency, Fort Meade, Maryland

The computers whirled, networking with the other terminals around the bustling world from Bangkok to Homer, Alaska. Their accumulated sounds hissing quietly, operating at top speed, processing the infinitude of information, calmed the soul of the operative known as Tinman. They eventually drove him into a hypnotic state after his tenth hour of his twelve hour shift.

The ocean played inside his mind, the waters swirling, the waves busting against the rocks, just like when he was a kid and he'd hear it inside a seashell perched on his ear. He longed for that ocean. Virginia Beach popped up. A portrait of his girlfriend Cindi in her designer bikini standing on the white sand looking hot, sizzling his brain, making his body unexpectedly give in to the moment as he recalled the last night they spent together.

His extraordinary mind, tweaked and seasoned like a veteran, momentarily lapsed. Trained like an athlete, it worked to the point of overload every minute during his shift. He never should have lost it like that. A break in concentration could be considered a breech in National security. The consequences could be a world catastrophe. He focused again, as he tortured himself relentlessly for the rest of his shift for breaking his attention during his watch.

Tinman appeared younger than his late forties, with his hair still light brown with only a speckling of gray at the sides. He dressed casually in light weight khaki pants and a white cotton shirt. He circled the room, listening intently, his ears and eyes sensitive to minuscule changes in the scanning equipment that watched the globe around the clock. His watch would soon end after hours of being glued to the monitors inside the antiseptic clean room of the DDO (Office of Signals Intelligence Operations) G Group at Fort Meade, Maryland. The group monitors communications and analyzes International telecommunications to and from the United States. It is connected by a central corridor to the National Security Agency's Operations.

The Unit contains state of the art equipment, and is the world's best kept secret, processing the activities of the world, quickly and efficiently. The super computer room, designed by the top US Defense Department's military planners and scientists in the Advanced Research Project Agency, integrated the evolution of aerospace products in research and the use of artificial satellite development. Together they used their unique capabilities and collaborated with other departments inside their top secret circle in a venture that gave them cutting edge electronics and communication software. It lead to a highly sophisticated system, superior and unknown to the private sector of the world. Its use was to spy on the rest of the world.

The operatives worked side by side, as they interpreted messages received from their computers, and coded return responses to others like them, scattered like dust in the wind in other states, Canada, and across every nation. The National Security Council sat at the helm, close to the hub of political and military entities inside the Pentagon in Arlington, Virginia, and across the Potomac in Washington DC. They existed together in its infrastructure of power to govern and keep world peace.

Tinman keyed into a message, scanning it for authenticity, decoding it. Captain John R. Brolins, USAF, G Group, Division I, Alpha Branch Commander, reported from Sector forty-eight, reporting a problem in Sector forty-one. He dialed the gray secure phone, a direct access line to Air Force Lieutenant General Garrity, the Director. His office was located on the third floor.

"General, Ground Squirrel flagged Montana in regard to BIG SKY." He swallowed a sip of water hoping to quench his dry mouth. "The operation is at strike command, but an incident has taken place that could alter the mission."

"Get him on the line."

"Yes, General. Right away."

Tinman dialed and pushed buttons, accessing the communication lines between the Director General and Ground Squirrel at his command center at Groom Lake inside Nellis AFB at Area 51 in the Nevada desert. His mouth felt parched, as if he'd been working in the desert with GS instead of the isolated center in humid Maryland. He reached for his ice water.

0100 Zulu (1:00 PST)

"Ground Squirrel, Tinman here. The General is waiting to speak with you about the developments you reported on watch 0100."

"I'm secure. I'll hook up."

"Captain, General Garrity. Brief me on the developments."

"Yes, sir. A concert in Bozeman, Montana became a shooting investigation. The victim turns out to be Jennica James. She is—"

"I know who she is. I'm thoroughly briefed with the whole file. This complicates the operation. Who's responsible?"

"All sides are scrambling, sir. Not a report on who, or why. It worries me at this point."

"It scares the hell out of me. This could mean several things."

"I have profiled the possibilities. I have to say that I didn't find a scenario I liked, not one that even made sense."

"Our existence doesn't require it making sense, nor does it require us to like it. We just have to do it. Follow your orders, Commander." The General hesitated, "Whatever it is, it's too late to pull the plug. You clean up whatever you have to clean up. The green light is on."

"Yes, sir. I'm flying in to coordinate Stage 3. It may not go as smooth as the course that was set."

"So be it. Director out."

Ground Squirrel disengaged the direct line, questioning for the first time just what he was doing. His life felt superimposed, magnifying a giant gaping hole in it, looming like a faceless ghost haunting him with questions, annoying him to the point of distraction. That luxury he could not afford, especially now. Never before had his mind started playing games like it was doing now, with the mission in Montana and its scheduled finish September 13 occupying it. That date even shook him. He didn't have a superstitious bone in his body, but, for some reason, he felt an uneasiness consume him after the news about Jennica James. Ending this on a Friday the 13th sent an unsettling feeling into his system. A total upheaval taking place inside, replacing his usual confidence.

The life he led, recollected and then regurgitated as he sat over the control panel switching it from manual to auto, sent him grieving as if he'd lost someone. His heart ached. It would be almost twenty years that he had given to his country so far, in specialized service, for what? His pension, if he lived to collect it one day, would be used for what? There were no family or friends to share it, or the rest of his life with now. He had to lead a secret life inside and outside of the military. It made his life solitary because it was an easy solution to his complicated position that warranted his work to remain classified to everyone but a select few within the structure of the government. Even the President was kept in the dark about certain missions. This mission in particular, was a total blackout from everyone inside the White House.

He didn't see any reason for anyone to want to follow him around the world chasing elusive enemies that never disappeared and kept him working twenty-four hours a day. It wasn't the kind of life most people would choose, and he adamantly believed that not many were successful at it. He picked the road, and he didn't expect anyone else to follow him. The option just wasn't there, even if he had wanted it to be.

Ground Squirrel slid off his chair, stretching his tired body, and stared aimlessly out the window at the wind blowing sand around. Millions of miniature swirls designed the surface in spiraling patterns in front of the runway. The overhead lights illuminated the metal hangar a few hundred yards ahead of him. He watched as the doors started sliding open in preparation for his flight. Under the lights the blistered green paint on the building looked as pathetic as he felt.

Ground Squirrel was forty-six, nearing the big fifty and he felt it bearing down on him like a speeding bullet. He had shiny coal black hair and penetrating dark eyes that vibrated from his athletic face like headlights on a dark night. Reaching up, he felt his unshaven face. Why did he feel as if he was bleeding uncontrollably from an imaginary wound? Was it his heart causing that insufferable pain?

He took one last look around. Picking up two silver briefcases, he walked through the doorway. He secured the building then headed to the plane that would take him back to the mission classified as BIG SKY in southwestern Montana.

"Hey, Mick, I'm ready." His trusted friend and Chief of Maintenance of Division I, Alpha Branch in G Group, Lieutenant Michael Anton, USAF, did an earlier flight check. Mick came aboard with him when he entered the organization in the late seventies. They went to Yale together, then became officers in the Air Force. The top officials in the National Security Agency, a top secret organization within itself, came to recruit them into one of their other secret organizations working parallel with the National Reconnaissance Office.

Spying fell into their paths pumping their adrenaline like buckshot, exciting them both like nothing they had ever experienced. It's been their way of life ever since, consuming them like a drug. They challenged each other in their missions like a couple of hot shots in a rapidly advancing firestorm. They were daredevils, cocky and sure.

They were both pilots educated and trained by the best at NASA. Mick specialized in mechanical and electrical engineering. He kept every gadget running smoothly so Ground Squirrel could concentrate on the human aspects of the operations.

"Pipes ready. You take it easy. I'll be flying the birds up to you, staging them on Wednesday," Mick said.

"Watch your tail. I don't know what I need to know, and that actually scares me."

"Buddy, you know, I have every reason to believe you'll figure it out, on time as always."

"I'm glad you think so, but something feels wrong this time. Don't you feel it? I can't shake it. You know what I'm talking about Mick? Like when you play poker, you can feel that winning hand, then at other times you fold because of the feeling you'll lose. Well, this one feels bad. I want to fold."

"Don't fill me full of this horse shit. It's too late to fold. Get out of here, man. You've been flying in the dark your whole life, just hanging on by the pockets on your skinny ass. Now go, before I mess with one of your toys before you're in the sky."

"Thanks for the sympathy in my first hour of real need. I always knew I could count on you to get me through it. What was I thinking?" He shook his head back and forth, laughing at Mick, taking out his dark glasses. He opened the door stepping into the pilot's seat. Mick stepped back and walked away, taking his cap out and flapping it in the wind above his head as Ground Squirrel watched his backside disappear. That was Mick's imitation of a ground crew giving a signal that the runway was clear. Not that he would ever have to worry. The runway was always clear on the deserted Air Force base.

Twenty minutes later he checked in, only to hear Mick's growling voice.

"You set me up, you sick freaking ass. I knew your little bleeding heart act was phony. You about sent my poor old heart into cardiac arrest when that short and sweet fireworks display exploded as I placed my hand on the doorknob. You're one crazy son of a bitch using that IED (Improvised Explosive Device). You know why? Cause' I'll hurt you for that one, hear me? Pay backs on its way, buddy. You watch your tail. Mick Finn out."

GS chuckled until his sides hurt. His eyes blurred from the tears, making it hard to fly the plane as he switched off and cruised through the clouds and rode above them. It amused him to shake Mick up at every opportunity. Of course, Mick would get him back. He always did. He couldn't wait to view the close circuit video on that one.

The joke was over. Wiping his eyes, the grin slipped quickly from his face. It was time to concentrate on the final aspects of the mission, the coordinates, and positioning his men. Timing was everything now, and it was running short. Lately, his own timing had been way off. He wondered if he was up to finishing this mission according to the plan that had been set years beforehand. He tried focusing on the details. They were as cloudy to him, as the clouds he flew through. His eyes watched the gages as his years of training worked to clear his mind from the debris. The plane popped out of the clouds as he took in the land spread below him. Montana's rich landscape brought his attention back to where it needed it to be, back to the mission that had already begun countdown.

Chapter 6

Saturday, the 7th day of September, 6:00 A.M.
Bozeman, Montana

"I pulled the job. Where's the money? I'm heading North while the heats on."

"Meet me at the Western Cafe in half an hour."

"Why? We don't need to meet. You just stow my dough in an envelope and leave it at the desk at the City-Center Motel with Beth. The arrangements we discussed. I've been waiting."

"We need to meet. Something else has come up that needs your expertise."

"What? Quit playing games. We struck a deal and you'll follow it through like we agreed. I don't like changes. Get the money now, or I'll come and get it."

"Listen. You need money? We have another job. It'll be quick and easy. Meet me if you want to increase the figure on the final amount due. I'll be at the Western at 6:30. If you don't show, I'll take it as a no, and I'll drop the payment off just as we agreed."

The line went dead in his ear. "He'll show. Greed's possessed his soul. If not, I'll deliver a bogus envelope to the motel and we'll grab him when he comes to collect."

"How did this become so fucked up? Where'd you find this idiot, The Soldier of Fortune's classified ads? You'd better see to it that you nail him, or the rest of the Sons of the Pioneers will come and destroy all of us for the incomprehensible mistake you made in judgment. If we're exposed, this will be the end to us all. The founding Fathers will remove their protection from us, and wreak havoc. It will be eminent then that nothing pure will be left to carry on in our tradition. Several generations of work will be forfeited."

Four men entered the Western Cafe and sat around the table against the back wall facing the door. Ordering coffee, they smoked cigarettes and waited.

At 6:32 a tall man entered wearing a long coat and large hat. His eyes darted to the back, and he moved quickly to the table. He took a seat, placing his large hands on the top of the table. Balling them up into a fist, he stared across at the man who had asked for his help.

"Thanks for coming."

"Cut the chit-chat. Give me the details. I'm in a hurry."

At the same time, the four men sitting, drew their revolvers from their concealed holsters under their jackets. They pointed them under the table at the man who had just sat down and spoke. In unison, they pulled back the hammer's of the guns, cocking them, and readying them to fire. The harmonious synchronized clicking of metal snapping back, emanated from beneath the table. The men smiled maliciously.

The man who joined them did not smile. His eyes grew large as he stared across at the men, recognizing the familiar sound.

"If you want, go ahead and peek. Four guns are pointed at your family jewels. Make one move and you'll be forced into our budget method of castration. Our members fill the cafe. We are going to get up, go out the door, and take a little joy ride in the country. The truck we're taking is parked at the curb, right outside the door." The man glanced around the table. The others nodded.

"Move to the door, now. The guns will be pointing at the back of your brainless head."

The tall man stood, along with the other four. The guns were concealed as they stood. The five left without incident. The driver motioned the man inside the cab. The other man slid in next and pulled his gun back out. The two younger men jumped in the back of the pickup truck and pounded the top of the cab with their fists. It was time to finish what they had started.

Pulling away from the curb, they headed east on Main Street to Bear Canyon. Forty-five minutes later, the truck stopped at the edge of a thick forest of pine, where a small private cemetery sat enclosed by a black wrought iron fence.

The man riding shotgun placed the barrel of his gun against the man's temple. "Out, you fucking imbecile."

The driver jumped out and came around to the passenger door and readjusted his aim.

Their quarry, dripping in sweat, slowly climbed from the cab. The two men in the back sat on the edge of the pickup bed. They held rifles in their arms, aimed directly between his piercing black eyes. In practice, the sights were dead on.

"What the fuck are you doing? Do you know who I am?"

"Yeah. You're the shit for brains we hired that is asking us for money for a job he fucked. You're a piss-poor killer. The target is alive. Now by our own virtue, you're soon to be a dead man lying at our feet." The sound of gun fire ricocheted through the tiny canyon as the weapons filled him full of holes. Red crimson sprayed the site like paint balls in one of their war games. The body jerked wildly, convulsing from side to side. Finally, it writhed one last time, then stopped.

"Throw him in the grave we prepared yesterday, and start filling it in. Let's not leave any evidence behind to come back and haunt us." He turned and stared into the clear sky. A Bald Eagle cruised by, circling for an early morning snack. "If we hurry, we'll still have time for breakfast before our meeting at 8:00."

Replacing their weapons for shovels, two of the men grabbed the body and dragged it to the site. They kicked the bullet riddled body into the crevice. The four heaved the rocky dirt upon the recently deceased man until the grave was filled. Packing and smoothing the top, they began covering up any trace of their deed. Leaving the cemetery, the driver raced to town. They'd leave the county's vehicle back in the lot at the Gallatin County Courthouse. Their regularly scheduled Saturday meeting of the Sons of the Pioneers was scheduled to begin inside their private meeting room at the Riverside Country Club, followed by nine holes of golf, weather permitting.

Chapter 7

Saturday, the 7th day of September, 6:00 A.M.
Bozeman, Montana

"Mom, I'm home." Dylan slipped off his black leather jacket, throwing it on the couch on the way to the kitchen. It had been a long day followed by an extremely long night. Now, at six o'clock in the morning, he arrived home just in time to eat with his mother and have a short snooze before getting back to the new case. He couldn't remember the last time he ate. He opened the refrigerator door, spying the pot roast sitting there carefully covered by cellophane. He couldn't count the number of dinners his mom cooked him that he ended up missing because of his job.

He wondered where his mom was. She usually sat at the table reading the newspaper this time of the morning.

He wandered through the house and searched for her. He quietly opened her bedroom door a crack and spied her curled up and under her quilt, sleeping soundly. Looking upon her peaceful face, he frowned. For her to be still sleeping, she must have waited up for him all night. He didn't think she would get use to his crazy hours. Worry consumed her.

He went back to the kitchen and cut a slab of roast beef. He threw it in the microwave with some carrots and baby potatoes and grabbed a large glass of milk. Breakfast is served.

He sat at the table and thought back to Friday evening. Taking out his notebook to read back the pages of notes, he studied and reviewed them for any clues that would lead to some answers to his questions. He scribbled more notes as he recalled other things about the previous night at the scene and at the hospital.

Dylan didn't understand why a person would shoot this woman in such a public place. Motive. He needed to interview the rest of the band, her family, and all of her friends to get a better background on her.

A killer was still out there, running around Bozeman free, getting away with attempted murder, if she died, murder. He seriously doubted the random shooting theory circling around town already. Someone wanted her dead. Jennica still clung to life, after being resuscitated during the code blue. Officers guarded her room. If the person responsible didn't accomplish their goal the first time, they might try again.

He started clustering thoughts on a page. Jealousy started the cluster.

"Oh honey, you're home."

Dylan looked up and smiled at his mother entering the kitchen. She wore a long flannel nightgown with Mickey Mouse covering the front and bright yellow Tweety Bird slippers that he had given to her last Christmas.

"I worried when you didn't come home. Are you all right?" Mrs. Drake walked behind his chair, stroking the top of his wavy hair, then bent down and gave him a kiss on the cheek.

"I'm fine, Mom. And you know you have to stop worrying about me."

"I'll never stop worrying about you, son. I'm your mother. That's my job."

"I know. But you do too much of it."

"Never. Not when it comes to you." She walked over and started to make coffee. "Don't you want some coffee?"

"No. I need to go to bed."

"Well, get then. You look terrible. I wish you'd find another line of work. If this job doesn't kill you, lack of sleep will. Now, go. I'll clean up." She walked over, picking up his half-full plate of food from the table. "Honey, you didn't eat much," she said.

"I'm sorry. It tasted great, but I'm ready to hit the sack. I'll eat later."

"Maybe if I cook you a real breakfast, like some bacon and eggs?"

"No, Mom. I'm fine."

A loud ring came from the living room. It was the telephone. Dylan stood to answer it.

"Oh no you don't, get to bed. I'll get it." His Mom hurried into the living room and Dylan followed.

"Mom, I have—"

"Hello. You've reached the Drake residence. May I help you?" Mrs. Drake turned, giving Dylan that mother look; her brows rose in a high arch in frustration because he hadn't followed her instructions. He shook his head, holding out his hand for the phone.

"Dylan?"

Dylan cut his mother off by grabbing the telephone out of her hand. "This is Dylan." He motioned for her to go away.

"Hey. It's Bobby."

"Just a minute." Dylan covered the phone as he whispered. "It's okay, Mom. I have to talk privately. Go on and get your coffee."

Mrs. Drake frowned back at her son. She turned around and went back into the kitchen.

"Okay. What's up?" Dylan said.

"I just wanted you to know the bullets they retrieved from the victim look like hollow points from a forty-four caliber."

"Thanks Bobby. Anything else?"

"No, not yet. We can't find any casings at the scene. We sent the bullets to the State Crime Lab in Missoula to get a complete ballistics report. They're backed up as usual."

"Call me if you turn up anything else."

"Sure, Dylan. You know I will. I love calling you. I just wish we had more stimulating things to talk about than the case we're working." She left the suggestion dangling for a response.

"Someday, I'd love to have a stimulating conversation with you that has nothing to do with a case, but right now, I'm lucky to be talking after working the last twenty-four hours and counting. This case has definitely pushed me into serious overtime. I'm sleepwalking as we speak."

"Do I hear a little bit of whining in the invincible Detective Drake's voice?"

"I don't know. Do you? I'll get back to you Monday. We'll talk then." Dylan hung up the phone, and walked past his mom. Turning around to her, he kissed her on the forehead and grinned. "Night, Mom."

"Goodnight, son."

Della entered her two story Victorian home, throwing her keys on the credenza. She dropped her coat on the floor on her way to the back porch.

She opened the sliding glass doors and jumped back instantaneously. A monstrous dog, white and fluffy, tried mowing her over in the doorway. She laughed, hitting the floor softly, pretending to be shocked.

"I let two macho males in one day knock me on my butt. I'd better watch my backside better. What do you say to that, you big overgrown sweetheart?" She wrestled him on the floor for a few minutes, growling at him playfully.

Her long legs wrapped around him as they rolled around on her hardwood floor. She rolled on her back and the Siberian Husky licked her face from chin to brow.

"Kiki, I love you." She said, releasing him. Kiki carried on with his barking, running over for his sock. He proudly carried it back to her and set it down in front of her. Drooling all over it with his thick pink tongue hanging out, Kiki sprang from his hind legs.

"Okay, I'll play sock with you for five minutes. I'm exhausted. I need some sleep."

Kiki barked again as if understanding Della's pitiful words.

Della grabbed the sock from the floor. Kiki jumped forward on his front paws, grabbing and pulling the other end of the sock. He started growling, thrashing his neck back and forth, trying to pull it out of her hands to win the tug of war. She held on with all her might, bracing herself on her oak coffee table. She felt him winning. She stood up where she could get some more leverage. She yanked, then he yanked. Finally she let go of it, leaving it hanging from his mouth. He dropped the sock in front of him, barking one last loud and deep bark, a signal of the triumphant one.

"Boy, I've got to get some sleep." Heading up the stairs, she shed her clothing as she went. She'd pick them up later. By the time she reached her room she stood in just her red silk bra and matching bikini brief. At the door, she reached behind her back, unhooking the bra, letting it fall at the doorway behind her.

The sun filled her room, making it hard for her even to think about going to sleep. She walked to the window, looking out at the Bridger Mountain range that already displayed a frosting of white snow along the top. She dropped the Venetian blinds after admiring the view, smiling as the room became dark. She slid her hand down and stepped out of her silky underwear. She dropped on her backside into the king sized waterbed, making waves slosh around her body. She pulled the goose down comforter over her eyes.

She tried drifting off to sleep. Her mind wouldn't slow down long enough to allow her to relax. It churned the shooting investigation over and over until she screamed loudly and begged herself to let it go. A crime like that just didn't happen here. She hoped that wasn't the beginning of the way things were going to be in the future.

She wondered if Dylan was having the same problem getting to sleep as she was. With her thoughts on Dylan, her mind slipped past the job and into their past. Would he ever be more than her best friend? She thought back to Josh Tate telling them about his friendship with Jennica and his love for her. She read more in his eyes and body than could be used to describe the word "friends". She felt empathy for his situation, as it mirrored her dilemma with Dylan. Her heart wanted and needed much more from him. She heard Kiki somewhere in the mist taking up his position on the floor at the foot of her bed. She concentrated on the voices telling her to go for it. Never give up on your dreams.

Chapter 8

**Saturday, the 7th day of September, 8:00 A.M. (PST)
Research and Design Facility, TransAmerican Telecommunications
Vancouver, British Columbia, Canada**

The telephone rang consistently, driving Jordan James further into the depths of despair. Finally, after losing a night of sleep from grief, he pulled himself together. Dialing a conference call, he waited for the other parties to pick up on their ends.

"The contract is still valid and we'll deliver on time. In the meantime, I want every available investigator we have to work exclusively with the shooting of my daughter in Montana. I want the bastard that did this. If it's our competitors, I want them destroyed. Destroyed beyond repair. Do you hear me?" Jordan said.

"Mr. James, as Chief of Security, I've taken care of it. Since the word of the shooting reached headquarters last night, I've put our team on it." Marcus said.

"We've sent word to Moscow to keep their ears open. We've been checking thoroughly our competitors." Bill said, clearing his throat. "Of course, there are others in Russia that would like to intercede for their own gain. It's more likely they would lie low and intercept once the products reach their delivery points."

"I'm speculating it might be a personal vendetta. Someone wants to make you suffer, Jordan." Clark Doherty's voice hesitated. "Whoever it might be, they may have more in store for you. Who would've used Jennica to get to you?"

"Hell, Clark. I can think of a million possibilities. The international commodity we've been proposing to the highest bidder overseas, upset some factions. I'm not a discriminating type of salesman when it comes to our buyers. I'd take the money from almost anyone who produces it. That might have pissed off some of our clientele. It could have sent any one of them fighting to pay me back for my lack of understanding when it comes to their political dilemmas.

"If China got wind of our current contract with Russia, they may want to put the skids on it. Hurting my daughter might be a technique to slow us down, but I believe they'd just cut to the chase. Profit and power are what it's all about to them. They see it as creating a ripple effect and unbalancing the world's power in a political move against them. They lose face.

"Even my former employers at the NRO (National Reconnaissance Office) would like to see me cut from the action in the industry. I've been a liability to them. They recruited me. I worked clandestinely, developing the advancements in their models of spy satellites during the eighties.

One evening, I copied my design and carried it out of the secure building. It was a big mistake, even though I designed and built it. I was caught red handed. The NRO promptly fired me, gave me a verbal slap in the face, and three papers to read and sign before they booted my ass out of their door forever.

"The first, disavowed me from working for any government operations. The second, was an affidavit stating the government or any government agency under its jurisdiction had no knowledge of me operating within the government, in the past, currently, or in the future. The last document I signed stated that I would never reveal any aspect of my occupation of employment, or any knowledge gained within the agency or about the agency. If caught selling secrets, the punishment would fit the crime. Their penalty would be death. The document was black and white and to the point. It made their intentions perfectly clear in a breech of National Security. The two words they signed up for life to preserve, protect, and defend.

"They know my capabilities. The advancing of their own satellites beyond their ability, and marketing it, wouldn't be a commodity that's on the list for free trade if they got wind of it.

"Who do you think brought the technology accelerating beyond imagination, not merely advancing? KH–12 and Milstar succeeded because of my team.

"With the smoke and mirrors we've put up on the operation around the world, they have never been able to infiltrate the mechanisms we positioned to maintain a target on me. I know they've tried keeping benign tabs on me since my forced retirement, but I know them. They won't touch me out in the open. It would be a lot of free advertisement for their carefully guarded secrets and its cloaked organization. So, it would be done very indiscreetly. It wouldn't benefit them to use my daughter against me. What would it have gained them? They'd just put an expiration stamp on my head and come get me. That's all it would take to blow our house down around our boots. I'd be six feet under before anyone noticed. A play for my daughter in light of the joy of killing me outright, just doesn't make sense."

"So, what do you think?" Bill said.

"I don't think. I know whoever is responsible is going down. If I have to spend every penny of the billions we've made to do it, I will."

"Have you thought that maybe this isn't about you? Your daughter may just have been an innocent victim of an obsessed fan. Or, she may have developed her own set of enemies working in the entertainment business."

"Impossible. Jennica didn't make enemies. And if it's a lunatic, I'll find out."

"Mr. James, I mean no disrespect, but your daughter was a very attractive young lady. Did she have a relationship that might have went sour? The statistics show that violent attacks such as this, are often times caused by jealously."

"I don't give a shit about statistics. Yes, I've considered all of these possibilities. It's your job to go and find out what did exactly happen. I want to give back a deserving bit of restitution to the person responsible. Hear me?" Mr. Jordan James's voice raised a decibel, booming across the lines to the other four men. "Marcus, add this to your list. Find out who my daughter has dated over the past couple of years and run the backgrounds. See what you turn up."

"Consider it done, boss."

Jordan James sat back in his deep leather chair and swiveled around to face the windows. "Joyce is devastated. The doctors put her on tranquilizers. The corporate jet will be leaving in an hour for Bozeman. I want the doctor's assurance they have everything available to them they need to pull her through this. The local law enforcement is guarding her room. At least, their concern for her safety is also my concern. I don't want whoever it is to come back and finish the job. After I'm through checking on her, I'll be flying to Moscow to finalize our clients' contract. I'll be back on Thursday to check on the operation at the warehouse.

"Friday the 13th, is going to be our lucky day. After this, Joyce and I will take an extended vacation to be with Jennica and our two other daughters. Is everyone clear at this point on the logistics and the procedure we will be using?"

"Everyone's been thoroughly briefed, sir. The arrangements are taken care of. The shipment will be ready to load on our cargo jet, when the last payment is wired and reaches Hans Gotbörg in Switzerland. We're sorry about Jennica. Don't worry, we'll find her shooter. Be extra careful dealing with our friends and watch your back. See you Friday," Ward said.

The conference call ended with all lines disconnecting on the open speaker.

At sixty-two, Jordan James, the founder of TransAmerican Telecommunications Corporation and Chairman of the Board, struggled for the last few years to remain as the lead manufacturing company of telecommunications equipment among his world competitors.

Distinguished looking in his tailored silk business suits, his appearance matched perfection. The perfection he demanded in every aspect of his life. Mr. James was a genius, and the most powerful CEO in the thriving telecommunications industry. His great mind drove him to succeed and brought his company leading the industry through his research.

His reputation for ingenuity and excellence in research and design in the field matched his aggressive negotiation skills and made him the leader in international sales. That drive made him the lead negotiator in high profile contracts. Fear did not enter his makeup. The powerhouse deals he struck with dangerous and high stakes international markets involving some of the most unscrupulous and unsavory buyers fueled his company to remain at the top, even in its current financial crisis.

The financing of his research projects became astronomical with the accelerated advancements in technology. Without the financial backing, his discoveries in science would never continue toward the future, or propel his company into the 21st century.

During his employment in the National Reconnaissance Office (NRO), the government funded his work. He engineered and designed their top secret projects. He never had a concern over cost. To achieve the results, he had free use of their secret funding. No questions or concerns over cost or budget were considered. Only results mattered to them.

His former employer, the NRO, was a "black" agency within the government. Veiled in its camouflage and classified operations, the government continually denied its existence. Its reconnaissance satellites, like the KH series, MILSTAR, and FORTE, were classified and code named for security. Its structure fell within the Pentagon. The Air Force, CIA, the black space program, and classified intelligence operations fell within the secret organizational framework in its mission to protect National Security. The reconnaissance satellites were their tools to aid in that mission. The National Security Agency (NSA), another secret agency within, kept the secrets safe.

The satellites used by the government and military intelligence were used for remote viewing and eavesdropping on other countries activities. The photographed images and audio received by the units were shot back to earth from space in real time. The intelligence agencies compiled and analyzed the information around the clock. The data retrieved aided the agencies with vital information, improving the future strategic planning of military operations against opposing threats.

TransAmerican Telecommunications Corporation, with Mr. Jordan James as CEO, designed and engineered commercial satellites for use in resource management issues around the world. He began altering, refining, and enhancing the basic satellite. He added key components and configurations within the satellite system, and its links, eventually changing its capabilities into a reconnaissance satellite.

From that design, he masterminded an evolution in the spy satellites. He developed it into the most powerful system among the reconnaissance satellites operating around the world. In the world of espionage, it was the most threatening spy satellite ever developed to date.

Mr. James transformed the satellite and perfected its enigmas encountered during its past missions in space. In doing so, he developed a new frontier in space reconnaissance. He achieved superior hardening surfaces, making the satellite resistant to attacks and impossible to destroy, even by nuclear blasts. It's information and imagery would transmit the world over at strategic and tactical locations simultaneously and instantaneously in real time. It would immediately aid actual commanders and their forces under attack in the field.

His prototype of the new ultra-reconnaissance satellite featured a worldwide jam resistant communication link that operated at the extremely highest frequency wavelengths to keep interception unattainable. He implemented an impenetrable encryption program for the communications, insuring its security.

Its stealth design and unprecedented maneuverability in very high orbits beyond synchronous kept the satellite out of range, deceptive, and efficient in its cloaking devices to enable it to disappear and change positions rapidly on any target.

The advanced technology in digital resolution imaging he perfected further by developing an advanced miniature supercomputer that contained a million microprocessors with concurrent computational capabilities. Ten computers were on board. They function assisted by automated computer control systems backed by artificial intelligence equipped to debug problems encountered after orbit. On its first test, crystal clear images returned to earth from its orbit in space.

The team specifically engineered the computer so it was not dependent on keyboards or graphical interface. They installed a new memory chip, a prototype they built, that could store 10 billion bits of information on a surface area a little larger than the palm of your hand.

Encrypting the writing of the CPU's programs protected it against hackers. An impenetrable immunization program was specifically written and installed into the system to protect it against deadly viruses attempting to destroy its superior capabilities. The ultra spy satellite he produced surpassed the United States current inventory. In space espionage, its threat would bring instantaneous world apprehension.

In order for TransAmerican and his family's future to survive the financial crisis it suffered, Mr. James secretly made an executive decision and added the ultra spy satellite to its inventory. He began negotiating with an underground network of counterintelligence operatives. The illegal ultra spy satellite he built would be the company's money train to the future.

Mr. James personally appointed his Board of Directors. It had nine members, the only ones in the organization aware of the black transaction with the Russian underground.

The top research and engineering team he called his Celestial Team, he hand picked among the top minds in the world. Enticing them away from private companies was easy using an enormous benefit package full of incentives. The employees he stole from his competitors had all previously worked under contract by the government, developing NASA's black space program.

The first three of his prototypes of his ultra-reconnaissance satellite he code named ETP (Extra Terrestrial Protection), rolled off the assembly line. After a year of negotiations, he had agreed to sell the units to Russia's underground network of Communists, X-KGB Officers, and the Russian Mafia.

The United States government ended up unknowingly financing the satellites that Russia's underground purchased. The government, in an attempt to help bail out the failing Russian economy after the Cold War, offered to help the New Federation promote democracy. It financed Russia's new government.

The former Communist line, along with the numerous X-KGB agents, and the powerful Russian Mafia with its tangled web grasping the throat of Russia, stole the money intended for investment into Russia's future. The same groups that ruled during the dictatorship, still kept the money from the citizens of Russia while their families starved and froze. The citizens were better off under Communism than under the new system.

Their powerful military forces, once the largest and most feared in the world, started suffering beyond recognition. They became a bleak skeleton crew, suffering endless maladies. Suicides were common place. The government promised paychecks, but the soldiers' families did not receive them on a regular basis, if at all. If they did, they came too late, and were a small pittance. The men who committed suicide believed the New Federation's government would pay their families the benefit from their life insurance policies after their deaths.

The corrupt Communists who lined their pockets with American money accomplished their number one priority after the fall of the Cold War. The satellites the Russian rogues raped their own country for would be used against the United States to secure their rightful legacy of power in the world, shedding the New Federation's Democratic Party.

The irony of the situation he became entangled with in his negotiations with the rogues affirmed Jordan James's plan to proceed and accomplish his personal objectives despite his doubts of appearing like a traitor to his country. Jordan believed his scheme was an excellent ruse to create a fusion within the current administration. If he was caught selling the satellites, he would be dealt with as a traitor. In his mind and heart, he saw himself as a patriot of the United States. It wasn't as if he was handing the Russians the most powerful nuclear weapon in the world to annihilate the United States. He merely moved a pawn in the world's political chess game. Selling the satellites to the Russian underground would be a crucial play to strengthen the American economy.

He laid out an intricate scheme of intrigue to motivate the United States into building the power back into the military. At the same time, add a financial bonanza for his company. Its shrinking funds caused from the inflation it had to endure by the governments mismanaged agencies inflamed him. When they started cutting the chief organs of the government that were vital to its freedom, his fiery temper flared into action. The military and intelligence units were cut to shreds by those budget concerns. What could be more important in the eyes of the Nation than being able to protect the country in an aggression of war and retain the freedom the generations of soldiers fought and died for? The outcome of his plot would go down in history, and be a matter of interpretation as to whether he was a betrayer of his country or a freedom fighter.

He resolutely believed the U.S. needed a perilous shake up of its structure, a head banging wake up call from the real powers in Russia that they cordially promoted, financed, and put faith in their future. The Russian's Democracy they forced, failed. And now, the plan by the U.S. government would soon backfire in their own neighborly face. The knowledge that they weren't the only country that held America dead on in their sights, spurred him to bring America on-line. He'd provide the beginning shake and watch in hopes that a reaction to save the trembling world would change lax attitudes across the nation.

The Rogue Russian Regime's aggression would force them to act swiftly to build their depleted military forces, update corrupted defense systems, and stockpile their empty warehouses with high-tech warfare equipment once again. The pulse of the military would be efficiently operational again, and ready to defend the country, a country that sat wide open and exposed.

The chain reaction rippling through the world, motivated by the threat, would produce another financial gain. Every world leader would need the ultra system to get back in the game of intelligence from the new threat he re-created by reviving Russia, the largest country in the world, back from the dead, and the end result would improve the world's economy.

If his plan worked to align the government and military again, to the real threat of a world war without actually hurting the citizens of the United States, it would be worth the risk. The citizens who denied any country would openly attack the U.S., that guns confiscated from citizens would protect them, and living in world peace was possible, needed a grave reality check. It was those kind of delusional fools sitting at the top rung of the government running the military with their heads buried in the sand. They desperately needed a direct sucker punch to secure their attention. Government responsibility called for action and accountability. Freedom founded on its powers needed preserving, and protected even against itself. Even after the bravest battles are fought and won, letting the country's guard down would only repeat history. Open doors and back doors left open, become inhabited by hostile enemies.

Jordan James wanted his country to get serious again. The world's composition of frightening and conspiring factions, were ready to pounce. He experienced their hatred, their rage, their vindictiveness first hand. Negotiating across conference tables at hardened eyes spewing violence forth from every pore of their bodies, he understood. America's ripe to pick. It was only a matter of time. At the current size of the active military, Jordan heard from his own intelligence reports that it would lose the country quickly if a foreign power hit swiftly on more than one unprotected area inside the U.S.. The military was capable of only fighting one battle at a time, where throughout history, it built itself to fight against aggression from an enemy at several places at the same time, anywhere in the world.

He stood by his conviction that the government would respond quickly to the news flash. They would react, prepare to catch up, move past it, and in the end, rise above it. They'd fight back and learn from the experience. It would come out still on top. A survivor. The country would remember the lesson, be wiser, and bond in their new found strength and power, restoring faith back into the system that failed them. A system that lost its citizen's hope for the future in the hands of the corrupt politicians running amok. The comedy of errors would end, and be regenerated with pride once again.

So, Mr. James initiated the plan, kept it simple, and it soon took shape. These days, International flights between Russia and the United States occurred daily, as easily as a flight from LA to New York. The United States, by promoting the democracy in the New Federation of Russia, helped ease the flight restrictions between the countries.

With the final stage of the plan in his hand, Russia's underground already paid three payments, well over fifty million dollars. The fourth payment would be transferred into various overseas accounts by wire before the delivery of the satellites from Montana to Russia, ending his foul conspiracy with them. He felt comfortable handing the satellites over. He engineered a back up plan written into the artificial intelligence's program aboard just encase the scenario he planned turned sour.

Mr. James reviewed the final operation again, making sure everything was ready. The papers in front of him blurred. He glanced at his watch.

He realized his concentration had left him the night he was informed of Jennica's shooting. The person responsible, he personally vowed to kill. No one messed with his family. Whoever did, would find that they made the biggest mistake of their lives. And it would be their last.

Grabbing the intelligence files laid neatly on his desk by his security team, he perused them again. Searching the files for a possible suspect to her shooting became his mission. He felt sure, somewhere in them would be the answer to the reason she was shot. Scanning all business transactions they conducted, it overwhelmed him when the multiple possibilities popped up from the page.

Every person he dealt with had a file. No buyer or group remained free from his thorough background checks before the contracts went into negotiations and signed. Full of seedy individuals and groups, from Iraqis to Colombians, the dossiers read like the CIA's most wanted list. The review of his files of his transactions, kept him busy, churning his mind to absolute revenge.

Checking his watch, he realized the jet waited for him. His wife would already be aboard. The flight to Montana to see his daughter caused a chill to race through him. A limousine would be waiting at the airport. He doubted his mind would be relieved of its torture when he visited his daughter. He expected the rage that consumed him earlier would return with a vengeance after he witnessed first hand the extent of the injuries his daughter Jennica battled to stay alive.

Chapter 9

Saturday, the 7th day of September, 5:00 P.M.
St. Angeline Catholic Church
Bozeman, Montana

"Let us pray." Father Murphy bowed his head as the congregation knelt down in front of their pews, hoping that God would be in their presence as they prayed for the healing of Jennica James.

"Tonight, we all gather under a cloak of uncertainty. Jennica James, a respected member of our church, who most of us had the joy of watching grow from a tiny child into the talented young women she is today, was shot last night. She lies in the hospital, clutching onto life with every fiber of her being. It's a terrible tragedy shrouding our small community, none of us expected this kind of thing to happen to one of our own. Let us take a moment to silently pray for her, her family, and her friends gathered here tonight. Let us know, dear God, that in our ailing hearts, our prayers to you will be heard and that you will see that Jennica makes a remarkable recovery."

The pews filled for the Saturday evening mass, with parishioners kneeling silently for a few minutes before crossing themselves and looking back to Father Murphy.

He glanced back at his parish, a lump catching in his throat. He felt the pain that he saw painted across each and every face. Sacred were the children. In their spirits, they hold the future in their hands.

As Jennica's priest, she held an extra special place in his heart since he arrived in Bozeman. After seeing her lying lifeless last night in the hospital, it tore a crevice the size of the Grand Canyon in his heart. He found himself traveling deep into a hole, searching a dark place he'd traveled to before and decided he never wanted to return again. He stared down the Devil wielding his shimmering pitch fork at him, hissing at him through the fire, glowering back as he basked in his latest glory. The Devil flaunted his quest, and turned his heart to ice. A smile painted hideously across his demon face, touched his soul once again, searing his human flesh with excruciating pain and making him scream out to God in his agony.

Father Murphy reached up and crossed himself ending with, "In the name of the Father, and of the Son, and of the Holy Ghost, amen." He walked off with his Bible to the back of the church to the confessional booth and waited for those who needed a confession.

He bowed his head and said another prayer for Jennica, his mind reeling with thoughts foreign to him as the devil prayed on his weakened state of mind, leaving him spent. A long night by Jennica's side left his spirit drained.

A voice started speaking from the other side of the wall. The voice of a young man whispering to him, so no one else could overhear. "Father, bless me for I have sinned. It has been eight months since my last confession."

"What is it that has brought you here my son?"

"I took the gun that shot Jennica James, and I have it here with me, Father."

Father Murphy jerked his head up in surprise. He did not recognize the voice. "Yes, go on." He held his voice steady. Panic started setting in at the thought of what the rest of the conversation might bring to light.

"I found it after the shooting, Father. I grabbed it out of the dirt in the fieldhouse as everyone ran out." He cleared his throat, trying to lower his voice. "I didn't shoot her, but I'm afraid."

"What are you afraid of?"

"I'm afraid the police will think I shot her. I didn't, I swear. I just saw it and without thinking I just picked it up."

"You wanted a gun?"

"Yes, Father. I was wrong, but I've seen the evil in my ways. I have sinned by taking this gun, and by wanting this gun. Can you forgive me?" His plea sounded desperate. His voice cracked as he spoke. He started crying. "Will you turn me in Father?"

"No son. What is spoken here is heard only by God and myself. I cannot and will not break the sanctity of this confession. You must do ten Hail Mary's and three Our Father's for penance, and leave the gun. I'll give it to the authorities with anonymity. Go now, and you shall be forgiven."

"Thank you Father." The man slipped out of the dark room, leaving the gun on the seat of the chair.

Father Murphy quickly left the booth. He walked around to the door, looking around as he opened it. The gun laid there, the silver barrel sparkling in the dim cast of light from the hall. He took it and hid it under his cassock. A peculiar feeling swept over him as he left the tiny room. The boy didn't tell him if he saw the person who shot Jennica. His anxiety heightened at the answer he posed from the question lurking in his mind.

Father Murphy went back and sat down in the booth, waiting for others to straggle in to him. Hearing a few more confessions from his flock who needed to cleanse their souls, he muddled through feeling unusually distracted. The Church emptied once again, leaving it quiet. He walked back through the empty church shutting the lights off in every room. The quietness stirred his thoughts into chaos.

Father Murphy craned his neck to stare up at the stained glass window under the dome. In the center of the church he prayed viewing the celestial heavens above him on the clear night. A short meditation helped him gather his strength on most nights. The stars glimmered back from the dark sky, sweeping an ominous breeze throughout his body. The gun pressed against his skin fanned the fire of confusion blazing in his mind, leaving him in an even weaker state than he had felt before. He prayed to God, wondering if he listened to him. He could not remember ever feeling so lonely or inadequate. It was as if his life work was just a sick joke. He shook his head to ward off the evil spirits engulfing him as he walked back to the rectory.

Father Murphy slipped the gun out of his robe and gently laid it on the table. He sat in front of it. Repulsion boiled from his gut from just the touch of it. Like a rabid dog he glared down at it. Curiosity replaced the disgust as he picked it up, turning it around to view it closer.

He realized it resembled the first pistol he learned to shoot at a friend's cabin the previous summer, much to his adamant misgivings towards doing just that. Turning it over in his hand, he discovered a piece of wood missing from the grips. Realizing it was the same sort of nick he caused the first time his friend instructed him while shooting the pistol. After he had pulled the trigger, the recoil startled him, making his hand jerk and the gun fall. It fell from a porch down about ten feet onto a huge boulder and skidded across it to the forest ground. There were scratches along one side on the silver metal from the skid it took, that appeared to still be on it. It made him feel bad he'd caused damage to one of Rob's guns. Rob said it was no big deal. Grips were interchangeable and the scratches easily fixed. His mind became bombarded with thoughts of Rob Browning and what his latest discovery might mean.

He loathed guns and everything they stood for in the world. Rob talked him into just target shooting for fun. In his mind, learning to shoot and handle a gun were handy things to know in the West. A man might need a gun at some point in his life, even if he used it for self-defense. Rob didn't see anything wrong with protecting family or himself. He didn't understand that a priest could never use a gun, even in his own defense.

Father Murphy jumped up like a man trying to get out of the electric chair. He dropped the gun, his hands jerking wildly, as if the charge of electricity from his imaginary chair reached his hands, rendering them uncontrollable. Rob Browning clouded his mind, mingling it with the night of the shooting. He couldn't have had anything to do with the shooting. He left town a month before for a while. Rob did attend the church and had met Jennica, but that was all there was to it. They were just acquaintances as far as he knew. Rob Browning had become a close friend of his over the past three years he attended the church.

Father Murphy wanted to talk with Rob right away, but decided the right thing to do would be to turn the gun over to the police. He'd then investigate the situation later. Rob had left his number before he left town. He'd try to contact him there.

He grabbed his gray coat and matching hat. He placed the gun in a brown paper bag, rolling the top down, and carefully tucked it under his right arm. A stroll under the clear night skies would do his heart good this evening. It would give him a chance to get a little exercise. And just maybe, the crisp evening air would help clear the fog from his mind and revive his spirit.

Some blocks to the southwest of the church stood the Law and Justice Center. He wove a path through the residential areas until he came into the backside of the building. Walking around to the front, he rang the button on the outside of the glass doors. The door buzzed, unlocking it. He passed to the inside and up the stairs to a window showcasing a young girl working behind it. She looked up acknowledging him with a smile.

"May I help you?"

"Yes, I need to speak with the Chief of Police. It's rather important. Is he in?" Father Murphy smiled back at her.

"You're in luck. He doesn't usually work on Saturday evening, but he's been here all day. Your name please?"

"Father Murphy."

"Just a minute." She dialed the phone. "A Father Murphy is here to see you."

She hung up the telephone. "He'll be right out to see you."

"Thank you." Father Murphy said.

A tall man about six foot two in height, wearing an immaculate blue suit, came out of the side door from where Father Murphy stood. He had wavy gray hair that spiraled out of control here and there. Before reaching his hand out to greet Father Murphy, he quickly reached up and slicked the top down and grinned.

"Father Murphy, what a surprise. What can I do for you?"

"Is there somewhere we could sit down and talk for a moment?" Father Murphy shifted the sack under his arm.

The Chief motioned for Father Murphy to follow. They walked in silence to his office.

They both entered the door. Chief Bishop took his seat at his desk. "Sit down Father."

"Thank you." Father Murphy sat down removing his hat and set it on the top of the desk.

"You have my full attention." Chief of Police Bishop leaned back in his chair, pulling his arms over his head and stretched.

"You look tired, Chief." Father Murphy said.

"I am. I'm sure you know by now, Jennica James was shot last night. We don't get a lot of attempted murder cases here, thank God. Oh, I'm sorry, Father."

"It's okay. I know what you mean. God *is* to be thanked. Most people don't do enough of it. Jennica James is also the reason that I am here." He set the paper bag up on the desk. "Go ahead and open it."

The Chief leaned forward and pulled the bag over to him. When he unrolled the top and opened it, his brows furled at the sight.

"This was taken at the fieldhouse last night after Jennica was shot," Father Murphy said. "It showed up in my confession booth. I'm sorry, but that is all I'm able to say in this matter."

"What? You're telling me someone gave you this gun and you can't tell me who this person is?"

"That's right, and I'm sorry."

"Great. That's just great. They could be the person who shot her and they may get away with it. Even if they didn't shoot her, they could have witnessed the whole thing and they could aid us in apprehending the right person. Do you understand that?"

"Yes, I do. I understand all the implications. I can only leave you with the gun."

"Father, this is important. Jennica James is a member of our church. Don't you want to bring the person who did this to her to justice?"

"I do, more than anything in my life, but I can't break my vows." Father Murphy stood up and retreated out the doors he came in from. His pace accelerated.

Chapter 10

Saturday, September 7 at 7:30 P.M.
Law and Justice Center, Bozeman, Montana

The Chief lifted the phone from its cradle and dialed a number off the top of his head. The telephone rang, and kept ringing. He was ready to hang up when he heard dialing in his ears.

"Hello. Hello?" the Chief said.

"Yes, who is this?"

He knew it was Dylan's overprotective mother, Mary Ann Drake. He attempted to squelch the aggravation he felt taking over his entire body like a bad flu bug.

"This is Chief of Police, Bishop. What's the matter? Your telephone kept ringing. I was about to hang up when I heard you dialing."

"Nothing's the matter. I had the phone unplugged. You can hang up now, I have to make a call."

"I can't. I need to talk to Dylan right away."

"He's sleeping, Chief Bishop. Someone kept him working all night."

"You'll have to wake him up. This can't wait." He ignored her remark.

Della and Dylan were always trying to fix the two of them up, never asking him what he thought about it. He didn't like her and he was sure that the feeling was mutual. She didn't suit him.

"Oh, all right. My poor boy looked like death warmed over. I'll just let you finish the job. Have it your way." She banged the receiver down on the side table with a bionic force.

"Damn," he took the receiver away from his ear, rubbing it. "Damn that woman."

"What?" Dylan said.

"Dylan?"

"Who else were you expecting?"

"Your Mother again. You got to the phone pretty fast for a poor boy looking like death warmed over."

"I heard her talking. I came out to see if she was screening my calls again. Sorry, you know her."

"Dylan, why don't you make her move?"

"I like her here. I want to take care of her."

"She doesn't need anyone to watch over her but—"

Dylan cut him off in mid-sentence. "What's got you singed around the edges today?" Dylan laughed.

"Your Mother, that's who."

"Got a thing for her, do you? Why don't you let her come live with you? The two of you in cohabitation would bring new meaning to the word."

"Hell, no! Dylan, let's drop this right now. I don't like where this conversation is heading. Go get Della and come over here right away. You're the lead detectives on the James shooting, right?"

"We are. I thought you would have known. You turned it over to the Sheriff's Department officially this morning. Captain Mitchell handed it to us. Why? You have something new?"

"Yes, I do. Get over here. I'll fill you in on it when both of you are here." He slammed the telephone down into the receiver, still agitated by Drake's sense of humor and his impossible mother.

Dylan grabbed his boots as he headed for the front door. Mrs. Drake followed, dangling his black leather jacket from her outstretched arm.

"You may need this, if you plan to stay out all night again."

"I hope not, but please don't wait up." Dylan stepped over and gave his mom a kiss on her cheek, relieving her of his coat.

"Thanks for looking out for me Mom, but it's my job. I have to go. You need to find something else to do around here besides worry about me all night. Go out, take in a movie."

"By myself? Sure, that would be fun. What would people think of me?"

"Nothing, Mom. People go out by themselves all the time."

"Sure, desperate people do."

"I have to go. I'll see you later." Dylan smiled at his mom.

He jogged to a fully dressed Harley. He cinched his helmet around his chin while jumping down on the kick-start. It came to life as he fed it more fuel, revving up the quiet engine purring under him.

Dylan backed the bike down the long drive, then sped through the dark streets on his way to Della's place, allowing the cool breeze in his face to wake him up tonight. Once he hit the forty-five mile an hour speed limit on Bridger Drive, the combination of speed and mountain air made the temperature in the canyon drop, blasting his face with frigid air. His tired mind became instantly alert, better than downing a giant sized mug of strong coffee. The mix made him feel alive again; ready for whatever the night would bring.

His bike felt good under him, as if they were one, gliding smoothly around the tight corners past the Fish Hatchery. Twisting between the mountain rocks on one side and the rushing river on the other on his bike, it thrilled him every time. It made his blood pump faster and his heart race, feeling as if it kept time with the speed of the bike. It boomed out like thunder beneath his shirt, charging through his body, igniting it like electricity in a storm.

He reached Della's house in Bridger Canyon in record time. Her freshly painted canary yellow house looked crisp under the softly glowing yard light. It sported a large yard fenced with white picket. He parked in her driveway and walked to the front door.

"Anybody home?" Dylan called, waiting briefly before knocking again. He turned the doorknob to find the door unlocked. He yelled again, louder this time as he walked inside. He didn't want to catch her by surprise. She just might shoot.

He walked in the living room, taking in the mess. Dishes in the sink, food out on the counter, and magazines dropped here and there.

"Della, it's me." He followed the clothes trail to the stairs then cautiously started up them, hoping a bullet wouldn't ricochet in his direction.

Suddenly a huge ball of white fluff jumped on him, growling viciously and taking him by complete surprise at the top of the stairs. His heart skipped two beats.

"Kiki boy, it's just me, Dylan."

Kiki stopped growling and started licking. Dylan petted him. He felt relieved the dog recognized him. Kiki wandered past him, down the stairs, and loped to the kitchen for his bowl of food nestled in the corner of Della's war zone she called a kitchen.

Dylan continued down the hall at the top of the stairs. Della didn't respond to the noise.

An image of Della formed in his mind stopping him cold, Della sharing her bed with another man. After all, she'd given him enough opportunities to join her there the past few months. Tired of asking him and being turned down, maybe she finally found someone else. That would explain the clothing found carelessly dropped on the way up to her bed.

Dylan started investigating, searching closer for clues, and playing his role as detective. The thought of her with another man sent a shiver rumbling through him. The feeling he recognized. Della would read him the riot act, then kill him for interfering in her private life. He visualized her as he reached down to pick up a piece of shiny red material off the floor. He fingered the red silk bra. That detail he definitely didn't need to know about his partner.

His thoughts wandered, taking him back ten years, when Della was still in high school. They met for the first time at the Police Officer's Ball. All night, she clung to the Chief of Police's arm, her date for the evening. Chief Bishop was proud of his daughter on his arm, and she was proud of her father escorting her. They stood out in the crowd like two beacons of bright light among the police officers and their families.

Dylan fell in love instantly with her sense of humor. She possessed a unique personality that was fun and energizing to be around, but knew the term jail bait and dropped all thoughts of ever being more than a friend to her. He enjoyed being around her. He was twenty-six and she just turned sweet sixteen. Robert Bishop was the Chief of the Bozeman Police Department and his boss at the time, before he made a switch to the Sheriff's Department. That was more than enough to keep him at a safe distance then.

Eventually they became close friends, though, in a friendship she instigated from the start by using her whole family. Dylan spent many weeknights and weekends when he was off duty at their home playing football and other games with her older brothers, and Della. They ate a lot of meals together around their family table. Chief Bishop sat at the head, treating him like one of his own sons.

The whole family made him feel welcome like one of their own. It filled up his own loneliness after leaving his mother after his father died in Salt Lake. His mom wouldn't move away from his father's grave and come to Montana to live with him. After his discharge from the Navy, he'd accepted a position with the Bozeman Police Department. He had no brothers or sisters and enjoyed being included as part of their large family.

Mrs. Bishop died when Della was five, leaving her father and three brothers to raise her. It's probably what made her into what she is today, he thought, an independent woman with a strong will and a definite mind of her own. She spent the summers in Italy with her Italian grandparents where her grandmother was the only womanly influence in her life.

Dylan was positive that if she didn't have that woman to influence her life as a child to smooth out her rough edges, she'd be intolerable to be around. Her brash personality became overbearing even to him at times. Woman hated her, and most men in their division didn't know how to take her. You had to know her like he did, to really appreciate her true character. Once he did, he knew he would love her forever.

The last thing her family wanted was for her to go into law enforcement. But of course, she drove herself obsessively to it to prove to the men in her life, including him, that she would do it, no matter what they wanted her to do. She drove herself hard, becoming a cop and then pushing until she made it to detective.

Lately, Della seemed to intrude into his mind more and more. Not because of the work they did together, but in a fantasy that tantalized him into instant arousal just from curiosity. She developed from a cute teen into a desirable woman. Very easy on his eyes. It had been hard to resist her and keep the close friendship that they developed years before under control.

Della wore her dark brown hair longer, down past her shoulders, sculpted in layers of fine silk around the front, along the perfect features of her face. Her mysterious violet-blue eyes lured Dylan in, speaking volumes to him without her ever having to talk.

He knew the rules and respected them. Their jobs depended on it. It might not have mattered if she picked another line of work, but now that she was his partner, the risks ran too high. It would be a fatal move for them both.

Della was a natural tease. She continually taunted him, knowing the way he felt about the whole situation. Her alluring female presence drove him mad, slithering into his thoughts frequently when they weren't together working on a case. He brushed the bra against his face, smelling the sweet scent of lilacs Della wore. He dropped the bra back on the floor deciding to go in further.

He stepped into the dark room, focusing on the huge bed in the middle of her bedroom. Della lay there on her side, resembling Sleeping Beauty, still and peaceful wrapped in a down comforter. Her long legs stuck out, curled around the end of the blanket.

She was a beautiful sight for his tired eyes. His mind wished he could go to her and have her wrap her exquisite legs around him that way. He shook back the thoughts escalating out of control in his mind, curbing them with a steely determination and years of practice. He stepped back into the hall and felt goose bumps forming on his neck. Ripples of relief swept over him. She was alone.

Chapter 11

Saturday, the 7th day of September, 8:00 P.M.

Dylan rapped on the solid doorframe of Della's room loudly, yelling to her at the same time. Since he went that far, he decided he might as well go all the way inside.

"Dylan?" A sleepy voice called from the bedroom. "Dylan." Della sat up, looking startled. She looked down, quickly grabbing the comforter, pulling it up around her. Della tried to hide her welcomed surprise playing across her face when she realized Dylan stared at her in the short distance inside her bedroom as if he'd never seen a woman naked.

Dylan edged inside closer to her and grinned. "Yeah, it's me. I tried staying at the front door, but you didn't answer. When I found your door unlocked, I came in to investigate. A cop who doesn't lock her door. That's not too smart, Del. I thought that maybe something happened to you when you didn't answer my loud call. You know this big mouth." He pointed at it and grinned. "Who couldn't hear it? So—, I followed the trail of clothes up the stairs. I had no idea you slept in the buff. Sorry."

He raised his brows and stared, eyeing the bra he left in the doorway, acting quite amused with himself. He picked it up and grinned. He felt like a teenager, caught red-handed spying on her. "Nice. I didn't know you were the Frederick's of Hollywood type." He twirled it around his index finger, laughing.

Della stomped over pulling her comforter along to Dylan who caressed the silky material. She snatched her bra out of his hand. "Give me that before you get overheated. Unless you want to borrow it. And there's a lot about me you don't know. You only know what you want to know." Her comforter slipped down revealing her breasts.

Dylan's eyes widened. His mouth dropped open before he could contain himself and think again of a comeback to her last comment.

She slowly pulled the comforter back up and smiled.

"Did you enjoy the view? Or would you like me to drop this comforter right now and let you see what you've been missing. Or, did you sneak a peek while I was sleeping? I wish I could figure you out. Do you want to play with me now?"

"No, we have work to do. I'm sorry I came up here," he said. His eyes turned away from her.

"What's wrong with you? I just want you to make love to me. That's all I've ever wanted since the day my father introduced me to you. Is that so awful? Am I so repulsing to you since I became your partner? What's pushing you farther away from me these days?"

She stared him down, her eyes holding his, waiting for him to say something. He lost his witty comeback, but he wasn't surprised by her dauntless manner of speaking. His face felt hot. Her eyes strayed from his, roaming his body. She knew he didn't find her repulsive after witnessing his physical reaction. She seductively smiled, her eyes slowly roaming down his body and returning to his face.

Dylan met her eyes, and turned to leave.

"I hope you're in excruciating pain Detective Drake. Maybe it will finally convince your confused mind it's the real thing. Or next time, maybe you'll use the doorbell." She said, as he disappeared.

"Get dressed, if you plan on working today." Dylan's voice dropped to a deep monotone. Minutes later, he heard her call to him from her bedroom door. Turning towards her voice, she walked slowly towards him clad in just her red panties and matching high heels. He took in a deep breath. He quickly recovered. Her body, fully exposed, except for the little velvet triangle he imagined behind her bikini panties, left him fumbling for his next line. "Della," he finally said through his shock. He stood paralyzed, not sure what to do next. He'd been through a lot in his life, but seeing her like that, rattled him more than meeting an enemy by surprise or being on the wrong end of a gun barrel. She had him, and she didn't seem the least bit shy in her show of indecency.

"Well, I thought as long as you're still hovering around here you could help me hook this damn thing." She slipped the bra on casually in front of him, pulling it down over her breasts slowly. Guiding them into the half cups, she looked at Dylan from the corner of her eyes.

An irresistible smile glistened across her full lips. Her offering, assaulted his body, tempting him to react and satisfy her wish.

Her breasts spilled from the half cups, bulging with cleavage. "Wonder Bra," she said. She turned her back to him, waiting for him to snap the hooks.

He stood locked in place. The thought of touching her flawless skin burned his fingers. His desire for her was as strong as the will he was using to resist the temptation.

"What's wrong Dylan?" Della said. She turned her head to look at him. Terror filled his face.

"Does the thought of touching me bother you? Come on, Dylan. We're partners, are we not? If we were both men, we'd be showering together in the locker room, sharing soap and everything." She laughed, throwing her head back and turning partially to see his face.

"This is not the same thing and you know it," he said. His hands carefully avoided touching her back. He slid the hooks together effortlessly.

"You have lots of experience at this, I've heard. You're an expert." She said.

Rage flared inside, her last comment fueling the fire building in him. She controlled him. She knew exactly what she was doing to him. Dylan stepped closer, smelling her scent of sweet lilacs. An unmerciful desire crept up on him and merged with his fiery passion. The beauty he held in his eyes staring at her, worked on freeing his conscience to respond in the way she wanted him to. It kept telling him to tread closer into her trap. The overwhelming feelings pushed him closer towards her, until he remembered his vow and all the risks involved if he fulfilled her wish. It tore him up. His insides shredded to pieces.

He reached for her silky hair, gliding his fingers through the thickness and grasped it. He pulled on the hair, jerking her head back close into his chest as his mouth reached her ear, trying to keep his breathing steady. He reached his other arm around her chest and pulled her harder against him. Melding his hard body into hers, his right leg wrapped around her thigh and pulled, squeezing and penning her in place so she could feel her creation throbbing against her. She reached out, grabbing the doorframe, her arms extended overhead.

He cupped his left hand hard around her right breast, massaging it gently, then squeezing the protruding nipple brutally and rolling it around with his fingers through the silky material. A quiet moaning sound escaped from her lips. He violently fondled her body to deliberately scare her from the fantasy she kept of him. It could never be what she deserved to have. After listening to her whimper, he eased up on his grip.

"Don't ever do this to me again." Dylan said. "Do you hear me? You infuriate me. I want to bend you over, take you right here, and let you have it. Finish what you started with me. Do you feel your wish?" Dylan leaned harder into her. She braced herself and grasped the frame of the door harder. "Do you hear me, Della? I want to rape you until you can't move. Do you know what being raped feels like? Is that what you want? Is that all you want from me? Why are you teasing me beyond my control and recklessly brandishing this exquisite body of yours in front of me? You've offered it to me like a piece of meat. I feel my body reacting to your enticing spell, but I'm your partner and I was your close friend. This isn't you, and this sure as hell isn't me. I'm a man. And I do enjoy a good piece of ass. Any man would want to take you right now, but I don't need a whore."

Della's eyes widened as she listened to him. His deep voice shouted his cruel words. Penetrating deeply inside, her anger flared in response. Turning swiftly, she slapped him across his face.

He held his stance over her. Not a muscle twitched in his body. His clenched jaws remained locked.

She recognized his murderous intent behind his dark green eyes. "Don't flatter yourself, Dylan. I don't tease. You know how I feel. Why don't you tell me what you really feel? The real reason you're denying your feelings and ruining the chance we have to be together. You know I love you. I also know you love me. I don't think I'm imagining it. We've both known it for years. You're the one who came up here to me, remember? What were you really hoping to find? Another man making love to me?" she said. "Is that what you wanted? Were you hoping I'd find a man so you could finally convince yourself to let me go? I wish it were that easy. I'd do it. I'm in as much pain from your denial as you are. I'm beginning to think you're gay."

Dylan released his grip, pushing her hard forward through the door, forcing her hands to give way. She lost her footing in her fancy high heels. Watching her fall to her knees, he turned his back to leave. Reacting out of blind rage towards her scenario and her last bitter insult to protect her from his rejections, he knew to get the hell out of there before he did hurt her. Being gay would be much easier than the torture he felt keeping his real reasons hidden from her.

"See, you can't take it, can you? You don't want me, but you sure don't want me to be with anybody else, do you? The thought scares the hell out of you, doesn't it? Just as it does me. And I can tell by your reaction it upsets you more than I thought it would," Della said. She watched him turn to leave. Pulling off one heel, she pitched it towards him. It bounced off the wall, knocking a picture off the dresser.

"You're right, Dylan. I'm not a whore. But I'm not a virgin that needs your protection anymore." She screamed loudly through the door at him. "I've grown up and I know you've noticed."

"If you care, I'm leaving in five minutes, with or without you. The investigation needs our attention, not this bullshit fantasy you've convinced yourself into believing." Dylan yelled back to her as he flew down the steps.

The veins at his temples and the arteries in his neck pulsed wildly. His rage boiled, filling him with more fire and crazy energy to burn. Using that rage and anger to strike out and bring down enemies he was sworn to kill, he had honed to perfection in specialized warfare in the Navy. The soldiers who killed without a bat of an eye were rewarded for the highest body counts. It earned him Sainthood within the teams.

He became part of a unique and classified unit of the sharpest and most deadly shooters in the OP–06 Delta (Navy SEALS) Specialized Warfare Unit. The unconventional Commander chosen to design and develop the top-secret team in his own image, solicited him to be part of his elite team. Eventually he promoted him to Lieutenant before a conspiracy split the unit apart. They were the number one team at infiltration and annihilation of its targets. They performed covert operations worldwide, eliminating and destroying national security threats. Their ultimate Commandment: "There are no rules—Thou shall win at all costs". Each one, lived and died by it.

Since his return from active duty ten years ago, he started a new life in Montana. Controlling the rage that erupted instantly from his murder and mayhem as a Navy SEAL, became his sole nightmare. The rage stayed with him, as if it were as vital to him as any other organ in his body. The rage, forged like steel, beat treacherously inside. It was a natural instinct bred in him he would never lose. It had brought a threat to his new way of life every day. He found it a daunting challenge since his return. He battled to keep it under control and hidden from the world.

Slamming the door on his way out, he hustled to his Harley. His fists came down on the seat. "Jesus." He stared towards the sky as if to apologize. Aversion replaced his rage. He felt disgusted at his lack of control dealing with Della.

She teased him past his control point. He almost gave into the blind lust she created inside of him. The conversation she tried to push him into later, he veered quickly from. He had his reasons, but she kept pushing him. Most of the reasons he explained, over and over again. The reasons should be crystal clear to her. The remaining ones, he'd never explain. His wish was to silently take them to his grave.

The craziness of the situation kept him on the edge of sanity. Hearing her tell him of her feelings, made the madness inside fester. He denied the truth she already knew as he told her another lie. She wanted a reaction out of him—and she knew the strings to pull. His temper reared its repulsive head and instead of getting what she needed, he tried to convince her she suffered from delusions. If she only knew how close he came to giving in to her, but instead, he cruelly played with her body and mind to scare her into backing away from him.

Did he go up the stairs hoping to find her with another man? The feelings consumed him causing him relentless pain. He'd been shot in combat and survived, but this felt much worse. Anxiety pumped the adrenaline in his system as if it had a high pressure pump attached. The shake in his hands alarmed him. When did his steel armor start to rust? He answered his own question.

He'd known for a long time, just as she said she did. The thing he feared the most was the feelings, connecting life back to his heart. She had been at the door knocking all these years as his loving friend. He needed her to stay that way. The door could never be opened. She'd turn and run, and be gone from his life forever. The danger in exposing the truth would put her in the path of destruction, the memory flashing in plain sight, reminded him. It told him to push the pain back down inside and squash the feelings building out of control before it was to late. He knew what he had to do.

Della kicked off the remaining heel, leaving it where it landed, the illusion over for now. She began picking up her clothing as she went, dressing on the run to catch up to Dylan.

Her head shook back and forth wildly. Reality hit her in the face. She instantly regretted her actions in front of Dylan. She forced him into a situation by her impulsiveness. She didn't know if she could look him in the eyes, knowing he hated being pushed into a situation. He explained his feelings to her many times before. She refused to listen after a while, because she realized, it was just an excuse for him to stay single. It would take him a long time to forgive her for this one.

Della couldn't apologize. It was not her style. She quickly made a decision to get past the remorse and stick with the business at hand. Pretending it didn't affect her in the least would be hard, but attainable. After all, she'd had years of practice. Grabbing her coat off the floor, she steadied her emotional state and gained her composure. She found Dylan still waiting for her.

Dylan straddled his motorcycle, resembling a warrior ready for battle. His dark mane gently blew back in the evening breeze, exposing a diamond stud he always wore in his left ear since the day she met him. His green eyes stared ominously back at her, reflecting a fire still raging inside. Sorrow filled his face, and his gentle and easy going appearance had turned to a stern composite. Set like stone, shadowing his handsome face.

Della's heart dipped as she tried looking into his eyes. He avoided her direct eye contact. When he finally did look at her to speak, she witnessed disgust in them. His eyes also told her he held onto his provoked anger. Her conscience burned a giant message from him to her in conclusion of her impulsive display. He pitied her.

"Get on. Your Dad's expecting us," Dylan said in his deepest voice.

"You sure? I should just drive."

"Get on before I leave you standing here eating my dust," he said it firmly, tossing her a helmet.

She put it on quickly before he changed his mind. Della slid on, and reached around his waist to hold on. Realizing she'd better back off tonight, she started to slide her hands away. She felt his hand reach down and stop her. She prayed it was a sign he was trying to forgive her.

Chapter 12

Saturday, the 7th day of September, 8:32 P.M.

Arriving downtown, Dylan and Della came into Chief Bishop's office, startling him from the newspaper.

Della kissed his cheek. "Hi, Dad."

"Della. Glad Dylan brought you."

"Yeah." She looked at Dylan, still hiding her shame. "Me too."

"Here's what I got." He pulled out a sack and opened it, displaying a stainless steel revolver. "I received this tonight."

"Is that the gun that shot the James woman?" Della said.

"It's a good possibility. It's yours to send to the crime lab. I'm sure there are plenty of prints on it you won't be able to use, but the chamber has four rounds left in it. A trace will be easy. Finding the owner may not be. "Dylan, you seem awfully quiet son, is everything all right?"

Chief Bishop observed them from across his desk.

"I'm fine. I just need more sleep. My mind and body are being overworked right now." He frowned at Della. He rubbed his stubble, looking over at the Chief. "This is a lucky break. Are you going to fill us in on how you got this?"

"Father Murphy walked in here with it less than an hour ago, saying it showed up in his Confessional. That's all he can say because of the sanctity of the confession. So, we take it from here."

Della shuffled her feet, staring down, half-listening.

"Della and I are on our way to finish the interviews and check back in at the hospital. I hear the James woman is doing better than expected. She may even come around so we can talk with her."

"I sure hope so." Chief Bishop said. "Let me know what you find out. Now go ahead and get on with your work so you can both call it a night before sunrise again. You both look like hell."

"Thanks, Dad," Della said.

"Thanks, Chief. I feel like hell." He shot another icy gaze towards Della as they left.

They mounted the bike, heading first for the hospital to check on Jennica James.

"Dylan?" Della said.

"I don't want you to say anything to me right now, nothing at all. I need time to cool first. You put my mind in overdrive. I need to concentrate on work. Later we'll talk."

Dylan hit another gear jerking their bodies backwards. They sailed up the long hill on East Main making a quick right turn that sent them horizontal with the pavement. Della instinctively grabbed Dylan tighter, laying her head on his back, leaning with him.

They parked at the Emergency Room entrance and headed through the doors to the reception desk. The person Dylan had mistaken for a nurse the previous night stood reading charts. Her copper hair fell down past her shoulders, pulled back loosely away from her face. She glanced up, giving them a warm smile this time. She engaged her deep hazel eyes with his.

"Hi, I'm Detective—".

"Drake," she said.

He wrinkled his face to her. "So you remember. I'm sorry I—"

"Was rude and assuming," she said.

"Yes, I was. I apologize. No excuses. Do you forgive me?" He pleaded with his eyes until she returned another smile.

"Sure. I always give someone a second chance to prove himself, especially if it's a man begging. Your sad puppy dog face won me without the plea." She slowly smiled back, grinning, revealing dimples on each side of her face.

Della observed the flirting. He charmed a snake once again. She'd never seen him get bit yet.

"I'm Dr. Greene, but you can call me Cait. Jennica James is doing quite well, considering what she's been through already. We do have miracles happen, even in Bozeman. I'm afraid she isn't ready to have visitors yet, but I'll let you know when that's possible."

"Great. Here's my card. My home phone is on the back. Call anytime day or night, please."

"I will. You look like you could use a break. Could I buy you two," she tilted her head past Dylan looking at Della, "a cup of coffee?"

Della stared at the floor absentmindedly.

"No. We have a lot of ground to cover tonight, but I'll certainly take a rain check Cait." Dr. Greene beamed, making her dimples appear even more pronounced as her smile widened.

Della watched the philandering long enough. She choked back the scene, wanting to puke. She stepped up to get a better peek at the lady doctor Dylan ogled over, knowing him all too well.

"Doctor, you wouldn't have any antacids around back there anywhere, would you? I seem to be feeling nauseous," Della said, interrupting the sparks flying back and forth between them.

"I can get some. Are you all right? Want to lie down?" Dr. Greene said.

Dylan stepped closer, grabbing Della's hand and peered deep into her eyes. Della stared back into his eyes, shooting him a look he knew well. He realized the invisible slap in the face she just gave him. He dropped her hand as if it had leprosy.

"She'll be fine," he said. Pulling a short pack of antacids from his pant's pocket. He reached for Della's hand and slapped the package into the palm of her hand. "Start eating," he whispered. He turned towards the doctor who was observing them. He smiled. "I'll be expecting to hear from you." He departed, walking briskly out the exit. In total silence, they reached his Harley.

"Great body. Didn't you think, partner? And I bet she's one hell of a doctor too."

Della fumed quietly behind him and loosened her grip. She tried to hate him on the short trip to the band's house. She realized it would be a futile exercise.

The obsessive love she felt for Dylan the past ten years, would remain in tact like it always had. She'd sat back when she was younger and kept a score card on all the women he dated. Each new one he showed interest in, hurt her more than the last one. At least, he never fell in love enough to marry one, or even keep one around for long. He definitely had a problem with commitment. It worked out to her advantage till now. She needed to find out what it would take to finally break through his armor.

Chapter 13

Saturday, the 7th day of September, 9:00 P.M.

Dylan slid to a stop, kicking his legs out, catching the bike as it tilted into the curb. He read the address on the house on Willson. Della slid off, slowly taking in the band's house, admiring the immaculately landscaped yard.

According to the information they received, once the band established themselves in the music industry, recording contracts started coming their way, along with real money. They pulled all of it together three years ago, purchasing the house. Their investment paid off. They bought it for next to nothing before the real estate market went crazy, inflating the prices to their present all-time high.

The band consisted of eight members. Five originated from Bozeman, Jennica James, Diana Edwards, Martin Meece, Scott and Josh Tate. The other three band members joined later. Kate Wood moved from Los Angeles, Perry White lived in Denver, and Taylor Young traveled all over during his parents' enlistment in the armed services.

The house, viewed from the front, consisted of three circular towers connected to one another like an ancient castle. It sat backed up to a small hill, surrounded by a personal forest. The only thing missing from the castle was the moat. Its red brick masonry had vines dangling down the sides from the towers. Each one had a walk out verandah at the top with a black wrought iron parapet surrounding the balconies.

Della sighed, bitterness filling her words. "Quite a place. It looks and smells like money. They must be doing something right." She turned, looking at Dylan. He kicked the stand down on his bike.

"If you ask me it looks creepy. Something you see in a horror movie. A skeleton-in-every-closet, type of house," he said.

"That's what happens when we stay right here all of our lives. We just snuggle down, nice and comfortable, in the middle of our huge state that most people couldn't point out on a map. All we are is good fodder for anyone in Hollywood needing a good line. I don't care what I'm watching on TV. There's always a crack about Montana. We're in nowheresville to everyone else. We'll never gain any class or wealth sticking around here satisfied with our old farmhouse fixer-uppers, watching Late Night with David Letterman and being cops in this one horse town."

"I'm comfortable with that. That's why I like Bozeman. I did like it better the way it was when I first came to town, but I think it's still a decent place. Unfortunately, I think we just graduated to a two-horse town. Famous singers shot down in cold blood pushes our plain old jobs into much more. I prefer they were kept boring. Money doesn't buy happiness or class. The only way to get them is by working hard to achieve it. You'll gain respect by earning it. And you sure as hell can do both, right here in Nowheresville, Montana." He looked back at the castle, "Hey, I can feel the skeletons calling us. Let's knock. Then we can play hide and seek."

"For a man who's content to never look outside of his own yard, you have developed quite an imagination," Della said.

Dylan laughed, leaning over to whisper in her ear. "Not so, my dear. I plan on finding all the buried pieces of this mystery inside. I bet there's more than one rack of bones hidden in there. I'm not imagining anything. It's my gut feeling." Dylan pointed to his stomach. "And you know it's usually right."

"Okay. I believe you Sherlock. Or are you Rhett Butler?"

"Both, my dear Scarlet. I'm the best of both." He turned and flashed his emerald eyes at her, slyly cracking a smile for the first time since leaving her house.

"Dylan, I don't know, but maybe that's why I like you. You're a damn scoundrel." She grinned. A tiny smirk appeared across her face.

"Frankly, my dear, I don't give a damn," he said, reaching for the doorbell.

"I guess this is the part where I—" Della stopped in mid-sentence. She gazed into the eyes of the most gorgeous man she's seen, standing casually on the other side of the door. He smiled politely, reaching out his hand and waving both of them inside.

"You two must be the detectives. Come on in and have a seat. We've been expecting you."

They followed him into the foyer to a sunken living room full of plush furniture whose new age look didn't fit the style of the house. A large fireplace covered one side of the room. Three overstuffed couches arranged together with two love seat recliners gathered around the other side of the room facing in a semi-circle by the fireplace.

"I'm Perry White." He reached out, shaking Dylan's hand.

"Detective Drake," Dylan said.

Della reached out, "I'm Detective Bishop." She smiled at him, trying hard not to stare. She realized now why there were groupies stalking band members around the country.

"I'll go get everybody. They're in the shop practicing. I went to the hospital to pick up Diana. They let her come home today. I just came in to check on her. She's upstairs sleeping. She's still upset by all of this and is taking things pretty hard. Jennica and Diana were best friends before they began the band. I gave her a sedative the doctor prescribed, and I don't want to wake her up."

"That's fine. We can get a line on her later." Dylan turned to look at Della..

Della's attention was focused on Perry.

Perry White matched Dylan's height of six foot, two inches. His broad shoulders and sculptured biceps were hard to miss in the white sleeveless sweatshirt he wore loose, unzipped halfway to his chest. A silver cross dangled around his thick neck.

His long wavy hair glistened with a spectrum of browns. The hair appeared wild and untamed, curling slightly around his face and ears just as his gray-blue eyes dazzled her with a sharp and daring glint behind them. The color and depth reminded her of the ocean. His eyes made her shy away when he returned a smile.

Della finally turned and tried to concentrate on the rest of the house.

"Would you like to see the place?" Perry said. "You can come to the shop with me to get everyone."

"We'll wait here. We have a lot of things to cover tonight. I'm sure we'll be back. There's no way we can get everything we need this time. Maybe next time." Dylan said.

"Sure." Perry walked through a set of French doors leading to a patio at the back.

"What was your first impression of this guy?"

"I think he's about the best looking man I've ever seen."

"You think he's the best looking man you've ever seen?" Dylan said.

"Yes, that's what I just said."

"You need to get a grip Della. Your mind is not on this case. I should pull you off right now before it's too late."

"What are you talking about? You asked me a question and I answered it. If you don't like what you hear, it doesn't give you the right to give me shit about doing my job. I do a damn good one, so get off my case. Next time, don't ask me what I think. You know I'll tell you exactly what I think. The truth." she said.

"Just see if you can pay attention when the band comes in, all right?"

She ignored his comment, walking around the living room snooping a little before they came back. She learned a lot about people by just observing their living areas. Their trash can be particularly informational. Dylan didn't speak to her again while they waited. Della sat down on the couch, staring at him. He paced the room, then stopped in front of the fireplace. Picking up a picture, he set it back on the mantle then did the same to the rest of the pictures placed there.

Della joined him, curious at what held his attention. She looked at a series of glamour photos of the band doing silly things with each other, looking casual and having fun.

When the door opened they both turned, watching the band straggle in. Their faces appeared tired and drawn, unlike the pictures they just studied.

"Here we are," Kate said.

The rest of the band sat down. They looked like they were waiting for one of them to take roll call.

"Let me introduce everybody here." Kate said. "Diana is upstairs resting. This is Taylor Young, and next to him is Martin Meece." They both faintly smiled. Kate walked over to the adjoining couch. "This is Scott Tate, and his brother, Josh. You've met Perry White." She pointed to him. "And of course, I'm Kate. We already talked the other night." She took a seat in the middle of Scott and Josh on the couch, pulling her legs in underneath her.

"Thanks for letting us in and talking to us." Dylan said. "I'm sorry we have to intrude, but it's necessary. We need any vital information that you may be able to supply us with so we can proceed in the case. We all want the person responsible for shooting Ms. James arrested and behind bars.

"We'll talk to you as a group, then we may need to talk individually with each of you later. We'll be setting up the appointments at the Law and Justice Center. You'll get to see our hang out." He laughed, trying to ease the tension. Gloom filled the room, but he understood their pain.

Dylan reached in his jacket and pulled his micro-recorder out. Setting it on the end table he turned it on. All eyes watched him. "We're just compiling general information right now to get a little background." He addressed the band. "How long has this band been together?"

A delicate voice penetrated the room from above them. Everyone turned, a petite figure descended the staircase, gripping the curved handrail moving slowly down. She kept flicking her long blonde hair away from her face.

"Runnin' Ragged formed in 1985. We haven't all been in the band since then, but it evolved when some of us were still in high school. We got serious in 1990. That's when we hired the rest of the band and worked on making a name for ourselves," Josh said.

Perry and Taylor hurried up the stairs to Diana. They each took an arm and helped her down.

"Diana, you need to rest. You don't need to answer any questions right now. The detectives said so." Perry grabbed her waist as she tumbled forward, slipping off a step and out of his grip. Taylor caught her. Between the two, they carried her to the bottom and sat her down in a chair.

"I want to." Her voice cracked slightly as she asked for a glass of water. "I'm all right." She crossed her bare legs. She pulled her short silky pink bathrobe down a bit, adjusting the belt around her tiny waist.

She looked fragile as a china doll, her pale color enhanced her bright blue eyes. Her platinum blonde hair fell straight down to the middle of her back.

"I'm Diana Edwards. Jennica and I started the band. I want you to get that son of a bitch who put Jennica in the hospital. I want to see him pay for this." Her face held her anger, her eyes sparking alive with the rage as she spoke.

"I'm Detective Drake. This is my partner Detective Bishop. We feel the same way. We'll find the person responsible but we need everyone's help. What makes you think it was a man?" Dylan said, studying her face.

"What do you mean? I didn't say, I knew it was a man."

"You said, you wanted to see him pay for this, " Dylan said.

"Oh. I didn't mean, I knew it was a man. I just meant, I want whoever it is to be found." Her eyes narrowed and fell to her lap. She clenched her hands. They were shaking. Her nervous appearance bothered Dylan. The little color she had, seemed to drain from her face. He saw something in her eyes change when she searched out the other band members sitting around the room watching her. Scared eyes faced him when she brought her face around again, much fuller than before. The weak smile she supplied when she noticed him studying her, he felt was for his benefit.

"Perry, maybe you're right. I'm very tired. I thought I could do this, but I can see I'm really not up to it right now. I would like to go back up and lie down. Is that all right?"

"Sure. You take it easy. We'll call you another day." Dylan walked over and helped her out of the chair. She glanced up at him, her eyes meeting his. The fear he saw, made him want to pull her up and whisk her away so he could get to the bottom of it. Something didn't feel right. He started wondering if she wasn't the key.

"It's okay, detective. I will take over from here." Perry came around and scooped Diana up in his arms. He carried her across the room and up the long staircase as easily as if he had a tiny child in his arms.

"Let's get back to my questions." Dylan walked over and stood leaning against the fireplace. "Who were the original members and who were the additions?" He watched the group, waiting for someone to talk.

"Jennica, Diana, Martin, Scott, and I," Josh said, as matter of fact. "Kate, Perry, and Taylor joined us in 1990." Josh walked across the floor. "Does anyone want anything? I could use a drink." No one answered. He shrugged and disappeared through a set of shiny silver doors.

"Who hired the three of you?" Dylan said.

"Jennica," Kate said.

"No, she didn't. We all made that decision together. Jennica—just never mind." Scott seemed upset. He stared up at the glass-covered dome above them.

"So, Jennica isn't the leader, or the one in charge of the band?" Della said.

"No." Scott turned his attention to Della. "No one here is in charge. We make all the decisions together. If we can't agree, we hash it out and end up working it out. Jennica is the lead singer, that's all."

Both Perry and Taylor shot Scott a face that told him they disagreed with him. Scott slapped his knee and stood quickly. He turned his back on everyone. His irritation with everyone became evident when he turned back to face them again. Josh returned sipping a beer.

"Okay. Sounds pretty easy. So, what if you don't agree? What do you do if the band is split?" Della said.

"It depends on what we're deciding on," Scott said.

"Sounds too easy. A band this size must have a few problems from time to time. Do you all get along?" Della said.

"Yes we do, Miss—" Scott stared at her with black piercing eyes.

"Detective Bishop."

"Ms. Bishop." His words sounded bitter.

He stared at her as if she created this mess. "You can drop the Ms. It's Detective Bishop. You sound angry. Are you mad? Mad at me maybe, or someone else in this room? Is there a problem? I know you just said you don't have any, but I have a hard time believing that. Everyone has problems. Are you holding something back?" Della said, hoping the question would cause a stir.

Everyone in the room squirmed. Kate approached Scott and tried to put her arm around him. He shrugged it off and backed away from her. She appeared irritated.

She turned to the detectives. "He's just upset. Jennica and Scott grew up together. He's furious with this whole scene and wants her shooter found just as much as we all do. He's mad at you two because you haven't placed anybody in custody." She gave them a sympathetic smile.

"I think he can speak for himself, please." Della waited, observing his coal black eyes. They bore a hole through her.

He stepped forward, then walked directly to her. "Yes, I do have one big problem. It's you, you bitch."

Dylan lunged towards Della, and grabbed Scott by the arm. He held him back away from her. Scott pointed his finger in Della's face. "Get out of my house, and stay out."

Josh bounded to the other side and held him by his other arm. "Scott, you're losing it man. Sit down before you do something I have to bail you out of jail for." Josh jerked his shirtsleeve, ripping it from the seam. Scott's stormy temper lashed out at his brother. "Let go of me." Scott jerked his arm away from his grip.

Dylan held his iron grip on his other side. Scott tried to pull away, but failed. Dylan held his ground using a hold he learned in the military. Pulling him far away from Della, he pushed him down in a chair. "Calm down and stay there. You don't want to try me on. You'd lose before you blinked your eye. I think a lesson on manners is appropriate. You owe an apology to my partner for starters. Then you better start explaining the problem you're having to us. We're here to listen. Be civil this time, or you can come down and explain it in custody. No one, and I mean no one, verbally abuses my partner, got that?" Dylan released his shirt and stood erect with his six foot two inch frame towering above him. Perspiration beaded on his forehead and his fists stayed clenched.

Scott's reaction stunned Della. Angry might not describe what she witnessed. She felt hot and needed fresh air.

"What's going on down there. Is everything all right? I heard Scott. Is he okay?" Diana stood at the top of the stairs.

Perry ran up the stairs to calm her.

Scott glanced up. He grinned for the first time since they arrived. "Diana, I'm all right. Go to bed." He glared at Della.

She sat stiffly in the chair staring straight at him.

His eyes softened. "I'm sorry, I fucked up. Seeing red made me react. I honestly don't know why I jumped you. I'm mad, mad as hell. The feeling that's taken over inside of me since Jennica was shot, is eating me alive. I'm here, penned up like a caged animal, and I needed to lash out. You were in my face and real handy. I've been crazy with fear for

Jennica. She's so vulnerable. The person is still out there, and I am frustrated that I can't do anything about it." He unclenched his fists then clenched them repeatedly. "We are relying on doctors and hoping they're not too busy to pay attention. I'm a nervous wreck just thinking that I have to put my faith in them." His eyes glazed over. "She didn't deserve this. I just want you to get this person and quit wasting your time on us. We all loved her very much. No one here would ever want to cause her harm."

"I accept your apology," Della said. "I understand your fear. We're all angry. The whole community is outraged. We will find this person. That's why we're here. We are just trying to find a starting place. A lead to follow. So far we have zip. All of you are closest to her. You can help us find this person by co-operating. We have a job to do here, and if it means talking in depth to everyone of you forward then backwards about your relationship with Jennica, then that's the way it is going to be. You may give us a clue to help us find the person who wanted her dead. You'll be our eyes and ears to her life. She can't talk for herself. If we wait until then, it may be too late."

Dylan studied them while Della talked.

Della tried to calm their fears, but at the same time, she did her job.

The detectives didn't need the band as enemies. They needed them on their side or no one would open up to them.

Dylan walked over to the end table and shut the tape off. He slipped it back in his pocket and joined Della.

"Thank you for seeing us tonight. This session ends here. You take a break from this for awhile. We'll be in touch." Dylan said.

They found their way to the door. The band sat in silence in the living room. A fragmented group of lost souls, alone with their own questions.

The shooting shattered their lives. The pain and doubt they suffered from would end when they did their job and apprehended the suspect. For right now, the questions they wanted to ask, they didn't dare. They were all under suspicion. Not just by the detectives, but by one another.

Chapter 14

Saturday, the 7th day of September, 10:00 P.M.

The detectives left together, walking into the darkness to the dimly lit street. Dylan hesitated at his bike, rolling his head from side to side. The muscles in his neck and back felt like a pretzel from the tension of the previous night and the long hours he'd been working this week. After he had a moment to rehash the last hour, his mind burst full of questions. Della's unusual silence brought his mind back to her, wondering what she thought. He glanced over at her. Her gaze held the sky. She studied it with a certain satisfaction he recognized behind the slight grin on her face. He decided to try to tell her what was next on his agenda for the evening.

"I—"

"What a beautiful night. Look at the stars. They're all visible tonight," she said. "It feels great just to be out here standing under them for a minute. I felt the tension bouncing off the walls back in there," she said.

Dylan dared to look up with her. The stars glowed in the black sky, dazzling him with their brilliance as if they were diamonds scattered across black velvet. The stars danced in patterns, twinkling brightly next to the full moon. On his first camping trip in Montana, he knew exactly why they called it the "The Big Sky Country". It lived up to its reputation as far as the eyes could see. "I agree," he said, "They are bold and beautiful and just as ominous as this case."

"Funny, I had just thought how mysterious they were. Just as mysterious as you, and by comparison, almost as intriguing."

Dylan cleared his throat, quickly changing the subject to the present. The place he intended to stay tonight. Tonight, he vowed to clear the air and tell her the decisions he made this afternoon. "The tension inside the house was normal, but I didn't like the interaction between them. Kate seemed to control the show, but I felt they were hiding something from us. I'm not sure, but I'm guessing one of them is holding something over one or all of their heads. Scott Tate blew without provocation. That tells me his stress level peaked. The situation he described is either true, or he almost blew whatever it is wide open.

"Diana disturbed me. She's scared. I witnessed it in her eyes. The agitation in her voice I picked up on when she heard Scott yelling from downstairs. I tuned into something. It concerns me." He mounted the bike.

"I'm wondering why Diana broke down and went into shock? The incident was devastating to all of them, yet her reaction was abnormal compared to the others closest to Jennica. The reaction might be fueled by more than just witnessing the shooting. So, I'll pursue it. I'll arrange to speak with her tomorrow. Her frightened eyes made me suspicious. She's hiding something or suspects something, but is scared to reveal it. It may involve the band."

Della slid on Dylan's bike. "I received the impression they were all scared. If a threat were made to them, you'd think they would've reported it before the concert. It might be something personal against Jennica that the band might have been aware of, or the whole band is involved in. It may be something that they are hiding for their own reasons. Hitting the lead singer of a band moving up, could slow them down. The competition could benefit. I guess I'll work on that aspect. It might be fun to dig into the music industry. I'll trace their past to the present. If I find any connections in the business tied to them, I'll run every check I can. My eyes will be on the look out for any close competition that's bad at losing their number one spot on the top ten chart." Della wrapped her arms around Dylan. "Maybe Jennica wasn't the angel everyone's claiming she was?"

"We'll get to the truth. I have no doubts about solving this case. There are a lot of questions to be answered first. Nothing makes sense at the moment, but it will. It always does in the end. I know that if we dig deep enough, we'll find a connection or at least the right lead from the other members of the band." Dylan said. He guided his bike south on Willson and took a right off the next side street, weaving around the MSU campus until he reached the duck ponds. He drove onto a driveway marked for service vehicles only and came to a stop. They were directly across from the duck ponds behind the tall pine trees away from the quiet street.

The deserted ponds appeared, still and serene. The late hour brought quietness and a relaxing atmosphere to break his news to Della. He pursued neutral ground with absolute privacy. This time of night he found it there. No one else appeared to be lurking and listening.

The ducks crowded together at the opposite end of the pond. It resembled a slick piece of mirrored glass, shimmering under the bright moonlit night. The backdrop of softly glowing street lamps around the pond wrapped him in a velvety peacefulness he needed. Peace was what he wanted to find tonight. He hoped the resolution of the problem would come peacefully and end the torment he'd been suffering the past few months working with Della. It was a priority tonight, something he needed to do for both of their sakes. She'd forgive him one day. In the end, she'd see his wisdom and thank him.

Della slid off the bike, puzzled at their destination. She understood when she glanced towards Dylan. She waited for him to speak.

"We need to talk," Dylan said, sitting Indian style on the grass at the edge of the pond. He motioned for her to join him there. The ducks, seeing motion and hoping for a handout of food, started swimming towards them.

Della sat in the same fashion next to him, smiling as she watched the ducks nearing them.

Dylan observed Della for a second. He pivoted his body around slightly to come face to face with her.

Della searched his eyes for a clue as to why he brought her here to talk. His eyes sparkled in a rich shade of green under the amber lights. The hesitation before beginning his talk, armed her anxiety about the subject he chose for tonight's discussion.

"I need to tell you a few things that have been on my mind. What happened between us today, should never have taken place. It's been bothering and distracting me ever since. Something changed between us. I think—" He struggled with what he knew he had to say to her. She stared down into her lap, nervously picking grass. He lifted her chin to get her attention. "Hey, are you listening? I'm trying to tell you something. Please look at me and listen, it's important."

Della's body tensed. She studied his face, trying to read his thoughts. His finger came up gently brushing a loose hair from her face.

"I'm asking for a new partner tomorrow," he said.

Della's eyes opened wide. In her worst nightmare, he never dropped a bomb on her like the one she just heard. Losing the words racing through her mind, she quickly tried to recover.

"You're a pretty fair partner," he said. "I have to admit that to you, even though I hated the idea. I'm glad I gave it a try. I've gained an invaluable experience by it. You even taught me a few things. It's time we split up and move on before the professional work we do, and the department's reputation, is compromised by our actions. It would be better if someone else finished training you."

"Dylan, no. You can't be serious. I'm sorry, but this is my entire fault. I didn't think today, I just reacted. Dylan, you can't split us up. We are an excellent team. What can I do?"

"I'm sorry, but I am serious. I have to do this, Dell. It wasn't your fault. It was all mine. I lost it."

"No, it wasn't your fault. I pushed you. I wanted you to lose it."

"That might have been, but that's the point. I wasn't in control, you were."

"We both lost it." Della said. "Please, it doesn't matter. Let's just forget it ever happened." Della reached for his hand, her face held a plea of mercy.

Dylan slid his hand away. "No. I can't continue this way Della. It did happen. I can't just forget it. That's not the whole issue here. Don't you realize what you do to me?" Dylan stared across at her, catching her eyes as they darted away from his.

Della gazed up through the pines at the stars. Tears moistened her eyes. She averted her eyes and turned slightly to avoid his direct stare. She wouldn't let him see the tears forming in her eyes. She wiped the first drops escaping from them before she turned back to him. "What can I say to change your mind?" She said. "Please?" Della stared at Dylan. She needed him to give in to her. He said it himself. She was in control. She needed that control now. Giving it her best shot was all she had left. Della watched his curly black hair gently flowing around his neck in the slight breeze. His expression remained the same.

"No. I'm doing this for both of us. It's as hard on me as it is on you."

Della's tears welled up in her eyes without her permission. The fuel behind them was the reality steam rolling through her emotions by the news. Turning quickly and standing, she needed to be alone. She intended to keep a small piece of her dignity tonight in front of him.

Dylan stopped her. He grabbed her by the shoulders and twisted her around to face him. "I want you to take a couple days off. In the end, you'll thank me for this." He noticed her tears.

She tried to turn away, before the uncontrollable sobbing started.

He pulled her to him and wrapped his arms around her. "I'm sorry, but you have to know this hurts me too."

She shook her head. "Please, leave me. I want to be alone."

"I'm not leaving you like this. Your car isn't here. I'll take you home." She fit perfectly inside his arms and felt good there. His chin came to rest on the top of her silky hair underneath his chin. Her body trembled slightly next to his. "You do know what you mean to me, don't you? I'm not doing this to personally or professionally hurt you. I need you in my life, just as you've always been since I've lived here." He gently squeezed her shoulders as he stepped back.

She turned her back to him. After a while, she turned back, her arms crossed in front of her. Dylan stood in silence waiting for her to speak again. He saw her lips trying to form words. She held his eyes for a moment, studying them and the face she knew so well. "I can't lose you, Dylan." Della swallowed hard, fighting back new tears.

Dylan stepped closer, catching a stray tear as he reached up and touched her face. "You'll never lose me. I'm not going anywhere. If you don't know by now that I'll always be here for you, believe it. I always have been and I always will. That's the point I'm trying to make. I need you to stay the friend you've always been. I need you too. You've been in my life ten years. That makes you my oldest and most prized and dearest friend. You're definitely not that spunky teenager I wrestled and tackled playing football when you were in high school. You've definitely changed like you said, and believe me, I noticed. A very long time ago, in fact. Do you remember my 30th birthday?"

"Yes. I remember the last ten birthdays."

"You gave me a birthday kiss that blew me away. From that moment on, I knew I'd better watch myself around you. I'm thirty-six now, and I've been struggling since then, not to blow that brother-sister type of relationship we've always kept.

"In six years, you've matured like a fine wine. Everyday I look at you, it's like another glimpse at heaven. You're one hell of a lady, Della. You deserve the best things in life. I can never give you all those things you'll want and need. You are too young to know what's best. When you get to my age, you might understand where I'm coming from. My life ended a long time ago. This is all I'm ever going to be. There are plenty of young men out there that would die to get a real chance to be with you. It will be the luckiest man in the world who will one day get to share your spirited nature and extraordinary beauty and be rewarded for capturing your heart by getting to spend the rest of his life with you."

"When I first met you, I fell instantly in love. You were the cutest teenager I'd ever laid eyes on. Today, well, you're still the most beautiful woman I've ever known. Back then, I thought of you like the sister I never had. Your spunky and rambunctious spirit kept me by your side like a big brother. That spirit thrilled me then.

"Recently however, the thrill I felt has changed. The spunkiness you display most of the time pisses me off now. It's different, because the situation is different. As senior detective, it's my top priority in this job to train you to the best of your ability. It's your life and all the other officer's lives, not to mention the public we're here to protect that are depending on that. I want to still protect you from all those bastards out there, but as my partner, I'm taking you right to them. I live in fear every day that we'll go out there and you're going to get hurt. It's my recurring nightmare. I can't stop worrying about it. I'd never forgive myself if something happened to you.

"It's that simple. I'm emotionally involved with you way past our co-worker relationship. I've felt like your big brother for a long time. That protective feeling I feel towards you will never change. If we stay together as partners, the temptation for me will be too much and eventually I'll make a mistake that will cost us dearly, because that brother thing? Well, it vanished on my 30th birthday and turned into a—well, an illusion. Now, the reality of all of this is, that the fantasy I have towards you and the desires you have for me, will never work. I'm old enough to know and understand it. I don't expect you to right now. One day, you'll understand. We'd ruin us.

"You want to get married, have children, and live happily ever after. I'm not the type of man that could stay and make you happy in that kind of environment. You know nothing of my past, just what I am now. I'd be using you if I let you pursue me, and you'd be trying to change me into someone I'm not. We would end up hating each other. I can't let that happen. Believe me, I've thought about this a lot."

"That would never happen. I love you, and I always will." Della watched him stiffen over her.

"You can't love me. I mean, in the way you think you do now." Dylan said. He couldn't take much more. He'd spilled his guts to her and exposed more about himself than he planned to tell. He needed her to understand a part of him. The only good part left in him. He wanted to let her down gently. He would never intentionally hurt her.

Watching her body shiver and shake, he put his arms around her. He held her tightly. He knew tears were falling. Gently he held her face close to his. Peering into her bold violet eyes, moist with tears and filled with pain disturbed him. He never had witnessed a time that anything caused her to cry. It hurt him deeply, much more than he ever thought it would. "I'm so sorry it has to be this way," he whispered in her ear. He kissed her then. First her right cheek he touched softly with his lips, then her left. He wiped the falling tears away. "Don't do this to yourself."

Studying her again, her lips trembled. He reacted with his heart not his mind this time. Gently he covered her lips with his. He wanted to comfort her from the pain he caused, and relieve his misery by kissing her salty tears away. Her soft lips responded gently with tenderness that spread a comforting and warm feeling rushing through him. The sweet taste on her lips and the passion in her kisses excited him. Her warm body against him felt natural. The tension he felt faded as she relaxed in his arms.

Embracing her in his arms, their lips danced together in slow motion. Dylan's hands slid under her shirt, up her sleek back. The touch of warm skin under his hands felt as smooth as the silk bra he quickly undid. Slipping it away, her firm breasts responded to his touch. It sent his pleasure sensors into full alert. He slowly pulled her down with him to the soft grass.

Dylan devoured Della's willing body. The sounds of the pleasure he heard from her drove his desire. His heart raced out of control. His fingers stopped at the first button on her jeans. His eyes opened to check on Della. Her eyes fluttered open as he hesitated. The delight he saw sparkling in her eyes relieved his confused mind. The smooth skin under his roaming hands enticed him deeper as he became lost in her powerful eyes. They disarmed him. He felt like a helpless victim drawn in by her irresistible charm. Rolling on top of her, he searched out her eager lips and lingered for a bit, enjoying them. After a few minutes, he pulled away from her. Kneeling over her, he searched those eyes for a sign to continue.

She reached his top button on his jeans, unbuttoning it.

Dry leaves crunched loudly directly behind them. They froze in their position and searched each other with surprised eyes. Another crunching sound approached closer. Their bodies frozen together like an ice sculpture, remained motionless.

Dylan silently signaled Della to move with him.

Rolling apart quietly, they listened for more sounds. They adjusted their clothing while scouting around the area.

Dylan signaled to her again of his intentions to case the area. He crept low until he crawled silently on his belly across the ground. After careful reconnaissance of the area, he finally stood and circled the area once again.

Della waited, then slipped over to Dylan. He squatted underneath and hid behind the huge pine with its massive trunk. His attention directed solely on the pond. She came up behind him and put her hands on his shoulders. Peering over them, she stared into the darkness.

"The ducks," he said.

"The ducks?"

"The ducks, Della, in the pond. They waddled out and over to that island to make a nest for the night."

"Good." Della slid her hands around his neck and hugged him. "Let's go to my place and finish what we started here." She planted a soft kiss on his neck.

"No, we can't," he said.

"No? We can't? You mean you can't. What the hell—"

"I'm sorry. We can't finish this. I'm glad the damn ducks stopped us. I can't believe me. I need my fucking head examined. I came here to stop this, and look at me. I took advantage of you. We were close to being buck naked and fucking each other in front of a bunch of ducks for Christ sakes. I have lost my damn mind. Fuck. I can see the headlines now." Dylan got up, and walked away. He turned back and paced in front of her.

"Dylan, it's meant to be. Face it," Della said.

"No, this isn't meant to be. I lost it again. You make me crazy. What would have happened if we made love?"

"What do you mean? I've wanted you to make love to me for most of my life. Now you aren't going to finish? Of course, I'm prepared. I've prepared for this moment for a long time. Shit, do you think I'm going to force you to marry me afterwards? I just want you on your terms."

"My terms? You haven't thought this through. Think a minute. Tell me what happens to us afterwards? What happens when everyone knows we are fucking one another? Tell me Della."

"Ah—" Della felt her face heating up in the chill of the night. "You're worried about your job." She turned away.

"I'm sorry."

"No, I'm sorry. I'm an idiot. If you don't know by now that all I want is you in my life, then I guess you'll never get a clue. Maybe, a bolt of lightning might penetrate that hard head of yours one day and you'll finally see it. I'll tell you though, that it may be too damn late by then." She turned around, frustrated beyond her limit.

Dylan came up behind her placing his hands on her shoulders and squeezed. "I'm sorry."

Della flung his hands from her shoulders, spinning around to face him. Fury covered her face. "Start up your God damned hog and take me home, damn it. And damn you, Dylan Drake. I'm tired of you and your—I'm sorry, shit. I'm so mad right now I'd like to—" Della pivoted sharply and started walking towards the bike. She stopped short, turned around and walked back to Dylan who stood staring after her. She slapped him hard across the face, piercing him with daggers from her daring eyes filled with tears.

His heart sunk, leaving it open and exposed, but he wasn't willing to let her know that he loved her too. The job meant nothing to him if he had to make a choice. His past pushed him to hold fast to his convictions to keep the life he knew before coming to Bozeman, hidden forever. She would never understand if he revealed the truth to her. Eventually she'd expect him to share everything with her, and when he couldn't, she'd feel betrayed by him, worse than him coveting another lover. It was inevitable, that the truth he hid would destroy even the heartiest of loves. The ultimate risk, suicide for them both. Danger would always be lurking till the end of his days by his past life. If he continued to allow them to follow their hearts, disaster after disaster could only follow them to their end.

Chapter 15

Sunday, the 8th of September, 7:00 A.M.

Father Murphy decided to check Rob Browning's cabin after Mass on Sunday. Rob left for Nevada in the middle part of August. He entrusted him with a key to his cabin and granted an open invitation to stay anytime.

Father Murphy met Rob one Sunday after Mass. Shaking hands with him, they talked and met for coffee later that evening. They became friends instantly. He found Rob a charismatic fellow. Some spiritual guidance in matters of the heart troubled him. The troubles he hid carefully behind a mask he wore. Eventually, he spoke openly and unveiled the burdens weighing him down. Father Murphy counseled him, easing his anxieties. Rob treated him with a respect to the robe and depended on his advice from that point on, as if he'd been his confidant forever. As their friendship developed, Rob invited him to his cabin at Teepee Creek to fish and commune with God in his true world, as he put it. Father Murphy discovered Rob's extraordinary intelligence as they carried on conversations debating world issues. Those conversations proved exhilarating. He hadn't found a chance to debate complex issues for a long time. They talked into the night on current affairs and philosophy, topics he enjoyed. As their personal philosophies became exposed, Rob gave him insight into a world he never imagined before.

Rob told him if he ever needed to escape from his responsibilities for a while, he could stay anytime. Father Murphy never took him up on his offer after that weekend, finding it hard to get away and be without a telephone. He hoped he remembered the way to the cabin and his vehicle could pass over the rugged terrain this time of year. September gloriously arrived and held winter back in its first weeks so far, even though he understood very well that in five minutes everything could change.

Packing his bag and leaving a message with the deacon, he'd return later in the evening if everything went according to his plan.

Driving the speed limit, he slowed each time he entered the sharp curves that slithered down and around up the highway like an enormous snake who fossilized making its trail through the canyon a trillion years ago on the way to snake heaven. Carefully driving along, he took in the clear river rushing beside him. The white rapids roared beside him, rumbling and raging, hissing at him. Taking a quick peek, he tipped his nose to the cracked window. He breathed in the pine scent floating alongside him. The fresh water of the currents sprayed against the huge boulders planted in the middle of the river, splitting between the rock and white-capping and continuing down its course. The air currents cruising beside him, smelled faintly fishy mixed with pine and smoke from the campfires blazing in the campgrounds below.

A moose standing in a shallow bog marked the last stage of his trip. The moose never disappointed him. It became a symbol, welcoming his journey through the regal Gallatin. He could count on the hefty moose to be there, just as he counted on Sunday turning to Monday.

His mind, cloudy from the past couple of days, needed the fresh air and quietness the cabin promised. Jennica stood out in his mind like a flashing beacon. The strong memories of her overpowered him, grasping at his aching heart. Her determined will kept her holding on, fighting to stay alive.

Father Murphy worried the investigators wouldn't catch the person responsible. He felt something had gone awry deep down in the pit of his stomach, but he couldn't pinpoint the gnawing eating at his insides. The most important pieces of the puzzle? Missing. Nothing made sense. He wondered if it ever would.

He turned right at the sign to Teepee Creek and weaved his way up the long trail to where the road ended in a fork. Stepping out, he breathed deeply. Locking the doors, he hiked in the backcountry six miles to the top of the mountain Rob nicknamed, Mole Hill.

At the top of the hill appeared Rob's mountain retreat. The cabin graced the top of a rise looking out at the Lee Metcalf Wilderness area. The majestic snow draped mountains towered like sentries to the valley below year round, like a picture perfect postcard.

Father Murphy loved the splendor. It brought joy in his heart to just breathe in the pine scented air and behold the glorious view. He walked to the back and unlocked the heavy wooden door.

He stopped turning the key as he heard leaves rustling and limbs breaking close to him off in the woods to his right. Turning around slowly like a statue on a turntable, he kept the key gripped firmly in his hand.

He peered into the trees, looking for any sign of motion. Squinting, he realized he had left his glasses back in his car. Hearing crunching leaves to his left and then on his right, brought the hair on his neck bristling with life. Looking again towards the sound, he met glassy black eyes as his vision focused on the shape. A large bear stood at the tree edge, staring back, watching him closely.

Father Murphy swallowed hard, standing perfectly still in his position. Viewing a bear at this close range for the first time sent a ribbon of fear through him. The bear boldly stared with his obsidian eyes. The huge face covered in thick coarse cinnamon fur dominated him. Powerful muscles encompassing the body looked formidable, even with his failing eyesight. A pronounced hump in the back enlightened him to the fact that he was looking face to face with a Grizzly.

Another crash sounded to his left. A smaller bear barreled out of the woodpile by the edge of the lot. The large grizzly bear growled, standing up on its hind legs, and swiped its claws through the air. The little bear lurched, then bounded over to the open space to the mother Grizzly. The bear crossed in front of him. Father Murphy held his breath and prayed. He watched with wonder as two more baby bears raced back to their mama from the same woodpile. The family of bears, amazed and astonished him, filling him briefly with blessedness to the glory of nature surrounded by the animals at home in the wilderness.

The three smaller bears followed the big mama bear back into the forest and disappeared in an instant. Father Murphy turned and opened the door, letting his breath out in one long sigh. Smiling to himself, he stepped safely inside.

The house, dusty and dimly lit by the afternoon sun streaming in the windows, displayed papers littered across the wooden floor of the cabin. He followed the trail down the hall. He peeked into the first room. Clothing covered the floor. Empty drawers lay upside down on the bed. Instinct told him, someone went through the place in Rob's absence. Rob kept his guns hidden in the back bedroom closet. Peeling back the shag carpet from the floor, he lifted the latch. He walked into the crawl space and crouched in front of the specially designed gun safe, noticing the door slightly ajar. Opening it, he saw his rifles and shotguns inside. He reached for the handguns stored in hard cases on the bottom shelf. Opening each one, he discovered empty cases. The three handguns, gone.

The empty cases confirmed the worry and the decision to make the trip to the cabin. After receiving the handgun, he recognized it as one he'd seen, belonging to Rob Browning. He rushed back up the hall, carefully scrutinizing the inside of the cabin for other things he might notice missing before he reported the robbery. A robbery could lead to a break in the case.

Back in the living room, everything appeared as he remembered it last summer—nothing else noticeably missing. The place resembled the after effects of a tornado. As if, somebody desperately searched every inch of the cabin for just the handguns.

Leaving the cabin, he pulled on his backpack and started down the trail and hurried along in search of the nearest telephone.

Apprehension built inside him as the memory of the Grizzly and her cubs popped into his mind. His step quickened with the memory, making him thrash louder through the woods purposely, making loud noises to avoid surprising any more Grizzly bears today.

Clearing the trail without further incidence, he drove seven miles back down the road, turned right into Eino's Tavern. At the corner of the Hebgen Lake turnoff, he pulled in the driveway. The pay telephone stood outside by the gas pumps in front of the irregular shaped bar. He dialed the Sheriff's Department.

The Dispatch Center radioed a Sheriff's Deputy out of West Yellowstone. The deputy would meet him at Einos in less than an hour. While he waited outside, he dialed another number.

"Rob Browning please."

"I'm sorry, he is unavailable at this time," the receptionist said. "Would you like to leave a message on his voice mail?"

"This is an emergency. Could you disturb him?"

"I'm sorry. He isn't in the office and can't be reached at this time. He has left instructions to refer all callers to voice mail. He'll return your call as soon as he can." She cleared her throat. "Do you wish to leave a message, sir?"

"Yes." He paused a moment to construct the sentences he'd relay. He didn't like talking to a machine. It seemed unnatural. He heard the electronic voice talking back to him, then the line squealed sharply in his ear followed by a loud beep.

"Rob, this is Father Murphy. I'm at your cabin. It appears someone came in and ransacked it. I called it in, and a deputy is on the way to make a report. All of your handguns are missing. I think your revolver showed up during an investigation of a shooting in Bozeman Friday night. The police have taken custody of it. I wanted to let you know right away. Please call me at the rectory in the evening if you receive this message."

He hung up, sitting on a bench next to the telephone booth, and waited for the deputy to arrive.

A half-hour later, a Gallatin County Sheriff's Deputy pulled in the lot. Father Murphy introduced himself and explained the situation: the location and the suspected break-in of the cabin. The deputy wrote everything on a notepad as he talked.

"Was the door locked or forced open? Is anything else missing besides the guns?" He asked.

"I unlocked the door. It didn't appear forced open. I'm not sure if anything else is missing." Father Murphy said. "This was the first time I checked out the cabin. I haven't been there for a while, not since the previous summer. I don't know what the owner might have taken when he left."

"I see. What makes you think there was a robbery with no forced entry?"

"Drawers were emptied and left upside down. The floor is covered with the contents. He wouldn't have just left clothes and papers all over. He always kept everything immaculate. You could bounce a quarter off his bed. Someone must have been looking for something. All three handguns are missing. Although, I really don't know for sure if he took any of them with him."

"He probably took them. Why would a man keep guns and not take them when he leaves? If someone robbed the place, they'd break in and take all of his weapons. Not just three. I also don't think the perpetrator would stop to lock the door on the way out."

"I don't know about that. I have tried to find out more before you arrived. I couldn't get through to the owner."

"Who is the owner?"

"Rob Browning. He leases the cabin. The land is Federal land."

"Where is he?"

"He travels extensively. I'm not aware of his exact location. He usually spends early spring through early fall here. He left a couple weeks ago. I do have his number. Let me copy it down."

Father Murphy scribbled down the number and handed it to the deputy.

The officer finished taking notes and informed him as he left that he had received a lot of calls about break-ins recently. "A bad group of kids turned robbing homes into their specialty. Their new career choice for the nineties. They pick places the owners leave vacant for long periods of time. Anything of value? They steal and pawn. The police keep tabs on the shops and their inventories in hopes of catching a hot item being sold," he said, as he finished filling out the report.

"I'll add this to the file when I get back to the station." The deputy swiped his hat off his head and smoothed down his slick hair. "I just don't see any reason to hike up to the cabin and investigate this further. You said yourself, the door to the gun safe was slightly opened and not forced. By the description of your report, it sounds to me like he might have opened the safe and took the guns and left in a hurry," he said. The deputy got back in his patrol car and headed south, back to West Yellowstone.

Father Murphy felt uneasy. The deputy left questions in his mind about the robbery. Why would a thief take three guns and not all of the weapons? He didn't know a criminal's mind. If he gambled? He'd bet they had another reason besides just stealing the guns. The deputy didn't believe anyone entered the cabin. He knew better. One of the guns ended up shooting Jennica James at her debut concert.

Now that he checked on the cabin and finished the business of reporting the robbery, he needed to relax. Commune with God for a while. He decided to stop and take a break before arriving in Bozeman. Driving north, he stopped in the canyon at a fishing access.

Retrieving a lounge chair from the trunk, he placed it between two Lodge Pole Pines at the edge of the towering forest. Lying back, he opened his Bible to the marked page, looking out the corners of his eyes sheepishly as the memory of the Grizzlies still lingered. It made it hard for him to close his eyes and completely relax and meditate.

He needed to inform Chief Bishop about the missing handguns at Rob's cabin the moment he arrived in town. He felt relieved now, knowing about the theft of the guns, and that Rob had left Montana.

He admired the man, but deep down he started questioning certain things about him he never paid much attention to before now. Drifting off, those thoughts crept unwillingly into his subconscious. He remembered a time Rob canceled a fishing trip telling him he had to fly out and take care of an emergency. Later that day, he thought he saw Rob, pulling out of a small cafe in Virginia City. He waved it off as someone that resembled him as he drove past on his way to Ennis Lake.

He rehashed incidents involving Rob that occurred in the past three years. Staring at the fine print in Proverbs while he repeated the verse over and over to lull him into a meditative state: 'He holds victory in store for the upright, he is a shield to those whose walk is blameless, for he guards the course of the just and protects the way of his faithful ones.'

He read another verse. The nagging in the back of his mind drew his attention away. He deliberately closed his Bible. He scoffed at himself to ever think that Rob had anything to do with shooting Jennica. What reason could he have? He only knew her because she attended the church now and then. She attended only when she had short breaks between tours. He recalled the two of them sitting together and talking at the back of the church one night a couple of weeks before. The night before Rob left town and only a day or so after Jennica arrived with her band to prepare for their debut concert.

He laid his chair back further, enjoying the slight breeze stirring through the opening in the trees. Feeling unnecessarily fatigued with thoughts of Jennica and Rob, he prayed silently in their behalf. The clouding of his spiritual mind baffled him. He closed his eyes, hoping to fall asleep for a while.

The ringing blared behind the voices speaking, calling to him and jarring him up from his lawn chair. His head reeled forward into his open hands. Fear hid behind his eyes. Squeezing them tighter, he prayed. The dream had found him here.

Slowly, he opened his eyes. Shaking his tired head, he firmly grasped the Bible and pulled it close to his body to ward off the recurrent nightmare. A monstrous chill possessed his body, overpowering his will. His body felt frozen, the warm blood coursing through it turned to ice. He staggered up from his chair. Reaching his car, he fumbled for the door. The creaking door swung open in time to catch him as he fell back across the seats. Exhaustion consumed him.

Chapter 16

Monday, the 9th day of September, 8:00 A.M.
Bozeman, Montana

Monday morning blew in like a tornado, covering the town with an early snow shower after days of sunshine. Dylan's mood matched the swirling snow blowing around outside. He felt a sense of foreboding, like the clouds, dark and cold. He thought about the letter stuck in his coat pocket.

Dylan left his bike parked in his garage to take his other pride and joy, his 1970 El Camino. He ran the heater on high and slipped in his favorite tape of Credence Clearwater Revival.

Parking his car at the Law and Justice Center, he leaped up the stairs at the side of the building and entered the security doors, shaking the wet snow from his hair. At Captain Mitchell's office he deposited the letter he had painfully composed on Sunday, putting it in clear view on top of his cluttered desk. His hand trembled slightly as he left. Quickly following the rich aroma drifting through the halls to the coffee, he got a cup before he had a chance to change his mind. A hot cup of coffee might warm him and perk his mind up, at least, he hoped enough to survive the day after tossing and turning until dawn.

Eating a maple bar and drinking his first cup of coffee, he sifted through the papers accumulating on his desk since he'd left it a couple of days ago. Sorting by priority, he filed them in his basket and then turned to do some work on his computer.

He entered his log-in code and leaned back, savoring the flavor of his coffee before starting the work of typing his notes from the previous

Friday night. His fingers were slowly warming up to the keys when his boss entered the room looking gloomier than usual.

"Morning, Dylan," Captain Mitchell said.

"Morning. I notice you didn't say, 'Good morning.' What's up?"

"That was my next question. I just sat down and opened the letter on my desk. You tell me."

"Just what the letter says."

"Just like that? You put in for a new partner. What happened? You two have some sort of misunderstanding?"

"You could say that."

"You can work it out."

"No. It isn't working. It's for the good of the department and her safety."

"You're talking in riddles. I can't just okay your request, splitting up the best team I have, and rearrange the whole department for you without a damn good reason. I don't think anything is that serious, unless you're covering up something that I should know about."

"It's nothing like that."

"Where is she, anyhow?"

"I don't know, I just got here," Dylan said. "With the weather outside, she probably got stuck behind a snow plow or a school bus creeping down Bridger."

A middle-aged women, dressed in a long denim skirt and dark sweater, silently entered the room holding slips of pink telephone messages in her hand. She slipped the first one to Captain Mitchell then dropped the second one on Dylan's desk and just as silently, turned and left.

Captain Mitchell, a man almost fifty with a full head of soft white hair, looked rather distinguished in his tailored suit as he skimmed the memo. He wore silver wire rimmed glasses over dauntless eyes that commanded attention in his presence. He stood over six feet tall, and his body was in excellent physical shape. He stood in the center of the room, scratching his head before looking down at Dylan reading his own pink memo.

Dylan quickly glanced at the note, rolled it into a ball, and disposed of it in the trash beside him.

"Della left this message. She's taking a personal day. What does that mean?" The Captain said.

"It means she's tired and needs some rest. We've been working this shooting since Friday night when our shift should have officially ended for the week."

"Okay, I'd buy that if it weren't for your letter I just read a few minutes ago. Coincidence? If Della's burnt out, then how about you? Maybe you both need a break today."

"No, I'm fine. I need to get some of this information processed and make some profiles. I need a bigger picture than we got. The leads just aren't falling together."

"Okay, but I'm denying your official request. I think you two can work it out," he motioned his long arms in the air like a conductor directing a band. "Whatever it is, between yourselves. I'm staying out of it at this point." He sat down on the corner of Dylan's desk and crossed his hands in his lap. "This is what partners do. They don't always see eye to eye, but they work their problems out and get on with it. They just don't hang it up at the first sign of trouble and be done with it. You're professionals, the best team I have here."

Dylan nodded, realizing he couldn't convince him at that point. He didn't have much fight left in him.

"Her father also happens to be a good friend of mine who thought my idea to put you two together in the first place was a wise choice. His opinion means a lot to me. I know you respect him too. I know I made the right decision here, so I'm sticking with it." He turned towards the door. Just as he reached it, he stopped and turned, holding onto the doorframe. "Have a good day."

Dylan watched him as he walked away, anger building inside of him. He stood, picking up his files, and slapped them back down on his desk. He felt lost in a sea of mixed emotions whipping him around wildly, with no sign of immediate rescue.

He swiveled around in his wooden slatted chair and stared out the snow plastered windows at the gray skies, thinking about Dell's note. He reached for the phone and dialed her number from memory, but slammed the receiver back down when her machine picked up and her voice haunted him. Black moved through him then dropped over him, blanketing him in the worst mood he could ever remember.

She held her control over him. He imagined her sitting by the phone waiting for his call, knowing she would let her machine pick up and laugh at him. She knew he would stop everything to drive up and check on her, regardless of the insult in the memo she left for him.

Thoughts of her simmered his blood, stirring him to life, uncontrollably making his senses aware of her absence as he remembered her softness, her sweet smell, the kisses eager and open to his will. Her eyes filled full of passion, touching him with the pure innocence they held. She felt so good clutching onto him, molding herself to him as if they were one.

Della, was the strong independent type, a woman who harnessed more intelligence in her beautiful head than any of the men in the department. Level headed and dedicated to her work, she climbed the ladder with fierce determination, never faltering or questioning her decision even when she was dished the worst possible crap in the department. The other officer's tried to unnerve her every chance they got, because they thought she shouldn't be on the force because she was a woman. In their eyes, woman couldn't cut it and were barely tolerated because of the fact they took the jobs from able-bodied men. Women were taking over, and most men in the department despised it. Dylan had to admit he felt the same way when he first was assigned Della, but knew she fought and worked hard every inch of the way to be there.

She had never shown a minute of vulnerability until the previous night. She held onto him like she felt safe in his arms and needed his protection. It felt good to him to hold her, to be able to feel like her protector. At that moment, she felt like the woman of his dreams, that special lady he wanted to protect from all the evil in the world. The lady that would love only him with each breath of life she took, and nothing else in life was more important to them both but one another.

It seemed for a short time like that last night, like they were the only ones on the planet. They both were happy to be in each other's arms. The memory kept burning stronger in his mind as it played again and again until he became so mad and disgusted with himself that he knew it was useless to try and work. Throwing up his hands, he wandered to the window. He leaned against it, staring down at the parking lot covered in inches of slush.

"Hey, Dylan. What's up?" Bobby came to him with her usual bright smile, looking much too happy for a snow covered Monday morning.

"Nothing. How's tricks?" He strained out a sound resembling his laugh. He found himself comparing her boyish looks to Della's natural beauty.

Bobby kept her blonde hair cut short, in a flat top. She had bright brown eyes that seemed to radiate a sparkle at all times. Although she used makeup, she still could be mistaken for the boy next door. Working out with weights kept her body toned and made her muscles powerful that added to her masculine features. She took control, staring back at his strained face. "Looks like you could use a good trick." She giggled, trying to force a genuine laugh out of him this morning.

"Do you have something for me?" Dylan said.

"Sure do. You don't think I would make a trip all the way over here just to look into those road maps you're wearing for eyes do you?" She moved in closer, handing the envelope to him. "The reports on the bullets, and the rest of the scene, not including the revolver, which should be in their hot little hands by now."

"Thanks." He opened the envelope and pulled out the pictures then read the computer readouts from the lab.

"I'll catch up with you later, when you want to talk," Bobby said. "I received an agenda this morning that you wouldn't believe." She reached out her hand and patted him on the shoulder as she went by. "You take care of yourself. You look pretty grizzled around the edges."

"Thanks for the compliment. One day maybe I'll be able to return it." He half-heartedly teased her back. "Later, Bobby." He watched as she left the room, then let out a big sigh of relief.

He sat back down, pushing files away, and rested his head on his arms. If he didn't get a grip on himself, his distraction would become evident to everyone that he came in contact with. He felt as bleak as the wind howling behind him. The dark grays of the day filled his soul with a dull emptiness that made him ache deep inside. His mind was still focused on the one person that usually made him smile on a day like this, only today, she was the person responsible for his misery.

He returned to his computer, entering the notes from the sessions they interviewed on the weekend, listing the people, then motives, and running checks on each of them through the NCIC computer base. He spent the morning pulling everything together, cross checking information, looking for anything he might have missed in the reports and in the conversations with the witnesses so far.

He stretched, then stood up just as the telephone rang.

"Detective Drake," he said.

"Dylan, this is Chief Bishop. Father Murphy visited me again. I'll come over and fill you both in, if you're going to be around in the next fifteen minutes."

Dylan hesitated before answering, clearing his throat. "Della called in this morning. She took the day off." He kept his voice light, trying not to give anything away.

"That doesn't sound like Della. Is she sick?"

"I don't know sir. I guess you'll have to ask her. I just received the message after I arrived at work."

"I see. I'll fill you in then. Come to my office in fifteen minutes."

"Fine. I'll be there."

Dylan hung up the phone, wondering about Father Murphy. He didn't include him on any profiles, so he decided to run a check. Working his way back into the system, he waited for the responses to be faxed in.

Promptly, Dylan walked into Chief Bishop's office and took a seat across from his desk.

"I called Della," the Chief said. "She didn't answer her telephone. Her damn machine did."

"She's probably sleeping like the dead. She's put in some long hard hours."

"I hope so. I started to worry after we hung up. You look like you could stand some sleep yourself. What are you two doing pushing yourselves so hard? There are other detectives and police in the department to work on this case."

"I know."

"Would you do a favor for me?"

"Sure, anything," Dylan said.

"Would you take a drive up and check on her. This isn't like Della, taking a day off without notice during one of the counties biggest cases of the year. Frankly, I've been concerned about her lately. It would ease my mind to know you checked on her."

"Yes, sir, I can do that if you think it's a good idea. I called a minute ago and got the machine also. I had been tossing it around in my mind all morning to stop and take a drive up there and check on her. Then I thought, maybe I should just leave her alone. Maybe she wants to be left alone. She's been acting different lately, even before this case."

"You noticed? You probably know her better than I do now, working so close with her. I tell you, I've been worried about her lately, but I just can't let her know that."

"I know. Excuse me for saying this, but she's as independent and stubborn as a mule. She'd hate us for doubting her ability to take care of herself, I'm afraid."

He chuckled deeply. "Don't I know it. Well, here's the scoop I brought. Father Murphy arrived back in town from a little excursion up to a cabin in Teepee Creek. Seems it's a cabin a friend of his leases up there. Says it was robbed at some point. That's the gun he turned in. The grip has a piece of the wood broken off and one side is scratched all to hell where he dropped it off a balcony at the man's house. His name is Rob Browning. The priest put it together after checking the cabin. He said three of Browning's handguns are missing."

"Where is he?"

"He travels. His answering service takes messages. Here's the number to call. The deputy from West turned in a report about Father Murphy's alleged robbery. It should be on your desk as we speak. He told Father Murphy that robberies were being reported daily around that area."

"I'm going to check this out myself," Dylan said.

"I thought so. I know you want this case solved ASAP."

"I do."

"I have an appointment. Get back to me right away when you find out about Della. Don't let her know I sent you."

"I won't. You have my every confidence, sir."

"Thanks, Dylan. I can't tell you how much that means to me."

He watched, as Chief Bishop left, meeting up with Captain Mitchell outside of his office. They stood in the hall carrying on a lengthy conversation with one another.

Dylan felt guilty thinking about Chief Bishop's last words. If he could read Dylan's mind right now, a hanging would take place.

Dylan left, leaving the work on his desk on hold for the time being. A ride up Bridger Canyon, slinging slush, sounded better than wading through the work on his desk that morning. Maybe by the time he returned his mind would be cleared enough to give his full attention to the work, after he'd have a chance to talk again with his partner.

A muddy road off the main highway led to her house. There were no fresh tracks on the driveway into her house.

He opened the gate, letting himself in the front yard to the porch, and rang the doorbell. When she didn't answer, he turned the door-knob, remembering his last visit vividly. Finding the door locked this time, he walked to the back yard where a snow covered Kiki greeted him by pawing at the fence. The dog shook his thick white jacket covered in slush and splattered Dylan square in the face.

"I bet Della trained you to do that didn't she?"

Kiki wagged his tail back and forth as he opened the gate and slipped in.

He pulled on the back patio doors but found them securely locked. Going around to the garage, he peeked in the windows, finding her car missing. It surprised him that she really wasn't home. Dylan headed back into town, wondering where Della could be as he stopped for the light at 7th and Main. He spied her car parked in front of the Scoop bar.

Pulling in front of the bar, he hesitated before killing his engine. It disturbed him to think she was sitting in a bar wasting herself while their work piled up.

The door was opened so he stepped in, adjusting his eyes from the bright snow to the darkness of what felt like a cave. The remainders of stale beer and cigarettes hit his nose and mingled with the smell of a strong disinfectant from the janitor working around the pool tables. Besides the janitor, a lady bartender looked at him as he circled back up to the bar.

"Hi. What can I get you?" she said, half smiling.

"I was just looking for someone. Has a woman in her twenties, with long dark brown hair, fairly good looking, about this tall," he lifted his arm up showing her where Della came up to him, "been in here this morning?"

"I'm sorry. I just opened. I haven't had anyone in here yet."

"There's a midnight blue Mustang parked outside your front door."

"It was parked there when I arrived." She cleared her voice yelling to the back of the room. "Hey, Marc, was that Mustang parked out front when you came in this morning?"

"Yeah. It was. Parked right in my damn way. I had to drag everything out of my van and squeeze by it. I should've knocked it out of gear and let it fly back away from the door. Lucky for them, I was a nice guy today." He turned back around, finishing with his mop and carried it to the back.

"There, you have your answer. Sorry," she said.

"I guess I do. Thanks." He walked out. The whiteness blinded him as he squinted, trying to dig in his pocket for his keys.

He stepped over to Della's car and peered inside. The doors were unlocked. Her coat was tossed over the back of the seat, so he grabbed it. Reaching in the pocket, he found a twenty-dollar bill, a pack of gum, and a comb. Feeling under her seats, his hand pulled out her car keys. His head shook in disbelief. Tossing her coat back over the seat he got out and locked the car doors. Fearing the worst possible scenario after leaving her in such a state as he had Saturday night, he hopped back in his car and took off. Frantically he drove around town thinking of where she may have gone without her car. He drove up several miles of alleys before he realized his search for her was ludicrous.

She left two messages at the office at 8:00, both vague. Could she have been taken against her will? Sweat poured down his face as he tried to think of every possible angle. He needed to talk to Angela. She took those messages. He ran up the steps, meeting Angela as she came out of the building.

"Angela, I'm glad I caught you. I need to talk to you about those messages you took this morning from Della." He caught his breath as he grabbed for the door.

"What's up? She called and left two messages."

"Are you sure it was her? Did she sound funny?"

"No. She sounded quite happy, actually."

"Happy?"

"Happier than I've ever heard her sound, if you want to know the truth. Usually she's so businesslike to us in the office. She laughed when she left that message for you. A private joke, I assume?"

Dylan turned, not wanting her to read his face as it filled with fury. Swiftly taking over his body, he felt it taking control. He had to get out of here, now. Sprinting back to his car, Angela called after him, but he couldn't hear a word she said because his own thoughts were screaming at him inside, driving him insane.

Chapter 17

Monday, the 9th day of September, 5:00 P.M.
Bozeman, Montana

Dylan screamed out of the parking lot, covering his El Camino in mud. "Damn, I wish they'd pave this lot," he yelled, as if his car had understood his mounting frustration. He lovingly patted her shiny dash, then admired the finish he had applied yesterday that kept her looking like new before apologizing to her. "Sorry old gal, I didn't mean to do that to you."

Dylan headed down Main Street and pulled into the BlockBuster Video parking lot. Della's Mustang was still parked directly across the street at the bar. Stooping so low as to actually spy on Della felt certifiable to him, but because he blamed himself that she was missing, and he was worried to death about her, he stayed where he was.

From past experience he knew Della could only handle about three drinks before she lost control. He witnessed one Christmas party in particular, where she had one too many. She apologized to him the following day because she couldn't remember much and was worried she had made a fool out of herself. She didn't do anything anyone could hold over her head, but the other officers didn't tell her that. They wanted her to believe she did and wanted to see her show a little vulnerability, a trait she didn't like anyone to see. That's why he convinced himself he was doing the right thing by being there, staring at her car from across the street, just waiting for something to happen.

She must have finally taken his advice and went out. He left her Sunday morning about 12:30. He stopped at her house and she slid off the bike and ran to her door without saying another word. After witnessing her anger that night towards him, he felt certain that whatever she was doing, she was doing it to pay him back for telling her that they could never be anything more to each other than just friends.

He couldn't believe she would actually pick up some guy or let herself be picked up in a bar, but he did feel he had driven her to it. He just hoped that nothing bad had happened to her. He could never forgive himself. She had said she loved him.

Dylan checked his watch. He'd been waiting more than an hour. Darkness fell and the street lamps came on. Waiting was driving him crazy, so he tried convincing himself to just hang it up. She'd probably met someone and was fine. He drove past and looked over again where Della's car sat. He hesitated, then pulled in, parking next to Della's car. Peering inside again, he found nothing disturbed since that morning. He realized if she did come back to her car, she wouldn't get far without her keys.

Dylan decided since he was officially off duty, he'd step inside the bar before going home and ask some more questions. He wondered just how long her car sat unlocked with the keys in it. Had it been there since Sunday morning? The thought scared him.

He looked around, hoping to find Della sitting in the bar. The place oozed with college kids shooting pool and watching the sports channel on the big screen TV. No sign of Della. He walked up to the bar. A different bartender hurried over to him.

"What can I get you?"

"Coffee, please," Dylan said.

"Coffee? That'll be just a minute. We don't usually start brewing it until closer to closing time." She grinned back at Dylan as he rapped on the Formica bar top like a drum roll.

"I guess I'll drink a beer then, " he said.

"You sure? It's no problem to start a pot, really."

"Yes, I'm sure. I haven't had a drink for a very long time."

"What flavor, then?"

"What do you have?"

"About anything your heart desires."

"Anything will do, just give me what's on tap."

"Okay, you got it." She started towards the cooler as Dylan yelled back to her from across the bar. She turned, hearing him over the loud music blaring out of the CD player against the wall. She came back toting a big smile.

"Give me a shot of Jack along with that," Dylan said.

"Sure." She walked to the end of the bar, grabbing the bottle off of the shelf, and walked back, placing the shot glass in front of him. She filled it to the top.

"There you go, one beer with a chaser. Now I'll have to take about three bucks from you."

Dylan paid for his drinks. He slammed the shot down then guzzled his beer. He bit back the bitterness in his mouth as he set the empty shot glass back down.

"Would you fill me up again when you get the chance?"

"Looks pretty serious for a Monday night," the bartender said.

"It is," Dylan said, as he felt the warm fluid burning deep in his stomach replacing the ache he felt earlier this morning. For just a little while, he wanted to feel numb. It had been a long time since anything sent him to a bottle for comfort. He shook his head, disgusted at himself, forgetting the bartender staring back at him. He finished the next shot and the beer, ordering his third round. The numbness swept through his body. It felt great.

He ordered another round when he remembered his mother would be waiting for him with dinner and that she'd worry herself to death if he didn't call her. Moving his mother in with him after his Dad died was the right thing to do, but it was hell on his social life. It was like being in high school all over again, making sure she knew where he was at all times so she didn't worry. What would he tell her? That he sat here getting shit faced by himself. That would brighten her day. He walked to the pay phone and dialed.

"Drake residence," his mother said.

"Hi, Mom. I won't be home at all tonight."

"Is everything all right?"

"Yes."

"Dylan, you sound strange. What are you doing?"

"Mom, I'm fine. I can't talk right now. I just wanted to let you know not to wait up for me."

"You can't keep up this schedule. You'll be an old man before you're due. I'm going to call Captain Mitchell up and give him a piece of my mind."

"Mom, don't do that. Remember, I can take care of myself. This is my life. I need to go now. I love you." Dylan hung up the telephone before she could say another word. He walked back to his bar stool feeling a little light headed.

He ordered another beer, knowing he'd have to walk across the street to rent a motel room for the night. In all his years before he quit drinking, he knew better than to drive drunk. He couldn't call a taxi to drive him safely home, because he couldn't let his mom see him like that.

Dylan focused on the bartender. His eyes felt fuzzy. He approximated her age to be about twenty-one. Much, much too young.

She had beautiful silky blonde hair pulled back in a French braid. She wore tight Levi's with a short midriff top that exposed a little cleavage on top and a flat stomach with a tiny diamond stud in her belly button. As she leaned over to clean some glasses he spied a tiny rose tattooed on her right breast, hidden underneath her flimsy shirt. He met her eyes as she looked back up to wait on a customer. Her smiled widened across her face as she turned to talk to him again. Dylan's face flushed from being caught peeping.

"I haven't seen you in here before," she said.

"That's because I have never been in here before."

"Just passing through?"

"No. I live here. I've lived here for many years, actually," Dylan said.

"Oh. This isn't the kind of place you usually hang out in then?"

"No, I don't make it a habit. I quit drinking a few years ago. I thought tonight I should try it again."

"I'm sorry."

"Sorry for what? Hell, don't feel sorry for me. I'm having fun."

"You are? You sure don't look like you're having much fun."

"Give me time to warm up. I'm a little out of practice."

"I get off at midnight. I could help you warm up." She giggled and turned around and poured another shot of Jack Daniels and slid it in front of him. "It's on the house."

"Bottoms up." Dylan jerked his head back, the shot sailing smoothly down his throat this time. "Where's the can?"

"Back there, to your right." She pointed. "Don't get lost. I'd like you to come back and keep me company. Monday nights are a drag around here."

"Okay, it's a deal." Dylan slipped off the stool, heading for the bathroom. He hit the doorframe as he went through it, then steadied himself before he bounced off the other wall and into the wrong door before apologizing to the woman coming out.

Managing to make his way back through to the front bar, he sat down and heard his name being called. Looking through the haze filled room he recognized the sound of the voice calling him the second time. Della and a man sat in the corner, looking up at him.

"Evening, Dylan," Della said. I thought that was your car parked by mine. Funny, this is the last place I thought you'd ever be." She studied his face.

"Della. It's nice of you, too—"

"Dylan, you're drunk."

"I am. And you—" Dylan reached down pulling Della up from her chair, "have some explaining to do."

"This isn't the place or the time. Please, let go of me." She pleaded with his eyes that burned like fire into hers. She knew he consumed his limit. He'd been sober for five years at least.

"Let her go, man. You're hurting her." The man sitting next to Della stood up and almost matched Dylan's height. He had short black hair and dark eyes and an athletic build with broad shoulders and was smartly dressed. Della sitting with a man threw him off guard. The man glared at him with his obsidian eyes. He didn't recognize him instantly, and then it hit him who he was, the son of one of the most notorious attorneys in the state.

"This is Matthew. He's an old friend from college. He just got back in town. He's looking for work. We accidentally bumped into each other and have been catching up on old times."

"We've met." Dylan said. "I'm sure Matthew remembers me. Detective Dylan Drake. Della's partner. Did she tell you she has a job? She's a detective now. A detective with a big case left piling up on her desk. Something that must have just slipped her mind today when she decided to take a personal day off." Dylan slapped his hand up to his forehead, exaggerating memory loss nearly knocking himself senseless. "Could that personal thing be you, Matthew?"

"Dylan, back off. You have no right to talk to him that way," Della said.

"I do have the right, and I'll talk to him any damn way I want. You're my partner, and I depend on you. I needed you today."

"Dylan, you're full of shit. You got rid of me, remember?"

"I do remember. But unfortunately for you, our boss wouldn't go for it."

Della pulled away from Dylan's grip, throwing his equilibrium off. It sent him staggering backwards. The bartender showed up behind Dylan just in time to catch him.

"Easy there." She slipped her arm around his waist to steady him.

Della flashed her a nasty look as she stepped up to Matthew and whispered quietly in his ear.

"Matthew. Could you excuse us for a moment? I think Dylan and I need to talk in private."

"Are you sure it's all right Della? He's hammered."

"I know, but he's harmless. He's got some problems he needs to work out. I'll be okay. I'll drive him home. I'll call you later."

"Okay. I'll be waiting to hear from you." He looked straight into Dylan's eyes. "I don't remember you and I'm not sure it was a pleasure to meet you. Della has said a lot of nice things about you. You're lucky she thinks so highly of you, man. I can't see it myself." He turned and strutted away to the rear door.

Dylan watched his bulky body as it disappeared around the corner, feeling happy he broke up their little get together.

"And who is this, Dylan?" Della pointed at the bartender. "She must be a good influence. I haven't seen you be this big of an asshole since, well, I guess yesterday."

"Hey lady, wait just a minute. I don't have to take this from you, and he doesn't either. I work here, and I believe you just 86'ed yourself out of here."

"I bet you do work here." Della flipped her badge out speaking calmly, "I'm Detective Bishop." She cleared her throat as she looked at Dylan. He was shaking his head and laughing uncontrollably. "I'm placing this man under arrest for public intoxication. If you'd like to join him, I could make the arrangements. All I have to do is call for a backup." She flipped out her handcuffs and grasped Dylan's left wrist, slapping a cuff on it, then put the other one around her right wrist.

"Hey, no thanks. I'm the bartender. Sober too." She raised both her arms up towards the ceiling, walking quickly away towards the bar.

"I should arrest you for allowing this man to become this intoxicated." She pulled Dylan along with her out the front door and to her car. She opened her passenger door and crawled in pulling Dylan in as she slid over to the driver's seat listening to Dylan still howling out of control.

"Are you sure that blonde babe didn't slip you something more than alcohol, Dylan? Would you try and shut up. This isn't very funny."

"Oh, but it is."

"I'm glad you think so. Tomorrow you may not be laughing so hard."

Della searched under her seat. "Damn." She tried reaching under Dylan's legs pulling his wrist with hers. She felt around with her long fingers around the floor.

"What are you looking for?" Dylan said.

"My keys."

"Your keys. On the floor?"

"Yeah. I left them under my seat."

"You kill me, Della. Under your seat. The lady detective leaving the keys to her shiny new Mustang under the seat of her car overnight at a God damn bar, of all places."

"Overnight?" Della looked back into Dylan's eyes. "What are you talking about?"

"I left you Sunday morning, and you came here and picked up that scum of an attorney."

Della reached out and slapped Dylan so hard it forced his head into the back of the seat.

"I guess I deserved that," he said.

"You're damn right you did. I didn't come here last night and get picked up by anyone."

"I found your car here this morning."

"That's right. I parked here to go next door and get my usual coffee and a bagel. And I sure as Hell don't know why I'm bothering to explain anything to you right now, you drunken idiot."

"Idiot?" He slurred more with each word.

"That's right. You're the biggest idiot I've ever met."

"Is that good?" He glanced over at her and grinned, feeling happier than he had felt all day.

"No, that's bad."

"Bad. Well, what can I do to make it up to you?"

"Let me drive you home."

"I thought you were arresting me."

"I should. You're a fool."

"I know. I'm a fool for you."

Della's head snapped around to look at Dylan. She obviously didn't hear that right. "What did you say?"

"I'm a fool."

"I heard that part. I'm the one that mentioned it, you damn fool. The second part."

"For you, Della." He turned around to face her reaching her with his free hand. Della slapped it away.

"Stay away from me. Don't pull this shit with me now. The alcohol is talking. You're totaled."

"Think so?"

"I know so, or else you would never tell me that."

"You're absolutely right. But I thought you would take advantage of me under these circumstances."

"Dream on, you jerk."

"Your keys are in my pants pocket."

"What? That's just great. You stole my keys. Give them here."

"I can't. My left hand is cuffed. I can't reach them, being all tangled up and crammed into your front seat. You'll have to get them, or uncuff me."

"I am not taking these cuffs off until I have you secured."

"Secured? You make me sound dangerous." He exaggerated a frown, then laughed.

"You are dangerous. I've known that since the day we met. But right now you're a danger to yourself."

He stopped suddenly, remaining quiet, his face turning stone serious. "A danger to you." His voice dropped to its deepest level, pain contorting his face then he shrieked like a madman, "I'm a fucking danger to you, Della."

"What the hell are you talking about? You're wasted." Della had to turn her head to look up Main and try and hide her face from Dylan because her eyes started filling with tears. She brushed them away with the back of her hand quickly. Caution signs flashed in her mind to take it easy on him tonight. Alcohol controlled him and anything could happen. She could finally get what she wanted from him right now, but she didn't want Dylan like this, she wanted him back first.

Dylan started sinking down deeper in her leather seats and his head bobbed forward.

"I don't feel..."

Della watched in horror as he crumpled forward hitting his head on the dash.

"Dylan, oh no, Dylan! Wake up, wake up Dylan." She scooted closer, as close as she could get to him with handcuffs, and tried pulling him up. "Shit, Dylan." She struggled to lift his head as she shook his jaw.

Blood gushed down from his forehead as she finally managed to push him back up into the seat. "Dylan, please wake up, come on." She retrieved her key to the cuffs, squirming until she worked it in and released the lock one handed. She tossed them off then quickly straddled him and grabbed him by the shoulders, shaking him to get a response.

Dylan started moaning her name faintly under his sour breath. She reached for the roll of paper towels stuck between the seats and grabbed what rolled freely then pressed them down on his head. She held him close, pressing steadily on his wound. She felt a jerk from underneath as her body rose and her head hit the ceiling. Dylan's arms reached around her and started to crush the life out of her. "Dylan, stop, wake up. You're crushing me!" Della squirmed until his grip loosened and she could breathe freely again. She looked down into Dylan's face. His eyes flew open like he'd seen a ghost that just brushed panic across his paling face.

"Della?"

"Of course it's me. Who did you expect, Florence Nightingale?"

"Della. Why are you sitting on my lap?"

Della rolled back off of him and told him to hold his head back as she reached his hand and placed it on the paper towels. "Hold that tight." She reached in his pocket feeling for her keys.

"Della?"

"What Dylan."

"That feels so good." He melted back into the seat.

"You son of a bitch. If you weren't already bleeding to death, I'd hurt you real bad."

She retrieved the key and fell back into her seat driving her car east. Dylan produced a gurgling sound as he turned a little, then flopped into her lap. She held onto him until she reached her house.

"Dylan, come on. You're going to have to help me a little. I am strong, but I don't think I can carry you upstairs to my bed."

Dylan stirred, as she pulled him out of her car and helped him to stand. The frigid air hit both of them giving her a second wind. A few stumbles later, Della helped the incapacitated Dylan up the stairs while he mumbled a whole string of unrecognizable sentences. She got him to her bed where he sprawled out.

Della undressed him carefully, trying not to disturb him. She didn't need him to move his head and make it bleed more. She took his bloody clothes into her laundry room to soak for awhile before washing them.

She grabbed a few first aid items from her bathroom and returned to clean the long gash across his forehead. After the bleeding stopped, she cleaned it. It looked to be superficial, not needing stitches she decided. She bandaged him up while listening to his serenade, a snore that could have raised the roof. He was right about one thing, he did sound like a freight train. Out cold for the rest of the night, she thought. She smiled, covering him up with her goose down comforter and walked out shutting the lights off.

She let Kiki in, then built a fire in her hearth. She positioned herself on the couch and fell asleep until the cold crept into her bones, filling her with a sudden chill that half woke her from her dream.

She shivered in the darkness, realizing her fire died. It left the downstairs frosty. Her wood needed splitting and carried in, but she couldn't possibly do it tonight. First thing in the morning she'd have to do it.

She sleepily sat up and wandered upstairs to her room through the dark, peeling her clothes off and leaving them beside her bed. She crawled in under her comforter for all the heat it offered her cold bones, pulling it up around her shivering body.

She stretched out and turned over when her leg met hot skin. Her mind jolted awake remembering the events of the evening. Dylan slept like a rock in her bed. A full grin covered her face as she snuggled closer to the heat radiating from underneath the covers, knowing she could get away with it for tonight. Her mind fell easily back to sleep, slipping into a heady dream.

Chapter 18

Tuesday, the 10th day of September
Bozeman, Montana

Della felt the light seeping in through her eyelids. She lay perfectly still, not wanting to start a new day. Opening her eyes slowly, she peeked at the sunrise outside her window. The huge orange ball elevated itself above the snow capped mountain ridge and came into view, making the rest of the skies look like they were gloriously spattered in crimson.

Taking in a deep breath, an arm slipped gently away from her waist, taking away the warmth and leaving a chill. She rolled onto her back, gasping out loud, as she remembered the previous night. Turning sideways she glimpsed at Dylan. He met her with his red-lined eyes and stared at her from his battered face. He looked unnaturally pale, but serene. He didn't speak.

The silence felt like a sentence to eternity bogging her down. It felt thick, so thick she was sure she could cut it with a knife.

He rolled onto his back, staring up at the ceiling, still not uttering a word in the light of the new day. Following his lead, Della kept her eyes up at the ceiling, waiting for him to speak first. She was curious about his lack of words and what he was thinking at that moment.

Minutes went by as they both stared up, their bodies touching each other.

"Della?" Dylan closed his eyes, squeezing them tightly, then blinking them rapidly as if he were trying to erase the scene he found himself in.

"Yeah?"

"I'm really sorry." He turned his head slightly looking over at Della. "Shit, I'm damn sorry."

"You don't have to be sorry for anything."

"Oh, yes I do." He turned his head a little more, moaning as he lifted his arm up to support his head.

"Don't be," Della said. She turned reaching for Dylan's face.

He jerked back, a small yelp escaping his lips. "Damn."

"Don't move so fast. You haven't seen all of your accomplishments from last night yet. I just wanted to check your bandage." She reached up gently, looking at him closer. Blood soaked through the bandage in the night, making him look like the survivor of a war.

Dylan reached up slowly, straining to reach his face. "Well, that explains one thing. That excruciating pain I'm feeling in my head. I was afraid to talk." He chuckled softly, sucking in short breaths of air.

"Oh, so that was the problem. I never witnessed you having a shortage of words at any given moment, but this one."

"Right. I have to admit."

"Admit what?" Della said.

"This is the most damnedest moment of my life."

"What? How can you say that?"

"Now, don't take offense. I just meant, well—"

"What way did you mean it. Are you trying to tell me something again?" Della glared at his face, trying to hide the sympathy she felt looking back into his pathetic face.

"I'm sorry, I—"

"I'm really tired of hearing, 'I'm sorry' from you," Della said. "You're starting to make me angry again. If you make me angry enough, I'll raise my voice. And this morning I don't think you want it any louder. Now what are you trying to tell me? Give it to me straight."

"I don't remember a thing."

"You don't remember anything?" Della held her eyes steady, trying to extract more information from him.

"Not one thing. That's why I'm sorry. I wanted this to be something we would always remember. I fucked that up, and I can't undo it."

Della furrowed her dark brows, looking confused until she realized Dylan really didn't know what had happened. He thought he had made love to her while he was drunk. She didn't know if she should be mad about that, but she decided to let him think whatever he chose to.

"I'm sorry too then, Dylan. I'm real sorry." She turned fully on her side, propping herself up on one elbow.

"What in the hell do you have to be sorry for?" Dylan said.

"Well, I'm looking at your face, a pitiable looking one at that, I might add, and I regret—"

"Don't. I have enough regret for both of us."

"I'm sorry because you told me—"

"Don't say it. I don't want to hear what I told you. Now you know why I quit drinking. I'm an ass, and I know it better than anyone else does. I just wish I could convince you of that." Dylan looked back up towards the ceiling. "This is the most uncomfortable moment of my life. I'm sorry, but I need to get up and get out of here. I should never have taken that first drink. Whatever I did, whatever I said, forget that it happened, please. Let's just get up and go to work and start over. You're a beautiful woman that any man would be crazy not to fall for. You deserve better than me. This isn't what you want, we both know it. Let's pick up where we left off a few days ago and get on with it. Our job is suffering. We both know that."

"I don't know anything of the sort," Della said. "Quit telling me what I know, what I feel, what I'm sorry for. I am sorry, but I do know a few things. For one, you said you wanted this to be something we would remember forever. Well, unless you happened to be a virgin last night and you were speaking in generalities here, that you meant to say, 'the first time you made love you wanted to remember it forever.' But I distinctly heard you say, 'when we did this.' So I'm interpreting that to mean you have thought about us rather intimately before last night, or even a couple of days ago. You just won't let yourself get involved because you're an ass."

"You're right. So why would you want me then?"

"I don't want you. I just want—" Della stretched her leg out, touching his. She felt a chill move up her spine, making her recoil. "I want nothing from you that you don't want to give. Okay. Let's forget this. I think we have exactly forty-five minutes to get to work."

Della rolled away from Dylan and stood up, walking over to the window to look down across the valley.

Dylan followed her to the window. Her arms were folded in thought, a perfect silhouette in his eyes.

Della slowly turned and stepped back over to Dylan. Their eyes met across the distance as she came forward. Dylan stared at her body.

"Oh, my god," he said. He fell forward, but caught himself in time for Della to make it around to his side and kneel beside him.

"Are you all right?" Della said. I think you should lie back. You might want to call in sick today." She reached out gently resting her hands on his knees.

"Please get dressed. I can't take this. I'm an old man, and now a disabled old man." Dylan shut his eyes.

"The showers yours in fifteen minutes, unless you'd like to shower with me now? I could help you stand." She spoke inches from his face, her breath touching his neck, raising the heat.

"No. I'll be all right. You get going before you have to dial 911. You're killing me." Dylan slid back under the covers gently laying back on the bed and holding his head. He sprawled out across the entire bed. "If I ever do this again, just shoot me."

"I don't know, I kind of enjoyed last night." She giggled, opening her drawers and grabbed some clothes before turning to leave.

"Della?"

"Yes, Dylan?"

"I have to ask. Tell me we used a condom?"

"Don't worry."

"I am worried. I said, tell me we used a condom?"

"Yeah, and I said don't worry." Della waltzed out, containing a private laugh that burst from her chest as she reached in, adjusting the water temperature before immersing her body into the hot steaming water. Enjoying Dylan squirm made her day, maybe even her week.

Chapter 19

Tuesday,the 10th day of September
Bozeman, Montana

Della sat sipping a cup of coffee, waiting for Dylan to get his act together. He insisted he didn't need any help. She heard the shower still running, and hoped he hadn't passed out.

Remembering she hadn't played back her messages on her machine, she hit the replay button. Her father had left several messages. The last one was from Matthew.

She smiled as she thought about meeting him so unexpectedly. He was a nice man. He left a message because he was worried about her after last night, reminding her she forgot to call him as promised.

She wondered why Dylan held him in contempt. He was the son of one of the top attorneys in town. He chose to follow in his father's footsteps, and was paving his own road to the top. His skills in prosecution proved successful by the number of cases he tried and had won in District Court. They met during his last year of law school in Missoula. They caught up on old times. He told her stories that made her laugh. She remembered his great sense of humor. Catching him up on her life didn't take too long.

She reached for the telephone, dialing the number he left. He picked up right away, scolding her for not calling.

"I think your partner is messed up, crazy if you want my opinion," He said.

"Dylan? Well, he usually doesn't act anything like that. I wouldn't have been impressed myself. In fact, I wasn't. He's having some problems right now."

Dylan came slowly down the stairs.

Della smiled, looking at him as he descended the stairs like an old man, holding the banister for dear life and holding onto his head for support. She knew he must have been suffering.

"Everything is all right," she said to Matthew. "You don't have to worry about me."

"Can I take you out for dinner tonight? Make up for last night. We were cheated out of dinner and dancing, you know?" Matthew said.

"Dinner and dancing tonight? Well, I don't know. Sounds fun. I can't believe you remembered I loved to dance. I'll have to check my desk when I get to work. I'll call you later."

"How about if I call you? I don't like waiting by a telephone. I waited all night for you to call."

"I'm really sorry. I feel really bad for not getting back to you. Call me at work. Talk to you then."

Della hung up the phone and stood up quickly to pour Dylan a cup of coffee. She handed it to him as his eyes questioned hers.

"Drink up," she said. "We have to go. I'll drop you off at your car."

"Matthew?" he said.

"Doesn't ring any bells?"

"Well, I might be remembering something. Yes, now I remember, Matthew. Ted's son."

"That's right. The one you ran off. You screwed up my date." Della said.

"I think it was a little more than that. You didn't make it to work, remember?"

"I remember everything. You accused me of sleeping with him the night before. Let me help you remember that part. I slapped you across the face. I didn't sleep with him, not yet anyway. You were not very nice. Remember?"

"I don't remember much, and I'm sorry. Do you like him?"

"No. I just took a personal day off to hang out with a slug. What do you think?"

"Are you in love with him?"

"I can't believe you. Love is a little strong for an old friend. He means a lot to me. We were great buds in college. A kind of replacement after I had to leave you here to go to college. I missed not having a friend like you to talk to. Any more questions?"

"No. I wish you luck, actually."

"What do you wish me luck for?"

"He's taking you out for a little dinner and dancing? Sounds like he may be interested in you in a different way than buds."

"Good. I always felt an attraction, but I never had the nerve to pursue it. Now, I do."

Dylan turned, setting his cup down next to the sink full of dirty dishes trying to hide his surprise. "I'm ready," he said as he moved quietly towards the door.

Della dropped Dylan off, arriving at work first. She walked into their office and sat down to play the messages off of the answering machine. She spotted a fax on the floor next to the machine. She picked it up and read it while waiting for Dylan to arrive.

Dylan walked in with a frown covering his face as he slowly sat down.

"You look like hell. You should just go home, " Della said.

"I feel like hell, but we have an important case to solve."

Della handed him the fax. "Look at this. It was on the floor."

Dylan read it. It was the information he requested about Father Murphy. No information was found since before he arrived in Bozeman. What did that mean? Who was he? Where did he come from? Questions started flowing through his mind, easing the pain behind it with his thought process warming up to something else besides Della.

"I guess this is our first order of the day. I think we should go talk with Father Murphy," Dylan said.

"I'm with you. You don't think he had anything to do with this, do you?"

"I don't think anything. Everyone is a suspect until we arrest one. This does leave a lot of questions in my mind. He's the one who turned in the gun and then coincidentally knew the owner. There may be a connection there we need. Let's go."

They left together, Della driving to the church. In the office they met an older woman with eyes that twinkled in a cherub face.

"I'm sorry, but Father Murphy is not here at the moment," she said, "He's visiting the nursing homes and the hospital today. I don't expect him until this evening."

"Thank you. If you could give him this card, and tell him we stopped by to talk with him."

"I'll do that, officer."

They left, discussing their next move. Dylan told Della he was going to check on the cabin. Rob Browning still hadn't made contact. They decided that Dylan would drive up to the cabin while Della made further inquiries about both Father Murphy and Rob Browning. Della parked her Mustang and let Dylan out by his own car. If he was scouting in unfamiliar territory, he liked to drive his own vehicle. An unmarked county car you could spot a mile away, tipping off the other side that someone is snooping.

"Are you sure you can drive up there in your condition? I don't feel good about letting you," Della said.

"You don't have a choice. I'm going. If I have to pull over, I'll remember why I quit drinking. Suffering is my best medicine."

"Okay, but I can't help worrying about you."

"Please don't start worrying about me. You know me. I'm a rough and tough sort of guy."

"I don't know about that. I think it's more like you're a hard headed, or maybe a better word would be pig headed, type of guy." She grinned at him, slamming the door hard.

Dylan winced.

Leaving Bozeman, he headed south on U.S. 191 and sailed down the winding road smoothly. His mind had started to clear with a little help from the open windows.

His thoughts turned to Della, and he wasn't sure what to do about his current predicament. He finally really went and did it, and didn't remember a damn thing. Feeling ashamed for taking advantage of her and even guiltier for not remembering it, he cursed to himself. She kept telling him it was meant to be, he knew better. He accepted the fact that he needed her, but he didn't know why that was. They had been friends for a long time before they were partners. The relationship changed in that instant. She was his partner that he depended on and a bond was definitely there. Did it really turn into much more for him?

The warning signs were always there, flashing danger. Becoming intimately involved with someone you worked closely with is against the rules. Was that the reason? A certain bond forming from the danger of their work, the risks they took together every day, turning them into nothing better than animals magnetized to each other. Drawing on the fear of the unknown, they both are hungry for a warm body to shield them against the crazy world. Trying to keep a hold of something in the face of change. It could only lead to a disaster that would crush the life out of them both if they didn't come to their senses.

She filled a part of him that now felt lonely and dismal. He recalled her perfect body glowing in the morning light that set him off like a rocket. Fooling her wasn't easy because he knew he was only fooling himself. He needed the distance this trip offered him.

Dylan reached Einos's bar and met with the deputy over coffee to discuss the robbery that Father Murphy reported. Driving back towards Teepee Creek, he prepared himself for the long hike to the cabin the deputy described, hoping he was physically up to it.

Hiking several miles, he heard the sounds of a motor off in the distance disturbing the quietness he had felt being way up on the mountain. It sounded like a truck engine rumbling, echoing back to him. He headed toward the sound. It led him to another trail that took off and was hidden by the tree line. He hiked back down along the trees, seeing a clearing. An antique Army truck was leaving a green metal building that sat hidden among the pines. A chain link fence that towered above the building enclosed it. It had razor sharp barbed wire strung in rows at the top. It looked like the fence surrounding the state penitentiary at Deer Lodge. The truck chugged away slowly up the hill, then left, heading away from him going further into the wilderness.

The structure looked like a forest service building, painted with the same green color they used on everything. He thought it was a strange place for it, sitting in the middle of the forest in the wilderness area where he believed motorized vehicles weren't allowed. At the Clerk and Recorder's office in Bozeman he'd try and pinpoint the ownership and see if the Forest Service owned it. Most of the area up here he understood to be within Forest Service boundaries. Maybe he was wrong.

He climbed around, searching carefully for anything else out of the ordinary. He stayed out of view, circling the area at the tree line. The place was as secure in its mountain hideaway as a bank vault. The building had no windows to peek in, and appeared to have a satellite link up. He ventured further into the woods, past the building in the direction the truck headed. Entering another clearing, he stopped in the trees. A shell casing glimmered in the dirt. As he checked it out, he discovered it was from a large caliber handgun and that he was standing in the middle of a shooting range that was carefully camouflaged from sight. Picking up a few more shells in the area that someone had missed when they cleaned the place, he found a bullet imbedded in a tree. The bullet was a Black Talon used only by law enforcement agencies. That may not have been what he came to investigate, but it was real interesting. Something didn't add up. Wandering back the way he came towards the cabin, he kept his eyes and ears peeled, feeling like he was at one of his weekend maneuvers with the Naval Reserves playing weekend warrior.

Once at the cabin, he let himself in and went through it, taking mental notes of everything. After he was finished, he descended the mountain. As he was turning to get back on the highway in the canyon, he called work from his cell phone.

"Detective Bishop."

"Della, get down to the Clerk and Recorder office and research the ownership of this area. I'll fill you in when I get there."

"I'll get down there right now, it's getting late. Father Murphy hasn't returned any calls. How are you feeling?"

"Better. There's just something about this fresh mountain air that does something for your head."

"I agree. See you when you get in."

"I'm on my way back now, but don't wait for me. I wouldn't want to interfere with your date. Just leave me the information on my desk. I'll pick it up when I get back."

"Fine. See you later then."

Dylan hung up the phone as he watched a Suburban signaling to turn up Teepee Creek towards him. Concentrating on getting the plate as it went by, he missed seeing the driver. He couldn't make out the numbers on the plate because they were partially covered by dirt, but was certain the plates were government issued. Spinning his car around in the road, he decided to pursue it.

The road forked to the right and left. The Suburban was on neither road. It must have turned off before the split. Dylan drove back to Bozeman in record time, feeling disappointed about losing the vehicle. He pulled in the office at 17:00.

Della was talking with Matthew on the phone with her back turned. "I have to work late." She paused, "I'd like that. I love Chinese. Pick me up here if you don't mind taking me out dressed in my work clothes. See you then."

"Hi." Dylan said, and came over and sat down at his desk. "Glad you're still here."

"You made great time. What did you find?"

"I found Rob Browning's cabin, and a huge warehouse off on the other side of the mountain. It looked like a Forest Service building. Did you get any information?"

"Yes, I did. Rob Browning leases the cabin from the federal government. It's a hundred-year lease. A quarter, quarter of that section on the border is owned by M.M.A. The rest is all Federal wilderness area and state forest service land."

"The M.M.A. What's that? Montana Medical Association?"

"I don't know. I couldn't find an address on them. They gave a P.O. Box on the deeds, but it's a post office box in British Columbia. The Assessor's office said the taxes were paid in full.

"Canada? That's all you could find? Hell, this isn't making any sense."

"So far. I tried to get through to the Canadian officials up there to trace the post office box."

"Father Murphy. Has he shown up or called?" Dylan said.

"No. He hasn't. I tried to reach him again. That sweet old lady said she hadn't heard from him all day. She said she would give him the message the minute he stepped in."

"I tried following a Suburban up Teepee Creek after I called you. I lost it. I think it was a government vehicle. See how many Suburbans are registered with the state or federal agencies in this county. See if Rob Browning is an employee of the state or federal government, and if a solid black Suburban is issued to him."

Dylan sat down at his desk picking up his memos. One stood out in his hand. Diana Edwards would like to speak to him privately. He picked up the phone dialing the number on the paper.

When a voice answered, he said, "Diana Edwards please."

"This is Diana."

"This is Detective Drake. I just got your message." Dylan turned his pencil around in his hand, waiting for her to say something.

"I have a doctor's appointment tomorrow at one o'clock with Dr. Greene at her office," Diana said. "If you could meet me there without anyone knowing about it, I'd appreciate it. Perry is taking me and will be waiting for me in the waiting room. Please be inside one of the rooms and not in the waiting room. Perry can't know I'm talking to you. It's very important that no one finds out. Can you do that?"

"I can. But are you sure you can wait till then?"

"I have to. I can't get away from here without someone finding out."

"Are you in danger?"

"I don't know. I have to hang up now." The phone went dead in Dylan's hand.

Della stared at him, waiting for him to fill her in.

"Diana Edwards," Dylan said. "She needs to speak to me privately. No one in the band can know. By the sound of her voice she's frightened and panicky."

"What do you make of it?"

"I could think of a million things. I just hope that whatever it is, she'll be okay until tomorrow, and until then, the suspense will be killing me."

"She seemed guarded when we were there. I mean, they all looked after her like some helpless child. Maybe they all know something, and Diana is the key. They don't want her talking."

"I agree. We may be closer to the truth by tomorrow. Scott Tate was out of control, and he raised my fur. I didn't like him or the way he snapped at you. Tension seemed to fill the air in that house."

Dylan wrote notes quickly, putting all his information together when the phone rang.

"Detective Drake."

"Hi, dear. I just wanted to know if you'd be home for dinner tonight. I was going to make your favorite meal, lasagna with fresh baked garlic bread."

"Oh Mom, that sounds great. I'd really like too, but—"

"You can stop for one hour and come home and eat a decent meal. If you don't, I'm going to call and ask your boss if he'll send you home to eat. You'll waste away to nothing."

"Okay, Mom. I'll be home. I'll be home about six thirty."

"You won't be sorry, I promise. I miss you, son."

Della filled the room with her laughter. Dylan smirked back at her.

"Mom?" Della said. She's worrying about her only son. Why, not coming home at all last night. What are you going to tell her, anyway? I know you would never tell her what really happened."

"No, you're right. And what did you tell your father when you returned his calls." I know you didn't tell him the truth, either."

"You think you got me? Well, no. I didn't exactly tell him what happened. I was afraid if I did, you'd be standing on the wrong side of a gun barrel."

"Direct and correct hit. But I was talking about yesterday, when you weren't at work. That's why I came looking for you. He asked me to check up on you."

"He did? Did he tell you to spy on me too?"

"No, and he will crucify me for telling you. He wanted to make sure you didn't need any help. I bet you didn't tell him you were out with Matthew, did you?"

"What? What difference would that make? He wouldn't care."

"Oh yes, he would. I know your father well. When it comes to his daughter having an intimate relationship with a man, it would make a difference on who it is."

"Where do you get this stuff from?" Della said. My dad would be happy for me no matter who that man was, as long as the man was a good man and good to me. Anyway, I'm not involved with Matthew. Not yet anyway. We do plan on spending some time together as friends, that's all."

"Are you trying to convince me of that, or yourself? Those aren't the words I heard this morning. You actually said you hadn't slept with him yet." He used special emphasizes on "yet".

Della stood up, spinning around, and bumped into Matthew as he entered the door.

"Oh, Matt. Hi. You surprised me. Someone let you in the security door. Well, I think I'm ready." She turned back to her desk in time to catch Dylan grinning back at Matt with a look of contempt in his eyes. She grabbed her coat from the wall.

"I thought we'd have a picnic at the duck ponds. You wouldn't have guessed it snowed yesterday. It's like a summer evening out there again." Matt said.

"The duck ponds?"

"Yes. They bring back a few memories for me. I haven't been there for awhile. I was hoping you'd like the idea."

"Like the idea? Sure. I love the idea. It brings back a memory for me, too." She shot a wicked look at Dylan as she painted a provocative smile on her lips to cover the surprised look on her face.

"I forgot. I won't be here tomorrow. I'm staking out the cabin tonight," Dylan said.

"I'm going with you."

"You have a date. I can do this by myself."

"I'm your partner, and I'm going, so when do we leave?"

"As soon as I go pack some gear. One hour. I'll pick you up."

She turned back to Matthew, "I'm sorry. I have to go. I hope you understand?" Della said.

"Just like that? You're going to leave for the rest of the night with him?" Matthew said, directing an icy stare towards her partner, Detective Drake.

"I'm sorry, that's just the way it is with my job, no warnings. Detective Drake is my partner, where he goes I go."

"He just told you, you didn't need to go. I don't understand." Matthew said.

"I'm sorry. When I get back, I'll explain it all to you, but right now I have to get packed," She said, giving him a kiss on his cheek. "I hope you give me another chance."

Matthew appeared devastated as he turned and walked out with his bags of Chinese food still in his hands. Dylan felt happy breaking up their date at the pond. The thought of them eating a cozy dinner together in the same spot where he almost made love to Della, provoked a misery in his heart he couldn't deny.

Dylan headed for home, sketching a scenario in his mind about the shooting at the campus. The pieces weren't falling together, but at least they were getting closer to turning up a few more leads to the puzzle.

A smell of fresh baked bread mixed with garlic filled his nose as he opened the door to his house. It made his stomach rumble and his mouth salivate. Dylan's mom came out of the kitchen.

"Dylan, oh no," she sighed, "What happened to your face?"

"Let's just say I encountered a situation I didn't handle very well, and leave it at that. And another thing, Della and I will be on a stake out tonight, so don't wait up and worry."

"How can you tell me that? Your face is all messed up and you look like the devil and you're running around packing enough guns and ammunition to protect the city and you tell me not to worry? Son, I hate to tell you this, but I think I need to worry."

"Okay, Mom. Worry then."

"At least I feel better knowing you won't be by yourself, " she said. "That beautiful partner of yours will keep you in line. I'm counting on it." She smiled.

"Yeah, right Mom." Dylan hurried and finished packing, trying to keep that subject out of his mind. He wondered at just how he was going to handle another night close to Della.

Chapter 20

Tuesday, the 10th day of September
Communications Branch, National Research Council
British Columbia, Canada

"There's been an inquiry into MMA, state side, by the local law enforcement in Gallatin County," the communications analyst said. "The reply was sent."

"Good. Relay the inquiry to all sectors and make damn sure that agent Ground Squirrel is aware that noses are sniffing his crotch. The bushes have already been shaken. Our target's daughter was shot Saturday night adding an unknown factor into the operation," he cleared his throat. "The operation is a go, and nothing can stop it now. If the local law comes down too hard on this and digs too much, we will have to pull out the skids and eliminate any yahoos that may get a big hard on and try and pursue our cover in depth. We can't allow any operatives to become exposed in the field nor can we risk them taking time away from their schedules. The clock is running and there is still a lot to set in motion before the thirteenth. This mission has the highest priority right now. The interception of this satellite tops the National Security's list. No one is going to interfere." Lieutenant General Garrity said.

"I will keep you posted, sir, out," the communications analyst said. He operated from one of the SIGINT (Signals Intelligence) sites in Canada, one of the many secret locations of the National Security Agencies code-breaking stations scattered around the world. He sent out the information as ordered.

Sluzba Vneshngo Razvedky (SVR) Headquarters
Russian Foreign Intelligence
Moscow, Russian Federation

"Yuri, the Big 7 reported in. Their finances are ready for transfer. They informed the Association that they now have support among the last of the clans that had been holding out. Their affiliations and political associations have been permanently severed. Politically they challenged the group in their own stupidity. They were quickly convinced. The rest of the bank leaders have made their transfers to the fund. They did see the economics of the situation. A bank without us, is a bank that will not be in business come Friday. We are now as one."

"We will rise again Sergey. The world will cower. We will emerge the great power again, mark my words. Our face restored, our humiliation turned to the rebirth of our great Mother Russia, the greatest power in the world, as it once was, and we shall hold it that way forever more. I will then take great enjoyment in seeing the United States of America pay dearly for its sins upon our soil." The phone disconnected.

Gallatin Field Airport
Bozeman, Montana

Jordan James held his wife's hand as they followed the security team and exited the plane. They were met by his driver in the car he kept housed at the airport. As they reached the car Mr. James cell phone rang. The Security team circled the car and moved inch by inch around it and then motioned to Mr. James that the car was clean. He opened the door for his wife and helped her inside. He closed the door and remained outside the car. "James here."

"Finances are in place. All is well in the land of opportunity." The voice said on the other end.

"I will order the product to be transported to the transfer point." Jordan James put his phone back in his pocket and smiled. "Let's get to the hospital."

The driver dropped Mr. James and his wife at the door. Two cars following a few car lengths back drove up and parked in the visitor's parking lot. His private security force would cover the perimeters and begin their own watch.

Law office of Black, Cameron, and Hill
Bozeman, Montana

He stared out the window contemplating the meeting he just left. The group seemed adamant to finish the job that became botched Saturday night. If it wasn't done, the risk of exposure became to high, a liability they could not afford. The hired hand who made the apparent mistake would never reveal his part in their plan. Now, the original target had to be taken care of before it was too late. The vote passed by a majority. There would be another killing in Bozeman.

He dialed the phone. "Hey, I need another job done. This time, Ed pick a reliable person. One with a little brain between the ears would you?"

"It can be arranged, if you will pay our supplier in full. Rob Browning still will only deal with us that way. One day maybe he will trust us totally. Another shipment is needed. With this one the MMA is armed and ready. Our militia will be the best armed and trained in the country. Our members have exceeded all expectations. This last shipment of supplies is just stockpile. Our guarantee we can defend our state against all enemies. Our contact wants the green now, however."

"How much this time?"

"Twenty-five grand."

"Deal."

"Same drill as last time. Put the money in the same account. My man will then contact you." The telephone disconnected.

Chapter 21

Tuesday, the 10th day of September

Dylan wove through town heading out Rouse and hooked up to Bridger Drive. His mind raced along with his bike that hummed underneath him. Replaying the rushed packing job he did, he wanted to be sure he didn't forget anything. A nagging worry played at the back of his mind despite his confidence.

As soon as Dylan arrived at her house, Della kissed her dog good-bye and jumped on the bike. The bike helmet slid on over her black hair that she had French braided. To blend in with the night for their stake out she dressed in all black, just as Dylan had instructed.

"I talked to the Captain. He wished us luck and told us to be careful. I about dropped from shock," Dylan said, turning some to talk with her before backing down her drive.

"You don't think he's behind us on this one?"

"No, I didn't mean that. It's just that he usually needs more information before he requisitions more hours for us to run on this kind of stake-out. I just thought he would tell us we were chasing our tails, or something else, spoken more true to his character in that natural style of speaking he uses. I'll spare you the details."

"I've heard most of his phrases. This time he knows we can do the job. We need to get some solid leads on this case. If you think there's a connection up the canyon, he knows you'll get it."

"I'm just surprised by how easy he sent us on our way."

"He's happy we're working together on this."

Dylan thought she might be right. The Captain was happy his team was going on an assignment after receiving the letter he'd written asking to be assigned a different partner. After he received his big 'no' and his long speech from a bona-fide short talker, he realized that he was following his sage advice and gave them the okay.

"Damn. I forgot. Diana and I are to meet at the hospital during her appointment tomorrow. I can't miss it. The information she gives to us could be the door we need. Diana is scared and has to keep this meeting a secret. That tells me volumes. How on earth could I have forgotten that? I knew something was bothering me."

"What time did she tell you to be there?"

"One o'clock tomorrow."

"That should be easy to make."

"I guess. It just screws up my plans to stay up on the mountain until I had something. This will be a short stay, but I can always return after the meeting."

Dylan turned out the driveway and headed back down Bridger. Taking Peach then Durston he turned on 19th and connected with Huffine Lane. Concentrating on reflector lights through the construction zone still hard at work, he slowed down. A flag lady turned her sign and made him stop. They were in front of the Main Mall.

"I guess my hope to make good time was a pipe dream. I'm tired of this construction around town. I thought at least at night we'd be able to sail up past Four-Corners by now."

"You need to just relax," Della said. "Take it in stride. Five minutes longer isn't going to make a difference. Trust me, it won't."

"Five minutes could mean the difference between being in place and seeing something, or not. Good. She just gave us the green light."

Dylan felt Della reach around him, tightening her grip as he took off down Highway 191. The night was pitch black and the traffic coming and going was almost non-existent. It felt like being in a long black tunnel.

Dylan glanced around as he sped through the night enjoying the stars above. Looking out into the huge sky made him feel small against the star filled sky. He controlled the bike through the obstacles of rock and river as they took one sharp curve after another. The pine trees lining the roads and the huge rock faces at every turn looked as if they wore faces and were staring back at them ominously.

The cold night air rushed across their bodies at fifty-five miles per hour, the speed limit Dylan was keeping. It chilled them to the bone. Dylan felt Della snuggle deeper into his back knowing she was trying to steal some warmth and cut the wind. The ride was going to come to an end soon, and the hike up the mountain would warm them back up.

Dylan came to an abrupt stop. When he looked up he saw an amber light glowing on a small building next to a bar and a gas station closed for business. A large telephone booth sat next to it in the sandy parking lot.

Dylan cut the engine and turned to face Della. "It's about twenty more miles up the road. This is the last stop before we turn."

Della slid off the bike, jumping up and down like her legs were made of springs.

"What's wrong? Did you get cold?" Dylan said.

"No, I just thought it was time to do some calisthenics. Warm up before the real exercise begins. Damn right I'm cold. I never rode a bike eighty miles in September up a damp and cold canyon before. I never let anyone talk me into something this stupid before." Della rubbed her arms with her hands, trying to unthaw them. If she had to shoot her gun right now, she'd be a goner.

"Stupid? You think this is stupid? If I remember right, I told you I was going to do this and you insisted on coming. Don't tell me I talked you into anything. I'd rather you be warm, and at home, tucked safely into your bed."

"You're right. I'm sorry. I just think we should have taken a truck that had four wheel drive. It could turn nasty tonight. It's not even safe in summer to be camping out in the mountains unless you're prepared for a snow storm this far up. If a snow storm does blow by, we'll turn into little snowmen waiting for someone to come along and put a scarf around our necks and raisins in our eyes." Della laughed, hoping Dylan might be humored.

Managing to give her a small grin, he got off the bike. "Della, come here." he laughed.

"Why?"

"Just come here."

She moved closer to him. "Okay, I'm here. Now what?"

Dylan put out his arms and gave her a big bear hug, covering her small body with his. He rubbed her arms up and down then spun her around to warm her back side. Della enjoyed the frisk.

"Warmer?" he said.

"Much."

"We'd better get our equipment out and get up the road and find a lookout point we can make camp at."

"Okay. I think my joints are mobile again. Thanks for the warm up."

"Anytime." Dylan smiled at her as he mounted the bike and she got on again. Up the dirt road he carefully maneuvered, scouting for the turn off he had seen earlier in the day. He found the two forks in the road. Cutting the engine, they got off of the bike and stopped and listened. Coyotes howled off in the distance. The pines whistled from the slight breeze sounding like snare drums. The trees formed a shroud of darkness around them, and he felt like they were inside of a black cave with the lights out instead of outside in the middle of the forest. The few stars breaking through the tree-tops didn't give them much light to go by.

Hiking deep into the woods, Dylan pushed his bike along until he came to a tall stand of trees at the top of a rise. Parking his bike behind the break, he took out his rifle, placing it over his shoulder, and grabbed extra ammunition and put it in his pockets for the two handguns he carried.

"Let's head up over this rise to the building that's below. We should camp on top. I'll have to leave the bike here." Placing it on its side, he cut some dead fall and placed the branches on top of the bike to hide it. "What a thing to have to do to eighteen grand."

"You paid that for it?"

"You bet, and I got a real deal. This one lists at a couple grand more."

"Man," Della said. "Men and their toys."

"It's not a toy. It's my alter ego. And worth every penny."

"I believe that." Della laughed, cinching her small pack and another small fanny pack around her waist that she kept her gun in.

"Here's your radio in case we have to split up," Dylan said.

She tucked it into the side of her backpack.

They hiked up the hill where it crested, and looked down across the valley to the building in the dark. It looked like a huge shadow. No lights came from anywhere on the mountain. Kneeling down, they stopped.

"That's the building. It has a tall chain link fence around it. I'd like to climb over it and see if I can get inside somehow."

"You know you can't do that," Della said. "You need a search warrant. You can't go break into someone's building."

"Watch me. If we wait for all the paperwork it might be too late. If I find something, we can get the paperwork."

"And what are you going to say? That you came across the door wide open and this is what you found?"

"Something like that. Right now, I'm going to go down there and try to get a closer look around."

"I'm coming with you," Della said.

"No. I need you up here to watch for anyone coming. You'll be able to spot anything from up here, and then you can let me know so I can haul ass out."

"I don't like this. I think we should both wait right here. That's what a stake out is, waiting and watching. It's not trying to be John Wayne in the middle of the night."

"Nothing's going to happen. Who's in charge here?"

"You, I guess."

"What do you mean, you guess? I'm the senior detective, and you, my fair lady, are the rookie."

"I know. You don't have to keep reminding me of that. Sometimes I think they should review their policy on that."

"Thanks a lot for your vote of confidence. Just sit back and relax. I'll be back in twenty minutes or so. Keep radio silence unless it's an emergency. If you need to warn me, break with 10–66. If someone is monitoring our station they won't get anything else. Got it?"

"Got it."

Dylan went down the side of the hill inching his way along the steep drop half sliding in a crouch all the way down to the bottom.

Della watched, peering into the darkness until he was out of sight. She took out her flashlight and laid it beside her. Sitting on the cold ground, she found a boulder in the tree line and took cover beside it. A crackling sounded behind her. Slowly turning to see, she froze when the sound grew louder and neared her.

Inching the zipper down on her fanny pack, she reached in, feeling the butt of her gun, and readied it. The possibility of a bear came to mind. She sat in bear country, no doubt about it, and it would be hungry, scavenging for the leftover's of the summer berries before hibernating. The thought of becoming dinner made the level of fear in her rise. She knew her revolver would only piss a bear off. Dylan had taken the rifle. She held her breath, listening harder for anymore sounds behind her. The sounds moved away from her. Every muscle in her body was taut. She sat as still as a statue, listening to her own heart pounding loudly.

Her knees, frozen in place, started to ache. She needed to stretch them. Sliding one leg out, she heard a limb break above her and then a whoosh beside her face. Pine needles filled her hair and scraped her face. Jumping up and stifling a scream, she pulled her gun out and aimed in the darkness. A squirrel ran in circles around the top of the boulder, then scampered off into the leaves. Della's sigh could be heard from the next county over if anybody out there was listening when the relief swept over her.

Twenty minutes went by, and Dylan didn't show up. It felt more like twenty hours had gone by. She prayed Dylan would change his crazy plan to break and enter. The Gallatin National Forest was a really big place for one to be sitting all alone in it, in the middle of a dark and cold night. It was crazy to let him go off like that, but what choice had he given her?

Dylan made his way a few hundred yards from the bottom of the hill, running in a half crouch through the open grassland trying to stay hidden even in the dark. The open range grass was long, and if he needed to, he could bury himself in it. Following the tree line to the back of the building, he crawled to the fence.

He searched in the darkness, not wanting to use his flashlight until he knew a security device couldn't detect him. He focused on trying to figure out the security system they were using on the premises. They were in place, but he just didn't know what kind, so he used extra care to avoid setting off any alarms.

He crawled around the boundary of the fence and found it charged with electricity. Searching along the rooftop of the building he spotted cameras at each corner, sweeping the perimeter. He might be able to beat the sweep of the camera and the electricity if he timed it just right and he was able to get high enough from the stand of trees at the back and jump inside the fence.

After twenty minutes slipped by, he checked his watch. He thought of Della waiting for him on the hill. Everything must have been going well. His radio maintained silence.

Creeping back to the tree line, he scouted out the trees closest to the fence and tried to find the tallest one. None appeared to be what he needed. The pines would eat him alive with their sticky pine cones and sharp needles before he could get up high enough, and the branches wouldn't be thick enough to hold him. He found some cottonwoods around the west side of the fence. They loomed the highest above the fence.

A thought stopped him as he started to climb. He didn't have a rope. Once he climbed up the tree and jumped inside, how was he going to get back out of the compound? The plan he made was failing, and the odds of getting inside were against him.

In the tree, he climbed higher and tried to get a better vantage point. Inching his way up the tree he had to stop. "Damn," Dylan said, and bit his tongue. A sharp point from a broken limb pierced through the flesh of his arm drawing blood. He unhooked his ripped sleeve and straddled the forked limbs. The back of the building had mini storage buildings clustered together. The visual in the dark wasn't good.

He studied the area for a while longer, deciding that the only possible way he might succeed was by digging his way under the fence.

He descended the tree, bark scraping under him, until he skidded to the ground. Creeping around the trees and into the side of the hill, he scaled back up through the forest. Circling back around in the opposite direction from where he came, he worked back to their lookout.

He sneaked up to the top of the hill and came around in the opposite direction to Della than he had left. Silently he walked up behind her as she sat leaning against the boulder. Reaching out his hand, he lightly touched her back. Della jumped up like a spring and turned with her gun leveled at him.

"Whoa, cowgirl. Put that thing down. It's just me."

"Have you lost your mind sneaking up on me like that? Thank God you're back and okay. Where have you been? I've been chewing my fingernails off waiting for you for the past hour. According to my watch, you either can't tell time, or forgot about your partner up here covering your back. I almost went looking for you. I thought maybe a bear had eaten you up and had spit you back out by now."

"I'm sorry. It's complicated down there. I need a shovel to dig my way in."

"You've got to be kidding, right? That would take the rest of the night."

"I know. That's why I'm going to come back here tomorrow night after I meet with Diana, equipped with a shovel. That's one thing I didn't pack, because I knew we wouldn't be building any fires out here tonight."

"What do you think is going on down there? Did you see anything? It was quiet up here."

"They have a security system that's top of the line. It isn't just to keep juveniles from trashing the place. They don't want anybody in there, and I mean nobody. It's about as secure as your family secrets." He laughed, grinning and waiting for her silver-tongued come back.

Della crinkled her face and stuck her tongue out.

"Cameras are constantly taking pictures, and I think the pictures are hooked into a satellite feed so the place can be watched from another location. An electric fence is set up around it to do more than give an intruder a little shock. If you got near it, I bet it would fry the hell out of you. And I'm sure the security has ears."

"That's terrible. There's so much wildlife that lives up here. What if they get too close and touch it?"

"They won't the second time. I can guarantee that. We'd better get out the sleeping bags and locate a flat piece of ground to make camp for the night. Sit back and relax, while we just watch like good little detectives. By the book, right Della?"

"Right, Dylan. I actually feel better knowing you couldn't break in. I had all sorts of scenarios playing in my mind."

"I bet you did. Come on, let's slip back to the bike and get the rest of our gear."

They carefully trekked back to the camouflaged bike and grabbed their stuff. As they started climbing back up to their lookout, Dylan grabbed Della's hand and stopped her in her tracks. They listened and heard an engine rumbling off in the distance. Stepping back in the brush and squatting down, they waited to see if it would come their way.

Five minutes passed before dim headlights bounced off the black sky and into the shadows of the trees as it wound up the road. A truck turned in and headed down the left fork. After it passed, Dylan motioned Della to follow him. They trotted all the way back through the trees to the base camp they had set up. The truck came down the narrow road and into the open pasture to the warehouse.

"Jackpot. We may learn something tonight after all. I have to get closer. I can't see enough from here. I'm going back down the hill."

"It's too risky," Della said.

"Yes, but it's the only way I can see anything or eavesdrop on one of their conversations. You stay here, and watch my back. I'm leaving my radio. It's too dangerous to have it go off." Dylan reached around and pulled his radio out, switching it off. Walking away, he started to circle north.

Della chased after him. "I'm going with you. Together we might see more. You circle around the other side of the hill, and I'll take this side, and maybe together one of us will get lucky enough to score."

"I really don't think that is a good idea. If one of us gets in trouble—"

"The other one will be right there to help."

"Okay. Then let's take the radios, change frequencies, and keep them off unless needed. I'll circle. You go straight down there. We'll meet back up here in one hour. If anything happens, get the hell out of here and back to my bike. Take off on it for help. We don't know who we're dealing with down there."

"Right. I'm all eyes and ears. See you in an hour. Hey, I'm just curious, but what time do you have?" Della said.

"Eleven fifty-five."

"Just checking. The last time we did this, twenty minutes became sixty, so I wanted to make sure we were in sync. You know, the agents in Mission Impossible couldn't have pulled off those capers without synchronizing their watches together."

"If we were those agents, we'd have all their fancy gadgets and we wouldn't be sitting in the middle of the forest freezing our asses off and just watching. Let's head out before the action does," Dylan whispered to her just before he leaped into the darkness and disappeared.

Della went down the ridge, angling farther north to avoid the slide.

The wind started to pick up. Moving through the trees, it sounded like the music in an eerie movie. A wave of chills started dancing through her body. Sucking in a deep breath, she moved on slowly in the dark. Tripping in a gopher hole, she flew forward through the air, skidding on the moist grass. She bit her tongue to keep from screaming. Grimacing from the pulsating pain in her ankle, she rolled up in a ball. She swore under her breath.

As she tried to scoot through the grass and position herself closer to the building before the truck reached the gates, they automatically opened. The truck's wheels barely slowed as it journeyed inside. A crash of thunder cracked over her and she flinched. It opened the black skies like a gusher and the rain began. Squinting against the pelting rain, she wished she would have taken Dylan's advice and stayed home. The lightning struck close, lighting the sky above.

The building's doors opened and the truck pulled inside. From her angle she could see nothing in the tall grass. Rolling flat onto her stomach, she wiggled a few more paces forward through the brush and waited.

Looking at her watch, she pressed the light and saw that it was twelve-thirty. Thirty-five minutes had passed. Feeling frozen and stuck to the slush on the ground, her teeth chattered loudly giving her a whopper of a headache. She felt numb and tired all over. A snooze started sounding good to her. Jumping around and getting warm became her next wish. It would be hard to take, but maybe her ankle was as numb as the rest of her, and when the time came for her to move, the pain would be deadened. It helped to keep positive thoughts.

Dylan sat up the hill closer to the front of the building, nestled in the tall overgrowth of the forest. He pulled out his pocket binoculars and focused on the door raising up, to see what was behind it. The darkness looked like tar through the lenses, the rain blurring his field of vision. Dim lights in the building were all he could see. He couldn't be sure of anything, except a few shapes that he guessed were more crates like outside.

Soaked to the bone and cold, he started to worry about Della. The rain turned to sleet, and he knew before long that the sleet would turn to thick wet snow. Nothing was working out the way he had planned. Della was right. Taking the bike was a mistake.

After another fifteen minutes, the truck left and headed back up the hill and out of sight. The doors and gates automatically shut behind it. After it was out of sight, he sprinted towards the lookout, pushing himself hard, hoping to get some body heat built up. Looking at his watch made him run even faster to make it back on time.

When he returned, Della was still out in the field. She had a few more minutes before being late. The sleet started turning to snow and it blew in around the point and started sticking. While he waited, he set their gear up. Placing the collapsible tent over a Space Blanket and then building a shelter over it with another tarp, he was able to throw their sleeping bags inside. He placed a can of Heat in the tent and zipped the flap down.

The hour had passed and there was still no sign of Della. If she hung back on purpose to prove a point and pay him back for being late earlier, he'd have her hide. Securing everything down, he glanced at his watch once again. Another fifteen minutes passed. If this was her idea of a joke, it wasn't funny. Shivering against the wind chill, he headed back down the way he told her to go and started searching.

Following the trail, he slipped down the wet rocks to the bottom. The trail was getting covered as the snow fell, getting heavier by the minute. His night vision decreased as the snow circled around him making a white out. Reaching for his radio, he clicked on. No response. Struggling ahead through the soggy mess, he turned and stopped. The field was white. A cold chill swept through him.

He kept trying the radio. Still no answer.

Della laid face down in the snow and had fallen asleep. Hearing Dylan's voice on the radio, she stirred. Pulling herself up, she tried reaching her radio. She fumbled around before her frozen fingers managed to key it. Her voice weakly squeaked out, "10–67."

"Dylan heard the weak voice. He took the risk and asked, "10–20?"

"Straight across, 300 yards from enclosure."

"10–4."

Dylan ran toward the building. His heart raced after hearing the panic in her voice. Finally, he spotted her lying on her side, the radio loosely in her hand and her eyes closed.

"What happened?" Kneeling beside her, he pulled her head up into his lap.

"My ankle."

Dylan examined her ankle and the rest of her, taking her vitals, and knew they were in trouble if she didn't get warmed up fast.

"Can you sit up?" he said. He watched her open both eyes. He pulled her up. "I'm going to get you out of here, but I'm going to have to carry you. It's not going to be easy. You with me?"

She nodded her head.

He pulled her to her feet. "Hold on. I'm going to carry you over my back. The fireman's carry. Remember that move in your training at the academy?"

Swinging her body over his shoulder, he moved through the gusting wind and snow through the dark. He climbed up the steepest side of the hill because it was the shortest and quickest route. Suddenly, he lost his footing and started slipping backwards. Della moaned as he regained his steps. At least he knew she was still conscious.

Finally reaching camp, he set her down on the rock. As he unzipped the tent he felt the heat. He focused on getting her wet clothes off and getting her into a sleeping bag quickly.

"Della, are you still with me?" He felt her pulse. "I'm going to get you undressed out here and then get you into the tent. It's warm in there. I wouldn't do this if it wasn't absolutely necessary."

Taking off her boots was easy, but stripping wet clothes off of a limp body wasn't. Della's head lolled to one side then fell forward into him. Her hand grasped his shoulder and tightened. It was a good sign. He carried her in his arms, then squatted down with her across his lap and worked his way inside the tent in a crouch. A thermal sleeping bag waited for her. He rolled her into it, then wrapped a dry towel around her head. Zipping it up around the top of her head, he left her.

Stepping back outside in the frigid air, he stripped himself. He entered the tent again and lit another can of heat before unzipping the sleeping bag Della was in. She shivered uncontrollably. Her eyes were tinged in blue, her lips white.

He slid in next to her and wrapped his body around hers. Underneath him, she felt like a block of ice. If he could keep his body wrapped tightly around her his body heat might bring her body temperature back up. Shivering himself, he fought the numbness and the fatigue that was taking over his body. She was suffering from hypothermia and he knew he wasn't far behind her. He shivered on top while she shook below. Together they formed a glacier.

All he could do now was to wait and see if it worked. Praying that Della would respond soon, before he lost consciousness, he tried to think of his next move before giving in to the weariness attacking him.

Chapter 22

Wednesday, the 11th day of September

Dreaming peacefully, Dylan snuggled closer to Della who was beside him, keeping him warm. In his dream, Della paraded around him, acting excited about the gift he had just given her, and then she seduced him with just her smile. She danced around him naked, wearing only a golden band on her finger, shouting at everyone that it was meant to be.

"Dylan?"

Dylan heard the change in her voice as it went from happiness to a question. His heart skipped across time as millions of doubts flew by him circling like vultures. They were ready to swoop down on her and take her away, when he quickly reassured her of his true feelings, and then the doubts flew away.

The heat moved up across his body, making it tingle. He smiled in his sleep. A breath swept across his cheek as soft lips touched his, caressing them with kisses. Kissing back, he craved the sweetness each taste gave, his hunger eager. The dream felt real. A soft hand glided down his side, returning his senses. He opened his eyes. The real world brought him back along with the horrifying memories from last night. Della was real and kissing him. She was okay.

Shooting straight up, he brought her to him and hugged her tight. "How do you feel?"

"I guess you can be the judge of that. How do I feel?"

"You finally feel hot." A grin covered his face as he smiled back at her. It was good to have her back. "Thank the Lord. I thought I lost you last night. Do you remember anything?"

"No. But I wished I did."

"This is the only thing I knew to do to save you." He released his hug and pulled away from her. "I'm so glad you are all right."

"Me too. This is nice. Now I know the secret of getting you to sleep with me." Della laughed moving her ankle slightly. The pain made her grit her teeth. "My ankle, it hurts like hell," Della tried taking a few deep breaths to ease the pain.

Unzipping the bag and crawling down to Della's foot, he examined her ankle. It was swollen badly with black, blue, and purple colors swirling around it

"I think it's broken," he said.

"Great. What do we do now?" Della said, as her eyes wandered over Dylan's nude body crouched at her feet.

"I have to get you out of here and to the hospital." Looking at her, he caught the worry in her eyes. "It's going to be okay." He put his hand on her thigh to reassure her.

"Where are our clothes?" She scanned the tent.

"Where I peeled them off of us. On the big rock outside, wet and covered with snow." He shivered and goose bumps filled his back.

"Why don't you get back in here while we think this one through. You're freezing."

Following her body up from where his hand was on her leg to her breasts, his eyes met hers. "I'd like too, but I don't think I would get the right problem solved. But never fear. I think I have a solution. I'll be back in half an hour."

Unzipping the tent, he jumped out before he did jump back in the sack with her. Every organ in his body was alive and telling him that getting warm wouldn't have been his only objective this morning. He relieved himself by the tree.

"Dylan, what are you doing?" Della called after him. The cold replaced the heat after Dylan left. She zipped the bag up and pulled it around her.

A lot of swear words came from Dylan's mouth, words he usually kept to himself. Getting back into clothes that were snow lined was a trick, one he hoped he never had to try again.

"Just stay there and keep warm," he said as he took off towards Browning's cabin. Where else would she go? No clothes and a broken ankle. He'd better hurry.

About an hour later, Della woke when she heard the tent unzipping.

Dylan crawled back in wearing dry clothes. "Here, these probably won't fit you, but we'll have to make do. At least they're dry and will keep you warm." Handing the clothes over to her he looked down, avoiding her eyes. "I'll be outside getting the bike uncovered. It's actually not bad outside. The sun is coming up over the valley warming things up fast. The snow is melting." He looked back up, "Are you all right?"

"Things could be better. My ankle hurts like hell."

"The sooner you get those clothes on, the sooner we can get you out of here and to a hospital. They'll fix you up and give you some really good dope for the pain."

"That's not what I need," she said.

"I'll be outside." Pacing back and forth he waited.

He had felt devastated when he found her. His plan had been just as she said, stupid. He put her in a dangerous situation that almost killed her. It could have taken them both.

In their line of work they needed to be level headed. Working with her distracted him and his brain stopped functioning. He thought of his Commander in the SEAL teams, his expert training, and his years of experience. If he could only see him now—His words to him would not be pretty. The next time they may not be so lucky. They had to talk.

"I'm ready, " Della said.

"Let me splint that ankle until we can do better."

"Fine."

Dylan worked on her ankle, being carefully not to move it, using supplies from the cabin to make a temporary splint. A few minutes later he sat back and admired his work.

"Okay, now let's get you out of here." He handed her a sweatshirt. "Put this on and wear the hood. I found this jacket to wear on the outside. That'll keep you warm on the ride down."

He carried her out the same way he brought her in, except this time Della was awake and in intense pain. Her broken ankle meant being taken out of action for a while and stuck doing office work.

"Where did you get these get-ups?" Della said.

"I borrowed them from Browning's cabin. I'll return them later."

"You're still not planning on coming back tonight, are you?"

Dylan didn't answer. Chuckling, he looked down as Della followed his eyes to see what he thought was so funny. The army fatigues she had put on fell down off of her hips and were resting at her knees.

"Here." Dylan lifted up his shirt and took off his belt and wrapped it around her waist. "That should help keep them on." He laughed again at her. She looked like some mountain man's trophy.

"You're finding this quite amusing, aren't you?"

"I'm sorry. I can't help it. You look so—"

"So what?"

"Undercover." He laughed. "Come on, let's get out of here. I also borrowed a toboggan for the ride down to the bike." He helped her onto the sled. "It'll just take me a minute to break camp."

They headed back down to where they had stashed the bike. He loaded up their gear and turned the key. The engine purred, making him feel a little satisfaction. Helping Della off of the sled and onto the bike, he hid the toboggan and drove back down the seven miles of mud and slush. Walking would have been faster.

Turning, he checked on Della. She looked like hell.

The bike dipped and rocked back and forth in the ruts as he went over them slowly, trying to keep Della's foot stable. The further they went down the road, the better the roads became. They were drying up. The snow must have hit only in the higher elevations.

"Doing okay?" he said.

Della's head rested on Dylan's back. She clung tightly to his body, trying to act courageous.

"Della?" Dylan turned, trying to see her. He stopped. "Della?"

"I'm okay. Don't stop again. Just get this thing in the wind and get me out of here."

Taking off again at her command, guilt burdened his heart. Della acted too tough for her own good sometimes.

Turning south on Highway 191, he stopped at Einos tavern. Calling in to dispatch, they called the ambulance from West to take her back to Bozeman to the hospital.

He'd ride back and make the meeting with Diana.

Dylan lifted Della off of the bike and carried her inside to wait. "I'm sorry," he said. "You were right. I was stupid to go on a stakeout without thinking the whole thing through. I hope my confession makes you feel better. Does it?"

"Say it again."

"You were right?" He looked straight into her eyes, searching for forgiveness before he had to leave her. "I was stupid?"

"Better." She giggled for the first time that morning. She stared into his eyes.

"What is it?" he said. "You're looking at me like—well, I don't know. Are you ready for a new partner now? One that isn't all brawn and no brains? Aren't you mad as hell at me and want to get rid of this compulsive asshole?" He pointed to himself, flexing his muscles to make her laugh.

"Nice try, Dylan. No, I don't want a new partner."

"This is the reason why I think we do."

"What are you talking about? This?" She waved her arms across in front of her.

"I didn't use my head. I should have listened to you. Something happens when I'm around you. This could have been far worse. I was lucky. Do you know how I felt last night?"

"Yes, I do. Damn good. I'm proud that you were my partner last night. You saved me. I have no doubts about you or your ability. Aren't you glad it was me you had to wrap your naked body around instead of one of the other guys? You would have felt worse then. I don't understand what you think is wrong with your head. If you're worried about it that much, why don't you make an appointment with that lady shrink you met the other night and get it examined while you're in her office today? Maybe she can get through to you that it's okay to love me."

"What? I'm sitting here trying to be nice. I'm telling you that you need a new partner because the one you have here can't think with his brains when he's around you. Our jobs require us to perform at our best at all times because of the high risks we take. I lose that concentration around you, and not because I'm in love with you. It's your body. It drives me insane every time you're in the same room. Have you ever looked at yourself? If I loved you, I wouldn't be thinking about you like that, but I don't want to just sleep with you either. We'd be too busy playing with each other to do our jobs. Understand?" Turning his head, he looked away towards the window.

"Bullshit." Della tried to stand and walk away, but remembered she couldn't. "Damn. Dylan, look at me."

Dylan looked at her as he heard the door slam. He turned and met the Emergency Medical Technicians as they walked inside carrying a stretcher. He waved them over.

"She's hurting pretty bad. Let's load her up and get her to town."

They carried her out and slid her in the back of the van.

She shut her eyes before tears came.

"I need to speak to her privately for a minute," Dylan said.

"Sure. I'll just get a cup of coffee for the road."

"Della. I'll come and see you when I get back."

"Don't bother."

"I—"

"Don't say you're sorry, damn it. If you say that to me one more time I'll scream."

"I wasn't going to say that. I think we need to sit down and really talk."

"That's funny. I thought we just were. I heard what you had to say."

"Della, look at me." He turned her face towards him. "You're my best friend. I need you to stay my best friend."

"That's where you're wrong. If I were your best friend, you wouldn't be thinking of my great tits and ass either. See it works both ways. Figure it out." She turned her head and looked the other way.

"We'll talk later." Dylan closed the doors. He got on his bike and put his head across his arms for a moment. He followed the ambulance and tried not to think about the lie he'd just told, hoping to convince himself that it was true.

Chapter 23

Wednesday, the 11th day of September

Dylan drove cautiously down the canyon as he kept an eye out for black ice, not wanting to slide around the shaded corners and into a solid rock wall or the rushing river running alongside of him.

Arriving back in Bozeman, he drove directly to the Law and Justice Center. A shower was what he really needed.

"Dylan, I have a bunch of messages for you." Angela handed him a fistful of pink notes.

"Thanks." Dylan headed for his office.

"Wait." Angela walked up to him, eyeing him closely.

"Don't tell me. I already know that I look like shit." He walked away briskly.

"No. It's your Mother."

"My Mother? What's happened?" He started walking back towards her, waiting for her to speak.

"She's is in the hospital. They think she might have had a heart attack."

His eyes turned away from hers.

"She's stable. The doctors have been trying to get a hold of you. I'm sorry." Angela touched his arm, giving him a little reassurance before turning away.

Dylan hurried to his office, and grabbed his gym bag, and ran for the showers at the academy. His mind leaped from his meeting with Diana to his Mother. He wasn't there for her and felt he had let her down again like he did when his father had died and he was up in Montana. She was alone.

Dylan rushed in the shower, saving a shave for next time. Hurrying to the hospital, he ran through the emergency entrance to the front desk.

"Maryanne Drake. What room is she in?"

"She's in the intensive care unit. Check in at the desk up there."

Jogging through the halls and up the stairs, he checked in with the young nurse who was flipping through a chart.

"I'd like to go in and see Mrs. Drake. I'm Dylan, her son." He fiddled with a pencil laid on the counter.

Grabbing another clipboard she stood up. "I'm glad they found you. She's awake and has been asking for you." She came around the counter.

"Can you fill me in on what happened?" he said.

"I'll let the doctor speak with you. Dr. Fergusson is in with her now. When he comes out, you can talk with him. Then I'll take you in to see her." She put down her clipboard, turning again to answer a call button that just blinked on. "Wait right here."

Dylan turned around and waited for the doctor to come out.

A young doctor, looking too young for a cardiologist, approached him. He stopped as the nurse came back to her station.

"Dr. Fergusson, this is Dylan Drake. He's here to see his mother."

"Nice to meet you. Your mother's doing fine. They thought she was having a heart attack when they brought her in last night, but after reviewing the tests I think her heart is fine. She seems to be under a lot of stress. It may have been an acute panic attack, but we're running more tests. Until then, we contacted Dr. Greene at her request. We'll be keeping her under observation for twenty-four hours until the rest of the tests are back and we're sure everything is normal. We'll be moving her out of the ICU later today, if she's doing as well as she seems to be doing right now."

Dylan listened intently as the doctor spoke, feeling relieved when he said his mom was doing fine. He'd been gone from the house too much lately, spending the past couple of nights away from her. He wasn't there to check up on her like he should have been. She might do better back in Utah; not knowing his job, which kept him always working. His crazy job worried her to death, and he didn't help her to understand it any. Now he wished he'd taken the time, so this might not have happened.

He needed to talk with Dr. Greene about her. Why did his mother ask for her? Whatever the reason, he wanted her advice so he could help his mother through this.

"You can go in and see her now. She needs her rest, so keep it short. I know when she sees you, she'll rest better."

Dylan stood, staring blankly at the wall behind the doctor; a gut wrenching feeling in the pit of his stomach took over.

"Mr. Drake. Go ahead. She's waiting."

"Thank you." He quietly stepped in and looked around at the dismal green walls. His mother looked peaceful lying in the bed with her eyes closed. Scooting a chair beside her bed, he let her sleep. Resting his head in his hands, he asked himself how he could be so insensitive to his own mother. If his dad were alive, he'd skin him.

"Dylan? Is that you?" His mother turned her head toward the sigh she heard from beside her bed.

"Hi, Mom." He stood up next to the bed and took her hand, squeezing it lightly. "I'm here. Don't worry now, you just go back to sleep. I'll be right here when you wake up. We can talk then."

"Dylan. I'm sorry."

"What are you sorry for Mom?"

"I didn't mean for this to happen. You need me at home."

"It's okay, Mom. You rest. Everything is going to be okay." Dylan kissed her hand as he sat back in the chair. A soft snoring embraced the room as she fell back into a deep sleep.

Dylan stretched completely, feeling tired, and looked at his watch. He quietly walked out and went back up to the floor desk. "I need to leave for a minute. I have a meeting downstairs. If she wakes before I get back, call me right away. Here's my number. Just tell her I'll be right there, that I just went to get something to eat."

She took the slip of paper with the number on it. "I will."

He left, heading to Dr. Greene's office. The receptionist told him she wasn't in yet. She didn't schedule patients until after one o'clock.

"Is she in the hospital?" he said.

"Yes. She does her rounds in the morning, and then usually she goes to the cafeteria to eat. She gave him a quick smile.

"Thanks." He ran down the hall towards the cafeteria. Dr. Greene sat alone, drinking a cup of coffee in the back of the room. Hurrying over, he interrupted her in the middle of a bite from her sandwich. "Excuse me, Dr. Greene?"

She took her eyes away from her paper and looked up at him. "Hi." She smiled.

"Could I talk with you?" Pulling out the chair, he took a seat across from her.

"What's up?" Dr. Greene said.

"My mother, Maryanne Drake. I was told she is a patient of yours?"

"Did she tell you I was?"

"No, but Dr. Fergusson upstairs just did. She's in the intensive care unit because they thought she was having a heart attack. He said they contacted you when she told them she was your patient. I just wanted to talk to you about it."

"I see. So you're the son she always talks about." She lifted her brows up, cocking her head to one side eyeing him. "Yes. Maryanne is my patient and has been since she moved here."

"I didn't know. I knew she saw a doctor now and then to get some medicine for an ulcer. I didn't know she needed a psychiatrist. She never told me. I'd like to know how serious this is?"

"She didn't want you to worry. It's part of the problem she has. She worries enough for a dozen people. It's something that we're working on. She does need to keep taking the medicine we have her on consistently, or the whole treatment will be in vain." She studied Dylan from across the table. "She didn't want you to know."

"Why?"

"Why do you think?"

"Damn." He slammed both his fists down on the table as he came up from his chair and spun around. He bowed his head and wrapped his arms around his chest, trying to think. Dr. Greene's hand touched his shoulders, as she moved to face him.

"It's okay. You have a right to be mad, but get over it. She needs you more than you need her right now." She gently grasped his upper arms. "You're going to have to make some changes if you want her to stay well."

"I just want to do what's best for her." He found his eyes searching hers for an answer.

"I can meet with you and we can talk then, but right now you'll have to excuse me. I have my first patient to see." She slid her hands away and squeezed his hand before turning and walking away.

"Wait." Dylan stepped back closer to her. "I'm your next patient. I almost didn't make it after all that has happened today." He noticed the funny look cross her face. "Well, I'm not exactly your next patient, Diana Edwards is. She needs to talk with me privately, and asked that I be in your office when she gets there. I'm sorry if this isn't making any sense, but take me with you to your office and I'll try to explain what I can before we get there."

"You'd better start talking right now. I don't like surprises. I should have known about this before now. You just can't waltz into my office anytime an investigative matter comes up and disturb my consultation. You should have asked me first."

"Wait a minute," Dylan said. "Calm down. I apologize. I had no idea you didn't know until just now. I assumed Diana arranged it with you before she contacted me, or I would have cleared it with you myself."

"So who's paying the bill?" she said.

"I will. Just add it to my bill that's getting bigger as we speak." He reached out and opened the door for her. A small grin crossed his lips as he made a mental note of her quick temper.

Her private office sat down the hall from her waiting room and patient rooms, accessible through a private door leading into it from a hall on the backside of her office. It made it easy for a doctor to slip in and out without walking through their reception area.

"Nice office. Is the other office by the emergency room your's also?" He sat down on a sofa as she sat across from him and crossed her legs.

She reached across her desk and picked up the telephone. "That's the office the county gives to me to use for all the emergency calls. I'm their staff psychiatrist. I get called in for everything." She motioned her hands around the room, "and this is my office I use in my private practice that I pay rent on. It doesn't come cheap, I might add." She buzzed the receptionist. "Is my first patient here?" She asked looking across to Dylan.

"Yes."

"Put her in examining room three. Buzz me from there." She sat back staring at Dylan, fiddling with his tie. "Your clandestine meeting is set."

"I appreciate your cooperation," Dylan said.

"You're welcome. I just expect a warning next time." She reached for the intercom on the phone as it buzzed a minute later.

"Will you bring her to my private office. I'll see her here." She hung up before her nurse could question her.

"I'll be in my library when you're through." She stood up and grabbed files from the top of her desk.

Feeling a bit awkward, Dylan stood, not knowing why he felt the way he did. He never had a problem making someone leave an area he needed, but he felt guilty making the doctor leave her own office.

A light tap on the door announced Diana's arrival. Dr. Greene opened the door and greeted her. She walked out and closed the door. She motioned for her nurse to follow her down to the library. Handing Diana's file to her, the nurse looked puzzled.

"Don't ask." She turned, walking into the library, and closed the door behind her.

Chapter 24

Wednesday, the 11th day of September

"Diana Edwards, Detective Drake." He reached out his hand, "We met briefly the other night. How are you feeling?" Dylan kept it light, letting her sit down and get comfortable.

She appeared calm, but resembled a stick figure wearing a black dress.

"Relax. I'm here at your request," Dylan said.

"I'm fine, Detective Drake." Her eyes wandered around the plush room for a moment before focusing back on Dylan, who leaned against the desk and folded his arms as he studied her like a photographer would before doing a take. It made her uncomfortable. "Something wrong?" she asked.

"I don't know. Tell me why we're meeting here today. When you're ready, of course." He walked over and sat across from her on the couch. Leaning back, he waited, observing every detail.

"I'm having a hard time dealing with Jennica's shooting, and I probably shouldn't have asked you to come today. It's just that there's been something that's been bothering me and I felt it necessary to talk to you about it. I want this off the record." She fidgeted and slipped her purse from her shoulder and set it down beside her.

"I'm the lead detective on this case, and whatever you have to say to me has to be on the record. I'm sorry."

Her blue eyes pleaded with his silently from across the couches. After a moment, she hesitated like she was about to speak, but then stood and grabbed her purse. "Then I can't talk to you." She quickly moved to the door.

The doorknob turned in her hand before Dylan reached her. "Are you in danger?" he said.

She nodded and turned to look at him. Tears filled her eyes.

"Let me help you. We can offer you protection." He guided her back to the couch and sat next to her. "I think you'd feel better if you'd tell me why you called me here. I'm here for you, and I'll help in any way I can if you'll just let me. Your safety is important to me and I'll make sure nothing happens to you. Finding the person who shot Jennica is what matters right now. You know that don't you? The person needs to be held responsible."

She shook her head of pale blonde hair.

"Okay. Do you want an attorney present?"

She shook her head again, and pulled her hands from her lap.

"You sure?"

"No," she whispered.

Dylan handed her a tissue from the top of Dr. Greene's desk. Wiping her eyes, she shook her long hair.

"Ready?" Dylan said.

"I think so."

He turned on his recorder. She stared at it for the longest time before speaking.

"A year or so ago, we were back in Bozeman on a break," she said. We had just recorded the single that's climbing the charts. The song Jennica was singing the night she was shot." Her voice faltered and she paused to clear her throat. "We were invited to a big barbecue up Kelly Canyon at the Tate home. Scott and Josh figured their father wanted to show off his sons, so we all came.

"We went a few hours early because Scott and Josh wanted to take us riding on their place before the other people his dad invited showed up. When we arrived there didn't seem to be a sign of anyone at the house or around the barns. His father has a few hundred acres on that side of the mountain.

"Saddling the horses, we headed for the open country. We came upon a bunch of pickups and four-wheelers parked by a huge pole barn in one of the winter pastures.

"Scott and Josh dismounted to check in with their father and tell him hello. It looked like they were having some sort of get together up there. All men. Nothing too out of the ordinary until their father came out and acted surprised to see us. We were invited at his invitation, but I got the distinct feeling we weren't welcome up at their meeting. He asked his sons to take us back and he'd meet us back at the ranch house.

"We rode back. Scott and Josh became quiet and didn't speak to anyone. Jennica tried to get the conversation going again, hoping to have a little fun on the way back. She rattled on, finally remarking that it looked to her as if the hired hands got caught spending their days around the pole barn telling lies and drinking beer instead of putting up the hay for the winter. By the time she finished her story, it sounded convincing. Their father didn't want us there because he didn't want us to see him reprimanding his help.

"Scott and Josh didn't comment, remaining silent and riding ahead of the group. Jennica caught up to them and asked them what was wrong. She knew they were upset. They kicked their horses and took off at a gallop and raced back to the stable.

"When we caught up to them in the barn, Jennica demanded to know what was wrong. They just pushed past her and left. The expressions they wore told me they knew what was happening, but they didn't want us to know.

"When their father arrived later he apologized to them, and the barbecue started.

"I like to take pictures. I've been snapping candid shots of the band ever since we were in high school. I got my camera and started taking pictures and shot a roll of film. I caught Martin perched on the fence right by the beer keg before he fell off and into the corral. I looked around for the rest of the band, but only found Kate and Jennica dancing with some of the guests.

"I needed a new roll of film, so I walked around the house to our van to get one. I saw Josh, Scott, Perry, Taylor, and Mr. Tate coming out of the hired hand's house across the road. I waved to them and started walking to them, but they hurried back across the road. They acted funny and asked me what I was doing away from the party. I told them I had gone to get some film. When I asked them what they were doing, they just ignored the question like I didn't even ask it.

"I became annoyed. I pulled Perry aside and asked him what the hell was going on. Something was up and he'd better tell me. He said I was overreacting and that Mr. Tate just wanted to show the 'city boys' a real working ranch. They were touring the hired hand's quarters. Well, I didn't give up. I approached the other three and asked them the same question and when I didn't get an answer, I watched them for the rest of our stay in Bozeman. I followed them one night after they all left the house. I still can't believe it's true." A buzzing sound stopped her before she finished her sentence. It was coming from Dylan sitting next to her.

Pulling a pager from his pocket he read the screen. He shut off the recorder. "I'm sorry, I have to go. I've been waiting for this call. I want to continue this. Could you wait for me? I'm not sure how long this will take."

She read the clock on the wall. "I don't have much time left. Perry will worry and may try to find me if I run later than expected."

"Will you be all right?" Apprehensive about letting her go without finding out the whole story, he asked her to meet him tomorrow. He felt like a stretched rubber band. Ready to snap. His mother would come first today.

"I'll have Dr. Greene's nurse call you and schedule the time. If anything comes up or you need me, call anytime night or day," he said before scribbling down his pager number.

"I'll be fine, thank you. I'd better let you go now, and get back to Perry before he gets suspicious." She straightened up, arching her back.

"Okay, tomorrow then?" He desperately wanted the whole story, but he promised his mother he'd be there when she woke up.

"Yes." She let herself out.

Dylan left out the back corridor. He ran up to the floor nurse to check in. Opening his mouth to speak, an old nurse with a wrinkled face wearing a cap of coarse gray hair wrapped tightly in a bun slid her chair back and took off down the hall, ignoring him.

"Ma'am?" He followed her.

"Not now." The snotty tone in her voice sounded gruff like an old man. Her squat body waddled into a room shutting the door in his face.

In exasperation, he hit the wall, then leaned into it staring at the tile on the floor. Taking in a deep breath he told himself to calm down. Getting angry wouldn't help the situation. He felt like a bomb ready to explode. Counting to three, he pushed away from the wall and spun into Dr. Greene.

He caught her as they fell against one another. Holding her for a moment, he apologized. Looking straight into her face and into her green eyes, he couldn't help notice they had yellow and gold flecks in them. Cat eyes, he thought. Releasing her, he felt annoyed at himself for being so clumsy.

"We meet again," she said.

"Sorry, I didn't know anyone was around."

"No need to explain. I'm a psychiatrist, remember?" She laughed. "You're not having one of your better days, are you?"

"Very perceptive of you," Dylan said.

"Feeling like the fireworks are being set off, but you're not the one lighting them?"

"Pretty descriptive way of putting it."

"Is it true?"

"I'm sorry, Doc, but I don't have time for a consultation right now. But I'm sure my partner and you would agree I need one."

They were inches apart from one another, each studying the other, waiting for the other to speak.

"It's hot in here today, or is it just me?" Dylan said.

"No, it's not just you, I'm feeling warm myself. They must have the boilers on full blast again. I just wanted to tell you I briefly visited your mom when I checked her charts. They told me you were to be paged when she woke up, so I went in and kept her busy to cover for you until you arrived. I just noticed you standing out here, so I came to get you. They're getting ready to move her out of intensive care."

"Thank you. I owe you big time. In fact, I'm going to probably owe you my life after today."

"I actually kind of like the sound of that. What is it now?"

"Diana didn't get to finish her talk with me. We need to meet tomorrow. Can we use your office again?" He pleaded with his eyes.

She hesitated, tapping her toe. "Okay, pick a time. Wednesday is good. I try not to schedule any regular patients on Thursdays, only in case of an extreme emergency. That's my only day off."

"Okay, how about tomorrow at one o'clock. You said your regular hours are from one to five. I'd like to keep it looking as normal as possible. If you have to reschedule a patient, I'm sorry. Maybe you'll let me make it up to you somehow?"

"I'll hold you to it. I better get back to the office. I'll be there tomorrow to help you carry on your ruse." She slipped him a card as she hurried down the corridor.

Dylan read the card. He turned over her business card and found her home number.

"What do you want young man?"

He turned in time to see the waddling nurse return to the desk. "Maryanne Drake." He tried to flash her his winning smile.

"Name?"

"Dylan."

"Full name."

"Drake. Dylan Drake. I'm her son." He frowned as he watched her thumbing through papers.

"I'll see if you're on the list." She kept scanning the papers until her eyes stopped on the last page.

His patience left him like a bad bet. He grabbed the clipboard out of her hand and firmly set it down on the countertop. "Trust me." he flashed his badge. "I'm on the list." The steel edge in his voice startled her.

"A cop? Well follow me then." Walking and mumbling to herself ahead of him just loud enough so he could hear all about how cops are so damn sure of themselves, she stopped at his mom's room.

Pointing her beaked nose up at him, she scowled before turning back to her guard post.

His mom watched him enter.

"They're moving me," she said.

"I know, Mom. I'm going with you. So take it easy. I'll be right here for as long as you want me to be."

"I want to go home. I can't sleep here all night. This place gives me the wally gags."

"That's the willies, Mom. I don't blame you. This place doesn't do much for me, either, but the doctors know best. They just want to make sure you're fine. Just one night, then you can come back to my house. I mean, our house."

"If you promise me, I'll have a room to myself."

"Promise, Mom. I'll go find out what room they're moving you into. I'll make sure it's a single. Do you need anything from home I can run and get?"

"I'd like my slippers. My little pigs are cold in this place. You'd think they were scared to turn on some heat."

"You got it. Let me go make the arrangements. I'll run home and be back in about an hour. How does that sound?"

"If you promise to stay until I fall asleep."

"I'll stay as long as you like," Dylan said.

"Then go, so you can get back."

Dylan leaned over and kissed his mom. "Take a nap."

"I should be telling you that," she said.

The shriveled up old bat glared at him as he left. He was glad that his mother was being moved off of her watch.

At admitting, he ran into Dr. Fergusson and Dr. Greene standing together talking.

"Excuse me, Doctor Fergusson? What room are you moving my mother into?" Dylan said.

"That's what we were just discussing. Dr. Greene thinks she should have a roommate. It would be good for her."

"No, that won't work. She wants to be alone. She asked me to make sure she is in a room by herself." Dylan caught Caitlin eyeing him from the side.

"Excuse me, Detective Drake," she said.

"You can call me Dylan. I don't want to scare the other people if they over hear a detective is hanging around. It worries some people."

"All right. Dylan. It would be good for your mother to have someone to talk to. Part of her problem is her self-imposed isolation. People have been known to bond with their roommates and form a special relationship."

"And what if she gets mixed up with someone she absolutely hates? That's been known to happen too." He cocked his brow, eager to hear her answer.

"She won't be here that long. If she doesn't like it we can move her tomorrow into a private room. Deal?"

Dylan thought a few moments. "I guess you know what's best. Go ahead and arrange it, but try and match her up with somebody that has a little life left to them yet. You know, not one foot in the grave like most of the people I've seen wandering the halls."

Both doctors laughed.

"You know, not everyone staying in this hospital is on their death bed," Dr. Greene said.

"Well, I wouldn't know. I have never had the opportunity to stay in one of these fine establishments, and I don't regret it. All I've noticed is the people in here don't look healthy. They scare me, and I'm a cop."

"Okay, you've convinced us. We'll work a little harder on the accommodations. Don't worry. We'll find a perfect match. Then everything will be just fine, you'll see." Dr. Greene turned as an emergency crew opened the doors, wheeling in a stretcher. A firefighter carried a tiny baby swaddled in blankets as another ambulance blared it's horn as it entered the garage arriving right behind the last one signaling a run on the ER.

"I'm leaving for a while to get some things for my mom. I'll be right back. Just leave me a note here with her room number. If her roommate isn't pleasing, you'll have to put up with her hot temper until then, because she was adamant about the 'no roommate' thing. I hope she'll be talking to me when I get back."

Dr. Greene heard her name being paged through the emergency room speakers. "I almost forgot to tell you. Jennica James is out of her comma. Excuse me please, I have to answer that call." Dr. Greene ran through the almond colored doors and into the emergency room.

Chapter 25

Wednesday, the 11th day of September

Dylan raced back to the hospital with the things for his mother. At home his mom wore Tweety Bird slippers and Mickey Mouse pajamas. Bringing her slippers into the hospital where the staff could see them made him feel peculiar. It embarrassed him now to think that maybe his mother was a little eccentric. He wondered what other things he didn't know about her. A surge of guilt crept inside him for thinking that his mom might embarrass him.

It was the craziest day in a run of bad days. Maybe that's why he felt so disjointed. He hadn't even checked on Della after hearing about his mother. The minute he settled his mom in for the evening, he would check on her condition. She had made it clear that she didn't want him checking on her.

Shaking his mane of dark hair, he rattled his brains, trying to exorcise Della's spirit from his mind. Her apparition floated there to drive him insane. His strong desire to keep her at a distance was being tested to the limit. Any more tests and he didn't know if he had the strength to push her away.

Turning on his radio, he was glad to be back in his El Camino after the cold bike ride through the canyon this morning. His veins felt like they had ice water running through them by the time he reached the Law and Justice Center. After the episode the previous night it was a wonder they both didn't have pneumonia.

Dr. Greene left him a message. It read, "Your mom is happy as a clam in 204."

As he passed the gift shop, a stained glass mobile caught his eye. He hesitated briefly before going in. A pleasant elderly lady waited on him.

She talked him into a fresh cut flower arrangement. It smelled sweet, with a hint of lilacs. The hint of lilac reminded him of Della. Staring at the deep violet vase, he realized it matched the color of her eyes. Those thoughts were killing him.

Paying for the flowers, he searched for room 204. After some dinner with his mom, he'd call Della and check on her.

The dinner cart rolled by as he found her room. He followed a boy into the room and slipped around to face the door, pulling the privacy curtain shut. Finding his mother with a mammoth grin on her face, he leaned over and kissed her.

"You didn't need to do that," his mom said.

"I'm sorry that I didn't get a single room for you." He felt weird talking to her with another person in the room. He should have stuck to her wishes. It would have made things easier.

"That's okay. Dr. Greene convinced me I'd enjoy it, and I'm so glad she did."

"That's good. I didn't want you mad at me." Remembering the flowers outside the door he said, "I'll be right back." Returning quickly, he set the vase on her nightstand.

"Darling, they're beautiful. Della, look at the flowers Dylan just brought me. I told you he's a wonderful son."

"Della?" His mouth dropped open.

"That's right. Open the curtain. She won't mind. She's my roommate."

Dylan pulled the curtain back slightly. She gave him one of her saucy smiles. He whipped the curtain back all the way.

"What are you doing here?"

"What do you think? I'm not here to—well, look." She pointed at the cast on her foot.

His eyes wandered from her cast to her knees before he could stop them and close his gaping mouth. "Tell me."

"It's broken. The bone had to be set with pins. I went into surgery shortly after I arrived. Tomorrow I can go home."

"You look better. They must be taking good care of the pain. Do you need me to bring you anything? Check on Kiki?"

"No. It's handled. I wouldn't want to trouble you any." She angled her body toward the window, looking out at the blue and white clouds streaking through the grayish sky.

"It's no trouble," Dylan said. "You know I'd do anything for you." Wanting her to look at him, he needed to see her eyes without contempt in them. Forgiveness is what he wanted to ask for, but not with his mom in the room. Catching that sharp edge in his voice that he used for protection, he made an effort to keep himself in check. "Well, if you need me, you know how to get a hold of me."

"Nice flower arrangement. Did you pick that out yourself? Very thoughtful of you." Della said. She laid back on her pillow and raised her arms above her head and drilled her eyes into him with a boldness he picked up on. She wanted to hurt him, and knew she was successful when his eyes turned darker and lost their sparkle.

Guilt hit his heart for the hundredth time that day and he couldn't stand much more. He rubbed his eyes, trying to get rid of the headache. He turned his attention to his mom.

The supper the attendant placed in front of her looked sterile in its Pepto-Bismol colored plastic dish. He opened the cover to inspect it. His nose wrinkled in disgust at the odor. His stomach lurched from the sight. Baked fish with rice surrounded by dried green beans the color of dead grass.

"Thank you young man," his mom said. "It looks marvelous. Now, Dylan, Della told me what happened last night."

His eyes widened. He tried recovering from his surprise quickly. He looked at Della from the corner of his eye. She was reading a magazine. As she started turning the next page she caught his eyes looking at her, and he saw the laughter hiding behind them. Straightening to his full height, the muscles in his neck started pounding and his blood pressure started to rise.

"What's the matter?" his mom said. "You look like you're not feeling well. Sit down next to me on the bed." She patted her hand on the pale peach spread.

"I'm just fine. All I need is a good night's sleep."

"And a shave."

"Yes, and a shave."

"Maybe you should try a haircut too."

"My hair's fine," Dylan said.

"I just like you with short hair. Like when you were in the military, that's all. I still keep that picture in my wallet. You wear it too long. I don't know why the department doesn't make its officers wear their hair short anymore."

"I'm a detective. I'm not suppose to look like a cop."

"And that earring, honey. It makes people wonder."

"Wonder? Wonder about what?"

"You know?"

"Do you think we could continue this discussion when you get home?" He glanced at Della, just waiting for her to explode with laughter. Dylan moved away from the bed and found a recliner in the corner of the room. He leaned back and stretched his long worn out body. He caught his eyes wandering towards Della. He needed to talk to her about Jennica James and Diana Edwards. He couldn't with his mother there.

The Wheel of Fortune was coming on the television as he quietly nodded off.

Dr. Greene entered the room. From the depths of his sleepy state he heard her voice, and jumped in the chair, his eyes popping open.

"I'm sorry," Dr. Greene said. "I didn't mean to wake you. I didn't know I had that affect on sleeping men."

"Dylan, this is Dr. Greene," his mom said.

"We've met." Dylan stood up, tucking in his shirt.

"You don't have to get up for me. I just wanted to check in with your mom before I leave for home." She reached for her hand and held it. "How do you feel?"

"Pretty good. Too good to be here," Dylan's mom said.

"Are you happy with the room?"

"Very happy. It just so happens Dylan's partner is my roommate. This is Della." She smiled as she introduced Dr. Greene to her.

"We've met also, Mrs. Drake." Della said, taking her nose out of the magazine.

"Detective Bishop. What happened to you?"

"It's a long story. The quick and dirty is Dylan and I were on a job. I broke my damn ankle and here I am. Stuck in this hole."

"I see." She followed Della's eyes that shot over to Dylan. He stood in the corner catching the round aimed at him.

"He saved her life last night. Della is eternally grateful to have a partner like Dylan. She said she has the best partner. Isn't that right Della? You told me that earlier," Dylan's mom said.

"Yes," she said softly.

Dylan opened the bathroom door and walked in, closing it behind him. Smiling, he caught his reflection in the mirror and had to wipe the grin from his face. Della gave herself away. She was still jealous of the lovely Dr. Greene.

When he returned to his chair the three women were unusually quiet. All three women were looking at him like they were waiting for him to answer a question.

"What?" he said.

"Oh, it's nothing dear. We had a funny to ourselves while you were gone. You know, a private joke just between us women."

"I see. I need to make some calls and finish up some business yet tonight. It sounds like now might be a good time to slip away. Then maybe I'll go get that haircut and shave." He gave her another kiss before he left, telling her to get some rest and not spend the entire night talking. "Della needs her rest too, you know."

Dylan walked over to Della. "Are you taking some R and R for a few days?"

She looked into his eyes, answering him directly. "No, I don't think this should slow me down. I want to keep on the case."

"Good."

Surprise showed on her face.

Dylan turned to Dr. Greene just as he heard a rap on the door. He turned to the sound. Matt walked in, looking rather dapper in a brown silk suit, carrying a long dress overcoat with a matching hat in his hands. A broad smile covered his face. Walking over to Della, he handed her a ruby red rose.

"Matt. What a surprise," Della said.

Matt kissed her on the cheek. Della smiled, running the flower under her nose. "Thank you. You're so thoughtful."

Dylan turned away from them and faced back towards his mother as they talked. "Caitlin, I need to speak with you privately for a moment. Can we step outside?" Dylan said.

They stepped outside of the hospital room.

Della jerked her head up as they left. She listened to his cowboy boots clicking down the hall until they disappeared. "Matt, I'm feeling really tired," she said.

"No problem. You rest and I'll see you in the morning."

"I hope to be out of here by then."

"Good. I'll come take care of you."

"I don't need to be taken care of, but thanks. I'll call you." She turned her head towards the wall.

"Take care, Della." Grabbing his coat and hat he quietly slipped out.

"Della, do you want to talk?" Mrs. Drake said, turning towards Della.

"No, Mrs. Drake. I'd rather not."

"That's fine. That young man really cares for you."

"I know. I wished I cared for him, but I don't. Don't get me wrong. I'd like to, but in the end, I know that I'd only hurt him. And that's something I can't help, and I feel real sorry about it too."

"I'm sorry too Della."

Chapter 26

Wednesday, the 11th day of September

"Caitlin, can you get me in to see Jennica?" Dylan said.

"I'm the psychiatrist assigned to her case, and she's responding to some stimuli. I'm worried she could still slip back into a coma. It happens a good percentage of the time. We're monitoring her closely. If we place her under stress too soon, her mind could shut down. I spent about fifteen minutes with her earlier today. Tomorrow, if she's responsive, you could ask her a few questions. Tonight, I don't think it would be beneficial to her health or your case. Can you understand my position?"

"Yes. She's lucky to have a compassionate doctor like you watching over her. Can you tell me to what she's responding to?"

"I can tell you what I've told her family. She's responding to sounds and turning her head in the direction of the sound. So her hearing is intact. Her vision is light and dark. She can't speak. She can squeeze your hand when asked a yes or no question. She knows her name and responds to her mother and father's names. She knows she's in Bozeman and in the hospital. I didn't see any evidence of memory loss so far. She doesn't know that she was shot. We didn't ask her that question. We saved the tougher stuff for later in her recovery process."

"Can I just go in and sit with her for a moment. I just want to see her, see for myself that she's going to get better. This's not for my job. It's just for me. I need to do this."

"I can arrange it. Follow me," she said.

They walked in silence past the hall to the critical care unit. She spoke with the nurse on duty and read her charts since her last examination.

Dylan stood in the background, listening to the conversation spoken in hush tones.

He mentally made a note of everything around him. The noises of machines humming in a repetitive tune in a quiet drawl alongside beeps intermingled with air escaping periodically that droned on into a sort of soothing rhythm he felt surprised at feeling. He could see the respirator breathing for her.

Her body lay covered by a white sheet. The wires running out of the sheet told him everything. His body tensed, feeling panicked. It was the look of death in waiting. He felt drawn to her, glued to her blank face. He needed to see it. He wished her eyes would open and her lips would speak to him. He needed something from her. A groan would lift his spirits, anything to let him know of her existence inside the pale outline of her still body. Her skin appeared transparent. The veins ran blue through the thin skin.

He carefully reached for her hand, touching it softy. He recoiled his hand instinctively and stepped back. It felt cold, as cold as Della last night. It could have been her lying there. The thought made him feel even sicker. She might have died because of his stupidity. He wanted to warm her up as he did Della.

"Dylan? Are you all right?" Dr. Greene touched his arm.

"I think so. I'm just beat. Where's her family?" he said.

"Her two sisters were called earlier. It seems her parents are out of the state. They're on their way."

He turned and wandered out of the room stopping at the drinking fountain. The cold drink tasted good.

Dr. Greene followed him, waiting. She reached out, touching his back as he stood drinking. "I think she'll make it. Does that help any?"

"It helps. She'd better make it. I can't understand how someone could do this to another human being. I never will. When I find the shooter, I'll make the son of a bitch pay." He hit the side of the metal drinking fountain. "I'm sorry. I'm just afraid when I do find him, I'll kill him with my bare hands."

"It's okay to feel rage. That's part of the reason you're a cop. You want to protect the world from harm. You do your best and you'll continue. You'll find the person responsible and bring him to justice. I know it. I want to ask you a favor?"

"Sure. Anything. I owe you a lot."

"I want you to take me home."

"That's easily done."

"I mean, I want you to take me home. And not because you owe me a lot." She stepped closer to him and reached for his hand.

Dylan hesitated, he didn't know what to say. She took him by surprise. "What's this all about?"

"I want you to take me home and stay the night. I'm sorry. I shouldn't have asked."

"You don't have to apologize. I feel something here too. I'm just not sure tonight would be a good night to find out what it is. I would only disappoint you. I need to get some real sleep." He leaned closer to her and brushed a piece of her hair back from her eyes.

"I don't think you could disappoint me. Only if you say no. Tell you what, I'll offer you a special deal. I give a great massage. I'd love to give you one. It'll relax you. It's a prescription this doctor can see you desperately need. I'll even let you sleep. I won't touch you again until the morning. How does that sound?"

"Like an offer I'm going to have to refuse, but it sounds like something I would enjoy, just not tonight. I hope you understand."

"I think I do. I think I keyed into it earlier today in your mother's room this afternoon."

"What are you talking about?"

"Della and you are more than partners. Am I correct? You're in love with her."

His basic instinct was to laugh in her face. "Della? No. She's like the sister I never had. She's my partner, and not by my choosing. In fact, I fought it. I still am fighting it. I feel protective of her, yes. I do care deeply for her, yes. Love her? Well, I guess I do. The way you love anybody that's in your immediate family. That's how it feels to me."

"I'm sorry. I didn't mean to upset you."

"You didn't upset me. It's just that I don't want you to take my saying no as a rejection from me. I just need time. The case I'm working on is important. Then there's my mom. She's in the hospital because I haven't paid attention. I let her down. And of course, there's Della. I blame myself for her being here too. I screwed up and didn't pay close enough attention to her on the job, and she's my responsibility."

"You're blaming yourself for things that are beyond your control. None of it's your fault."

"Then why do I feel like it is? Anyway, the point is I don't want to get involved right now, because my heart would only be half in it. I've waited this long, so when I fall, I really want to fall." He chuckled. "And, as you can see, I'm too busy screwing up to give one hundred percent to a relationship. It wouldn't be fair. I hope you can understand where I'm coming from."

"I'll try to accept that, but when you're ready, will you tell me? I think you're the person I've been waiting for all of my life."

Dylan took her chin and leaned into her face holding her eyes with his. He brushed his lips across hers, then kissed her slowly, standing in the hallway. He pulled her into him. She felt good in his arms. He held her for a few moments before pulling away and letting her go.

"I have to make some important phone calls before I leave. Do you still need a ride home?"

"No. I have my car." She slipped him her key ring. "The gold key is to my office upstairs. You can use the phone there if you promise not to snoop in my files. I'll see you tomorrow."

Dylan counted three keys on the ring. "Thanks. I promise I won't disturb a thing. You sure you don't need these other keys?" he asked.

"No, I won't be needing them. It's a spare set I keep around. Keep them. That one's to my office, one to my car and the last is to my house. So, if you change your mind just let yourself in."

Dylan found her office, let himself in, and turned on a lamp. Her office was left immaculate.

He dialed directly to room 204. He crossed his fingers and hoped Della would answer.

"Hello?" Della said.

"Della, it's Dylan. Don't say anything. I need to talk to you, and I don't need my mother getting upset because I couldn't talk to you with her in the room. Understand?"

"Hi, Matt. Of course, I understand. And I'm sorry for snapping at you this afternoon."

"You really snapped at Matt, or are you trying to apologize to me for the unfair treatment you've been giving me all day. You've been treating me like shit."

"I did, and you are."

"I see you're not going to make this easy. Well, I thought you might want to be filled in on the case and my meeting with Diana Edwards. I can tell that you really don't want to talk to me, so I'll just hang up."

"No, wait. Don't hang up. I do want to hear about it. Please?"

"Then tell me you're sorry. Tell me you hate yourself for treating me that way and that you were out of your mind in pain. Then I might reconsider hanging up on you. Tell me."

"Really? I'm sorry. There, are you satisfied you jerk?" she whispered back in the receiver.

"Now, Della. You can't call me names. Agreed?" He loved every minute of this game. He could see her squirming and doing anything he asked to get the information he promised.

"Okay. You'd better hurry. They gave me a sedative and I might not last, but I want you to know that I'm glad your voice is the last one I hear before I slip away into my dreams tonight."

"Isn't that sweet. Okay, Diana met me, but I got paged before she could finish. Tomorrow we meet again here."

"Where's here?" She said.

"Cait's office. That's where I'm calling you from." Pay back time, he thought.

"You're there?"

"Yes, she's given me a set of her keys."

"You're about the most—"

"Now, Della. You promised."

"That's all you have to tell me? Tell me something else before I have a change of heart."

"I went and saw Jennica James. She came out of her coma today," Dylan said.

"Great. One good thing happened today."

"You still with me?"

"Barely. Did you get to talk to her?"

"Not yet. Cait is going to work on that."

"That's not all she's been working on."

"And what's that supposed to mean?" He grinned.

"We'll have to talk more about this later. I have to go. I'm tired. I wish you were here to tuck me in. Tell me you're thinking about me and you'll come take me home tomorrow. I changed my mind. I'll let you stay and take care of me, Matt."

"You know you're all I think about. You've bewitched me you little seductress into coming for you tomorrow. Don't worry, I'll take special care with you because I love you." He stopped whispering returning his voice to normal. "There. Is that what you wanted to hear? From Matt or from me?" He slipped the phone quietly into the receiver.

He felt so many things, and he couldn't handle all of them. He'd sort some out in the morning when his mind could join him in the process. He started nodding off.

He spied the plush couch and swore he heard it invite him to rest for a few minutes before driving home. His body was empty, feeling weaker than water. He fell into the couch with a contented sigh and the instant gratification of slumber before the room got dark.

Chapter 27

Thursday, the 12th day of September

The bells were ringing as he ran away, running against the freezing winds. The chill catching him. He shivered against the black night. Lost in the trees he couldn't see the stars, the frozen ground beneath made him fumble with each slow step. He fell, tumbling down the cliff, into the dark abyss. "No," he yelled.

He felt himself hit the ground. He opened his eyes slowly, and carefully patted himself down, reassured he had survived the ordeal. Urgently sitting up, he searched the room he found himself in. He had fallen off the doctor's couch in the throw of a wild dream. Dylan wiped the sweat that had accumulated on his eyebrows and faced the ringing telephone on the desk. He rolled over picking it up as he pulled himself up and sat back in the chair. "Hello?"

"Dr. Greene?" a voice said.

"No, this is her answering service. She's unavailable right now. May I take a message?" He tried to sound as business like as he could, being caught off guard answering the doctor's private line. She probably wouldn't appreciate the help.

"I need to speak with her right now. How can I get a hold of her?"

"I can take your name and number and have her return your call."

"I can't do that. Can you give me her number? This is an emergency."

"I'm sorry, but I can't. I will—" The phone went dead in his hand. The person hung up, the voice sounding somehow familiar to him. A hint of an accent. He wished he'd stayed on the phone a little longer. Whoever it was sounded paranoid. He wondered if all her patients acted that way. That person sounded in trouble and was reaching out for help. He didn't know what to do. Deciding to call Cait, he hoped he could explain the situation so she would understand and not be too angry with him. Falling asleep in her office all night wasn't intentionally planned. Neither was answering her phone.

Searching his pockets for the card she gave him, he came up empty. He searched around the couch and floor before he decided to try a telephone book. With that thought, he slid open a drawer looking for her directory. He reached her appointment book, pulling it out. Shuffling around some more, he came up empty handed.

He didn't find her telephone book in the first drawer, so he reached to place her appointment book back from the spot he found it in. Hesitating, he decided to look through it to see if her number might be written on the inside. Opening it, he turned it to the first page.

It wasn't there. He flipped through it. He stopped at a page, a month at a glance. On every Thursday there were initials highlighted at 9:00 a.m. He flipped to the next month and saw the same entry. She didn't see patients on Thursdays, she had said. That must be a person she was seeing. Professionally or personally, he began to wonder.

He shut the book, letting the initials F.M. run through his mind. He placed the book back in the drawer, finally concluding that it wasn't any of his business. She said she reserved Thursdays for her day off. He was most likely the reason. He couldn't help wonder why she asked him to go home with her if she was seeing someone?

She probably kept several men on a leash. He felt foolish for almost falling for her line. He liked the thought of someone taking care of him and loving him totally. Someone to share the good with the bad and everything in between. She tempted him and he kissed her willingly and he couldn't deny there was an attraction there.

Feeling guilty for going through her drawers and reading her appointment book, he put everything away like he found it. His head jerked up when he heard a key rattling in the door. He quickly smoothed back his hair and moved to the couch.

Dr. Greene slipped in, fumbling with her key and was surprised to see Dylan. "What are you doing here? It's 6:45." She walked over and set her briefcase on her desk.

"Would you believe I slept on your couch all night? I just woke up."

"I believe it. And to think you could've slept in a real bed with a shower waiting for you. I would have fixed you breakfast." She laughed watching his face. She moved closer to him.

"I did need the sleep. Thanks for the use of your couch. It made a fine bed. I apologize. I better get going. They're expecting me at work for a briefing."

"Sorry to see you go. I hope I'll see you later," she said.

"I'll be back to visit my mom, of course, and to check Della out and get her home. Also, I hope you'll still let me talk to Jennica."

"Right. I'll let you know. I'll be in and out, but I'll be here for the meeting with Ms. Edwards."

"Thanks. I'm sorry if I messed up any of your plans for the day." He watched her closely.

"It's okay. I'm use to it."

"I was just trying to call you. I woke up to your telephone ringing, and answered it before I realized what I was doing. It was a man, who sounded desperate to talk with you, but he wouldn't leave his name or number and then he hung up on me. I detected a hint of an accent. It sounded almost like a brogue. I'm sorry."

She looked concerned. "No problem. I record all my calls, and have caller ID. I'll play it back. Don't worry."

"Why?"

"Why do I record all of my calls? Lots of reasons. A patient is in trouble and sometimes they will only talk to me. If I'm not here they hang up. My patients aren't known to think with clear heads." She smiled back.

"I see. Well, I guess you're in a hurry to rescue that caller, so I'll just let myself out and catch back up with you later."

"I hope so."

He felt she was hiding something from him. He understood from her body language that something worried her after he told her about the call. Of course, she wasn't about to let him in on it.

He hurried to his car, hoping it hadn't been towed away during the night. Lady luck smiled on him. The El Camino sat parked in the corner of the lot where he had left it.

He rushed home.

Shaving off his three day growth and trying to cover up some of the damage done to his face in that time, he stepped into the shower. Enjoying the hot water rolling over his stiff body, it eased some of the tension away along with the grit.

He had more aches and pain than he could ever remember, and he hoped it wasn't a sign he was entering into his golden years. The thought made him suck up and will his pain away. Turning off the shower, he stepped out and examined himself at the mirror.

The cut over his eyebrow was healing into a pink scab and was only lightly bruised. A detailed examination of his front and back displayed seventeen years of battle scars from his years in the military and his years of service as a police officer.

Noticing a long scratch running down the back of his arm that looked raw and weepy, he vaguely recalled puncturing it on a limb while in the tree during the stake-out.

He studied his physique and decided he wouldn't give in to the aches and he'd have to work out even harder than he already did to keep in top physical shape. If he was hurting that much, he wasn't pushing his muscles to the limit during training.

He dressed casually and drove to the office. Walking in and sitting down, he rifled through the mound of papers still sitting on his desk waiting for his attention.

Captain Mitchell leaned in the door. "Morning, Dylan. The meeting is in the conference room in ten." He left as quickly as he came.

"Dylan, how's it going?" Will said.

William Wainwright was a detective with the Bozeman City Police Department. He'd joined their force about three years ago after leaving Los Angeles. Dylan worked with him on occasion, finding him to be amiable and easy to work with. The Bozeman City Police Department and the city offices moved in with them consolidating the law enforcement agencies into one building, forcing them to be one big happy family. They were all living in glass offices and trying to keep the shades down.

"Where's Della? She's going to be at this briefing isn't she?" Will said.

"I guess the scuttlebutt isn't spreading through the ranks as quickly as I thought if you haven't heard that Della is in the hospital."

"I didn't know. What happened? Is she okay?"

"She's going to be fine. Nothing could keep her away from here, I can tell you that. She fell in a goddamn gopher hole and broke her ankle during a stakeout we were on the night before last. We were close to the Lee Metcalf Wilderness area. She should get out today."

"What in the hell were you doing out there?"

"Well, I'm sure if you're joining our briefing you'll get to hear all about it in about two minutes."

"I'm glad she's fine. Della is one tough lady. That's why I'm here. I was hoping to get you alone for a minute before the meeting to talk about Della. She called me the other night. She wanted to know if I wanted to switch and work for the county because an opening would be coming up after Perty's retirement in a couple months. She said she would like to work with a partner like me, that I would be an asset to the department. It took me by surprise. I didn't know what to say to her. I still don't, but I've caught myself thinking about it a lot since. I think she's great. Smart, quick instincts, expert shot. She'd make a hell of a partner."

"She is, and yes, she would."

"Not to mention she's the most gorgeous detective I've ever seen. Of course, I've only met a handful, but I've worked in Los Angeles. You should meet some of the women on the force there. It would make you appreciate her a lot more. Della isn't your average stereotype of a woman cop. That's for sure."

"You're absolutely right."

"What's going on then? Why would she call me like that? Was she serious? Are you two splitting up?"

"Will, I think you need to talk to her about this." He knew why she called him. He felt that stab of possessiveness taking over. She acted quickly in her hurt state the other night.

He started thinking about Will. He would make a fine replacement for him. They were about the same age. They both kept in excellent physical shape. He proved to be one of the best detectives in the city. He joked around like Dylan. Both of them we're thorough to the point of being called 'abusively dedicated to their work'. He had light brown hair flecked with blonde streaks, wearing it a little longer like Dylan. The physical build was a little bit different. Will stood a head shorter and was barrel chested and thicker through the waist and thighs.

"Okay, I'll talk to her. I just thought I'd ask you first," Will said.

"You don't need to ask me to talk with Della. She's her own person."

"I know that. I just meant, I thought I'd ask you if there's a problem. If you were making this decision or if she was?"

"Why?"

"Because I might consider her offer."

"Really." Dylan considered what Will said, feeling competitive in light of his own comparisons of the two. "I asked for a new partner."

"You did?"

"That's what I just said. I did."

"Why?"

"I've taken her as far as I think I can. I think a rookie should train with different people, get a bigger picture. We're the only team right now and only because she's training with me. The partner thing is just temporary.

Of course, things change pretty fast around here." Dylan went on to tell him his reasons, sounding like he had rehearsed his speech.

"That's not it at all is it," Will said. "You're blowing smoke up my ass. You're fucking her, aren't you? You got her to give you a piece of her tight little ass and now you're dumping her."

Dylan slugged him square in the nose. It sent Will reeling backwards. Dylan caught the front of his shirt as he started to go down. Pulling him up, he held onto his shirt and spoke inches from his dazed face.

"It's no one's damn business about what goes on between Della and I. If I hear of any stories floating around about us, I'll personally stalk you and finish knocking your block off." He released his shirt with a jerk, sending him falling backwards again.

"Hey, I'm sorry," Will said. "What can I say? No harm done. I was out of line." He reached out his hand and walked towards Dylan.

Dylan hesitated before taking his and shaking it.

Will rubbed his nose. "You sure have one hell of a right," he said. "Does it look broke?"

"No, just bigger." Dylan cracked a smile. "And bloodier."

"I guess I deserved that. I'd better take care of it before the briefing." He turned, almost running for the door.

Dylan threw the memos into a pile and rested his head on his desk. He knew that one punch wouldn't stop the rumors from flying at warp speed through the two units. People would naturally speculate. Della needed her reputation intact. Her father ran that department. He would come gunning for Dylan if he even thought he'd laid a hand on his daughter.

"Dylan we're waiting. Get in here," Captain Mitchell yelled impatiently from the door.

"Yes, sir." He hurried to the conference room.

The room contained about ten chairs. They were filled with law enforcement personnel. Captain Mitchell took a seat at the front with Chief Bishop of the Bozeman Police Department. The city had jurisdiction, but had asked the Gallatin County Sheriff's Department to take over the case because of the swelling caseload the city was under and the violent nature of the crime. The county detectives division took the case officially, with Detective Drake leading the investigation.

The front contained an easel with a marker board next to a podium. Two city dicks and a detective from his division with the Sheriff's Department were seated around, facing the Captain and the Chief. Scattered around the room were a lieutenant and a sergeant from the Bozeman City Police Department, a Montana State University campus police officer, and a few members of the five county drug task force.

Captain Mitchell asked everyone to be seated. They discussed the James shooting in detail. With the evidence presented to the investigative team, they studied the information that they had collected so far from the night of the shooting along with the witness interviews, reports from the crime lab in Missoula, and their own technicians that reviewed the actual scene.

It was complete with drawings, photographs, and computer printouts. They estimated the shots were fired from a distance of fifty yards in the center of the floor area below the front of the stage. Two shots were fired, one bullet entering her chest missing the heart. The other entered from the front and embedded in her tenth thoracic vertebra. A copy of the doctor's report was read. The doctors could only speculate on her recovery process. She may never recover and that meant she might never be able to answer their questions. If she knew her killer, she couldn't communicate it to them as of right now.

He briefed them on the gun, the bullets, and the possible suspects with the usual motive and opportunity theories based on the whole picture. A picture that was full of blanks. He didn't believe they had a solid lead, except the gun and the owner. The priest couldn't be subpoenaed to testify and identify the person who gave it to him. A lawyer would make sure of that detail. The gun was missing from the owner's collection and he was out of the state when the shooting took place. He concluded his report and waited to be dismissed.

"That's all for today. I'll expect more from all of you tomorrow." Captain Mitchell walked out.

Captain Bishop grabbed Dylan as he tried to leave. "I'd like to have a word with you Detective Drake."

"We can talk in my office."

They walked back together and entered Dylan's office.

"I wanted to express my sincere gratitude on saving Della's life. I owe you."

"What? Where did you hear that?" Dylan said.

"First from Della, then Captain Mitchell told me that after he talked with her at the hospital."

"I just did what I was trained to do. I don't feel I did anything anybody else wouldn't have done. In fact, if I had stuck by my original plan, Della wouldn't have been there in jeopardy in the first place."

"What are you saying?" Chief Bishop said.

"I shouldn't have let her go on that stakeout with me. She's too green. It was risky."

"You're wrong. She's a little green, but ready. You know she wouldn't let you go without her. You're her mentor. Training in the field is the best way for her to learn. How else is she going to get out on her own. You're to be together in every inch of the investigative process. Teamwork it's called."

"Yes sir, I know all of that and that's the problem. I think I should work solo. I'm not very good working with a partner. Ask Della, I'm moody, self-serving and reckless at times. It's those traits that make it dangerous for her to be my partner."

"You don't have a very high opinion of yourself, son, but I want you to know that I want Della trained by you. You're the best this town has got to offer and I feel better knowing she's in your hands. I'm secure in the knowledge that you'll treat her with respect and keep her safe, since she's my only daughter. I know you'd never take advantage of the situation like others might."

"I don't know what to say, except it means a lot to me to have your support. Speaking of Della, you'll have to excuse me. I should go check up on her. I promised her I'd take her home."

"I know, she told me when I called her. I wanted to check in with her before the meeting and she asked me to tell you she'll be released at three o'clock today."

"I'll be there. Unless of course, you wanted to take her home yourself. She really should be taken care of for at least a couple of nights," Dylan said.

"She told me that's exactly what you're intending to do."

"She did?" Dylan felt heat returning to his neck. Remembering the whispered words he spoke into the phone, she either didn't hear the end of his sentence as he hung up or she was holding him to his false words to spite him.

"She did. You sound surprised. Did she jump to conclusions here? Because if you can't, I'll take her home. It's just that she'd have a hard time without that damn dog of hers, and she knows I won't allow a flea-infested mutt to enter my home. She would be miserable. I tried to convince her to come home with me before she told me you were already taking on that responsibility."

He caught himself grinning outright at the thought of her having to be waited on by her father in his sterile house. The meticulous Chief would drive her crazy if she had to spend more than an afternoon with him.

"I did tell her I would if she needed me. It looks like my mom isn't going to get out of the hospital for a couple of days. I'll be taking care of her then."

"MaryAnne? She's sick?"

"She was admitted to the hospital yesterday. She's okay, but they're running some more tests before they'll let her go."

"I'm sorry to hear that, Dylan. Send her my regards."

"Why don't you do that yourself. She'd probably love to talk to someone other than me for a change."

The Chief eyed Dylan suspiciously with contempt in his eyes.

"It wouldn't kill you," Dylan said.

"Oh, all right."

"Better yet, go see her. You can visit your daughter at the same time. Keep them both from being bored until I get there. I have a few things to run down before I can get over there."

"Your mother and Della are roommates?" He said skeptically.

"They sure are."

"Lord have mercy. I feel sorry for the staff at the hospital. Putting them together is like rubbing two sticks together, eventually you'll get fire."

"I thought the same thing myself. Bring plenty of water with you. You might need it." He laughed as he grabbed his coat and left for the church. Father Murphy left several messages while he was away from his desk. Finally, he would get the opportunity to pick his brain.

Chapter 28

Thursday, the 12th day of September

At the church, the secretary seated at the desk told him he'd have to wait.

"I'm on a tight schedule, if you would just let him know I'm here," Dylan said, feeling like he was getting nowhere with the woman. She had grit in her voice with steel gray hair cut bluntly to her head. It made her appear more like a guard than a church secretary taking appointments.

"He'll be right with you, officer. He can't be interrupted right now," she said, studying him from underneath her thick-framed glasses.

"How long do you think it will be?" he said.

"One can never tell about these things." She started writing in a book filled full of numbers.

Dylan gave up his pacing and finally sat down. He crossed and uncrossed his legs, squirming around in the old wooden church pew out in the hall. Finally, a door opened and Father Murphy walked out, motioning him to come in.

He stepped towards him. F.M. popped into his mind. Father Murphy, F.M. he repeated it several times to himself. Coincidence? Maybe. He laughed quietly to himself that he would think of such a thing. It was highly unlikely; after all, lots of names could have those abbreviations. His mind couldn't drop it. What if it was his initials? Why would the doctor have to see him every day on her day off? All sorts of scenarios played through his mind. The worst scenario was the one he finished with, what if Father Murphy and Dr. Greene were having an affair? Of course, they would have to keep it a secret.

He eyed Father Murphy, speculating. After a careful once over, he found many characteristics that might attract a woman of Cait's stature. The priest looked energetic and young, he estimated middle fifties. The man had gracious eyes that commanded you while in his presence. He spoke in rich and lively tones. His celibacy might attract a woman who knew the mind and body well enough to divide and conquer vulnerable souls. After all, she had made a move on him out of left field. Maybe that was her deep and dark secret. She was addicted to that power she could take from men.

"You look like you've drifted off somewhere, detective. Some people find it uncomfortable being inside a church."

"I'm sorry, I just have a lot on my mind today. Churches don't bother me a bit. It's just a structure." It was just that he wanted to ask him so much more than he had planned to in light of his suspicions, but he knew he'd be out of line. "I'd just like to ask you a few questions."

Detective Drake pulled out his notebook, retrieving the fax, unfolding it in front of him. He scanned the contents once again before choosing his words carefully. "When did you arrive in Bozeman?"

"It was 1977. I arrived shortly after graduating from the seminary in St. Paul, Minnesota. I spent many years there." He turned in his chair slightly looking down towards his lap. "I worked hard to get here."

"I have all of that. It's the rest I'm trying to fill in. Let's just start from the beginning. Where were you born?"

His eyebrows raised high on his forehead. "Scotland." He smiled.

"What year?"

"Is this really going to help you?"

"Please just answer the questions and we can be done."

"1940."

"Do you have a birth certificate to verify that?"

The priest laughed. "Not on me, no."

"Well, do you have one?"

"Of course."

"Then I'll need you to get it. I'll have to verify it by seeing the official certificate."

"Fine. How long do I have? If I don't rush it to your office are you going to arrest me?" He chuckled again.

"I'm glad you're finding this so amusing, but it's for a background check." Dylan started feeling irritated.

"Excuse me for finding it just that. A killer's loose and you are wondering how old I am, where I was born, and God only knows what else you have on your list. I fail to see the importance of my birth fifty-six years ago to a shooting that happened almost a week ago. I have high regards for the police and their jobs in this community and that's the reason I turned the gun in to Chief Bishop, a respected member of this church. Unless I'm a suspect. If that's the case, do you really think I would hand it over so readily to him? Only a fool would think they wouldn't be caught." Facing Dylan directly, he looked him over carefully. "What motive would I possibly have for such a crazy act as this?"

"Like I said, I'm just filling in background. I don't know, maybe you were having an affair with her."

Father Murphy gasped. "What? How dare you come in my private quarters and assault me with an unfounded and serious accusation as that. Where in damnation did you get that from? Jennica is just a child. I'm a priest for God's sake. You're stepping way out of line here, detective. You'll destroy the Church and my good name if you start speculating with such an outrageous story as that one. I'm afraid I'll have to report this to your Captain. This conversation is over. If you need to insult me further you'll have to do it with an official warrant next time. Cooperation works both ways. I'm highly offended and would like you to leave. The door, Detective Drake. Good day." His face turned to stone as he swiveled and turned completely around to face the wall.

"I'm sorry, Father Murphy, but it's my job to ask tough questions of everyone involved in the case. You're involved. I wasn't accusing you of anything, it was just an example of a motive. Of course, if you were having an affair you wouldn't admit to it. No one does right away. You'd be surprised at what people try and hide. What they don't realize is, their reaction to such questions makes us start asking more questions. It's a popular motive, and just because a priest is a priest doesn't mean I'm not going to ask that kind of question. It's a motive that's on the top of our list, and I know that priests are human and can make mistakes. I know it's happened before."

Father Murphy glared at him, his face turning blood red. The calm exterior he started with had turned to anger against him. Reading faces was part of his job also. Dylan put away his notebook and stood while Father Murphy remained quiet facing the wall.

Dylan hit a nerve. He wondered if he got too close to the truth. He'd like to pursue it, but it had nothing to do with the case except to satisfy his own growing curiosity about Cait's appointment book.

"I'll need that birth certificate," Dylan said.

"You'll have to get it on your own. Like I said, I've lost all respect for you, detective. I won't help you anymore. I can see you don't respect this robe or this church or you would have never made such a ghastly insinuation, even as you say, just for an example."

"Have it your way." Dylan left, mulling over the change that came over Father Murphy. He didn't get any answers, but he had a place to start with, the location and date of his birth, if it did indeed matter.

Dylan drove back to the hospital, climbing the steep hill following the traffic. He passed a few people running the hill. He used it himself to build up his endurance.

He pulled in and parked in the patient parking lot. He'd check in with his mom and speak to Della. The meeting with Jennica loomed in his mind. His days felt like they were all caught up in a swirling tunnel. The investigation was stalling out. He needed something to grasp onto that he could run with.

Strolling to his mom's room and carrying a dozen red roses, his mother became ecstatic. "Dylan, you didn't have to bring me more flowers."

"I didn't, Mom. These are for Della." Her face lost some of its exuberance when he turned and handed them to Della. "These are for you." He kissed her on the cheek.

"Thanks. They're beautiful." She reached for his hand and grasped it for a brief moment.

He grinned because he knew his peace offer was genuinely accepted. Turning towards his mother, he noticed she was trying not to look disappointed.

"So, how are the two most beautiful women in my life doing?" He gazed at both of them like he was studying portraits hanging in a gallery. They both were remarkably beautiful. His mother had a grace that surrounded her that was hard to miss. For her age, she was stunning, even in her hospital bed. Then there was Della, no words could articulate her breathtaking beauty. She looked a little pale, but in spite of it all, she looked radiant.

"You seem to be in a good mood today. I must admit, Son, you look ten times better than you did last night. I can see you didn't get that haircut like you promised though."

"It's amazing what a good night's rest can do for you," Dylan said. "And yes, Mom. I didn't make it to the barber, but I will soon. In the meantime, I just came by to talk a minute. I have an appointment at 1:00. Della, can you come with me for a minute?"

"I can try. They gave me these crutches. They did put a walking cast on, but the doctor wants me to wait a couple more days before I start walking on it."

"Listen to the doctor. I'll get a wheel chair. One's sitting outside down the hall." He returned pushing a silver wheel chair. "Get in." He pointed towards the chair.

Della swung her long legs around the side of the bed slowly, standing up on one foot. "Can you get my robe?"

Dylan reached for the red silk robe thrown at the foot of the bed. He held it up as she slid into it. It matched the long red silk lingerie she had on. Wondering who had brought her these things, Matt flashed through his mind. He let his eyes linger too long on her bare shoulders and back before stopping on the thin red spaghetti straps. He wondered how they held it all up. A grin secretly passed across his face behind her.

Della swiveled around on one foot, her robe flowing out. He let his eyes enjoy the view. He rolled the chair behind her. "There you are, your coach."

Carefully she sat down. "I don't know if I trust you to drive." She giggled.

"Do we always have to have this argument about my driving?" He laughed a hearty laugh then remembered his mom watching them.

"We'll be right back. It's official police business." He watched his mom who smiled back at them.

"You two just run along and have some fun and don't worry about me. I'm fine."

Dylan pushed her to the elevator and backed her inside.

"What's this all about?" Della said. "Where are you taking me?"

"Just down the hall to day surgery. They have a private room we can use to talk in. I don't need everybody staring at us." He cleared his throat and mumbled under his breath.

"What was that last comment you intentionally muffled so I would have to ask you this dumb question?" She wiggled around in her chair so she could see his face.

He bent low to her and whispered. "I said, you look like a red flare in that lingerie and people are staring at us. It's not exactly the type of bed clothes people wear during their stay at a hospital."

"Am I suppose to take that as flattery, or did you just do one of your world famous put downs to make me feel stupid?"

"Take it as a compliment. You look like a million bucks. I bet someone would pay that to take it off of you right now." He started to laugh, but Della pushed herself up and out of the chair, spinning around on her good leg. She slapped him across the face. He instinctively blocked the blow and grabbed her wrist as her other arm swung around. He was quicker and grabbed it. Now he held both. He could see the fire behind her eyes when they met his.

"It was just a personal observation and wish Della," he said. He tried to sound apologetic.

"I didn't sound like that at all. It sounded as if you were calling me a whore. Whores dress like that to get someone to pay to take it off of them. Whores get paid for that." Her chest heaved up and down as her anger escalated with each sentence. She finished firing her angry words and a silent stare remained.

He watched her chest rise and fall, her cleavage exposed from her quick turn. He felt a stirring inside of him that made him outwardly shiver. "I'm sorry. I didn't mean it to sound that way. I just meant—" He stepped in closer to her, still holding her arms tightly. He pulled them down between them. An overwhelming urge to just put his arms around her and hold her close took over. He noticed her face change color. "Are you all right?"

Della's head went down. When she looked back up, a tear rolled down her cheek.

"I didn't mean to make you cry," Dylan said. "I was just teasing. I've always been able to tease you. This crying thing is really new with you. What's it all about?" He brushed the tear gently away and pulled her into his arms.

She instantly pulled away and shook her head. "I feel a little nauseous right now, that's all. The pain pills must be making me sick."

"Let me get you back into your chair. Do you want to go back and lie down?"

He reached his arms around her and helped her slide back around into the chair.

"No, I'm feeling better. Let's just get to that room," she said.

Dylan honored her request and opened the door to the small conference room. Once inside, he sat across from her and set his tape recorder on the table.

"The taped recording is the meeting I had with Diana yesterday. I want you to listen to it." He smiled at her. Della stared blankly back. He waited for a response to her closed off eyes. "Can I at least get one smile before we begin?" Her color looked better.

Della finally gave in and gave him her quirky grin.

Dylan hit the start button and Diana's voice recounted the first half of the tale. "That's why we're meeting today, to finish it. I don't have a clue where this will all lead, but I hope it's our key to unlocking this mystery."

"I hope so too."

Dylan stretched. "I almost forgot. I talked with Father Murphy today. I pissed him off, actually." He sat back down.

"You pissed off a priest? What did you do that for?"

"I accused him of having an affair. At least that's the way he took it. Sort of like you and your response to my lingerie statement." He winked at her. "He isn't speaking to me anymore. By the time I get back to my desk, I expect an order to be in my box to see the Captain." A sly grin covered his face.

"You didn't?" Della gasped studying his face carefully.

"He interpreted it that way. I was just trying to get the background filled in, since our search wasn't complete on him. He became arrogant with me over the questions. He didn't think the questioning was appropriate. He laughed when I told him everyone is a suspect until cleared. He asked me what motive could he possibly have? I just threw that one out there. He went ballistic on me. I think I hit a raw nerve."

"That's crazy, Dylan. He thinks it was an accusation by you that he was having an affair with Jennica? That he shot Jennica because of what? She loved him and wanted a commitment that he couldn't give to her? I think that's about the most disrespectful thing you have ever done, not to mention cruel to someone you've questioned." She tipped her head back and laughed fully. "It would make some real good fiction though, but really Dylan."

"I have another news flash."

"Please, by all means tell me." She laughed directly in his face.

"I happened to find Dr. Greene's appointment book. Every Thursday was marked off with the initials F.M. at the top. When I walked into Father Murphy's office it hit me like a ton of bricks. That's his initials, F.M., Father Murphy."

"So?" she said.

"So, I think he's having an affair. He's having an affair with Cait." He watched as Della fell into a fit of laughter. "Now, what's so funny?" he asked.

"You. The way a man thinks. Instantly, your doctor friend is having an affair with the priest all because she has F.M. written in her appointment book every Thursday."

"What would you think? She told me she has Thursdays off. She doesn't schedule any appointments that day unless it's an emergency."

"So you rush right in with her having an affair with him. Well, I have a news flash. Why would a woman who is in love or having an affair have to pencil in the initials of the person she spends her day off with every week? It doesn't make sense. Think about it, she would know she spends Thursdays with him. I think she's too young to have a poor memory and have to keep track. Did you ever consider it might not be initials of a person, but something else? An activity or a club she belongs to that meets on that day?

"Well, Father Murphy did overreact."

"I would have thrown you out on your ass if I was him. I wouldn't have given you another second of my time. What did you expect?"

"Him to take everything just as it was meant. Hypothetical."

"Dylan, I don't think you wanted that at all. I think you went in there with this little bit of information you stole, and you wanted to find out if he was having an affair because it involved Cait. She's the reason, the only reason. Jennica and the shooting had nothing to do with your motive. You wanted to know if the woman you're taking to bed is in fact, sleeping with him too. Isn't that the truth?"

"The truth? Do you really want to hear it?" He kept his voice steady, not wanting to lose control.

"Yes. If you feel like sharing."

"I don't know where you get off thinking that I'm sleeping with Cait, but I do want to clear a few things up. First, I didn't steal Dr. Greene's appointment book. She—"

"No, it probably was as easily available as she's made herself to you. It probably sits by her telephone by her bed. You casually flipped through it while waiting for her to return to you in her bed."

He faked a laugh as his anger started to boil over with her wild accusation. "Okay, have it your way. You tell me what happened."

Della sat quietly as she looked across at him. Her face glowed from the heat rising up from her embarrassment. She met his angry eyes. "I'm sorry. It's none of my business."

"That's right, it isn't. Besides, I really don't feel like sharing." He tried to keep a smile across his face. He walked around behind her, his anger out of control. It compounded inside of him until he let loose, slamming his fist into the wall. He groaned from the pain and wildly turned to Della. Kneeling down and leveling his eyes with hers, he fought to gain control. His jaw muscles clenched tightly and he white knuckled her chair, squeezing down with his brute strength. "Now, can we move past this? We have a very important case waiting for us that needs us."

His face held its fury. He pushed her back to her hospital room in silence. He kissed his mom. "I'll be back to get you at 3:00," he said to Della. He abruptly left with his black mood and turned the corner. Ahead, he saw Cait. She was leading a group of people to the room they had just occupied. He stared at the group as they filed past him. Two men dressed in dark suits cased the area as they entered. The tall man in the middle turned, catching Dylan staring at them. He thought he looked familiar. It hit him. If the photographs he'd seen didn't mistake him, the man was Mr. James, Jennica's father. Dylan knew he was finally in the right place at the right time.

Chapter 29

Thursday the 12th day of September

Dylan marched down the hall feeling angrier with every step he took, mad at himself for losing control and letting her see it. His happy mood of the morning rapidly turned to rage and confusion clouded his mind. He didn't need to be thinking about Della right now while his meeting with Diana waited.

He strolled to Dr. Greene's office, finding the door locked. Just as he was leaving, his pager vibrated against his hip. It alerted him silently someone was trying to reach him. Using the key she gave him earlier, he let himself in and dialed the number displayed.

"Detectives. Vicki speaking. May I help you?"

"This is Detective Drake. I just received a call."

"Good morning, Dylan. I'm sorry about your mother. You did get a call. It was a woman who wanted to let you know she couldn't make her appointment with you today. She made a point to make sure you were reached."

"What woman?"

"She said her name was Diana."

"Who talked with her?"

"I did."

"Tell me exactly what she said."

"Word for word?"

"Yes. That's what I just said. Exactly as you remember it. Try not to leave anything out."

"Okay. What's eating you today?"

"Nothing. Just that this call was very important. Now just tell me," he said. "Please?" trying to sound more accommodating.

"You said the magic word, I'll try. She said, 'Could I speak to Detective Drake please?' I said, he's not in the building right now. Would you like to leave him a message? She said, 'Yes. Please tell him I have to cancel our meeting. Please make sure he knows right away, so I don't keep him waiting needlessly.' I told her I would. That was the extent of our conversation word for word. I'm sorry if you were stood up. That would put me in a bad mood too."

"I'm not in a bad mood. This isn't personal, Vic. This is business. For Christ's sake, I wish everyone would see fit to leave my personal life out of their speculative minds. Why in God's name does everyone think I'm dating everyone I come in contact with if it happens to be a woman? Answer me that, would you?"

"You're single, attractive, and available. Haven't you ever heard of fantasies? "

"Of course I have, I'm serious here. What does that have to do with it?"

"It's just what keeps the world alive, that's all. I guess you don't know you're most women's private fantasy around here."

"No. I didn't know that, great, this is just great. Thanks for telling me. It makes me feel a hell of a lot better. Now I'm in a really bad mood."

"You're welcome. I was hoping it would lighten you up some. Lord knows you sound like you need it. You usually make me laugh. I was just trying to return the favor for once. Don't take offense to it. I'm married, but woman can ogle too you know. It's only fair."

"I do take offense to it. Nothing is going to lighten me up some until all you women get off of my case and leave me the hell alone."

"I'm sorry. I wish I hadn't told you."

"That makes two of us. In the future, please leave these kinds of little secrets to yourself, would you?" He slammed the phone down as Dr. Greene entered with a smile that quickly turned to concern over his flushed and frantic looking face.

"Is everything all right?" she said.

"Hell no. Everything isn't all right. Diana isn't coming in. I just received word and I'm really worried about what this might mean."

"I can tell."

"Will you do me another favor?"

"Anything if it will help you."

"Please call her and talk with her, see how she sounds. I think she's scared. I want to make sure she's okay. I'd really like you to talk her into coming in if you can convince her to. I need to find out what's behind all of this. The people in her band seem to be holding her hostage."

"Why would they be doing that?

"I don't know. I just get a feeling there's more to this than being a little overprotective of her. Maybe you could talk to Perry, the man who was suppose to bring her here today. Appeal to him. Tell him she really needs to be re-evaluated or something, anything. Say you feel she could do something to herself. Suggest she should check back into the hospital, that you were premature in letting her go."

"But it's not true. She's fine. Why would I do that?"

"For me. I feel something is very wrong here, and I don't want something to happen to her too."

"Okay. If your instincts telling you she's in danger, I'll trust you. I'll try to help you. I'll make the phone call right now."

"Here's her number."

Dylan handed the number to her. She dialed, hitting the hands free button on her telephone so Dylan could listen to the conversation. She pulled out a drawer retrieving a pen, doodling as she waited for someone to answer.

An answering machine picked up. "This is Dr. Greene. I'm calling in regards to Diana Edwards. It's very important that I reach her. Please have her call my office." She gave her office number, slowly enunciating it. She repeated her number again as a click sounded over the speaker. A person picked up the line.

"I'm sorry. Are you still there?"

"Yes. This is Dr. Greene. I'm Diana Edwards' doctor. I need to speak with her please."

"I'm sorry. She's not here. An emergency has taken her away and I don't expect her back for several days. I'll tell her you called."

"Who am I speaking with?"

"Scott."

"Scott. Will you please have her contact me as soon as possible when she calls? It's imperative that I speak with her. I've come across something in her blood work she should be aware of that we should check. It's important that she know and we have a talk about it."

"What is it, doctor?"

"I can't say. It's confidential. The only thing I can stress to you is that it's extremely important that she know right away. It's crucial to her well being. Can you understand what I'm telling you Scott?"

"Yes. I'll try and get in touch with her."

"Thank you."

Dylan gave her a nod, grinning with satisfaction at her performance. "You handled that very well."

"I just hope it helps you. I guess I better make plans to stick close by in case she gets the message and tries to call."

"Unless she's running," Dylan said.

"What do you mean?"

"I mean, she may have canceled this appointment and left all on her own because she didn't want to finish her story she began yesterday. She almost ran out on me then and might have had too much time to think about it and left town."

"She still may call if she thinks I really did find something. We did run a lot of routine tests and that's usually where we find abnormalities when we aren't looking for something specific. At least, not what an individual is usually being seen for by the doctor."

"I sure hope she does. If she puts it together you're helping me, she may run further. That's assuming, it is her call right now."

"And if it isn't?"

"Then I'm afraid she is in immediate danger. If she knows anything about who shot Jennica or the circumstances surrounding it, that puts her head on a platter. It could get her killed."

"I don't like the sound of this. What can I do?" Dr. Greene said.

"Just what you said, stay here and answer your phones today. If she does call, you said you record them. Your Caller ID will tell us where she is if the phone doesn't have a block on it."

"Right. Anything else?"

"I can't think of anything right now. Page me right away if she calls. Let me write down the number. I'll be busy running back and forth. I want to cover every angle possible. I'm taking all the precautions on this one. It could involve lots of people, for all I know. Damn, I hope she calls." Dylan stood handing her his card. "Thanks Cait."

"Lucky for you, I like you."

Dylan started walking past her and studied her face. She wasn't easy to read. "Oh, by the way, I do need to ask you a couple questions before I take off, since you're familiar with this hospital."

"Sure. Anything to help."

Dylan reached for her hand. They walked to the couch together. He stopped and dropped her hand and motioned her to sit. He sat directly opposite her in the overstuffed chair. She crossed one leg over the other, giving him a rather demure smile that surprised him. Scooting to the edge of his chair, he hesitated briefly before choosing the right words to begin with. Masking his real intentions and justifying them by believing it might be relevant to the case, he asked her exactly what was on his mind.

"Dr. Greene." He cleared his throat, and decided to start again. "Cait."

"Yes, Detective Drake? I do believe you're stalling."

"I'm not trying to, I'm just finding it a little hard to concentrate right now."

"You are?"

"I am, but let me go ahead and begin. Do you know a priest by the name of Murphy?"

"Yes. I know Father Murphy."

"How well do you know him?" He watched her eyebrows rise slightly. Noticing her uncross and cross her legs again, he thought the questioned bothered her. She folded her hands together and placed them in her lap.

"I've worked with him in this hospital. The most recent, being the night Jennica was brought in here. I believe he came that night because the family called him."

"That's all?"

"You want more? I hate to disappoint you, but that is it. Why do I get the feeling that my answer wasn't the one you wanted to hear?"

"I don't know. You tell me."

"Tell you what? Shoot straight with me here," Dr. Greene said. "What are you trying to get at? Yes, I answered your question. I do know Father Murphy. What more do you need to know? Do you want documentation of every time? I fail to see where you're headed with this Dylan. You know I'm trying to help you. What is it?"

"I guess nothing. I'd better go."

"Not yet. Why is Father Murphy important to you right now? Are you investigating him? Tell me."

"I can't, but yes, I have to look at everyone who is involved with Jennica. He may be a priest, but he seems to be involved with the family intimately."

"How so?"

"You said yourself, they called him."

"Of course they did, she wasn't expected to live. That's a normal thing for a family to do if they can."

"I know. I just have a job to do and part of it is finding out about everyone who is involved with the victim. I have to be suspicious of everyone."

"Are you adding me to that list because I know him?"

"Of course not."

"You say that like you really mean it. Like I'm a suspect. Why? Because I stood up for Father Murphy?"

"No. It's nothing like that. Unless, of course, Jennica had been a patient of yours previous to the shooting, then maybe I would need to question you further."

"Is that the question you really wanted to ask me? You could have just come out with it. I don't appreciate this cat and mouse game you detectives think you're so good at playing. It stinks."

"I'm just doing my job."

"I know. I thought you were different than the rest of the cops I've had the privilege to meet in my line of work. I gave you credit for being a little more original than this. You just used the most standard line as a defense. I just figured you out, Detective Drake. It's always the job first with you guys, isn't it? Can't you still treat me like a human being while you're doing it? An intelligent one at that, that can see through all your bullshit in between?"

"Okay. I'm sorry. What would you have told me if I asked you if Jennica was a patient of yours?"

"I'd say it's privileged."

"That so?"

"Yes. It is. So where do we go from here?"

"I'd have to say, you win. I hope we can go on from here." He didn't want to risk losing her help. Whatever the truth was, he knew he would keep digging until he found out what he needed to know. Things always had a way of turning up when you least expected them to.

"You're not as dumb—"

"Don't finish it," Dylan said. You might have to eat those words later." He stood and helped her up from the couch.

They stood in a precarious silence facing one another.

Dylan turned and walked out the door. Father Murphy would have to answer a few more questions. After all, he was the connection to the gun and Rob Browning. Finding Mr. Browning and having an up close and personal chat with him became Dylan's number one goal.

Chapter 30

Thursday the 12th day of September

Dylan arrived at the office and picked up his messages in his box. He hurried to his computer and logged on. Shuffling through the messages and sorting as he went, his eyes stopped at the name on the one in his hand. He set the others down. Bingo. Rob Browning finally called him. He dialed and waited.

A voice answered the line announcing it was his answering service and telling him that Mr. Browning was unavailable at this time. Dylan left a polite message to get in touch with him leaving his pager and cell number. The lady attentively took down the information and said she'd do her best to reach him.

"Drake, get in here." Captain Mitchell bobbed in the door long enough to command the order then left.

Dylan stood up, taking his jacket off, and placed it around his chair. Walking to the Captain's office, he took a seat. Captain Mitchell tapped his pen on the desk, a habit Dylan recognized well. It was a preliminary to shit hitting the fan.

"I had a visit today with Father Murphy. I believe he's not a fan of yours. Can you enlighten me on the cause of this visit that interrupted my whole entire schedule?"

"Yes, sir. I interviewed Father Murphy after discovering his background check had come back incomplete. There was no information prior to 1970. I went in to have him fill in the gaps for me, such as where he was born and the year, so I could check him out further. He laughed at me, thinking these questions were inappropriate and irrelevant to solving this case. He then asked me if he was being investigated. I told him the usual. He laughed and asked what motive that he would have to shoot Jennica. I said having an affair with her, meaning that as an example of a person's motive, not what I thought his motive was at the time. I know he misunderstood me, because he became highly upset and told me to leave. I tried to apologize, but he remained hostile towards me."

"I can't believe you actually would tell a priest he might be having an affair." The Captain shook his head back and forth and then burst out laughing. "I would have liked to have been there."

"It wasn't pleasant, sir. He threatened to end my career."

"Don't worry. It would take a hell of a lot more than a pissed off priest. The Chaplain happens to be a good friend of Father Murphy's, so he went to him for advice. That's where I got involved. He filed an official complaint about the matter and I have to turn it over to the review board. I'm sorry, it's just the policy. I know you didn't slander his good name or the church, but he's not taking what you said lying down."

"Doesn't it make you wonder why he would make such an issue out of it?"

"I hadn't really thought about it, but if I were him, I suppose I'd be hot under the collar too. No pun intended."

"He's blowing this all out of proportion. I still need to finish his background check."

"Just be careful and use a little more tact, would you?"

"I don't think he'll let me near him again."

"I don't think you'll need any more face to face meetings to complete his background, just run with what you've got. If you need more answers, we'll have to set a meeting up here with a mediator to watch over your ass."

"Sounds like fun," Dylan said.

"I thought you'd like that." Captain Mitchell stood up. "Keep me posted, will you?"

"I will. Right now, I'm trying to get a handle on Rob Browning. He might have been out of the country, but it was his gun, according to the priest. We've been operating under that assumption. I haven't been able to confirm it from Browning or with the ATF. He might have his gun with him for all we know. The scratches could just be similar to what Father Murphy remembers. When we ran a trace on the ownership to confirm it was his, we came up empty-handed. The factory said that serial number is issued to the government. I called ATF and they told me the information I am requesting is classified. So, you see I'm at a standstill right now without Browning. If he can come forward and identify the gun as his own, then it makes my mind start working overtime. If he tells me it's not his gun, he's off the hook. If he can show me the gun that Father Murphy thought was his, that is."

"Do what ever you have to do. This is our investigation and we have to thoroughly exhaust all leads. Bring him in and get your answers, just don't piss off any more priests while you're at it. One in my office in a lifetime is enough for me."

"Gotcha." Dylan strolled to his office cleaning up the paperwork on his desk for the next two hours. He ran every check he could on Father Murphy, still finding absolutely nothing. The social security number he had for him was not correct. The problem must lie in the number. Accessing records under that number didn't get him anything. The number had to be wrong.

There were many things that bothered him with the investigation. Why was the identity of the person assigned to the government issued gun classified? And if it was assigned to a classified government agent, what are they doing in Bozeman in the first place? Was it planned, merely a coincidence, or a big mistake that it ended up involved in the Jennica James shooting? And why couldn't he find anything on the priest? Father Murphy couldn't be a government agent working undercover as a priest, could he? Was it all a set up for a larger agenda? The questions led to more questions. Dylan would keep on digging until he uncovered the answers.

Dylan followed up a few more leads, and called his mom to check in. "Mom, I just wanted to check in and see how you're feeling?"

"I'm fine, son, but Della isn't. I'm afraid she's going to have to stay here."

"What happened? I'll be right there."

Dropping the phone, he ran out and left a message with Vickie.

Arriving at the hospital, he flew up the stairs and ran into room 204. Della laid in bed attached to a couple of machines. Her face looked pale and she was sleeping.

"What happened?" Dylan said.

"A fever. They haven't been able to get it down. They hooked her up to that heart monitor and have another machine to make sure she is breathing okay."

Dylan reached her bed. Scared and full of anxiety from hearing about Della's condition, he leaned over and brushed her face with his hand. "Della, don't fail me now." He reached for her hand and held it, pulling up a chair.

Dylan felt Della squeezing his hand.

"Did you come for me?" she said in a weak voice.

"You bet I did. What's going on?"

"After you left, I just fell apart."

"I guess you did. What are you trying to do? Put me in an early grave by worrying me to death?"

"I'm sorry. Look at the bright side. You're off the hook for today. You don't have to take care of me. They won't release me now until they figure this out."

"I was actually really looking forward to it," he said.

"You're lying, Detective Drake. I can see right through you."

"You're right. You can be such a pain in my ass that I was dreading it."

"That's better." She closed her eyes.

A few minutes passed and she started coughing. He held her hand and helped her sit up. "I'm okay now," she said. "You don't have to stay. I'll be better in the morning. Then I'll hold you to your promise."

"You're not getting rid of me that easy. I'm spending the night right by your side. I'm your partner, and I'm here for you. I know you'd be right here for me."

She laid back and smiled closing her eyes.

Dylan reached in his jacket and pulled out the cellular he grabbed at the office. He dialed Dr. Greene. She answered on the first ring.

"Have you heard from Diana?" Dylan said.

"Not yet, and we're running out of time," Dr. Greene said. "She knows my office hours. If she doesn't call before five we won't hear from her today. We can hope for tomorrow."

"Yeah, and I hope she's still breathing. I've put patrols around the house and an APB for her across the state. I'm covering a few bases. Look, Della is really ill. I'll be in her room the rest of the night. Call me here if she calls. Get her to meet with you tomorrow."

"I'll do that. Take care. Della's a fighter, and she'll pull through it."

"Damn straight she will. That's why I'm going to stay here and kick her ass all night if I have to."

Chapter 31

Thursday the 12th day of September

"Ground squirrel, you have to come in." The voice crackled over the airwaves.

"Now? It's too soon. Our objective is near. It's too early."

"I know."

"Is this a direct order?"

"From the top."

"It's a crash then?"

"Negative. Ground to the pines. Foods arriving 2200. Over."

"10–4, out."

The single engine Piper Cub rattled a bit before the engine smoothed out for take off. He sat back in his seat, checking his gauges over once more while waiting for clearance from the tower. His flight plan in place, he received a green light from the traffic controller. He pushed the throttle up and steered onto the runway, easing down the asphalt. Smoothly the plane lifted to a crisp take off. He climbed up to cruising altitude and began enjoying the view as he flew north from Mountain Home AFB in Idaho, where he had been the past few days finalizing stage 3 with Montana in his sights.

GS set the plans out in front of his mind, making sure he took care of every detail. He would land at the Gallatin Air Field after two o'clock. His Jeep sat fueled and ready to go. That would put him at the cabin early so he could get changed and prepare himself for the meeting. He hated changes in the schedule at the last minute.

All that time and expense wasted all because he overlooked one small detail when he left town. He left his government issued revolver and it was stolen. If the locals traced it back to the department, it would put the skids on the whole operation. It took five years to set up and bring in their payday. They were too close to end it now. Infiltrating one group to spy on another hadn't been the easiest mission he'd been assigned to.

He couldn't make any sense out of it. Jennica James shot. Who could have done such a thing? It appalled him that someone in the organization could have retaliated and taken such a low blow against him, to take his gun, involve an innocent victim, then try and set him up for it. It just didn't make any sense when he mulled it over in his mind. He worked every angle and came up with nothing.

Who knew the two of them were intimate? To make a hit on Jennica didn't make any sense. Her father ran the show. Would he have put the word out to hit his own daughter? If they uncovered the ruse and wanted him back, it didn't take shooting Jennica to get him back. Her murder wouldn't have changed anything in the scheme of things, unless they were sending a clear signal that they were willing to risk it all to accomplish their objective. They were risking exposing their whole operation by playing this kind of game at a time like this.

He started wondering if there wasn't a third party out in the field, playing the game that none of them had figured on before now. He knew things were getting messy, but somehow someone just made it messier. He'd have to investigate it further when he arrived and try to find out some answers on his own. He shook his head as he came out of a cloud, wishing his long flight to be over so he could get to town and to the bottom of it. A thorough briefing would take place on the mountain and then he would have to decide if seeing Jennica would be wise.

He landed at the airport on time. The afternoon was clear and the mountains sparkled with fresh white snow. He parked the plane in its hanger and jumped out, grabbing his bags. He hurried across the parking lot to his Jeep. He glanced at his watch. Ahead of schedule, he could use a quick bite to eat before heading up the canyon. The cupboards were bare.

He felt a wave of guilt climbing out of his gut and up into his throat. He felt ultimately responsible for Jennica laying in the hospital. Somehow she became a target. The agency forced him to pursue the relationship three years ago to stack the deck in their favor against her father their bitter enemy, and now she was paying the price for his dirty little war.

Meeting Jennica James and drawing her in was easy. He joined the church and met her. One Saturday evening after Mass he asked her out. He was the bait and she was reeled in like a sucker. Having a woman to talk to turned out to be the nicest part of the job, and it wasn't such a hard part to have to play. Loneliness was a big part of an agent's life, and after years of being alone her company became a comfort. It had been a long time since he met someone he dared to let his shield down with.

Falling for her was easy, so easy that the game turned real. Looking into her crystal blue eyes that lit the room up made him fall hard. She laughed at his stupid jokes and it intoxicated him. Like a drug, he became addicted. Three years of her love and now it would've ended with the mission. Only he hoped he'd have the chance to say it was over and good-bye in person. After the next day, he would have flown out of her life permanently, but he had hoped to make love to her one last time. Now it was impossible. The only way he could say good-bye was to slip in her room and whisper it to her while she laid there sleeping. Praying that when he did, she'd hear him and know that he did love her. She'd always be his pin-up girl.

Friday the 13th was the night staged for their final act. After that, he'd be given new orders and he'd be off in another country somewhere and working out another deadly situation. There would always be orders and other women, but he'd carry her in his heart until his last days.

Those feelings jeopardized them both. Now they were both paying the price. She was an innocent victim. She couldn't know what put her in the hospital. She told him she loved him. He vowed when he found the person who did shoot her, he would pay the ultimate price and be marked for death.

As his thoughts drifted to Jennica and captured all the special memories he held during their time together, he faltered. "Hell with them," he muttered out loud, as he tried to convince himself that it would be okay to quickly see Jennica. Taking a left out of the airport and onto the old highway, he drove towards Bozeman. Seeing Jennica might ease his mind from the torment he felt since he found out about the shooting. He needed to see her alive, fighting those bastards that put her there. Knowing that, he could have a clear head for what he had to do.

Chapter 32

Thursday the 12th day of September
Gallatin County General Hospital, Bozeman, Montana

Dr. Greene met him privately like she did every Thursday. Today was no different. Frank Morrow arrived precisely at one o'clock. She'd spent the previous months working with him, making little progress in his therapy. She'd made a few small breakthroughs that gave her hope that they would one day uncover the mystery. It lurked just below the surface, she convinced herself, and whatever it was they'd unlock it and expose it together.

He'd spent years in therapy in different places and now he looked to her for the truth. The truth became his hope for normalcy. He said his time was running out. She'd encouraged him to stay with her for a little while longer and convinced him they were close to a breakthrough.

She knew it must be hell for him. He said it felt like being dropped into time and struggling from that point on, surviving one day at a time. He'd felt like a sewer grate, cold and full of holes. Frank Morrow was a survivor. He'd fought his way blindly ahead trying to fill in the holes. At one point, he'd thought he was finally free of it all and for the first time in his life he felt normal. Then it started happening all over again, time was missing and had moved forward. The holes were back and he feared himself once again.

Dr. Greene observed her patient and noticed uneasiness. He held his body rigid, following the tension to his strained face. It carried through to his eyes seeming more intense as they watched her today. She decided she'd better be extra careful with him. She thought back to the day he came, begging her to try and help him. He was a desperate man on the verge of killing himself. They agreed to meet on Thursdays when her office was normally closed for appointments. A private confidential meeting that kept anyone from knowing he was her patient. That was the deal they struck. She knew she needed to help him. A man that was so full of his own fears, he needed a guarantee he would have total privacy. A sanctuary to retreat to where he could come and be saved, then healed.

The case fascinated Dr. Greene from the very beginning and their exclusive meeting benefited them both. It became their time to work close together as doctor and patient, exposing the raw sewage lying just below the surface that had taken on a life of its own. Several months had passed before they made their first breakthrough, and now she felt they were close to opening it wide open, the whole ungodly truth.

"Let's begin today where we left off last week. Are you comfortable with that?"

"I don't know. I haven't been feeling like myself. Since last week, I've lost hours here and there, just like before. I thought I was past all of that, and it's scaring the living hell out of me. I feel it's getting worse, not better, and we're not getting anywhere with this. I'm wasting my time and yours."

"I certainly don't agree with you. In the past few months you've made remarkable steps forward. I know this is very hard on you, bringing your past out from the darkness within yourself, but it's the only way for you to be free of it and get on with your life, your real life. Don't give up on yourself now. You're so close to a real breakthrough. I know it. You are just scared. That's all. It's natural for you to feel that way. We have to keep pushing. Eventually, we'll get past this point and it will get easier. I promise."

"I'm not sure I can do this again. It's making me crazier than I already feel."

"You can do it. You have tremendous strength. I've witnessed it time and time again. You aren't crazy. It's just plain human emotions surfacing from deep within you. They've been buried for a very long time. It's a good thing. And the only way if you want to get better."

He got up and paced around her office. He finally stopped and settled on her couch. She kept watching him, hoping he would consent to more sessions. His case was the first she'd ever treated who displayed genuine multiple personalities. She believed that they were real and she knew she could help him beat them. Dr. Greene found she had learned more from working with him in the past months, than all the years in school studying the textbooks. She felt she needed him now as much as he needed her. It might take him years of counseling, but she was willing to stick by him every inch of the way. The depth of his problems went all the way to hell.

"Let's relax for a bit and talk about what we have uncovered." She walked towards him and reached for his hands that he had laced in front of him.

He stared at the painting on the wall. Gently holding his hand, she waited until he turned toward her. The pain was visible on his face like shattered glass. His anguish tore at her insides, in spite of her attempts to remain objective.

"Dr. Greene, I know I am who I am. This isn't going to change any of it. My past is my past. It has turned my life into a mockery of itself. I no longer know who I am anymore and I just want to stop. I should just end it once and for all."

"No. Don't ever say that. You can stand up to it. Don't let it take over again. You're a strong man with a bright future still ahead of you, if you'll let yourself accomplish that for yourself. Come on. You trust me don't you?"

"Of course I do. You know you're the only one I do trust. I wouldn't be here if I didn't, and I sure wouldn't have been coming here for the past year and a half. That's part of my problem. I feel normal when I'm here. When I leave, I fall apart. I'm dependent on you for my normalcy. You won't be here for me forever." He dropped his gaze towards the floor.

"I'll be here for you as long as you need me, you know that." Dr. Greene felt her heart leap at the sound of her own words. A big promise she vowed she would keep.

Frank steadied his eyes and looked at hers through his dark lenses. "Okay. I'll try."

"I know you can."

They sat and she told him to lie back and get comfortable.

"Let's begin with a relaxation exercise before we move on to the hypnosis."

Taking off his jacket, he set it on the arm of the couch.

She instructed him to get as comfortable as possible and relax his mind and body by beginning to tense each muscle, starting with his right foot. She guided him through the process; working up his body as he squeezed each muscle then relaxed them until he reached his head. "Your entire body is now relaxed and heavy. From the top of your head, your face and neck, through your shoulders, chest and arms and midsection, down into your legs and feet. Your whole body is heavy and warm, sinking right down into the couch. Take a moment and enjoy this heavy, warm, relaxed sensation. Your body is floating down, down, down, right down into the couch, " She said in a soothing voice, bringing him to total relaxation.

From her experience with him in the previous months, he'd taken longer to relax today. Relaxation was as important as a prelude to the hypnotic state. It was hard at first to get him relaxed the first few times. Now, she knew when he reached that point when she could begin hypnosis. She studied his form. He appeared calm, very quiet, his eyes closed like he was sleeping. She began to put him under hypnosis.

He thrashed about like a wild dog on the couch, lashing out again and again. She watched as he cried before he was finished as he relived the same ugly scene they had uncovered from the very beginning. He shook violently; screaming out as if his body were on fire as Dr. Greene brought him out of his trance. His face was drawn tight in horror, the color of cherries, and beaded with heavy perspiration. He was weeping like a child. She held him in her arms, rocking him gently until the calm returned and he was able to speak.

"It's going to be all right, it is. I just want you to keep believing that, and never give up hope. You've been through such a hideous experience that your real soul couldn't handle it. You shut down, and other personalities took over for you. It's a way for the human mind to cope with the monstrosities that no human being should have ever had to endure. Take all the time you need. Rest for a while here, and I'll be in the next room if you need me. Then, when you're ready, I'd like to take some extra time today and just talk." She stepped to a drawer and pulled out an afghan and placed it around his shivering body, like a mother taking care of her sick child. Flicking the light off, she listened to his stifled sobs as she left him.

Dr. Greene played back her calls from her machine. There was not a single call from Diana Edwards. Dylan needed her, and she wanted to help him get her back to shed some light on his investigation.

Returning a couple calls, one to a pharmacist and one to a patient, she turned back to check on Mr. Morrow. The telephone rang. It was Diana Edwards. Pulling in a slow breath, she prepared herself to tell a lie.

"Ms. Edwards. I'm glad you received my message. Is everything all right?"

"Yes. I'm just fine. You needed to talk to me?"

"Yes, I do Diana. But, I need to see you in person, face to face. Please can you come into my office for a consultation today?"

"Today? I'm afraid that's impossible. I can't. I'm not in town right now. Whatever it is you can just tell me over the telephone. I give you my permission."

"I'm afraid I can't. I really need to sit down with you and show you these tests and explain everything in detail. When do you think you can come in? It really shouldn't wait."

"I don't know. I'm in Billings right now with my ill grandmother, and I may be here for a while. I don't want to leave her. Please just tell me. I can take it. What can be so horrible you wouldn't tell me over the phone? Am I dying?"

Cait remembered Dylan's last words he spoke; worried she might be in extreme danger. He was fearful for her life. "No. It's a very serious matter, however. But that's why I need you in here to go over everything thoroughly, and start a plan of treatment."

"You're worrying me. You should just tell me now. A plan of treatment?"

"Yes. That's all I'm going to say. Please, it will only take a couple of hours and a few more tests at the hospital to be one-hundred percent sure. You can return to your grandmother after that, Please? It's essential to your immediate well being we find out for sure and get you on medication."

"You aren't giving me any choice in this matter are you?" Diana said.

"No, I can't. I'm sorry."

"I'll leave here now and drive back. Will you see me right away when I get in?"

"Yes. That's what I planned on. I'm at the hospital. Just page me in the ER. I'll meet you there."

"I'll see you at around four o'clock or so."

"Good. I'll set up those tests in the meantime. I'm sorry about your grandmother, but this is just as important for you to take care of right now, or I wouldn't be putting you through it. You'll understand more when you get here." Cait squeezed her eyes shut, thinking she might not understand any of this later.

They broke the connection and she sighed. Tension had built from trying to sound convincing. Thinking of her integrity as a doctor, she grimaced for out and out lying to a patient to get her to come back under false pretenses.

Dr. Greene dialed the number Dylan had given her, waiting impatiently for him to answer. Frank was still in her office, and she hadn't checked back with him. It had been ten minutes. She decided that he might need a little more time to get back to his dominant personality before they could talk about the session. Ten minutes later, Dylan returned her call.

"Dylan, Diana just called, she's on her way up from Billings. It's a two hour drive, right?"

"Right. What did she say?"

"She'd meet me right away and page me in the ER."

"Thanks. I knew you could pull it off. I'm on my way there now. Della is better this morning. They might even release her by this afternoon."

"That's good news."

"The best."

"I think you care for her a lot more than you led on to the other night. I heard it in your voice just now."

"Don't turn this conversation into a discussion about me," Dylan said. "I'm tired of everyone telling me what I feel."

"Well, I'm sorry. I can see Della has your attention, and that's what she wants."

"I'll see you at your office in a half hour or so."

"You sure can change the subject when it's convenient. You're scared to death, aren't you?"

"Like I said, I'll see you in a minute. I think this discussion is going nowhere."

"Nowhere? Only the places you let it. I'll see you, and then let's finish this discussion. I'm a good listener. I get paid to untangle people's deepest darkest feelings."

Dr. Greene hurried to her office, opening the door quietly. She turned on a small lamp on her desk. Frank was asleep on the couch curled in a fetal position looking pathetic. Her first impression of him was that he was a fit man with an athletic grace that made him appear much younger than his fifty odd years. His hair was the color of chestnuts streaked with a hint of gold and not many gray hairs in sight. Now, however, he looked old.

Deeply etched lines were visible on his face in the dim light of the lamp that she had never noticed before. Deep as the secrets buried inside him she thought. She prayed he could survive the reality of them when the whole picture revealed itself.

Deciding to let him sleep for a bit longer, she left again for a moment to collect her thoughts and prepare for their talk.

Walking down the hall to the drinking fountain, she heard her name paged through the hospital intercom. She walked back into her reception office to dial the front desk.

"Dr. Greene. What is it?"

"I'm sorry, Dr. Greene. I know you aren't on the schedule, but someone told me you were in here today. A man has been trying to get in to see the James girl. He says he's family and wants clearance. He says he would like to talk to her doctor."

"I'm not the doctor in charge of her case."

"I know. He said he wants to talk with someone who knows what's going on. All the other doctors on her team, except for you, are unavailable. I was told you have been working with her. I thought you would talk to him."

"Okay. Where is he?" She heard the agitation in her own voice.

"He's in the chapel. His name is, let me find it. I wrote it down. Oh, here it is. It's Rob Browning."

"Rob Browning?" The name seemed to send an alarm off in her head. "Okay, tell him I'll meet with him, but I have another patient I'm working with right now. I can't be sure when I'll be done. I'll come up there afterwards. It might be an hour or so."

"I'll tell him that Dr. Greene and thank you. I'm sorry for calling you, but he was demanding and he wasn't giving up."

"It's all right. I'll be glad to help if I can."

Dr. Greene walked into her office, reaching over her desk to flip the desk lamp on to check on Frank again. She felt a warm hand run up her nylon, sending a chill up her spine. She turned around and found herself standing two inches from Frank in the amber light. He stood in front of her totally naked, with a wicked smile on his face, his hands reached out to her. Her mouth dropped open in shock as she felt her throat constricting when she tried to scream. His hands shut the scream off instantly like shutting a valve off from a pipe.

She knew if she acted scared it could feed him into frenzy. She felt panic rise in her throat. She didn't know who he was at this moment. The other personalities were all small children. None resembled the devil that stood leering at her as his squeeze tightened even more.

She cut off her last attempt to scream, deciding it might scare him into a more excited state than he already was.

His grip released while he rubbed himself, reaching for her hand, his eyes darting around the room and back to her. Figuring out who he was before he was on her might trigger him to stop before things escalated and got out of hand.

Her mind raced through all the textbooks like a computer sorting data.

Frank pulled her to him hard, sliding her dress up above her hips. Reaching for her throat, he stopped. Slowly he let his hand slide down to her breasts as he unbuttoned the first button, then the second, as his darting eyes followed each movement. Screaming out like he was in excruciating pain, he finished by ripping every button off on his way down. Tugging roughly and yanking her dress off of her shoulders, it fell to the ground. Her belt popped off and landed behind the desk.

Tears spilled onto her cheeks. As he saw them, his eyes widened, briefly stopping him as if in shock. Then his large hand came up and slapped her across the mouth so hard she fell back against the desk. Her head throbbed as the taste of blood filled her mouth. Crawling on top of her, he eagerly pulled at her bra. Her heart raced. Hands groped along her bare skin, his wet tongue felt hot on her neck. His breathing became quicker, hot and stale. She felt the vomit swelling in her throat and she realized how foolish she'd been. He was raping her and she wasn't even fighting it. Her mind screamed back at her to fight before it was too late.

Chapter 33

Thursday, the 12th day of September

Dr. Greene opened her eyes and remembered the room spinning out of control, then nothing as if the lights had been turned off. She felt the knot left on her forehead, biting back the throbbing pain. Licking her lips, she tasted the crusted blood. Slowly, she sat up and tried getting her bearings. Before the blackness consumed her, all she could remember was being pushed on top of her desk.

Flashing back, she replayed through her last memories, trying to figure out what had happened to her. Questions flooded her mind like a run away freight train. With no answers, her questions turned to fright and then hysteria. Her eyes darted around the room, trying to find Frank. Bile rose in her throat. Crawling towards the door, she tried to make it to the bathroom off of her private office. Spying a garbage can by her desk, she grabbed it, heaving the remains of her late breakfast. She sputtered, gagging until she regained control. Crying and coughing in between sobs, she wiped at her mouth. She felt dirty.

Breathing in deeply, she desperately tried to force her tears to stop as they flowed down her cheeks and down onto her bare breasts causing another icy chill.

As she tried standing, the room twirled, making her disorientated and then, violently ill again. Putting her head between her legs, she took in more deep breaths and tried getting past the feeling that was drowning her.

Dr. Greene pulled herself up and into her office chair, willing herself enough strength to do what needed to be done. Looking at the clock, she realized a short time had passed since she found Frank in her office. Her heart raced with her mind as it chased each question.

Grappling the chair, she peered around her office, searching all the places he could be hiding. Finally, deciding if he was hiding, he'd stay hidden if anyone else came in, gave her a glimmer of hope that she might still have time to repair the damage. Of course, if he wasn't back to his dominant personality, anything could happen. Surrendering her last sliver of hope, she knew the person he was ten minutes ago could attack again. Finding that thought too disconcerting, she screamed silently and prayed. Shoving the thought to the far recesses of her mind, she thought denial would be better for now, because at the moment, she didn't have time to deal with it right now. She hurried to do what she could for now.

The important thing she decided was to straighten the place up and get a shower. Her body needed cleaning and she hoped she could manage it all before Dylan arrived. Straightening the papers that had been scattered and picking up the other items on the floor, she gathered her clothing, circling the area for anything else she might have missed. Noticing a couple buttons from her dress, she rescued them from the thick carpeting.

Grabbing her gym bag from the closet, she limped to the bathroom. Turning on hot water, she held herself under the full blast. The hotter the water, the better. It would clean her if she had to burn him off of her. Crying out in pain from the searing water, she remained, letting her skin burn until her body felt numb.

Soaping down her body with antibacterial soap, she scrubbed vigorously. The smell of him was on her, the odor pungent and sour. Scrubbing again and again, she finally understood the woman she counseled who spoke to her after they'd been raped of their feeling of never being clean again. Wincing, she washed her hair, trying not to touch the front of her scalp that left her head feeling like a balloon ready to burst.

She dressed in her jeans and T-shirt and stashed her gym bag before combing out her hair. Staring at her swollen lip and forehead, she tried in vain to touch them up with makeup. One eye appeared to be turning black and blue. A firm knock came from behind the door. She stiffened and tried to think of a quick cover story.

"Cait? Cait are you in there?"

She opened the door standing back behind it as Dylan strolled in, then leaned against it for support.

Dylan turned and noticed her casual wear and commented. "You are here, bare feet, jeans, T-shirt, wet hair?"

"Yes, I'm here. I wanted to shower quickly before you arrived." She tried to keep the strain from her voice.

She noticed he watched her in the darkness. She took a few steps slowly, then stopped. She knew her movements were stiff an awkward. Reaching the couch, she sat down.

"A shower? Don't you usually do that at home?" he said.

"Usually, unless I want to take one here." She tilted her head slightly, then quickly put it back down. "After Diana called, I decided I had time for a quick run. I ran down Highland Boulevard and back up the hill. It's convenient having a bathroom equipped with a shower for just that reason. I often shower here."

"If I would have known there was a shower here, I would have used it the other night."

"If I knew you planned to use my office for a motel, I would have let you in on my little secret."

"Direct hit, doctor. Do I detect a little sarcasm? You haven't forgiven me for that night, have you? It wasn't meant to hurt you. I'm sorry you don't understand. I thought you did."

"I do understand."

"So why so sullen? I get an adrenaline rush after a good run. I run the hill myself at least five times a week. It's an excellent work out."

"It is, and I'm not sullen or angry at you," she said.

"Damn, I should've detected your happy go lucky mood. I mean, just hearing all that excitement in your voice should have given it away." He frowned and turned on the office lights.

Cait shielded her eyes pretending the light had blinded her.

"Sorry, I thought we could use some light. What's the matter?"

"I have a raging headache, that's all."

"Okay, I'll turn off the big lights and turn on the lamp on your desk." Walking over, he wondered why she was acting strange. She did a three sixty. It must have been their earlier conversation, he decided. He had ended it by hanging up on her.

Casually strolling towards the desk, a shimmer reflected in the corner of his eye coming from the floor. It appeared to be a round metal object like a button, then he noticed a belt curled up and discarded in the corner close to it. She wore it earlier with her dress. She seemed totally preoccupied, so much so he thought he might as well be invisible. Reaching over her desk, he switched the desk lamp on. His hand brushed something wet. As he looked down, he saw a red smudge. Blood? Why would blood be on her desk? His mind switched into high gear. "Is everything all right Cait?" he said.

"Of course, everything's just fine."

"That's what you keep saying. Why am I not convinced?"

She looked up, then quickly bowed her head. Dylan sat down on the chair facing her, a determined look in his eyes.

"Then you're still mad at me for this morning, as much as you're trying to deny it? I didn't want to talk about my personal life, remember?"

"Of course, I remember. And no, I'm not mad. What do I have to say to convince you I'm not mad at you for anything? It's your business. If you don't want to talk about it, it's up to you."

"I'm glad you feel that way." They sat in silence for a few moments. "Look at me, would you?" Dylan said.

Raising up and leaning heavily on the couch, she let out a small cry.

"Cait? Why won't you look at me?" He reached out touching her chin and turned her face to him. Flinching, she put her head down. "What's going on here?" Her swollen lip, her black and blue eyes, and the lump on her forehead the size of an egg scared him. "What in the hell happened to you? Answer me, would you?"

"Nothing happened."

"What do you mean, nothing happened? Your lips look like you tried silicon injections only the experiment went bad."

"Very funny."

"You have two black eyes that look worse than my opponents when I boxed in the Navy." He brushed a piece of hair away from her face, "And that bump on your forehead? That wasn't there last time I saw you. So, come on, give it up."

"It's nothing—It's just I feel like an idiot telling you what happened. While I was running, I wasn't paying attention to where I was and slipped on a long patch of black ice in a shady spot by the park. I did a flying free fall, landing on my face." She looked up and grimaced. "That's why I'd rather not speak right now."

"Here, let me take a closer look." He turned the overhead lights back on and examined her face close up. She winced at his touch and tried to get away. The bruises and bumps weren't consistent with a fall. She had no scrapes or cuts that she should have had if she really did skid along the pavement on her face as she had said. His gut feeling told him she was hiding the truth from him.

Something had happened here in her office he thought. Anger mounted as he tried to imagine what could have happened, but after a few seconds of scenarios, he told himself to back off. It was her personal life. After all, she just finished agreeing with him that his personal life was just that, his business. He couldn't butt into her life after she consented to staying out of his.

Did her secret meeting with F.M. get rough, an argument that escalated into a violent confrontation between the two, or was he just a man that liked to abuse his women?

He couldn't make her tell him the truth, but one thing he was sure of was that he really didn't know Doctor Caitlin Greene very well. Meeting her less than a week ago, after the Jennica James shooting, she kept surprising him. The thought of a woman being physically abused by another man made him physically sick. In his line of work, he saw it too frequently.

"All I can say is, I'm not the doctor here," Dylan said. "Don't you think you should have one of your colleagues look at you? You might have a concussion. It looks like your nose may be broken." Staring intently, he hoped she could read the doubt and questions covering his face.

"No. I'm fine. I don't need a doctor."

"I think you do."

"Who're you to question me? I'm a doctor, remember? I think I know when I need one."

"I think doctors could be their own worst enemy and probably make the worst patients. I would feel better if you went down and had one of the emergency room doctors look at you."

"No, Dylan, I said, I'm just fine. I am. Diana should be here soon."

"You'll scare the hell out of her looking like that."

"I can't do much about that right now, can I? I won't look any better in a half-hour, even if a doctor examined me. If you want that information out of Diana, you'd better drop this, and I mean right now." She glared at him.

"For the record, I don't believe a word you just said to me. I'll drop it, but you can be sure that before this day is through, you'll tell me everything." He flipped off the overhead lights as he reached the door. "I'll be back in ten minutes. You'd better pick up your belt on the floor and wipe the blood off of your desk before Diana arrives."

Chapter 34

Thursday, the 12th day of September

Leaving from the back exit out of Dr. Greene's suite, Dylan reached the corner of the hall and stopped. He hesitated as he thought about her prefabricated story and whether or not he should go back and play the bad cop. It would ease his mind to know her injuries were being looked after.

Turning his head, he glanced down the hall. A figure raced by and hurried down the hall as if, the building were on fire. From the back, the figure wore a long black duster and a black hat. He reached the end of the hall as another man approached him. The two collided. A newspaper flew from the other man's hand. The person in black pushed past him and disappeared. The other man recovered, shook his head angrily and picked up his paper from the floor. The man stopped at the front of Dr. Green's door. Finding it locked, he quickly glanced around and noticed Dylan as their eyes met as he stood at the other end of the hall. The man turned quickly and left.

Dylan caught up to him, inspecting the man as he walked a safe distance behind. He followed him to the intensive care unit. The man sat down in the waiting area outside and unrolled his paper and started to read. He couldn't help wonder about his identity since he had been trying to enter Dr. Greene's office. A patient would have known the office was closed on Thursdays. Was he wrong about the identity of FM and was this the man in her appointment book? Could he be the one who beat her earlier? Did he come back to apologize?

The man dressed casually in loose tan slacks and a white dress shirt with no tie. The top buttons were open, revealing an expensive gold chain. He judged his age to be in his late forties. His wore his hair cut short, slick jet black the color of thick oil.

Their eyes met again briefly. He studied the door to the ICU as two nurses walked in. His eyes appeared as glossy as his hair and the color of obsidian. His face was surveying the area in a cool manner, listening doggedly to the conversations around him. Whatever he was doing there, it must have had something to do with a person in the intensive care. Glancing at his watch, Dylan noticed it was an expensive Rolex that had as much gold and jewels on the band to pale the brilliance of the rings on his hands. The man reeked of money.

Dylan moved through the double doors to check on Ms. James. The nurses stopped giggling and ended their conversation when he flashed his shield and asked about Jennica.

"The man sitting just outside in the waiting area, do you know him?" Dylan said.

"No. We just came back from a break. I've never seen him before. Have you, Debby?"

The other young woman casually strolled to the glass, looked out, and studied the lobby. She turned back and sat down. "No, I haven't seen him before."

"So, what's this all about? Who is he? A movie star? He looks like he could be, he's so tall, dark, and handsome, kind of like yourself, officer."

"Debby." The other girl gave her a nudge. Her face blushed cranberry red.

"Excuse me, I was out of line. Don't arrest me." She gave him a coy smile and giggled innocently.

"I don't know who he is, or I wouldn't have came in here to ask, now would I? I was hoping you could tell me," Dylan said, grinning a bit.

"Why do you need to know?"

"Because it's my business to know. You have a patient in here that's being guarded, or haven't you noticed? Pay attention to your jobs in here please, it is very important that you do. How many patients are in here?"

"Only two. The James woman and a young boy."

"Keep an eye on him. If he tries to come in here, page me. Here's my number."

Dylan went to Jennica's room and talked with the guard, then stepped in to see her. Her color looked better. She had a little pink in her cheeks. He touched her hand. It felt warmer. Feeling movement under his hand, he looked in her face. Her eyes fluttered open, reminding him of blue diamonds. They stared through him, then shut.

Jennica moved her lips slightly. A sound like a whisper escaped.

The intercom buzzed loudly over his head. "Rob Browning please, dial extension 2020."

Dylan jumped when he recognized the name. He ran out of the room past the two nurses. As he reached the doors, he noticed the man had left. He turned to an elderly man sitting at the volunteer's desk outside the waiting area doing a crossword puzzle. "Sir, can you tell me whose extension is 2020?"

He grasped at some papers, flipping through several pages before he stopped. He looked over the top of his bifocals and pointed at the name. Dylan bent so he could hear him.

"Dr. Greene, MD, Psychiatric Services, room 2020 on the second floor."

"Thank you." He spun around and immediately headed back to Dr. Greene's office.

He reached it and entered by the back entrance with the key she had given him. Quietly he stepped over to the door of her private office and stopped to listen. Finally, he heard a door open and noticed light seeping out from under it. He stepped to the side, realizing she must have let him in through the front door.

He let himself out and went around the front to the reception area and peeked around the corner making sure no one waited for them. Quickly, he slid along the wall, working his way past the reception window and towards the hall to the examination rooms. Peering around the corner toward her office, he saw that the door was open and the light on.

Easing himself down the wall, he got close enough to eavesdrop on their conversation.

"Ms. James is still on our critical list. She's still in grave danger," Dr. Greene said. "No one is allowed in to see her unless they're her immediate family. Even then, it's still supervised by a law enforcement officer because of the attempt on her life. The person responsible for this is still not in custody."

"What if I were to tell you I was her husband?" the man said.

"I'd say Jennica James isn't married." She noticed his large dark eyes probing hers, and heard desperation in his voice. A plea to bargain to spend a few minutes in Jennica's room.

"Jennica and I are married. It's not a public record, but true. Our wish was to keep it secret. It's imperative at this point not to have it public knowledge. Please, it would help her."

"I'm sorry. I'd need more proof than your word on a matter as serious as this, Mr. Browning. A marriage certificate, maybe?"

"What? You think that I carry it with me?"

"I would, if I had a secret to prove. I have to follow certain protocols. It doesn't allow secret husbands to slip in unattended, I'm afraid. Without proof it's just the request of a desperate man, maybe one that wants to do her more harm than good."

"What are you saying?" His voice deepened, losing the controlled English and slipped into an accent. "That's ridiculous. If I wanted to harm her, I would have done it by now. You think a rent-a-cop posted outside her door would stop a real killer? Think again. I wouldn't be showing my face and asking for your permission. Please, I'm begging you. I want to do this for her. Can't you understand that? I need your okay. I want to be on the right side of the law, if you'll allow me. I'm not going to harm her. I just want a moment alone with her."

"I hear the conviction in your voice. Even if I believed your story and understood your situation, I couldn't do anything about it without clearing you first. I'm very sorry. It's not my call."

Dylan praised Dr. Greene for holding her own against a man so obviously used to getting his own way. A man desperate to obtain his wishes could be dangerous. If his suspicions were right, Mr. Browning was toxic. Dr. Greene put herself in harm's way by meeting him alone in her office.

Rob Browning secretly married to Jennica James. It could help to explain a few things. A solid connection between the two would rule out a coincidence.

Now that the elusive Rob Browning had appeared, he needed to have that conversation with him. Suspecting he had just learned a hell of a lot more from their conversation than he ever would when he questioned him, he kept listening. If he were telling the truth to Dr. Greene, it would place him into position as their prime suspect. He'd try and run down that marriage certificate.

It was supposedly Browning's gun that shot Jennica. If it turned out the two were married, it was a perfect situation for him to get away with murder. No one would tie the two together, if he suddenly didn't want to be married to her. She certainly couldn't tell the world she was his wife. The job was botched and she lay in a coma. She might survive and she might not. He had to plan for all the contingencies.

Why would he want her killed? Perhaps she found out something that she shouldn't have about certain business practices to do with the cabin and the warehouse up the canyon, his operation. Whatever it was, she became dispensable to him when she put her nose where she shouldn't have. He needed to find out exactly what his operation really entailed.

Dylan suspected Rob Browning was prospering in something illegal. Secrecy was of utmost importance to keep him alive and free from what little he observed that night. If she uncovered her husband's covert operation, it would explain why she had to be taken out.

The plan made sense. Leave town, leave your gun, and have it stolen and used in a shooting. Contract a hit on her, and when it came down to him being a suspect, it looked like it was too easy, a setup. He couldn't be so stupid as to use his own gun?

He eliminated his problem and can continue his business as usual.

Dylan brought his head up as he heard Dr. Greene's name paged over the speaker again. It must be Diana. He tiptoed down the hall as he heard Dr. Greene tell Browning she had a call to respond to in the ER. He slipped back down the hall and hid behind the reception window. She led him out to the front of the lobby. A bell tinkled above, signaling their departure.

Dr. Greene hesitated at the door. "I'm sorry, Mr. Browning, I need to call my associate. If you'll excuse me."

Dylan melded his body against the wall. He hoped she didn't come around and find him hiding. His pager vibrated on his hip, alerting him to her call. He heard her frustration as she replaced the phone in its cradle.

"Mr. Browning? We're finished here. I trust you can find your way back to the main wing alone?"

"I trust I can, Dr. Greene, but you'll be seeing me again. I don't give up easily."

Dylan heard her pick up the receiver and slam it back down again and swear. A few minutes passed before he heard the bell above the door sound and the door being locked. She had finally left. He felt relieved at not getting caught, but mad that he never got to see Rob Browning's face. The only way he could identify him if he ran into him was by the faint Latino accent apparent in his voice.

He ran out the back and down the stairwell to the hall. It led to the Emergency Room. He would catch her and cut her off at the pass. She turned the corner as he ran out of from the stairwell. He grabbed her and pulled her into the swinging doors of the day surgery unit.

"Dylan. Thank God. Diana is waiting in the ER for me. I just tried paging you."

"I know. You gave up on me too fast. I tried to commandeer a telephone from a grouchy nurse in ICU, but she said it was against the rules. Emergency lines only, cop or no cop. How do you like that?"

"Policies have to be followed."

"I can understand all that, but she directed me to the pay telephone down the hall. I realized I didn't have any change."

"You'd better get moving. Go in the back way. Here's my key."

"I still have yours, remember?"

"Thanks for reminding me. Now get going, please. You're making me nervous. She can't see us together here. I'm crossing my fingers until she's in my office safe and sound."

"Thanks, Cait."

Dylan watched as she walked through the doors of the ER. He quickly organized his thoughts while hurrying to her office. Dr. Green's office proved easy to slip in unnoticed. He'd just proved it could be done successfully.

Chapter 35

Thursday, the 12th day of September

"Diana, I'm so glad you're here," Dr. Greene said. "If you'll follow me, I'll take you to my office where we can get comfortable, and go over your tests."

Her lips drawn into a thin line, Diana nodded her head and followed as Dr. Greene led her through the Emergency Room.

"Excuse me, Dr. Greene?" A young male nurse called to her from behind the counter at the emergency room desk.

"Yes?"

"A few minutes ago a visitor found a man lying unconscious on the floor in the chapel. When we arrived, he was incoherent and thrashing about in distress, speaking nonsense. He never opened his eyes or regained total consciousness. We looked for identification on him, but found none. We admitted him to your wing for evaluation. A real nut case."

"A nut case? Do you like working here?"

"Yes."

"Then I'd highly recommend you not refer to any patient that way again."

"I didn't mean anything by it. I just—"

"Just don't let it happen again." Dr. Greene felt her legs wobble underneath her as she grasped the counter. An instant wave of nausea took over her body. She felt her hands and forehead start to perspire. She needed time to think. What else could go wrong today? "I'm on my way to my office. I have a patient scheduled right now for a consultation. You'll need to call in someone else." She felt her hands tremble. Letting them fall, she placed them into the coat of her examining jacket.

"I tried Dr. Laffnesse, but he's had a family emergency and must have already left. I saw you here and just thought, well, you were here already. You're the doctor on call?"

"Yes, I am, tomorrow and the weekend. But today, I'm suppose to be off." A hysterical laugh leaped from her throat. "I'm sorry, but this person standing over there drove from Billings to see me. I'll be down after this consultation. Did the doctor that first responded to the patient medicate him?"

"Yes, they had to. We put him in full restraints."

"Good. Monitor him closely and put a nurse in the room until I can get there."

"It's a done deal." The nurse smiled back at her.

"See that it is," she snapped back. She turned quickly, motioning Diana to follow her. They walked in silence to the elevator. She hesitated, looking back at the ER. It had to be Frank.

The elevator door opened and they stepped inside. Dr. Greene wanted to speak, but couldn't find the right words to begin. Before she knew it, the doors opened and she found herself walking out of the elevator with Diana following her. She unlocked the door leading to her private office. She noticed the light was on, stepped aside, and let Diana slip by her. "Have a seat, I'll just go get us some coffee."

Diana turned at the door. "Dr. Greene, I'd just rather get on with this. I don't need any coffee." She took a seat on the couch.

"Then I'll be right back with your file. I'll just be a sec."

The bathroom door opened and Detective Drake walked out, surprising both women. Dylan threw her a smile from across the room.

"Ladies," he said.

"Detective Drake? What are you doing here?"

"I needed to hear the rest of your story." He sat down next to her as Dr. Greene left.

"Then this is a set up? Dr. Greene isn't going to tell me I'm dying of some rare disease? Damn it. I just drove like a mad woman to get here and talk to her. My grandmother is sick and—"

"Calm down. I think you need to hear this Diana." Dylan stood quickly, switching to the chair opposite the couch, so he could maintain eye contact. He scooted closer to her until they were almost touching. "Your life may be in danger. I don't want the same thing to happen to you that has happened to Jennica. The only way I can keep that from happening is for you to talk to me. I need you to tell me the rest of the story you were going to tell me. Do you understand?"

Diana paled. She bit down on her lip, picking on her nails, and stared at him from her seat. "I can't understand any of this. I want to get back to Billings." She started to rise from the couch.

Dylan jumped up, leaning over her, gently touching both of her shoulders. He eased her back down. "Wait. Give me a moment, please. I need your help. Jennica needs your help. Have you forgotten her?"

"Of course I haven't forgotten her. I just can't help you. I don't know anything."

"I think you do. I think you know lots of things. I think you may be the only person that knows something that can help me."

"What makes you so sure?" She glared back at him, her deep blue eyes penetrating his.

"My gut instincts tell me. I became a detective because I'm good at what I do, and I'm good at reading people. Your body language tells me volumes, without you even speaking. Did you know that? I can tell you're really scared, and it's not because you're scared of me."

"Damn right I'm scared." She hopped out of the couch like a rabbit bounding for the door. Dylan reached her as she grabbed for the handle. He stepped in front of her and blocked her way.

"Then I hope you'll tell me why, so I can protect you." He searched her eyes as they glared at him with all the intensity of a storm brewing, changing color from light to dark blue.

"Please, let me go. I have to get back to my grandmother."

"I can't just let you go. If you know something, you need to tell me. Tell me now, before I have to drag it out of you. I can bring you in as a suspect in this you know. A conspiracy to murder."

"What? How dare you threaten me. I haven't done anything. I don't know who shot Jennica, or why. That's the question I've been asking myself over and over."

"Finish the story you started to tell me then." He kept his eyes pinned to hers and waited.

She turned quickly, dropping her hand off the door handle, and walked to the couch. He followed as she turned again and bumped into his chest.

"I'm past being scared. I know I'm going to die if you make me tell you."

She fell into his arms, and buried her head in his chest. He held her shaking body tightly until the calm returned. Then she would tell him her tale.

Dr. Greene rushed out of her office and down to the psychiatric wing, trying to formulate a plan in her mind. Frank had snapped. She didn't know how to put him back together again. His psyche shattered into a thousand different pieces. She needed to find one person in his mind that she could recognize, and bring him back to her. Fright took over her aching body as the thoughts of him overwhelmed her for the hundredth time since that afternoon. As each uneasy step took her closer to him, she worried at what she would find when she entered his room. She braced herself for the worse as she entered.

The attendant acknowledged the doctor's entrance with a nod. Dr. Greene gazed over at the person in the bed. He lay on a narrow hospital bed wrapped in white restraints at the hands, feet, legs, arms, and around the middle of his chest. His eyes remained closed. Her fear heightened. Her throat constricted. "Nurse, I'll be a few minutes if you want to take a break." She turned toward the patient, her anxiety level heightened as she touched him, checking his vital signs. It was Frank.

Della checked her watch and anxiously waited for Dylan to arrive. He promised to take her home, and they finally decided to let her check out at three o'clock. She waited for him all day leaving several messages for him that had not been returned. She hated waiting. Mrs. Drake sat up reading a magazine, adding her comments in here and there, as Della half listened. She'd had her fill of the hospital. Her only wish was to leave with Dylan soon and to never return as a patient again. She needed to get back to work. Dylan needed her, even though he would never admit it to her. Their case was getting colder as she just laid around getting fat from no exercise.

"What do you think is keeping Dylan?" Mrs. Drake said, as she eyed Della.

"I hope nothing. He'll be here. He said he would. A few more minutes and he'll be here. I know it."

"Then why don't you relax and set your bag down. You're starting to worry me. I thought it was strange that Dylan hasn't been in at all today after he left you early this morning. Now you have me wondering."

"Worry you? I'm sorry. I didn't realize I looked so anxious."

"You look like someone on death row waiting to hear from his lawyer about his appeal."

"That's about how I feel. I miss my dog. I want to go home and be with him."

"Is that all?"

"Not exactly."

"I didn't think so."

Diana turned her head towards Dylan, brushing her hair back from her eyes. "I guess I'll never get out of here and back to my grandmother, until I tell you everything I know about this damn story," she said.

"You're a smart woman. Did anyone come here with you?" Dylan said.

"No."

"Good. Does anyone in your band know you're here?"

"No. No one knows I left Billings today."

"Good. Then we have plenty of time for you to finish your story."

"No, I don't. My grandmother doesn't even know that I left. She still expects me sometime today."

"We'll get you there, safe and sound. Don't worry. I need to make a quick call to my partner, Detective Bishop. Come and sit down. I'll be just a minute." Dylan strolled down the hall, looking for Dr. Greene. He grabbed the reception telephone and dialed Della's room.

"Dylan? Where are you?" Della said.

"I'm upstairs with Diana."

"Diana Edwards?"

"Yes, of course, the very one. What other Diana would there be?"

"It's hard telling with you, Don Juan."

"Thanks, sweetheart. Anyway, she's going to tell me the rest of her story, and I'd like you to come up for it. Do you think you can, or do you want to wait for me?"

"Of course I can. I've been waiting all day to see you as it is."

"And a wait worth waiting for, don't you think? I've been quite busy."

"I'm sure you have been, Detective. All in the name of justice, right?"

"Darlin, I don't have time to mince words with you right now, but I thought I'd get Cait to wheel you up here, but she must have left."

"I can get up there. Just give me five minutes. I'll send your mother your warmest regards while I'm at it."

"Will you? How kind, thanks. You're a real doll."

"Don't I know it. See you soon."

He paged Cait. He needed her to do one more favor for him.

"Dr. Greene."

"Cait. I have to ask you to do one more thing. Please stall Rob Browning until I can get finished here. Do anything to keep him here.

If he leaves, I may not be able to question him. I need to. He may be my link to this whole thing."

"How did you know?"

"I just know. I'll fill you in later. Just keep him busy."

"I already let him go. I don't know where he is right now."

"Go find him, please. Find him and detain him if you can. He probably went back to the ICU."

"I'll do my best."

Crossing his fingers, Dylan hurried to Cait's office before Diana got any ideas to run again.

Chapter 36

Thursday, the 12th day of September

"Detective Bishop will be here shortly," Dylan said. "You met her the night we visited your house."

"Yes, I remember. Scott blew up in her face. I heard about it later."

"Yes, he did. I sensed more anger in him than most people direct at us as investigators, under the circumstances. He's a time bomb with his fuse already lit."

"I know. He's dealing with some problems right now. It hasn't been easy for him with Jennica gone. He felt bad after you left."

"Good. He should have. Are any of his problems pertinent to this investigation?"

"No, not directly, I don't think."

"I have no room for doubts here. You said you don't think. Let me be the judge."

"It's just that Jennica and Scott were really close. This shooting has stripped him of his good judgment. He's worried about her, that's all."

"Did you know Jennica is married?"

Diana laughed. She dropped her head back. Her long blonde hair whipped back and forth as she brought her facial expression back under control. She closed her mouth, covering it with both hands and looked at the stern expression covering Dylan's face. "You're serious?" she said.
"I am. What if she is?"

"She's not. To Scott? That's funny. Really funny."

"Why do you say that? You just told me they were close and wanted to keep it a secret. Maybe they got married and kept it a secret even from you."

"That's ludicrous. She isn't in this thing with Scott for love. Just for sex. With Josh it was different. She's mentally attached to Josh, if you want to know the truth."

"You're telling me she's using Scott for sex, while in love with Josh?"

"No, I'm not saying that at all. I really don't think Jennica can love anybody in that sense of the word, but she's closest to Josh. They can talk to each other about anything."

"It doesn't sound like that to me."

"Well, almost anything. Jennica likes men. I'll concede that it's a power trip. She doesn't want to marry anybody. I know that. She's made that point to me more than once."

A light knock came from the door. Diana's head turned quickly towards the door. A cat couldn't have been more nervous than she appeared ready to spring from the couch and flee.

"It's just my partner. Relax." He stood up. "It's open. I'm sorry, but this conversation is exceptionally important in this investigation. It puts a motive behind everyone in your band, including yourself."

"I've had enough, Detective Drake. I was on stage when she was shot. I saw her fall. I couldn't have shot her."

Della wheeled herself inside. "No, but you could've hired someone to do it," she said.

"That's it, I'm leaving." She stood, her pale face suddenly rosy. Her top lip feverishly biting on her lower lip. She sailed towards the door. Dylan lunged and caught her arm, grasping it tightly.

"Not until you tell me the rest of your story," he said. "I can't wait any longer. If I have to drag it out of you, I will. If it makes you feel any better, I don't really believe you arranged to have Jennica shot, but I believe your eyes are wide open and you just might go to her room and finish the job someone started after you leave here. She's slept with Perry also, and that's why you're so bitching mad at me. You want to poke my eyes out for opening up yours. You can thank me later."

She reached out and slapped his face so hard, his head jolted backwards. He recovered from the shock and massaged his jaw with his left hand, while still holding her firmly with his right. His eyes narrowed. He kept his breathing under control and faced her.

"The truth sometimes hurts, so I'll excuse you because I know you're in pain. Now, if you'll sit back down, we can get on with it." He released her arm, pulling her into the couch with him.

"You son of a bitch." She turned her face away, the fire in her eyes danced to a savage beat. She faced Dylan square again, going off like a banshee, swinging her fists furiously towards his chest as she yelled at him, "I hate you, you bastard. I hate you for making me feel this way. All of you goddamn men are, is a bunch of pigs. You're all assholes."

Protecting his head and eyes, Dylan let her beat on him like it was open season. She finally slowed down her slapping until she broke down and fell in his lap and cried. Dylan knew she needed to lash out, and he let himself be the target. Dylan let his shield down, glancing at Della. He placed his hand protectively on top of her head and stroked her hair. "It's all true, I know. But this pig isn't the enemy. I want to help."

He turned his eyes towards Della and grinned. He included himself in that category and conveyed the message clearly with his eyes, that all men were alike. Complete assholes, with a capital A. One day she'd agree with him.

"Ms. Edwards, I'm sorry," Della said. Here, have a tissue. We can wait until you're ready to talk again. You have to excuse Detective Drake. He's over zealous at times, and I think this is one of those times. I'm sorry I wasn't here from the beginning. I would have prevented him from crossing that line with you."

"I would like to get this over with," Diana said. "I have a sick grandmother back in Billings." She rubbed her eyes.

"That's what we all want, so let's begin. I believe you left off at finding something out after your suspicions were raised after the barbecue up at the Tate home in Kelly Canyon. Why don't you pick it up from there." Dylan turned the recorder on and pulled his notebook out.

Della followed suit and started taking notes as Diana began her story.

"I dogged Perry, Scott, Josh, and Taylor, trying to get them to open up to me. I felt they all were hiding something. They kept eluding my questions and ignoring me. I finally let them think I gave up and changed my strategy. I don't like secrets. I can keep them, but they always have a way of turning sour on you. So, like I said, I started following them. One night it led me to the north side of town on a dead-end road, to a warehouse down there. It was dark as the ace of spades on that side of town, and felt spooky. Vehicles surrounded the building and were parked on both sides of the road.

"I spotted the band's van and couldn't believe it. I parked and checked it out. Before I knew it, a crazy woman grabbed me. She yelled for help. A few men came out from the sides of the building and brought me in. They dragged me to the front of the building where it looked like a meeting was taking place. They accused me of being a reporter trying to get a story with my own agenda in mind. They told me I was trespassing on private property. I was pushed to the front, facing a panel of seven men.

"I turned my head to the side. That's when I saw Scott, Josh, Taylor and Perry sitting in the front row. I saw surprise on their faces, but no one acknowledged that they knew me. Not one of them said a thing. I felt hurt by it, but then turned back to the panel. On the panel, Mr. Tate sat, staring at me in disgust. I decided I'd keep quiet. They searched me and then bombarded me with questions. I was in shock."

"What questions did they ask you?" Dylan said.

"Who sent me to spy on them. Which of the media I represented, local, state, or national? Where was my recording device and photography equipment hidden? They sent one of the men holding me to search my vehicle.

"I lied when they asked me my name. I left my purse at home when I left in such a hurry to follow Scott, so I didn't have any identification on me for them to find. I tried looking around the room to see if I could recognize any other faces in the crowd, but one of the men standing next to me jerked my head back to face the panel. He leaned over and told me to pay attention and answer the questions.

"After they didn't find what they were looking for, they asked me what I was doing snooping around. I told them I was from out of town and took a wrong turn. I was looking for the house I was staying at. I saw all the cars and thought I could borrow a telephone. They finally let me go."

"So, you must have found out what was going on inside?"

"I'm not sure I did, but I did find out a few things. When I left, I drove straight home. My hands and body were still shaking when I arrived. I felt drained, and never so exposed as that night. I sing on stage to thousands of people and have never felt that way. I couldn't believe they all sat there while I was being humiliated in front of all these people. I went home and locked my bedroom door and took a long hot shower. I went to bed furious.

"Later, I found out that Mr. Tate belonged to a group of men from this valley calling themselves the Sons of the Pioneers."

"Sons of the Pioneers? That name sounds familiar," Della said.

"It's a name used in many places, even in Bozeman. The historical society has used a similar name, but this isn't the same."

"Like Daughters of the Revolution? I've heard of that group back east. They put on shows depicting historical events during Revolutionary times. Don't women belong, too? I thought the name was Sons and Daughters of the Pioneers?" Della said.

"Could be, I didn't get a history lesson. Just that it was a group of men that formed back in the late 1800's when this valley was first incorporated into a city. The members are all direct descendants of the founding fathers of the settlers from this area. They have to be, it's the first rule of their secret society. An exclusive membership. It dates back to when Montana was still a territory.

"Its members are secret and many it appeared. It's far from the historical society group. In this society, a secret group of men are appointed to watch over the community as sort of vigilantes, stemming from their great-grandfathers', grandfathers', and fathers' own days. They keep the peace under their own written code, established back in the late 1800's.

"They keep the outsiders with their crazy ideas out of the county. They infiltrate groups, and then tear them apart before they get out of hand. It's an overwhelming job these days."

"Don't tell me these are the Freemen?"

"No. That's one group they adamantly oppose. They believe in local government and want to protect its integrity. After all, it was their ancestors who built the city. They were elected as some of the first judges, county attorneys, and commissioners all throughout the county. Where do you think all the names of the streets came from? The founding fathers, of course. They're protecting their family heritage.

"They believe in paying taxes, license plates, and supporting their community. Without money to run it, it would deteriorate quickly and rot with these so called Freemen and militia movements running in, denouncing government officials and charging them with million dollar fines. The Sons of the Pioneers are like having your own county CIA agents. You never know they're there, but you can guess they got it covered."

"I can't believe this. Why would they have a meeting in some old warehouse full of people, and shake you down?"

"That's just it, it wasn't a meeting of the Sons of the Pioneers, it was a meeting of the local chapter of the militia. The woman that grabbed me was actually one of their so-called leaders. I tell you, I had one look into her smoky black eyes and I saw the madness."

"What was her name?"

"I didn't get it. I didn't get to ask any questions."

"You said Mr. Tate sat on a panel up front?"

"That's right, I did. Because he's on their board. They've infiltrated them. Now, they are going to exterminate them. They know who they are. That's why I'm scared."

"Why should you be scared of the militia, or these so called Sons of the Pioneers?"

"Because I know their plan. I know the members of both groups. They all saw me that night. I believe they've made a plan to get rid of me. I look so much like Jennica that maybe it was me they were trying to kill that night. We're always being mistaken for one another."

"Which group are you accusing of putting a price on your head?" Dylan said.

"I'm afraid the Sons of the Pioneers. I don't think the militia would care if they found out who I really was, do you? They would probably chalk it up to a curious civilian. They let the public in their meetings, advertise in the paper. It's not against the law to be a militia member. They claim everyone is a member of the militia in the state, if you're a citizen. You just have to sign in at the door and sit down. They just don't like people lurking around outside of the meeting like I was, trying to get a story and making bad press. They have enough of that as it is."

"I don't understand. You said you knew the Sons of the Pioneers plan. I think a secret organization operating since the 1800's that has never been exposed by now would be a little more discreet in who it tells its plans to." Dylan wiped at his brow, watching Diana fidget with the button on her shirt. He didn't believe anyone would let her know the real story. It was so farfetched in his mind that he decided she must really be gullible to take that as the gospel truth.

"I don't understand all of it either. That's just what I was told," Diana said.

"Who told you?"

"I can't tell you that. I just know Scott and Josh have known about this since they were old enough to understand. You don't automatically become a member when you turn of age, but they're groomed from childhood to participate. They go through extensive education and training. Scott and Josh both have degrees. They disappointed their dad when they chose to form this band and left town. Strangers are invading and taking over the state and local governments. It's hard to pass something like a secret society off these days on your kids. They're much more interested in world events than what's happening in their own backyards."

"Okay, so, we have our own little original western Mafia or something like that here. Do they actually commit crimes like murder to accomplish their goals?"

"No. They never have. They use all the legal arenas where they hold the power. They're everywhere they need to be. That's why Mr. Tate is getting in deeper with the militia. He's further up than the local chapter. It's probably been a plan in the works for years, before we ever started hearing about the militias and the freemen movements."

"You said Mr. Tate was going to exterminate them all. That sounds like murder to me."

"I did say that because I was told they tear them apart piece by piece, exposing their ignorance of the laws and all that they stand for. Eventually, they'll be looking for another state to hide in instead of being put behind bars for a long time here. The movements don't have any credibility, and all that they've tried to gain will back fire in their faces like it has so far, thanks to them.

"Nothing has happened here in Gallatin County that they didn't want to happen in all these years. It makes sense, if you study the history of this place. You start realizing why a small town like Bozeman has taken so long to develop the kind of problems that other states have been dealing with for years. They're the enforcers that keep it all away

"It sounds like a line of bullshit to me. You don't believe all of this, do you?"

"I do."

"You told me on one hand, they do everything legally, but then you told me you thought they might have put a hit out on your head because of your knowledge of their secret society."

"I did. Organizations with their own agendas, including our own government, always contain some unhappy person or minority within them that doesn't agree with everything that's done. They end up taking justice into their own hands to find an end to their own means. They operate out of that group on their own accord. I've been convinced that is the case here. Someone didn't like me knowing about this, and decided on their own it would be in the best interest of the society if they got rid of me."

"That would give them real power. To uphold the law while a renegade group, operating under the same society does their own vigilante justice. Sounds like someone has been reading too many dime store novels about the old West to me."

"You wanted to hear it. That's what I found out." She picked at her fingernails.

"So, assuming all of this is believable, which I'm having a hard time swallowing, you think this whole shooting happened because of you? Why, then didn't that person decide to take Perry and Taylor out, if that's correct?"

"Because they are part of the society. I don't really know, but that's why I think they're watching me."

"Don't you think they would have finished the job, realizing they shot the wrong woman?"

"That's what I'm scared of. It's still early. Jennica was shot less than a week ago."

"I know, but it's a little like doggie years in cop time. A week is a long time with no suspects in custody. The evidence is fading quickly, and if we don't get on the right trail soon," Dylan glanced down at his watch as he turned the page in his notebook.

Della cleared her throat. "Diana, we need to know who told you this information. We need to verify your story."

"I'm sorry, I can't answer that. I don't know how to contact him, or his true identity. All I know is this man is in deep, and knows the truth about the situation. I believed everything."

"This is important. You're telling me you can't get us in touch with this man."

"No," Diana said.

"How do you know he wasn't feeding you false information."

"Why would he? He has no reason to."

"Do you know Rob Browning?" Dylan said. Her eyes remained clear and motionless. He wanted to see if the name brought about a reaction, since she was Jennica's best friend, and possibly the keeper of deeper secrets.

"No. I don't recall hearing that name before. Rob Browning? Should I?"

"According to Mr. Browning, he's Jennica's husband."

Diana's eyes and mouth opened as wide as the Montana sky, stunning her into silence. Della's pen slipped from her hand and onto the floor. She retrieved it, staring at Dylan in disbelief.

"You're free to go. Drive safely back to Billings. If you think of anything else, call. If you notice anything unusual pick up the phone. Your life may be in danger, as well as the rest of your band. Until we figure this out, we'll go under that assumption. Take all precautions to stay safe and don't advertise your location to anyone. We will be investigating what was said today." He pulled the door open wide and waved her through.

Chapter 37

Thursday, the 12th day of September

Dr. Greene marched down the hall towards the Intensive Care Unit, hoping to find Rob Browning there; her thoughts raced ahead trying to find a way to hold him for Dylan. Letting him see Jennica, and spend time with her, would be the only way that she could guarantee he would stay. It's just that helping Dylan, and letting Mr. Browning see Jennica, meant a breach in hospital security and protocol. It could get her dismissed from the hospital and it might cause her to lose her license in the State of Montana.

Shaking her head, it disgusted her to think how easily she would throw her entire life away for him. Stopping in her tracks, she berated herself for being the queen of fools. That price was a price she wasn't willing to pay for anybody, not even for Dylan. Browning wasn't her problem. None of that was. Why was she teetering along that precarious line for him? She asked herself over and over what spell he had put on her to make her act that out of character. She decided to think of something else to keep Browning long enough for Dylan to catch up.

Hearing her name being paged to go to the third floor, her heart stopped. She couldn't deal with that, not now. Needing time to think, she fled, ignoring the page. Hearing her name three more times throughout the hospital, she retreated quickly into the bathroom.

Covering her ears tightly, she blocked out the sounds of the intercom. She pushed open an empty stall, slamming it behind her. Heaving, she held onto the cold porcelain bowl, gripping it for dear life. Sweat ran down her temples, mixing with her tears. She brought her head up, willing the tears to disappear. "Leave me alone," she shrieked, as she turned and hit the back of the stall. It swung open to her surprise.

"Dr. Greene? Are you all right?" A perplexed sounding voice said to her. She looked up to find a floor nurse she worked closely with staring back at her.

"I'm fine now." She cleared her throat, giving the nurse a coy smile. "I think I must be catching that flu bug going around already."

"They have been paging you for the last twenty minutes. That man you admitted on three disappeared."

"What? How could he? He was heavily medicated and restraints were in place. For God's sake he was in lockdown."

"I know. The other nurses are calling him Houdini."

"Great. Did they search the floor thoroughly? He couldn't have gone far and gotten out." She bored her eyes straight into Pat's before she gave into the flashing nightmare fleeting through her last thought. "Could he?"

"Looks like it. They're still searching, but there seems to be no sign of him. Like I said, he's some magician, pulling an escape act like that from there. The only person that has come and gone through the locked doors was a doctor with clearance. Not one person saw him try to leave."

"What was the doctor's name?"

"I don't know. I wasn't there. I just heard about it. You'll have to ask Jess when you get up there."

"Thanks. This is turning out to be one hell of a day," she said as she ran out.

Dr. Greene retreated, running to her office for cover. Everyone was probably looking for her. The whole situation whirled out of control. Maybe it was best he did escape. She had his address in her file and she could pursue that on her own.

The Detectives still sat talking in Dr. Greene's office.

Dr. Greene walked in, moving straight past them and into the bathroom, slamming the door.

Dylan leaped to the door. "Cait? Cait, are you all right?"

"I'm fine, but I need my office. Something has come up." She reached in the medicine cabinet for some tranquilizers. Her fingers trembled as she pried off the lid. She kept a few meds around for her patients in case of an emergency situation. That seemed like an emergency worth breaking into her stash for, except she always thought she would have to use them on a patient, not to medicate herself.

"Okay. We were just finishing up. You sure you're all right?" Dylan said. "Cait. We'll leave when you come out. I need to ask you about Rob Browning."

She opened the door slightly and looked through the crack. "I couldn't find him. I think he must have left."

"What's the matter?"

"Nothing." She stepped past him to her desk and acknowledged Della with a nod. Sitting down, she dialed a hospital extension of four numbers.

"This is Dr. Greene." She kept her head staring down at the swirls in the wood on her oak desk. "I know. Have they found him?" She looked up at the detectives still standing inches from her, listening. She covered the receiver. "Do you two mind?"

"No." Dylan said, quickly scanning the area. "Not at all. We were just leaving. Thanks for the use of your office."

The two walked down to exit out the front door of her offices. "How do you feel?" Dylan said.

"I feel fine. I think I look better than she does too, " Della said.

"My thoughts exactly. And if I told you the rest of what I suspect, you'll just say I'm pathetic. So, I'll just take you home. I have to find Rob Browning."

"Wait. I know I've been laid up for a couple of days, but where did you come up with Rob Browning being married to Jennica?"

"He said it today in the hospital talking to Cait. I don't know that it's true, but if it is, it could explain a few things. Let's get you home and into your own bed."

"Not so fast, Drake. I'm part of this, and I want to finish it. Just because I have one broken bone doesn't mean I have to lie down and play dead. I'm going with you, because I know what you plan to do. You need me there."

"No I don't. You're on a hiatus."

"Says who?"

"Says the Captain, that's who. He told me I already reached my limit on risking your life for this week." He winked at her, watching her violet eyes fire up instantly. She flexed her spine and leaned forward to give him her usual grief.

"Now, Della. Please, don't. You need rest. I could wait until you're better, then we could go back up to the cabin, but by then the trail will be cold. Hell, it will be an ice jam. I have to do this tonight. I can't wait until tomorrow. I'm going up there and I don't need backup because I'm not going to be sneaking around this time. I'm just going to talk with him, that's all. He knows I'm coming."

"So, take me then. I shouldn't have to do any fancy foot work."

"And if it turns out bad, then what? I don't think I can carry you out of there while dodging bullets."

"Get off of it, Dylan. Stop right now. If you don't take me, then I'll get in my car and follow you up there."

"Not if I tie you up first."

"Very funny. You'd like that, wouldn't you?"

"Maybe. If I were you, I wouldn't tempt me."

"Come on. You're wasting our time. Rob Browning might get away while we're sitting here debating the issue. I win, you lose, let's go."

"No," he said.

"Okay, you heard your option." She stood up and walked away from him, a proud strut in her hobble as she touched down and her bad ankle bore the weight.

Dylan followed at her slow pace. Untying his necktie, he let it hang loose around his neck. Reaching and unbuttoning his black pouch, he brought his handcuffs out quietly. He methodically reached for Della's left wrist, grasping it firmly, bending her arm backwards. He slapped the first cold cuff around it.

"What are you doing?" Della tried jerking away from him. "This better be a joke."

He deftly latched the other cuff tightly, satisfied with himself for acting quickly to her bold act of insubordination. "No joke, partner. I'm taking you into custody. I hope you understand. It's for your own safety." He leered at her as she wiggled her body in agitation. Slipping off his jacket, he wrapped it around her. He used the sleeves for leverage, like a straight jacket, helping him to pull her backward towards the wheelchair. Reaching the chair, he pulled her down into it with force.

She kept up fighting him like a fool. She had no chance to win. Cursing at him in a string of hearty words that made him cringe, he pulled his necktie off of his neck. Wadding it up, he shoved it into her open mouth in an attempt to stop the battalion of words being hurled.

Heading for the west doors, he pushed fast and hard, flashing his badge at a couple of bystanders who happened to walk by at the moment he gagged her. They scurried past the half empty parking lot to his car. Hauling his cargo that still floundered around, he reached the passenger door. Releasing the jacket, and putting it on, he walked to the front of the chair to face her fury and to take the gag out of her mouth. He couldn't contain himself any longer. He laughed hearty and loud. Seeing her like that made his day.

She reacted with a swift kick with her good foot, aiming high and hard between his legs as he stood laughing at her.

Her heavily booted foot made contact, making him double over and almost fall on top of her and the wheel chair. Falling to the side, jerking the chair backwards, he made contact with the asphalt. Moaning, he rolled over.

Rage took over, building at an alarming level. He writhed with the hot burning pains shooting up his entire body from his crotch like a rocket's red glare racing across the sky. His mind had only two thoughts. He would have to kill her, then die.

Chapter 38

Thursday, the 12th day of September

Rob Browning stood by his Jeep smoking a cigarette. Glancing at his watch, he still had some time before he needed to leave town. Crushing the cigarette out, he blew the last puff of smoke into the crisp mountain air. Turning slightly, he heard a fight. Stepping to the rear of his vehicle, he looked for the source of the noise and spotted it.

A man lying prone to the ground pushed himself up with one hand, holding his groin with the other. He was shouting at a woman sitting in a wheel chair. His hand moved swiftly to her face. Thinking he was about to strike her, he instinctively jogged towards them. The man pulled a piece of cloth out of her mouth. Stopping just short of them, he watched as she spit on the ground. Yelling in his face, she matched word for word with him.

"It serves you right you arrogant son of a bitch," she said.

Her one foot was in a cast. She squirmed, standing long enough for him to see the handcuffs on her wrists. The tall man pushed her back into the seat, then came around the back of the chair and put her in a chest lock, pinning her head and neck back in the crook of his arm. Putting his mouth next to her ear, he spoke quietly into it.

The back of the man's jacket blew open as the wind gusted from the top of the hill where the hospital sat overlooking the valley. Browning picked up a silver flash. A badge hung on his belt. A carefully concealed handgun was tucked up under his armpit.

Rob turned away, to his own business at hand. He concluded that she was in his custody. Somewhere along the line, he had lost control of his prisoner. He thought he recognized the same man at the ICU earlier. Walking back towards his Jeep, he unlocked the door.

Jennica's face danced around in his mind, haunting him like a preview of a suspense thriller. Not being able to take it anymore, he finished his last thought and turned it to action. He would see her now, even if it meant exposing himself to the world. He reached under the seat and placed his forty-five into his shoulder harness beneath his white coat. Slamming the door and locking it, he confidently walked towards the hospital, formulating his plan.

Dylan released Della from his iron grip. Picking up on the man heading for the hospital entrance, he realized the form resembled the man he needed to find, Rob Browning. The height, hair color, and his clothes matched the same style and color as the man he tried to follow earlier.

"Della, shut up for a minute. I think our man Browning is still here. It looks like he just entered the hospital."

"Well, what are we waiting for? Let's go talk to him."

"I guess you do win. Let's go get him."

"Of course I win. When are you going to trust me on this?"

"Probably not until the day I die."

"You better wake up, Dylan. I don't think I can wait that long. Besides, I don't want to do hard time for killing you."

"Killing me? Why I could have saved you the trouble by killing you first back there a second ago. And don't laugh. It wasn't so funny then. It was all I could do to hold myself back from doing just that. Don't kid yourself, Della. We're poison to one another. The sooner you realize that plain and simple fact, the sooner we can get on with the rest of our lives." He hit an uneven piece of ground, almost tipping the chair. "Hold on, this is going to be one bumpy ride." He dodged potholes in the parking lot.

Dylan wheeled her into the same door he saw Browning enter, searching the hall and offices as they strolled by.

"Do you think you could take these cuffs off? I'm about to die here, already," Della said.

"I don't know. Maybe I'd better keep them on for my own protection."

"Come on." Her back hit the back of the chair, and Dylan stopped instantly.

"Okay, but you have to promise me one thing."

"What?"

"You have to promise me that after this, you'll let me take you home and you'll take the next couple of days off."

"No way."

"Then I'll just handcuff you to a chair and find Mr. Browning myself."

"Oh, no you don't. That's not fair. Come on," she pleaded, changing her voice to a whine.

Dylan cringed, hating to hear the desperation in her voice. "Promise then."

"Oh, all right. I promise."

Dylan reached behind her and took the handcuffs off. He rubbed each wrist a little as he released them. Seeing the red marks the bracelets left, he felt guilty he had used such extreme measures. Slipping them back into the case, he walked around to the side of her and squatted low and faced her. "If you ever try a stunt like that again, I'm giving you fair warning that next time, I may just have to kill you."

He followed her eyes as they met his, her long black hair swinging to one side. She never blinked, keeping her gaze steady. She cocked her head to the side. "You had it coming. Now, let's get to work."

They stared at one another stubbornly before Dylan gave the first hint of a smile. Della shot him a grin. They both laughed for a second, then Dylan pushed her down the hall and they continued to sweep the area for Rob Browning.

Rob entered the hospital and headed for Dr. Greene's office. She might think differently about the whole situation if he presented his needs in a better light. A gun in your face made all the difference in the world. Hoping she would give in, and he wouldn't have to resort to it, he prepared himself for the confrontation.

Arriving at the front of her offices, he found the door locked. Checking other doors, he found them all locked. Trying a buzzer at the back door, he waited. No one answered. Walking back to the wing where a nurse worked, monitoring rooms and telephones on the psychiatric unit, he stopped to ask her some questions.

"I need to speak with Dr. Greene. Have you seen her?"

"You too? Well, we've been trying to locate her for at least a half hour now, and she hasn't responded to her pages." She gave him a weary look. "And you are?"

"A personal friend."

Her eyebrows lifted slightly. "I see. Well, she might have gone home by now, is what I am figuring. After all, it's her day off. She just comes here every Thursday. For what reason, I don't know. I think she's lonely and doesn't have anything else in her life, but her work." She grabbed the telephone, pressing buttons. "I'll try her again. Maybe you can save her from drowning in all of this." She paged Dr. Greene while he waited.

Deciding to give her ten more minutes, he heard footsteps from behind. Turning, he faced Dr. Greene walking towards him.

He put on a guarded smile. "Dr. Greene."

"Mr. Browning."

"I need to talk with you."

"You do? I need to talk with you, also. I tried to find you after you left, but an emergency called me away again. I'm glad you didn't leave. Let's step into my office. I have to make a quick call first."

"Good." Rob followed her into the doors. She walked down the hall and into her private office as he followed her. He pulled out his gun, dangling it at his side behind his back.

Dr. Greene turned slightly. "You can wait out in the reception area. It will only be a few minutes. This call is important and can't wait."

Browning followed her and pointed the gun.

She gasped. "What are you doing?"

"I'm a desperate man, Dr. Greene. Now forget about that phone call and get back over here. You and I are taking a trip to see Jennica. You'll clear the rent-a-cop from her door long enough for me to get in to see her for ten minutes. If you give me away, I'll shoot you and whoever gets in my way. Do you understand?"

"I do. Please put that away. I'll do it without you pointing that thing at me."

"I thought you'd see it my way. I'll put it away when we get out of your office, but it will be right here in case you go against your word."

"Mr. Browning, I won't go against my word. I'll do anything you want. The last thing I want is a shootout in this hospital. I don't want to see anybody hurt. I'm a doctor. I save lives."

"I knew you were a wise lady from the first time we met. Now get over here and take me to Jennica. I'm running out of time."

Dr. Greene walked out the door, his gun aimed at her back as he followed her out of the room.

Dr. Greene heard a thud then a crash from behind her. She turned as Mr. Browning fell to the floor. A body in a white doctor's coat picked up the gun that fell from Browning's hand and turned towards her.

Feeling the room start to spin, she grabbed the high counter top at the reception window. "Frank? Frank put that down. It's Dr. Greene. Come on Frank, do you know where you are? Frank please snap out of this. You've gone too far this time. Frank," she yelled, as he started towards her, a blank look on his face.

"How dare you lock me up in your hospital. Who do you think you are?" he said.

"I didn't lock you up. They found you passed out. You snapped."

He laughed. Then his laugh became louder and louder until his eyes watered like a broken pipe. Stopping suddenly from his uncontrollable fit, he said, "I loved her."

"What are you talking about? Please put that gun down. Let's get you comfortable. We can talk. I think something happened today inside of you. We need to work this out."

"Ha. Something did happen. That's why I'm here. To finish it."

"Please Frank, don't do this. I can help you."

She started backing away from him. He slowly walked towards her, setting the gun on the tall counter as he passed it. He reached for her and pulled her towards him.

"Frank, please. Don't hurt me again. Please." She started to cry.

His eyes grew larger, watching her face in the light. Pulling her face to his, he kissed her hard. Releasing her after several minutes, he licked away her tears.

"Salty are the tears, my love." He released her, and then pushed her away. He let out a blood-curdling scream that made her ears ring. "Love is my pain." He picked the gun back up and tried handing it to her. "Here. Shoot me, please. It's the only way to end this. I can't go on like this anymore."

"Do you know me?"

"Shoot me now, or you'll be sorry for what's going to happen next."

"No, I can't shoot you. I want to help you. Please. I love you." She couldn't think of anything else to say to convince him he needed her help.

"You love me? You've only been toying with me. I don't want to play any more games with you, so just shoot me and let's get this over with."

"Frank, please, I can't." She hesitated, watching as Rob lifted his head up slowly from the floor behind them. Looking like a cat, slinking slowly and crawling down the hall, he stood, ready to leap.

Watching both men carefully, not sure what to do, she had to pick the lesser of two evils. They both were threatening her life.

Rob motioned to her to take the gun being offered.

"Okay, I'll take the gun." She reached for it, grasping the handle of the gun as he offered it to her, holding it out to her, his hand on the barrel.

The floor creaked behind them as he started to loosen his grip. Instinctively, Frank pulled the gun back towards him in a tug a war that ended with a blast.

The gun accidentally fired, blinding her with flash and leaving a ringing in her ears. Frank staggered backwards and into the wall like a crash dummy. He slid down the wall.

"Thank you, Dr. Greene," he whispered. Blood flowed from his chest, pooling on the carpet beside him.

"Oh my God." Dr. Greene froze. The horror consumed her.

"Dr. Greene, get a hold of yourself, now is not the time to lose it." Rob Browning said as he bent down, "Father Murphy?" Turning to Dr. Greene with his face full of surprise and then anguish at the identity, he said, "This is Father Murphy. What's going on here?" He felt for a pulse.

"Father Murphy?" Dr. Greene said. "What are you talking about? This is a patient of mine. His name is Frank." She knelt beside Mr. Browning, staring at his face.

Mr. Browning reached up and removed a wig "You've been had this is Father Murphy. I should know, I considered him a friend of mine."

"Oh my god, how can this be. I've been treating him for a year. I don't know how this could have happened. I've been in the same areas as Father Murphy at the hospital, but I never talked to him." Her tears were falling freely. "I never knew." She sobbed quietly, staring at the person she thought she was beginning to really know. She felt she had broken new ground with him. The startling reality of it all hit her, and she realized she didn't even begin to hit the mark. She failed him miserably and protected him to the point it hurt him. How could she be that wrong? She abruptly stood and paced.

"Father Murphy? Can you hear me?" Browning said.

"Hush, my son. God is here, talking to me. Please be quiet, so I can hear his words in my final journey home. The angels accompany him and they're so beautiful." His eyes shut, then flew open. He started screaming, "No, get away Lucifer. Get out. Leave me alone. I won't fall prey to any more of your tricks. You controlled me, making me perform your evil. Controlling my hand and eyes and closing my heart by filling my body with searing fire, making me crazy until I did your deed. I shot Jennica." He coughed, spitting up blood.

Dr. Greene spun back around towards them, hearing Jennica's name in his rambling. She knelt down to get closer. His voice became quieter, weakening from the loss of blood. "God, please listen to me. Don't leave me alone with him. You see him don't you? The devil, he took over my will, he wants me. Please, God it wasn't me. I loved her. I'm sorry, Father. Save me, please. I would have never hurt her of my own volition. I lived my life in Hell and I won't be sentenced to it for eternity." His eyes shut slowly, his chin dropped to his chest. Slumping further to the ground, his hands opened.

Rob reached over and checked his pulse. "He's dead."

"No, he can't be. Check again, please, this can't be happening. Move over, I'll try CPR."

She tried shoving Rob aside. He held her tightly. She fought him to get near the body.

"It's no use, he's gone." He released her from his grip.

She turned, staring back at Father Murphy, the sadness consuming her. "No, this can't be." Her body swayed. Running to the telephone, she dialed a number from heart. Pacing wildly waiting for her telephone to ring, she prayed Dylan would answer his page. Her prayer was answered. The phone rang.

"Detective Drake."

"Dylan, this is Cait. Come to my office now. There's been a shooting and a man is dead. Trust me when I tell you we don't need the media here if we call this one out over 911. I want you to handle this." She held her voice firm, holding in her breath. Grinding her teeth, hysteria screamed from behind her eyes, trying to take over her body.

"I'll be there in two minutes," Dylan said. He slammed the pay telephone down and turned to Della. "Let's get the hell up to Cait's office. Some man is dead and she's in deep shit by the sounds of it."

"And it's not even Saturday night," Della said.

"No time for jokes. This one is going to be big. We'll secure the scene then call it in using a secured line. Damn it, I knew something was going on with her today. Why didn't I get to the bottom of it then?"

"Because you can't save everyone. You've been busy trying to find a shooting suspect, remember? Not to mention, taking care of your partner."

"Thanks for the pep talk, but I don't need it, nor do I deserve it. We need to get there ASAP. I'm going to carry you up the stairs, instead of waiting for the elevator."

"I guess you've done it before. Just as long as you don't leave me here waiting."

"Don't worry, I won't leave you. I have a feeling I'm going to need you more than I've ever needed you on a case before. You can be the objective pair of eyes. I'm too involved."

"I thought so."

"Not the way you think. I just haven't told you everything yet."

"When are you going to start?"

"Just as soon as I can."

He abruptly stopped in front of the stairwell. "Hang on. You were out last time I tried this. You might not feel the same when I get done."

"I should hope not."

Swinging her over his shoulder, he ran up the three flights of stairs and to Dr. Greene's suite of offices. Huffing a little, he felt perspiration beading on his forehead.

"You must have gained a couple of pounds staying in the hospital." He felt a slap on his back. "Don't worry, it's good someone fed you. I know you don't feed yourself. A few pounds would look good."

Reaching the door, he slid her to the ground. He held her there briefly with his arms around her, looking into her sparkling eyes. "I don't know what we're going to find in there, but prepare yourself for the worst."

Chapter 39

Thursday, the 12th day of September 12

Dr. Greene let the detectives in, swiftly locking the door behind her. Leaning against the heavy door, her arms clasped tightly around her waist, she averted her eyes to the floor. She tried to hide her swollen and red lined eyes. "I can't believe he's dead."

Taking a hold of her hand, Dylan told her to go into her office and sit down for a moment. He'd take care of everything. Walking over to the body, he knelt down and examined it.

Della stood behind him.

"Della, get on the phone and call the Captain on his direct line. We'll need Bobby down here right away. Then call the Vet Doc and tell him he has a customer."

"The Vet Doc?" Cait sputtered looking confused.

Dylan turned, looking back up at her. "The Gallatin County Coroner. He's a retired veterinarian. He'll have to do an autopsy with the state boys on this one, I'm afraid. Cait, please move into your office. You don't need to be here listening to this. We'll be in to talk to you as soon as the others are here to take over."

"I shot him. I shot Father Murphy." Dr. Greene shook violently, her face strained against the florescent lighting in the waiting area. "I didn't know it was him."

"Don't say anything more. You'd better be thinking about calling in a lawyer before we question you. It's for your own protection."

"A lawyer? It was an accident. The gun went off." Cait bowed her head and crossed her arms tightly in front of her, sniffling and wiping at her eyes with her sleeve.

Dylan handed her a tissue. "Please call a lawyer and don't say anything else until he's with you. Do you understand what I'm saying to you?" He touched her arm cautiously. She looked up, tears streamed down her face. Blindly, she fell into his arms and sobbed quietly.

After a few seconds she turned to Dylan. "Rob Browning is here. He was here."

"Where is he?"

"He went into my office to use the bathroom. I didn't question him. His tan paled when he realized it was Father Murphy. He died in his arms. I think he's in shock. They were friends."

Dylan pulled her away, scanning the hallway. Rob Browning walked out of her office.

Both detectives turned to each other as he approached them from the hallway.

"Mr. Browning, we've been looking for you," Dylan said.

"Is that so? And why would that be?"

"We heard you were in town. We have questions about Jennica James."

"I do to. That's why I'm here."

"Good. I'm glad we finally met. It looks like we'll be detaining you for two reasons now. I can't help wonder if this isn't much more than a coincidence here."

"It's not. I can assure you of that fact." He stood eyeing them with a certain brashness for an individual who just witnessed a killing.

"I can't wait to hear your explanation, but for right now, it will have to wait. I'll transport Dr. Greene and you back to the Justice Center for questioning. It will be safer for the both of you there. People will be crawling all over here in a minute or two. You should also be thinking about retaining a lawyer."

"I'm confident I won't be needing one. All I'll need will be waiting for me down at your headquarters." His eyes blazed across the room meeting Dylan's eyes.

Dylan observed his righteous self-assurance.

Browning lifted up his arm to read his watch. He pressed a sequence of buttons on the side, creating a symphony of odd beeps. A knock came from the door.

Dylan rushed to it, opening it a crack. Bobby poked her head in. A couple other officers stood behind her.

"Heard you needed me," she said.

"I do, in the worst way."

"It's good to finally hear you say that. You just made my day. I'll take it from here." She crossed the room, giving commands to the first two technicians entering.

One man videotaped the entire room inch by inch, while a woman photographed the scene.

"We got it covered here, take off. Do what you have to do. The van you requested is parked in the emergency room parking lot." Bobby said.

Dylan found Dr. Greene and came back to where Mr. Browning stood. "If you'll exit this way down the hall, we'll leave through the private entrance." He spoke directly, looking into Dr. Greene's eyes.

Dylan turned to Della who nodded in agreement. "We'll enter the service elevator, then out the east doors to the van."

Mr. Browning followed Dr. Greene as she led them down the hall. Dylan turned to Bobby. "See you back at the farm. We'll share notes then."

She nodded her blonde head and placed a ball cap on it. "You got it Drake. That's something I always look forward to." She smiled. Her brown eyes twinkled with excitement.

Dylan caught up to Della, Dr. Greene, and Mr. Browning. His mind should have been arrested for speeding as it sorted the details of the scene while he worked each one over and over. The revelation that Father Murphy was the dead man played havoc with him. He hated learning his suspicions were correct when the outcome turned devastating. If he'd pursued the matter when he first started piecing things together, instead of backing off and following other leads, his death might have been prevented. He blamed himself, and he couldn't deny there had been something between Dr. Greene and Father Murphy all along.

Dr. Greene stood slightly slumped over and still in her jeans and T-shirt. Her hair hung straight down off of her shoulders, hiding her face. Her appearance reminded him more of a frightened young schoolgirl than the self-confident doctor he had begun to know and like. He dreaded the upcoming interviews with her, knowing somewhere along the line he had become personally involved with her. Fear of that filled his mind, as he worried at what the justice system might do to her. He would help her pick the best lawyer money could buy.

Standing in an eerie silence, they descended to the first floor in the elevator. All eyes stared straight ahead. The doors opened, jarring them into reality. Stepping out and moving forward, they hurried as a group to the van. Dylan led the way. Bringing up the rear, Della limped along looking tired as hell.

The Law & Justice Center buzzed with the latest shooting at the hospital. Detective Drake and Bishop arrived, herding Mr. Rob Browning and Dr. Caitlin Greene into separate interview rooms.

Waiting to get a full report from the detectives stood Chief Bishop of the Bozeman Police Department and Captain Mitchell of the Gallatin County Sheriff's Department.

Hurrying through the facts with them, Dylan reviewed the scene and what little details he had learned. He explained that the victim of the shooting was identified as Father Murphy. He had been shot by a forty-five semi-automatic handgun through the chest at point blank range and died at the scene. The gun was retrieved. He reported that Rob Browning and Dr. Greene both were present during the shooting and were being held for questioning. Both of them had been advised to seek an attorney before giving their statements to the police.

"It's good you kept a lid on this. We need to keep it that way. It isn't going to be easy by the way it is spreading through the ranks in our own building. That's why I didn't want all of these departments sandwiched together. Chief of Police Bishop has given us his blessing and turned this one over to us also. So, the ball is still in our court. I'll inform the County Attorney before this gets loose and out into the public, and they demand some answers from him. The Coroner just left the hospital with the body and is on his way to Missoula to meet with the boys at the state lab for an autopsy."

Captain Mitchell stretched. "Get in there and get solid statements from those two. Don't leave any loose ends. Bring the statements back to me as soon as you're finished. It's been one hell of a week around here."

"Yes sir. Detective Bishop and I will start with Dr. Greene. After we finish with her, we'll talk to Mr. Browning. His will take a while. We need to question him on this shooting, and the James shooting. It seems Mr. Browning knows both victims well. We'll follow up with you as soon as we can."

"You both have another long evening staring at you. Della, are you sure you're up to it?" Captain Bishop said. "You look tired."

Della frowned at her father. "I'm fine and would like to be in on these interviews. I've been laid up in the hospital with nothing to do. That's why I look tired. I was bored into it."

"I'll keep an eye on her, sir. I'll take her home if it gets to be too much," Dylan said, acknowledging he was aware of his concern for his only daughter.

"Excuse me," Della said. "If I were a man standing here with a broken ankle you all would have sent him on his next assignment, no questions asked. I demand that same respect."

"Del, I think you're acting a bit childish. We're interested in all of our officers' welfare. We wouldn't have just sent him off like you say. You have our respect."

"Then address me as Detective Bishop, not Del."

"Okay, Detective Bishop. Get off your feminist high horse and get your skinny ass to work. Enough time has been wasted already while you were convalescing in that hospital. Vacations over Detective. Is that better?"

"Yes, sir." She cracked a tiny smile at her father, while the others kept their poker faces drawn tight.

"What? You think this is funny?" Captain Bishop's eyes drilled into her from across the room.

"Excuse me, sir, but I do."

"Well, we'll see how funny you take it when I write you up for insubordination to a commanding officer."

"But, Dad you aren't my commanding officer." Della wiped the growing smirk off of her face and replaced it with a solemn look.

"It's Chief Bishop to you, Detective. And it's a good thing I'm not your commanding officer." He grinned at her, catching her in her own folly. "Get out of here."

Dylan turned and followed Della.

"I guess my buttons aren't the only ones you like to push," Dylan said. "You did a good job at raising his fur in there." He chuckled with his thought lingering of the Chief chewing Della's ass out in front of her commanding officer, Captain Mitchell.

"Don't even start with me." She kept her head straight ahead and tried to hurry to the interview room, but found it hard to move fast with her weighted foot.

"I wouldn't think of it." Dylan laughed loudly, watching her spine stiffen straighter as he followed her uneven gait.

She stopped in front of the break room, turning to face Dylan. She pushed him backward slightly into the wall. "You're a liar, Drake. As I remember, you're pretty good with buttons too, remember?" She lifted her dark brows seductively, watching his smile turn from a smirk to a scowl. "Speechless? You're trying to get at my buttons right now. And what?" She reached out and ran her fingers slowly down across the buttons on the front of his shirt to his silver belt buckle. "You don't want to play with me anymore?"

Della shook her silky black hair at him trying to egg him on. Tilting her head up towards him, she laughed in his face.

Seething, Dylan kept quiet.

A few sheriff's deputies were taking a break. Waiting to pour a cup of coffee, they overheard the two in the hall. One deputy stuck his head out and made a crack. "If he won't play with you, I certainly will. Buttons are my specialty."

Dylan grabbed the deputy by his shirt collar. "Watch your mouth. It's become disengaged from your brain. Makes life dangerous." He released his shirt and pushed him back.

The deputy sailed back into a chair, knocking it over. The other officers quickly scattered, their laughter dying into a welcomed silence. Della had disappeared from sight.

Dylan marched to the interview room and found Della waiting for him just outside the door. She flashed him her smile and turned up her seductive powers. It sucked him straight in and blew him away. Wanting to stay mad as hell at her for blatantly starting an altercation with him in front of the other officers, he decided he'd better let it ride.

Her words could be taken out of context and used against her if she wasn't more careful. Rumors already flew around the building at warp speed. They didn't need to add fuel to the fires.

"I hope you enjoyed yourself back there darling, because pay backs are a bitch." With that he started opening the door, but Della's hand went out and stopped him.

They stood inches from each other. Their eyes connected and held. Reaching up after a bit, Della grasped his tie. "Your tie. I think it's seen better days."

"I agree. I should have left it in your big mouth. Then I wouldn't have to listen to all of the crap that's constantly coming out of it. I'm just discovering that you have a long line of bullshit that comes with you. That's disturbing. And I have to be honest here, I don't know what I'm going to do about it either."

"At least you're honest." She finished fixing his tie and dared to look back in his eyes.

"Honesty is about all I can make good on. Let's get in there and get to work."

He opened the door and held it as Della wobbled in. Taking a seat on the other side of the table, they both geared up for another long night of unraveling the mystery.

Chapter 40

Thursday, the 12th of September

"Sorry we kept you waiting, Dr. Greene. Did you contact an attorney?"

"No. I've found it fortunate that I have never had to use one. I don't know any. So, I think I'll pass. I just want to get this over with."

"That's not advisable. This could get complicated. Lawyers make sure your rights are being protected. You've heard us cops are all a bunch of lowlifes?"

"I know better. Quit trying to make me feel better. Just take my statement. If you arrest me, then I'll retain one."

"It's your call, but you'll have to sign this before we can start. Can I get you a cup of coffee?" He slid the paper to her and she signed it handing it back.

"No. I'm fine. I just want to get this over with and go home."

"Okay, let's start. Just tell me everything as you remember it." Dylan turned on the tape recorder.

"Father Murphy—" Her words stalled out when she spoke his name. She bowed her head slightly. "I'm sorry. It's just that I didn't know this person as Father Murphy. Frank Morrow was a patient of mine. I knew him by that name only. Over a year ago, he came to me and asked me for help.

"Playing a cloak and dagger number on me from the beginning and maintaining it successfully throughout, it appears, he presented me with a list of things I would have to do in order for him to consent to therapy and trust me to be his doctor. He'd been burned in the past. I didn't think it abnormal in my line of work. It was a typical paranoid schizophrenic behavior.

"Fascinating me from the very beginning, I agreed on all of his terms. As the weeks and months progressed, I became obsessed with his case, because my initial diagnosis was dead wrong. I unearthed he was a bona fide multiple personality.

"It was a thrilling discovery for me, the day it became apparent. I have video footage of all of our sessions. That's one thing he was unaware of and would have never agreed to. I consider it to be an essential tool in my practice. After the initial session with the patient, I view it again after the session is over to get a different angle from the one I experienced as it's taking place. You don't get everything the first time. I pick up on things I've missed sometimes the third and fourth time around. It benefits the patient, because it aids the doctor.

"I became totally driven, trying to find a way for him to come to terms with the diagnosis, so he would be able to lead a better quality of life than he had been living.

"A tragic and delicate case to handle, with the odds against success. His life took over my life. I studied all the case histories and research done on similar cases documented all over the world. I looked forward to each week because he taught me so much. So much more than I ever learned in all of my education and training. I never once thought I couldn't handle it, that he was out of control, until today." Her voice cracked as she looked across at Dylan who read the anguish.

"Let me get you some water." He returned quickly with a tall glass of water in one hand and carried a box of tissues in the other. He set them in front of her. "Please, continue when you're ready."

She lifted the glass to her lips, hesitating. Her hand shook, spilling some water down her shirt. Instantly, she set the glass down and pulled her hands into her lap. "Frank showed up as expected. I started the same therapy as he was accustomed to. We talked, covering the week, reviewing what happened during our session the week before. I determine if he's handling the new information, then with his consent, we take another step and begin digging again.

"Let me explain it to you both in simple terms here. It's like being an archeologist uncovering prehistoric bones. We dig and excavate all the feelings and experiences buried deep down in his psyche, uncovering his past. A past full of horrors obliterated from his mind because a safety mechanism in his brain took over for him. It took over after he had been subjected to endless tortures, rapes, and other vile things too sordid for me to repeat to you. He's lucky that mechanism took over, because a normal human being couldn't function after such hideous abuses if they weren't wiped from the person's memory.

"That's where all the personalities start emerging from. They assist his everyday living, coming to his aid to protect him from further assaults. I can't tell you how it happens in scientific terms. No one can. Severe trauma and abuses are linked with every confirmed case. You just aren't born with a multiple personality.

"We did a few relaxation exercises, then I put him under hypnosis. Under hypnosis I bring him back to his childhood. He turns into a small boy. We've worked our way from that point on.

"I have found five personalities and now I witnessed the sixth. One is a baby boy almost three. Then there is a boy at age eleven and one at age fifteen. One is a young girl about to reach puberty, and another female personality, age about twenty. The personality I witnessed today must be his projection of the world's evil all wrapped up into one soul. The one responsible for killing a monk back in Scotland when he was just fourteen."

Both detectives shot each other a questioning glance, reading the other's surprise.

"They all have introduced themselves at some point during our sessions with the exception of that one, which showed up today. It's disconcerting to watch them unfold. My skepticism of multiple personalities changed quickly. I now believe they do exist, after bearing witness to his.

"This is what I've found to believe are the holes in his past. I put together a case history from all the bits and pieces I've managed to extract from our sessions this past year. I'm sure there's much more to the story that I'll never know now." Her voice dropped as a sob escaped her throat.

Wiping a tear from her eye, she continued. "Apparently, he is a byproduct of a priest and a nun engaging in sins of the flesh. That's his way of saying it. The priest and his coveted nun covered their impropriety by hiding the pregnancy. Then, at the time of birth, the priest turned him over to a monastery as an orphan. This all took place somewhere in Scotland.

"Raised by the monks from that time on, he survived. The one monk put in charge of him abused him from the beginning. That monk was to teach him obedience to God and the Church. It seems the monk chose to teach a different type of obedience. Obedience to serve him as he so desired. From the time he was a toddler, throughout his young adult life, he was sexually assaulted many times daily and made to do the most vile things ever imagined.

"In the years that these things took place, the monk taunted him with stories full of his evil and wickedness. He suffered endless days and nights of sexual abuse and mental and physical torture. He ridiculed him mercilessly, telling him daily they were bastard brothers. He learned from him about the identity of his mother and father. This monk was another one of the priest's offspring that he had cast away two decades before.

"One day, he finally snaps, taking revenge on the monk, murdering him with an ax. Chopped his head off over the chopping block as he waited to be mounted by him at his order. It was his last act of sexual abuse.

"The Church, protecting their own, whisked him off to America, sending him to a seminary school in Minneapolis. A long way away from the scandal that would have rocked the strong foundations of the Roman Catholic Church.

"He worked hard, educating himself, and developed a fine reputation in Minneapolis. None knew of his tragic past. Unknown to anybody in his new environment, he lived a double life that kept him in his own private hell.

"The years in Scotland had changed his development from a naive baby to a person with several personalities. This evolution took place gradually in the years he endured his captivity by that monster. That's how he lived with himself and his surroundings until finally one personality, the dominant one full of hate, took over killing his abuser, his own brother. This evil personality of his, if you were to witness it yourselves, would make the monk I've been talking about sound like Mother Teresa.

"His mind kept snapping like a rubber band, in and out of different personalities, like being a marionette attached to strings on a stage all the while excelling in every area of his life in the seminary. He couldn't control the personalities that entered him. They would take over, wiping out his memory. He'd often wake up and find himself in another part of the city, lost and confused. It started occurring more and more frequently during his first few years in Minnesota.

"No one witnessed these changes that happened unexpectedly to him, but he feared every waking moment that one would emerge at the wrong time and ruin his chances at becoming a priest. Becoming a priest meant everything to him. Deciding to seek help, he was burned by a doctor there. Rumors quickly started flying around the seminary, but he kept them at bay until he finally became a priest, and was sent to Montana in the early eighties.

"On his own, he breathed easier and became totally committed to the Church. Working endless hours for the good of God and the community. They couldn't know his tortured soul. He blossomed here, thinking his problems were in his past, until a year or so ago, when they started taking over his life again, haunting him at inconvenient times.

"He became suicidal. That's when he accepted the fact he needed professional help if he were to ever lead a life free of them. He needed to sort out the past that was one big black hole for him, with a little memory here and there that would surface, then cause a split in his personality. But once again, he needed to find a totally private setting with a professional who would keep his case on a one on one basis. Total client patient confidentiality, which I was more than willing to provide."

Dr. Greene pushed her chair back and stood. She circled behind it, then turned away from the two detectives. She turned, brushing tears away from her face. "I'm sorry. I just can't seem to stay in control. I hate myself. I guess I became personally involved."

"It's okay," Dylan said. It happens to all of us in our line of work. I've learned lots more from being out there in real life living the experiences than just reading about them. That's what life is all about. Sometimes you get back more valuable lessons than you think you've lost. You did nothing wrong by following through on your client's wishes."

"I did do him wrong in the most unprofessional way," Dr. Greene said.

"How's that?"

"I wasn't experienced enough to really help. I should have referred him to an expert in the field of multiple personalities. I shouldn't have been so self-centered, thinking I could handle such a sensitive and mind boggling case. I really thought I could make a difference and break through all his mental trappings and free him. Me." A hideous laugh escaped her lips. She slapped both hands on top of the table, leaning over the back of her chair. She slid them back and straightened up again and wrapped her arms around her waist.

"I should have known better. I kept ignoring my better judgment, missing all the signs." Her eyes were fixed straight ahead in a trance.

"I think you're being too hard on yourself," Dylan said. "Look, tell me what signs you missed."

"I'm responsible for this whole mess, even for Jennica getting shot," she said.

"What?" Dylan said, looking back at Della as they questioned each other again with their eyes. "How could you be responsible for that?"

"Father Murphy said he shot her. He loved her. That's why he wanted me to shoot him. He knew I knew his history and that he couldn't control his actions. Killing him would free him from the nightmare of his life. I believe he snapped back and found himself with a gun in his hand staring at me, his doctor. What could he do? He didn't want to hurt anybody else. He never wanted to hurt anybody. If you really knew him like I had begun to know him, he was the most gentle and compassionate man I had ever met."

"This can't be for real," Dylan said, astonished at what he heard. He leaned closer to Dr. Greene. "He told you all of this?"

"Yes, in the moments before he died. Mr. Browning heard it all too."

"I can't believe this, Father Murphy shot Jennica James? Were they sexually involved?"

"I don't know that for fact. I can't even tell you who he was at that moment he told us. It wasn't any of the personalities I was familiar with. All I know is this is torturing me right now, and it feels like a bad dream. I had no clue to the life he was leading right here in Bozeman. I thought we were really working on the truth. I didn't even know his true identity. I knew he was a priest, but I didn't know he lived here in Bozeman. He told me he came to town every Thursday from a larger city. He never actually told me where he lived."

"You can't change what happened," Dylan said. "Don't beat yourself up. I wouldn't have known the man was Father Murphy if I hadn't been told. You take off a priest's clothes put regular clothes on him, a wig, some different style of glasses, and he looks like all he rest of the middle age men out there."

"I should've figured it out, sensed somehow that he wasn't being totally honest with me. For God's sake we've been in the same areas of the hospital with patients before. If I would've investigated this further instead of believing in him blindly, maybe I could've prevented all of this from happening."

"Let's just concentrate right now on what happened today that lead up to the shooting."

"I don't know if you'll ever be able to forgive me."

"I don't think you should be worrying about that right now. I'm a big boy. I can handle whatever it is. I just need you to tell me exactly what happened today, starting from your meeting with Father Murphy." Dylan sat back against his chair, studying her face for a sign of what was to come. He couldn't imagine why she thought he wouldn't forgive her, unless she was sleeping with her patient. That would really put this investigation into a tailspin.

Della squirmed in her chair. "Dr. Greene, it's important to remember that we're doing our job now and taking down your statement of the facts surrounding the shooting of Father Murphy. We're here for that purpose only. We can't get involved in this matter personally."

"I'm sorry. I know I'm not conducting myself very well."

"Don't worry about it. Let's take a break. Can I get you anything?" Dylan pushed himself up from his chair and leaned over, turning slightly to Della.

She eyed him suspiciously.

"Detective Bishop, we'll need another tape," Dylan said.

"Right. I'll get another one from our office."

"Cait. We'll be back in five minutes," Dylan said. He locked onto Della's eyes, motioning her to follow him. "Just try and relax."

"I'll try." Folding her arms tightly around herself, she rocked back and forth. The detectives slipped out of the room.

As they left the room, Della turned on Dylan. "What do you think you're doing in there?"

"What? I'm not doing anything. I'm trying to find out what happened. What's eating at your brain now?"

"All I know is I think you're personally involved with Dr. Greene and you aren't using your head. You're not conducting an interview. You're babying her along and treating her like a child. You're trying to make her feel good about all of this. I'm sure you're not aware of it, however, but you'll hear it when we replay the tape."

"I'm trying to get her through this before she falls apart. If she does fall apart, then we have nothing. It's not exactly easy for her. Put yourself in her shoes."

"That's exactly what I'm talking about. Putting ourselves in her shoes is not what we've been trained to do. It interferes with our objectivity."

"Okay, so I'm personally involved to a certain extent, but not the way you're insinuating."

"You told me you would tell me about it later. I know you slept with her once, but did you have to continue?"

"I don't think my sex life is any of your damn business Della. Who I decide to sleep with on my own time is just that, my decision. I don't badger you about the details of your latest affair do I?"

"My latest affair?"

"Yes, with Matthew Justus."

"Matt? How did you know his last name—? What did you do check him out?"

"I can't tell a lie." He smiled, hoping for a time-out. It was getting too intense for a five minute break."

"How dare you." She turned away, then turned back. "We're getting off the subject here. Matt isn't involved in this case. Dr. Greene is. That makes it my business. It affects us both. We have a dead priest and a woman lying in the hospital critically injured. We're here to obtain the facts, collecting evidence to finally link what pieces we've gotten with what we're getting now, and hoping they'll tie in somehow. I don't think you can remain objective when it comes to Dr. Greene telling us her side of the story. She looks like she's in it deep. The other person is dead so he can't speak for himself."

"What are you really trying to say to me?" Dylan said. "I don't think you're acting totally objective either. I think you're jealous of the beautiful Dr. Greene. Am I right, Detective Bishop?" He stepped closer in, brushing a piece of hair away from her eyes. She dropped her gaze to the floor. Reaching up, he tilted her chin to him, forcing her to look at him. "Admit it, Della. You've hated her since the first day we met her at the hospital after the night of the shooting."

"Hate? That's a strong word. I don't hate her. I don't feel anything for her. And I don't especially feel any jealousy towards her. All I know is in the room back there, I felt like I was the only one thinking with my brain."

"Is that right? Well let me clue you in on something. I am using my brain in there, so don't start making something out of nothing and don't keep putting me in places I'm not. It only adds fuel to feed that hot temper of yours. And that temper of yours is something I'm not willing to go a round with tonight. When this case is finished, then we can finish this—." Waving his hands through the air at her in exasperation, his tongue stumbled over the words he was trying to say. "I don't know, this shit between us. I'm aware we have some problems to work out, but now isn't the time or the place to do it. Let's just call a truce for tonight, please? You're the only person I've a hard time remaining objective with." He turned and walked into their office.

Della started to follow him, but he came back out and turned in her direction. He tossed a box of tapes at her through the air. She caught it as he reached her.

"It's time." He moved passed her, brushing his body lightly against hers, glancing back at her to see if she was coming. She stood in the same place with a pleasant smile on her face. Wondering how she could change her expressions so easily, he didn't know if he would ever figure her out. "Ready?"

"Yes. I'm right behind you."

Chapter 41

Thursday, the 12th day of September

Dylan and Della entered the interview where Dr. Greene waited, and found her in the corner of the room, her head against the wall. Turning quickly, she realized that the two detectives were back in the room with her. Taking her seat at the table, she took a drink.

"Let's finish talking about your session with Father Murphy today," Dylan said.

"I'll try. Like I said, I really didn't think he was a danger to himself or to anyone in this hospital until today. I want you to believe me. The thought that he was dangerous never crossed my mind."

"What changed today?" Della said.

"Everything changed in an instant. I mean, not at first. We did the same type of therapy we always have done. It triggered something this time that I had never witnessed before. After I brought him out of hypnosis, I left him on the couch to rest before facing the world again. This particular session drained him more than any other that I remember. It's natural, the more he deals with, the more taxing it becomes to the system." She stopped, drawing her eyes away from them. She turned and sat sideways in her chair. Crossing her arms across her chest, she bit at her lip, then softly started to cry.

"Go ahead. It's okay. Tell us exactly what happened. I know this is difficult, but you'll feel better telling us. Trust me." Dylan reached for her hand, but quickly withdrew it. Della's reminder to stay objective crossed his mind.

"I don't think it's going to be okay. I've been replaying it in my mind for most of the day. I didn't want anybody to ever know about this."

"Come on, what happened?" Dylan said.

Standing and turning towards the wall, she paused a few seconds. "I came into the room and he was standing in the dark, totally naked. I didn't know what to do. I tried talking to him, but he didn't hear me because it wasn't him. It was a personality I'd never met before. If this personality would've surfaced before in our therapy, I might have known the dangers." She leaned against the wall, turning her head away with a sob. "He ripped my clothes from me while he beat me."

Jumping up and rushing to her, Dylan held her in his arms and tried to comfort her. "It's okay. You're safe. You have nothing to be scared of anymore."

She slid down in his arms. He pulled her up and tried holding her to him.

"I think he raped me," she said.

Della came around the other side of her. "You think? Why do you say that? You must know?"

"He knocked me out. I woke up lying on my desk. I don't remember anything else. I just remember the sinister laugh and him hitting me and ripping my clothes off as he pushed me on the desk and climbed on top of me. I tried to fight, but the next thing I knew, I woke up in the dark, alone and hurting."

"Where was he?" Dylan said.

"I didn't know, and I wasn't thinking straight. I prayed he had snapped back and fled after he saw what he had done. I didn't want to report it. I couldn't. I didn't want to admit I couldn't handle him. I know I should have called you right away."

She turned and collapsed into his chest sobbing again. Holding her there in his arms, he stared at Della's eyes, pleading for her help. He found himself at a loss for words.

Dylan walked her back to the table after she stopped crying, and sat her back down. "So, you didn't fall running down the hill?"

She grabbed for a tissue and wiped her eyes. "I'm sorry, I lied about that. I couldn't tell you then, and I wish you hadn't made me tell you now."

"Christ, Cait. I was right here in the hospital. Why didn't you let me help you? He could have killed you or some other innocent victim. Is that why you shot him? He came back to kill you?"

"No, No." She yelled, shaking her head furiously. "I didn't shoot him. I could never kill anybody. He handed the gun to me, then pulled it away when he realized Mr. Browning woke up and was coming up behind him. He shot himself."

"What was Mr. Browning doing sleeping in your office?" Della said.

"Father Murphy was hiding in my suite. Mr. Browning came back to my office, pointing a gun in my face, telling me I would take him to see Ms. James or he would start hurting people. I told him I would do it without the gun pointed in my face. He was walking me down the hall to the outside of my office when Father Murphy jumped him from behind. He took the gun after it fell out of his hand and hit the floor. That's when he started talking crazy, pointing the gun at me. Then he turned the gun around in his hand and held it out to me to take. He asked me to kill him and put him out of his misery.

"He rambled on about god and the angels, and the devil turning his heart to stone, making him shoot Jennica against his will. It sounded as if he was in love with her. He said he wanted to give up his life to God and just be a man who would be free to love her.

"It must have wrenched everything inside of him loose again. I can see now, that if I'd known that one secret he kept from me, I might have stopped all of this from ever happening. It must have been the pinnacle that sent him spiraling down out of control. It all makes sense to me in retrospect, considering how he came into this world.

"His violent past set in motion because of a priest that couldn't control his sexual appetites and breaking his vow to God. The shrapnel from that era of sin, still destroying his life even after fifty some years. He was forced into becoming a priest with no choices back then. The monastery sheltered him because of the circumstances surrounding his birth in his early years.

"He would put himself to the test, knowing he could withstand anything that God would hand him during the rest of his life. He educated himself beyond his studies, pushing himself, testing his strength and will, doing the work God had set before him. He finally thinks he is over the test and settles in with a small hope that he'll find happiness in a new place. He does, but it soon starts to crumble. His demons return.

"Love is something he never experienced in its truest form. It was a term alien to him. It probably became a symbol representing a part of each individual personality trapped inside of him. The infant needing the love of a mother to nurture him into adulthood. The young boys protecting the innocent child, giving him their love as brothers normally would try to do. The young girl always appearing innocent, full of love and understanding. Other times, she acted scared and cowered. She would protect the little boy from the evil in the world, but often cried to me that she failed. That one is what he imagined his mother to be.

"I believe he saw his real mother a victim of the priest and his power over her. His mother might have been raped by the priest and forced into keeping the act a secret, and the offspring banished from her.

"His mind had many years to spin the abuses into the personalities he became, turning one into the worst evil imaginable and another one into the exact opposite, his perfect vision of innocence and purity. Good versus evil, God versus the devil. Easily broken down that way into a simple explanation of life. The personality of the young innocent baby boy was the one I worked with almost every week. The others came out unexpectedly, usually when a subject that was too painful for him was suggested.

"He may have never actually had sexual relations with Ms. James, but he must have loved her intensely in his own confused mind. In fact, I would say most likely he never did have any sexual relationship with her. She may not even be aware of the depth of his love for her. She may have just thought of him as her priest, a bond that formed insidiously, because she felt comfortable with him and confessed everything to him as the years progressed. He always absolved her."

"I doubt she was naive to it. In fact, I bet she played it for all it was worth." Dylan set back, wishing to recant his last sentence.

"Why would you say that? Did you find something to the contrary?" Dr. Greene said. She gazed across at him with her reddened eyes and blinked back a tear. Shaking her head in disbelief at Dylan's response, she waited for his answer.

"Let's just say, I suspect her of having an affair with many men at the same time. It seems every man I've talked to has confessed their love for her, and I have concluded the reason is because she has had an affair with all of them. I suspect her of being a sex addict. That's the correct term I would use to describe her, in my investigation to date." He rapped his knuckles against the top of the table watching her reaction.

"If that's so, then that may be what triggered this episode with Father Murphy. She was his angel, and in another personality she was his devil. This could almost make sense to me from a clinical standpoint. If she confessed to him her acts of carnal pleasures with different men, it could've set him off. He developed a love for her early on. Remember now, his perception of love. One that is pure, like the Virgin Mary, let's say. She must have attended his church when she was a small child and continued until she became a woman. One personality locked inside of him became her protector somewhere along the way, trying to protect her from her own desires that would block her way to God. The other personality wanted to covet this virgin child for his own purposes. His evil twin, you might say. So the battle began. Are you following me on this?" She stopped for a minute, letting them soak in her theory.

"I'm following you, but I'm finding this very disturbing. To think someone went through this metamorphosis because of someone else's abuse. How many more people are living with time bombs ready to explode them to hell here?" Della said.

"We'll never know until a tragedy occurs like this one. Father Murphy fought his battle with courage. A survivor." She looked away. "He started experiencing blackouts again. I think Jennica James became more than a symbol for him. I truly believe now, after listening to him talk of her that he fell in love for real. This was the real Father Murphy. He knew it was wrong, but fought it steadily through the years he was her priest. He wanted to protect her from the wicked ways of the world. When she confessed each time to having sex with these different men, he snapped. His virgin child soiled. It set him off. His demons took over, fighting self against self.

"One probably stalked her to take what was his, angry that she had given herself to another. She was to remain a virgin for him. This one, thinking himself as God. Another one, probably planned on taking her life to protect her from further transgressions. If he absolved her, then killed her, she would still be pure in his mind. I really couldn't say whether the two of them ever experienced a sexual relationship together or not. It could be the motivating tool into his spiraling demise of the past months. It could be the reason he solicited me in the first place, over a year ago."

The detectives stared at one another incredulously. Their eyebrows both cocked above their eyes questioning each other in silence. They let it soak in, filtering it through their minds like a fine sieve.

"I guess we'll have to wait and see if Jennica can answer that question, if she makes it. You told me you taped your sessions with Father Murphy," Dylan said.

"Yes."

"Were you taping him today?"

"Yes."

"When did you turn it off."

"I always turn it off after he collects himself and we engage in a regular conversation again. Oh my god. I didn't turn the tape off. After I woke up, I panicked. All I could think about was to get the mess cleaned up because you were on your way up to my office. I didn't want you to find me like that. That means—" She broke down in hysterics and put her head on the table. Covering her head with her arms, she tried to hide from her thoughts.

"It's okay. It will tell us everything we need to know. It's evidence. It'll show us if, in fact, he did rape you. It's too late for you to go through an examination. You showered, but I would like a doctor to document the bruises covering your body."

"No. I don't want to know. I just want to go home. I don't want anyone else to know about this, especially another doctor. I don't want anyone to see that tape. You can't get it. You can't. It's confidential. My client should be protected." She straightened up in her chair, taking her arms away from her face. Her eyes glazed over, pleading with him to give in to her demands.

"Your client's dead, Cait. You can't protect him anymore. You could be charged with his murder if the evidence isn't consistent with your statements here."

"How can that be? I didn't do anything. I can't believe you just said that. You don't believe me? I knew you would be upset with me over this, but I didn't believe you'd think I killed him willingly."

"No, Cait, listen to me. You're not hearing what I'm trying to tell you. I'm not accusing you of anything. I just have to submit the facts. Without the concrete evidence to support them, your version of the truth could be turned upside down by a prosecutor if this ends up in court. You're upset right now. I know you aren't thinking about the whole picture here clearly. You refused to obtain a lawyer. You need to enter those tapes into evidence. I'm telling you this to help you. The tape will only confirm your story. It'll show what frame of mind the victim was in during the attack, and later in your office. It could prove your motive, that being one of self-defense. Rob Browning might lie. He did, after all, come after you with a gun. He may try and contrive a story that puts you out of his way and clears him from any wrong doing here. As it is, you could press charges against him for threatening bodily harm. He knows this and could sway the story to keep you from doing just that. It's your word against his."

"Motive? Self-defense? I didn't shoot him on purpose. I couldn't shoot him even then. I was taking the gun, so he wouldn't snap into one of his other personalities again and use it on the two of us. I saved Mr. Browning. He better back me up, because it's the truth."

"The truth has to be proved in a court of law. I don't need your permission to retrieve those tapes, but I'd like your consent. I promise you that Della and I will be the only ones in this building to watch them. We'll keep them under strict security. Please agree with me that this should be done for your benefit, or call a goddamn lawyer now, before we get any further." Dylan's voice struck like thunder at her. His anger took over. Turning, he slammed his fists into the wall. Trying to gain control of his exploding temper, he walked out the door. A few seconds later, he returned, and sat down like nothing had happened.

"Cait, can't you see?" he said. "The tape will make this all just come to an end. No charges filed. No damn trial. No media to plaster this man's dreadful life, not to mention yours, all over the front page of every newspaper in this state, probably the country. Believe me, a story like this one would rock out of our quaint and quiet little town into every home in the nation. Do you want that?"

She kept her head down on the table, moving it back and forth, hiding her face inside the cushion of her arms.

"Please," Dylan said. "I know this is hard, and it's more of an issue for you than breaking a doctor-patient confidence. I know you think it's better if you don't know the true facts here, but in the end we all have to know exactly what took place. As a doctor you know you have to deal with this now. Help yourself and give yourself your own professional advice. Then follow it."

She pulled her head up slowly, sitting back against the chair. Her eyes studied Dylan's face as he held his eyes on hers until she spoke. "I want to see the tape with you."

"I think you've been through enough today already. I'll take you home. I'll pick you up in the morning. You can look at it then."

"No. I want to be with you when you watch it."

"Please. Give yourself a break for tonight."

"You said yourself, I should know. Well, I want to know tonight."

"I'll consent, but it's against my better judgment. You're the doctor. Do you think you can handle much more? Think about it. You'll have to wait until we've questioned Mr. Browning. Then we can go back to your office and retrieve the film. Are you sure you want to wait that long? It may be another couple of hours?"

"Yes." She bowed her head and placed it back on the table.

"We have a room equipped with a bed. Why don't you let me take you to it? You can rest until we are through," Della said.

"Thank you. I think, I could stand getting away from this cramped room. The walls feel like they are closing in on me."

Della stood and Dylan helped Cait out of her chair. Della led her carefully down the hall and left her in the room. She hurried back to join Dylan and the next interview with Mr. Rob Browning.

Chapter 42

Thursday, the 12th day of September

Dylan stepped out of the interview room towards his office.

"Drake I need to see you now," Captain Mitchell yelled.

Dylan stopped in his tracks, turning towards him. The look on his face told him something was terribly wrong.

"Captain?" Dylan stood just inside the door, hesitating before entering. He hid his surprise at seeing the Captain's small office full of people. Chief of Police Bishop and three individuals he'd never met before, sat around the room. Blank expressions covered their faces.

"Have a seat," Captain Mitchell said, as he directed Dylan's attention to the other people. "These men are from Washington."

Dylan stepped up to them, reaching out his hand, "Detective Drake."

The individuals turned their attention to him, but ignored the hand he offered and turned their concentration back to the Captain.

"Rob Browning is remanded into their custody as of now," the Captain said, as he straightened in his chair.

"Sir, I haven't questioned Mr. Browning. I need to interrogate him."

"Interrogate him?" one of the three men said, his voice sharp and surly as he stood to face Dylan.

"Yes, interrogate him. He committed a felony."

"You have the charges? Evidence to support this?"

"No. I just finished with the victim. I'll have her statement to you, Captain, by the end of the hour. The recorded interview can be reviewed."

"Gentleman, if you'll excuse us for a moment, there's a break room down the hall."

"We have our orders." The man held a stern stance, darting his eyes between the two.

"Yes, so I've been notified. A moment please." The Captain pushed back his chair and motioned his hand in the direction of the door.

The three stood, exiting his office, honoring his request for a moment alone with his detective.

"What's this all about? Tell me quickly what you have on Browning."

"Sir, as you know, Father Murphy was shot today in the hospital. At the time, Dr. Greene and Rob Browning were in her office. Browning pulled a gun on her and ordered her to take him to the James woman. That's an assault with a deadly weapon, a felony."

"Yes, I know the law. Go on."

"The shooting was accidental on Dr. Greene's part. Browning is her witness to that. I would like him to corroborate her statement, so we can let her go. No charges will be filed. It appears Browning's involvement with Ms. James is more than a coincidental burglary, in which, his gun was taken and used in the crime against her. Father Murphy confessed to shooting Ms. James before he died in Dr. Greene's office. Browning is also a convenient witness to that confession. I need him to verify that fact for the record. It was his gun that shot Father Murphy accidentally at the hand of Dr. Greene. The James case could be closed if the facts support the evidence and statements here. There're just a few loose ends I need to tie up in this whole matter that were brought out during our investigation of the James shooting. I need Browning to be able to do it."

"What loose ends? You have a confession."

"A confession from a dying man who wasn't exactly the man everybody thought he was."

"Obviously priests don't go around shooting people."

"Exactly. He was a patient of Dr. Greene's. Her diagnosis was multiple personality disorder."

"Lord."

"I don't think his last words could be used as fact, until proved beyond a reasonable doubt by us that he actually committed the crime. Who knows if he really did it, or witnessed it, acting out another person's confession to it? He was a priest who heard many confessions. It was his confessional where the gun originally turned up. He then gave it to Chief Bishop. I'm not an expert on multiple personalities, that's for sure, but I'd like to investigate this further before I finalize this case. I'd like a chance to study up on this and call in an expert to help us. I need Rob Browning. At least to make a statement here as to what he witnessed to substantiate Dr. Greene's statement."

"You're starting to sound like a stiff-peckered lawyer." He cracked a benign smile at Dylan, laughing at his own style of humor.

"Good. That should make you proud." He passed a smirk back to the Captain as he returned Dylan's comment with a rolling of his eyes. "What? It should be your prototype, Captain. If every cop concentrated on fine-tuning their reasoning skills and using more of their brain capabilities in situations, instead of stimulating the testosterone levels in their muscles every time they have a confrontation, we wouldn't continue to get such a bad rap."

"Now you're starting to sound like a woman. I think I may have made a mistake pairing you with Detective Bishop. She's screwed with your mind somehow."

Dylan maintained a poker face at the Captain's last remark. She did seem to preoccupy it lately, and screwing with it seemed to be her forte, but she certainly couldn't be guilty of teaching him to use his brains. They went into hibernation in her presence. "I'm only trying to cover all the bases here. I like to think our hard work will pay off in the end. I don't like mistakes thrown back at me when it comes time for our day in court. I believe in the system. We all have to do our best here, in order to succeed in putting the bad guys in prison and keeping the innocent ones from entering it."

The Captain shook his head. "I know you and I trust you. I just like to give you shit back once in a while to watch you eat it, then spit it back in my face."

"Thanks."

"You're welcome. I suppose the Feds are getting anxious to depart with Browning."

"I don't understand sir. Why are these men taking Browning? Has he committed a crime against the federal government?"

"I haven't a clue. They walked in flashing their badges, informing me that Rob Browning is to be turned over to them. It was followed by a phone call from the Justice Department. They don't explain themselves. They gave me a directive that they expect me to follow. I have to tell you, I don't like it when these stiff suits come in here and start ordering me around in my own Goddamn town. I especially don't like it when it is affecting one of my cases at a crucial point in it. What in the hell do you think is going on here? Any ideas?"

"No, sir. All I can tell you is Mr. Rob Browning is untraceable. I think that speaks for itself. These men whisk him away to protect something they have no intention of exposing. I can't even guess at this point, but I intend to find out."

"Any suspicions?" Captain Mitchell said.

"The night Detective Bishop and I ran surveillance up to the cabin he leases, we watched trucks moving crates into a warehouse located on forest service land a couple miles from the cabin site. I couldn't get in close enough to verify what was in the containers. And guess who leases the cabin to him? The Federal government. I found shells scattered around like an army had been up there target shooting behind the warehouse. I was starting to wonder if it was arms they were stockpiling. At the time, I was trying to tie the two together, the cabin and the activity at the warehouse. Now, I'm thinking the location of the cabin owned by the Federal government and leased to Browning and the warehouse on forest service property, isn't just a coincidence. They must be related somehow. I'd bet he is directly involved in the activity in some way. The Federal boys showing up to bail him out tells me that much."

"You've never mentioned this to me. When were you going to let me in on the surveillance?"

"I'm sorry, sir. After Detective Bishop entered the hospital and I found out my mother was admitted also, I haven't been back here to finish my reports. I planned on another stakeout to confirm my suspicions that something illegal was taking place up there. Since I stumbled onto it by accident, and it had nothing to do with the James case, I thought I'd just check it out on my own time. I was leaving this evening. Now, I'd like to find out for sure what's going down, whether Browning, the cabin, and the warehouse are connected. I know that Browning and the James woman are connected in some way. He was at the hospital trying to get to the James woman. If Father Murphy hadn't been in Dr. Greene's office, she would've led him right to the James woman. He had a gun and was threatening Dr. Greene he would hurt people if she didn't oblige him. I overheard part of his conversation that he was secretly married to Ms. James. I'm almost positive that was a ploy to get Dr. Greene to let him in to see her. Maybe he was going to finish the job someone screwed up. It baffles me though, I have to admit. He may be a protected witness for the Feds and they need him, so they are taking him into custody to keep a lid on it. The James woman must have known something that was serious enough to have her killed. Serious enough maybe to risk trying to kill her a second time in the hospital surrounded by guards. Whatever it is, I'm going to get to the bottom of it."

"I don't know what I should do here. I can't detain Browning with a Federal warrant in my face. I don't like the way this is shaping up. In light of your last surveillance going sour, I don't think it's the best idea for you to leave again tonight. The weather up there is still tenacious."

"I planned on being prepared this time."

"How about Della?"

"I'm taking her home first."

"That's good. What about backup?"

"I'm just doing surveillance. I'm not going in and shaking any trees tonight. I just want to sit back and observe. It'll probably be a waste of time. If the Feds are taking Rob out of here, I would bet they are not taking him back to the cabin. It's hard to say for certain, but whatever he's been up to, the Feds are involved. Whatever it is, they don't want us messing in it, or getting in their way."

"I don't like this. There are too many loose ends. We just can't wait in line for Browning to answer our questions. This shooting is too important and I'm sure when word gets around about Father Murphy's death, we'd better have all our little ducks in a row when people start coming around for the answers. You can bet it won't be too long before those numbnuts from the paper come storming in here and demand to read our logs."

"I understand. What are you going to do?"

"I'm going to call their bluff. I need Browning, damn it. They will just have to wait for a piece of him. They expect me to bend over backwards while they fuck me, but I'm going to try and negotiate with them my way. I hope it works."

"I have to leave for about a half hour. I'll return quickly. By then, you'll have cleared the way for me to talk with Browning. Right?"

"You can count on it, or I'll be taken away into Federal custody along with Browning. I don't think they want the publicity that might stir up. Speaking of the reporters, I think I'll just call the one friend I do have down at the paper and have him ready and heavily armed. Maybe I should call in the television station. They can be standing here when the shit hits the fan with their cameras rolling. It's going to come down, so I might as well try and work it to our advantage."

"Good plan. I'll check back in soon."

Dylan left and headed down the hall. Della sat at her desk, straightening things up, looking at him with a weariness in her eyes he could plainly see. He wanted to make her go to bed. The telephone on his desk rang, and he lunged for it, picking it up before it rang the second time.

"Dylan, Bobby. I found a video camera running. I have the camera and tape. I thought you'd want to see it right away."

"You bet I do. I was headed there myself to retrieve it after interviewing Dr. Greene. You saved me the trip." Walking back to his partner, he saw that she sat motionless like a stuffed doll molded in her seat.

"Della, I think I should take you home. You look beat. I don't want you running yourself down. I can't let that happen."

"Cut the crap. I'm here for the duration. I want to see that video. You're going back to the hospital to get it, aren't you?"

"I don't have to. That was Bobby. She swept the place and found the video camera and took the tapes. She's bringing them to us as we speak." Dylan pulled up his chair and slid it closer to Della at her desk. "Look at me. I know I promised you that you could accompany me back up the canyon, but now that things have changed, I'm taking you home. Captain Mitchell is going to force the Feds to at least let me ask Rob Browning a few questions. Then we have to release him into their custody. I'm going back up to his cabin to observe again tonight. If I don't get anything, I'll spend every night up there until I figure out what's going on. There's no way in hell I'm going to let you come with me. It may turn nasty, and you're in no shape to handle it. Look at yourself. You are falling asleep and you need the rest. I asked Colton to drive up and bring a couple more of the deputies from Big Sky to meet me. It'll give them a chance to try out their new equipment they got for playing around in the mountains."

"Fine," Della said. "But I want to watch that tape and be involved in the Browning interview. Then I'll let you take me home." She picked up a pen and twirled it around on top of her desk calendar. After a second of doodling, she stopped and dropped her pen. Facing Dylan, she looked into his eyes. "I'll expect you to come back and take care of me like you promised. That's one promise I won't let you get out of. I'd like to see you in an apron with dish pan hands."

"A promise is a promise, right?" he said, grinning.

"I'll expect you to keep it or I'll come looking for you." She smiled. Her violet eyes gave him a stern warning. Reaching for her lip balm, she slowly parted her lips and applied a thin coat.

Prying his eyes off of Della and her lips, he fought against an urge that was devouring his entire body. He tried unplugging himself by turning completely away from her. When his thinking became clearer, he turned back and saw Bobby enter. Jumping from his chair, he moved swiftly to the door.

She sat a box on the floor. Slipping her jacket off, and tying it around her waist, she conversed with Dylan in the corner of the big room.

Returning to his desk, he said, "The tapes are here. Let's get this over with. I'll go get Cait. Get the set ready and we'll be there shortly."

Dylan entered the room quietly. Dr. Greene slept on the small bed. Laying on top of the covers, her long russet hair covered her sleeping face. Brushing it aside, he gently shook her. "Cait. Wake up."

Moaning softly, she opened her eyes partially, looking in Dylan's face. "I can't believe it's been two hours."

"It hasn't been. Something came up unexpectedly. I have the tapes, so I thought we'd get this over with first, so you can get home and get some real sleep."

"Did anyone see them?"

"No. I told you, no one but Della and I will see them."

Raising up on one elbow, she reached over to Dylan, who had sat on the bed next to her. She ran her finger around his jaw and traced his features as if she were blind. "I want to remember your face as I see it now. You won't have the same look on it after seeing this tape."

"Cait. Stop." He pushed her hand away. "I'm a detective and I'm observing this tape to substantiate that a crime has been committed against you. I'm not here to judge you. I just need to view this tape and enter it into evidence in this case. I would never think less of you because you were raped, if that's what you're thinking. My God, my only concern here is for you and your well being.

"I came in here, hoping to change your mind about seeing the tape. I can tell you the information after I've seen it. If I just tell you, it might make it easier. You won't have to relive the terror. I think you're a pretty tough person, but I think you also have your limits. I know I have mine, everybody does. It's not a sign of weakness. Seeing the details might hurt you and do more damage. I don't want you falling apart at the seams on me. Understand?"

"I understand, but I have to see it. I just don't want to be alone when I watch it this time."

"What do you mean this time? This has happened before today?" He clenched his teeth, keeping himself from yelling.

"No. It's not like that." Tears filled her vacant eyes as she squeezed his hand tighter.

Dylan released her hand, and grasped her by both shoulders. His large hands pulled her to him, turning her face to him. "Tell me everything this time, without pulling any more punches. Start talking and quickly. I don't want anymore surprises when we get into that room."

Chapter 43

Thursday, the 12th day of September

Della studied Dr. Greene and Dylan as they entered the tiny room, and found Dylan looking anxious. The veins on the sides of his neck were pronounced, drawing her attention to them. Grinding his teeth, she watched him as his jaw moved back and forth slightly. Recognizing his anger from the many occasions she's been on the receiving end, her curiosity became aroused as to its source. Noticing that Dr. Greene kept her head down and her eyes directed to the floor, she couldn't help but wonder what was up.

They both sat quickly and silently.

Dylan crossed his legs and stretched back into the chair, then crossed his arms in front of his chest.

"Dr. Greene, I have the tape ready. I found a marker date for today's session. I believe I rewound it to the beginning. I noticed there's more than one session on this tape. I think Detective Drake would agree that we'll need to review all the other appointments you taped throughout the year with Father Murphy. We'll keep them safe. Are you sure you're up to seeing this at the present time?"

"I am."

Flipping the lights off, she pressed the remote. The three sat in total silence. The only sounds came from the machine as it started running the tape.

The session started out routinely, just as Dr. Greene stated in their interview. Then after twenty minutes or so, Della perked up. Listening closely, and watching Father Murphy's actions on tape, brought her a sense of fascination. She wouldn't have recognized Father Murphy from the other night at the hospital either, now that she saw the tape. It made her a believer. She could see now how Dr. Greene never clued in to his identity.

The skepticism she felt before disappeared as she watched the tape. It sent a frosty chill through her, making her stiffen back in her chair. With each personality that emerged there came a total change in appearance that was apparent even to her. The differences were striking even to an untrained eye.

Her skin tingled with the exposure of the metamorphoses taking place in front of her, making her feel like she was watching a science fiction movie. It didn't take long before she gasped and upgraded it to the status of a horror movie. The doctor was beaten and raped viciously by a maniac while she lay unconscious. Every nerve and muscle became taut, like guitar strings being tightened. She felt they might pop, and spring out from inside of her at any moment. It frightened her to the core.

Della felt horrified by the image in front of her. Quickly she pulled her eyes away and glanced at Dr. Greene. She worried about her stability. Tears streamed down her eyes as she watched her own horror show. Turning slightly towards Dylan, she wanted to see his reaction. His face read like a stone, not an expression of any kind showing in it.

Della hit the stop button then the rewind. For the first time she could remember she couldn't speak. She didn't know what to say.

Dylan silently stood and moved to turn the lights back on. Just as he moved past Della, the video made a few noises again, and the screen filled with images.

"What are you doing? Turn that off," Dylan said. He hurried over to Della and tried to grab the remote out of her hand.

Della pulled her hand back instinctively. "What's gotten into you?" Della said. "I just wanted to see the previous session from the beginning. We have time."

Grabbing the remote out of her hands, he tried furiously to stop the tape. He threw it at her and it landed in her lap. Stepping to the machine to try and turn it off, he was too late.

"Oh my God. What's this?" she stammered as she looked at the two bodies on screen. A startled expression covered her face. "It looks like Dr. Greene is—"

Dylan pressed the off button on the VCR. The room blackened, blanketing their faces in gray shades. "She already informed me of this and explained the situation to me, but there is not enough time for me to explain it you right now. Rob Browning is our priority. We need to focus on him." He turned towards Dr. Greene. She stared at the floor and leaned against the wall for support. "I'll have an officer take you home."

She lifted her head and nodded.

"Don't leave town unless you notify the department."

Dr. Greene left, moving into the light in the hall. Dylan followed her.

Della digested the images she saw floating on the screen. It hit her full force, and it explained why Dylan acted so strange. Dr. Greene and Father Murphy were naked and engaged in sex on the floor of her office. In her opinion, after viewing the brief segment, that both Dr. Greene and Father Murphy found enjoyment in the sex act by the sight and sounds she witnessed. Ejecting the tape, she placed it back in the box and carried it to the evidence room. Placing it securely in the vault, she rotated the dial. Returning quickly to the interview room, she looked for Dylan for an explanation. She peered inside. Dylan sat on a chair, his arms resting on his knees, and his head between them.

"Dylan?" Della said.

Dylan straightened up. "Have a seat. It's going to be a while longer."

Moving across from him, she kept standing, staring at him, her hands on her hips. "Sorry."

"Sorry? I thought that was my line. Sorry for what?"

"Sorry that Dr. Greene was sleeping with him."

"She wasn't. It happened just that one time. She explained it all to me."

"And you believe her?" She kept the jealousy towards Dr. Greene out of her voice. It festered just below the surface.

"It doesn't matter what I believe," Dylan said.

"The hell it doesn't. You can't just sit there and tell me this is not relevant to this case."

"I didn't say that. I told you I don't have time to discuss this right now. Do you hear me? Can you understand what I'm trying to tell you?" He glared at her. "We'll go back and go over it all, I promise. Rob Browning is on his way here, and I'm trying to concentrate on that. Okay? Will you please just sit down."

"If you weren't personally involved with Dr. Greene, and trying to protect her, you wouldn't have any trouble concentrating."

"I'm not protecting her, and quit telling me I'm personally involved with her," he shouted with vengeance glowing behind his eyes. "If I tell you I'm not, I'm not." Standing, he paced around the room. "I don't know what I have to say to convince you of that." He turned abruptly, coming up behind her, and pulled her up and out of the chair. "What do I have to do to convince you, she only helped me during this case?"

"Sleeping with her helped you on this investigation? Now that's an explanation I can believe coming from you." She laughed in his face. "She didn't tell you all her secrets while you were in bed though, did she?" She kept her eyes riveted to his. "She only told you after she knew you would find out, because she knows you're thorough in everything you do, not only in bed, but at your job as well. She figured you would watch all of her preceding tapes eventually. She forgot about the camera in the room during her rape, but she also forgot it when she obviously lost control and got carried away with Father Murphy. I just wonder why she kept such damning evidence, unless she's just as sick as Father Murphy was?

"She enjoys sex. Of course, you already knew that. Why did you turn the tape off so suddenly? Were you next on the tape? That's why you're mad as hell right now? Isn't it? That's just another thing she forgot to tell you? Am I getting warm? That's why you became upset when I turned it back on and you couldn't shut it off quick enough. You weren't worried about Dr. Greene's indiscretion being seen, you were worried about yours. I feel for you Dylan. She turns out to be just another sicko."

He reached out with his fist to strike her. He pulled back, before doing so, but her head snapped back instinctively and she lost her footing trying to back away.

Catching her before she fell, he grabbed her and pulled her back up. "I'm sorry. I didn't mean to raise my fist at you. I reacted instinctively. I don't know what came over me. Scratch that last sentence. I lied. If you were a man, I would have beat the hell out of you just now." He squeezed her waist between his hands. "But, you're not a man, are you? I can't beat the shit out of you as much as I'd like to right now. I'll curse the Captain and your father until the day I die for pairing you with me. It's a curse on me."

He released the pressure on her waist. She gulped for air.

"I do know what caused my reaction," Dylan said. "You do too! You. You bring it out in me. You've everything twisted in that mind of yours. I don't know when, or how, but your mouth has over-ridden your ass. It doesn't suit you. Be careful in the future. I may not be able to control myself the next time. I'm going to let you in on something, even though it's none of your goddamn business. Dr. Greene and I have never slept together. Got it? I'm not saying that I didn't want to, because I did. She's an attractive woman. End of story." Releasing his grip, he left his hands around her waist.

"If you want me to believe you, then you have to tell me why you didn't. I mean, you said you wanted to," Della said.

"You're a detective, darling. I thought you might have figured some of those reasons out by now. And I don't give a damn whether or not you believe me."

"Detectives?" the Captain said.

Immediately, Dylan's hands slid from Della's waist.

"What's going on in here? I hope you two are acting out a scenario from the crime scene, because we don't have time for personal agendas here. Do I make myself clear?"

"Very clear, sir," they said in unison, standing side by side, facing Captain Mitchell.

"We'll meet in the briefing room at twenty hundred hours." He left, leaving the door wide open in his wake.

Dylan glanced at his watch and turned to Della. He hunted her with his eyes, searching hers for acknowledgment that she was aware as much as he was, of their caustic relationship. The shock value from the Captain walking in on them was like taking an ice cold shower.

"I can see we're in serious trouble here. You're my problem, Della. One big serious pain in my ass problem. I know I have to find a solution to this before we lose the one thing we both need. Our jobs."

"Spoken like a true asshole." Della walked away and stopped just inside the door. Turning her face to him, she saw a forlorn look in the dark expression covering his face.

He turned his head up and stared back at her. "Don't—," he held his hand up, stood, then pushed past her in the doorway and disappeared down the hall.

Chapter 44

Thursday, the 12th day of September

"What in the fuck were you thinking Major?" the Colonel said. He stepped back peering into Rob Browning's eyes. "I knew I should've pulled you out a long time ago. I saw it. I just didn't want to believe you of all people would be compromised. Fuck me. You had to know you were way out of bounds on this one. Why didn't you pull your own goddamn self out?" The General slammed his fist into the wall.

"Now it's sink or swim and by god we'd better be swimming out of this shit hole real quick or you're going to be facing a court martial like you have never seen before. The Joint Chiefs will cut your sorry balls off and mine too and eat them as appetizers at their next staff meeting if we don't fix and repair. And I mean right now. The bomb is ticking and the detonation can't be stopped.

"You're set to meet those local shit for brains little militants in only two hours. If you don't show, we don't need a bunch of hot-headed, Yahweh screaming, bomb toting psychopaths loose, looking for you while you're intercepting that satellite from the mother fucking Russians and our very own traitor, Mr. James. Your cover is compromised. Shit!

"It's always hoped that an agent's first cover wasn't exposed, but if it is, that's why we design multiple cover and contingencies. We'll use the U.S. Marshall dossier if we have too. Since we've worked three years here establishing that cover for you, I really don't want to expose you as an agent intercepting firearms between the local militant group and a major arms supplier tonight. It could complicate matters instead of undo the damage you've created. You need to get released right now and quietly.

"Jesus. If we do hand them that story, it sure as hell won't do us any good if you don't get out of here and swap merchandise and make it up the goddamn mountain to lead the operation as scheduled.

"It would be harder to retrieve James's satellite after it's left the airport. We'd have to blow it out of the sky, and that, Captain Brolins, will get even messier. We'd also lose James's prototype that proves we've lost our best kept secret and the lead in our stealth satellite technology we've had in the works. It looks as if our high priced army of scientists in the National Reconnaissance Office has been sitting on their fat asses and picking them instead of getting the job we're paying them to do done. Right under our noses, he designs the grand master of satellites, small and undetectable to the rest of the world and the whole package at a third of the cost ours is estimated at. He's left our asses exposed and eating our own shit. I have to hand it to him, he created one hell of a system. Light years ahead of us. The rest of the world can't, I repeat, can't get a hold of it.

"You're the only one at this stage of the game that can run the operation from the mountain and succeed. Replacing you at this point is out of the question. I might as well chew off my own feet right now, if I tried replacing you with anyone else. If we're going to accomplish our mission, you're our only chance. If we don't succeed, you know billions of dollars and resources have been lost and Russia will end up with our stealth satellite technology. If James is successful at handing over this satellite package, that would give Russia their super power status back and put us groveling at their feet. They will take that power and nail our American asses to the fucking wall and bury us with our own technology and nuclear power. That's all they need is that little window of opportunity. You know they'll take it just to restore their face to the world again. Paybacks are a bitch.

"If we don't succeed, the future as we know it is history. Our whole fucking operation will be fucked beyond repair if your face and name are flashed all over the local news tonight and connected with James's daughter. Their security force will make us, and we'll all be finished. Hear me? Not a pot left in the world to piss in. If the Associated Press gets a hold of this, the repercussions of your face being in the spotlight during primetime in every fucking part of the world, in which you've operated, sends me right over the edge. Why did you put all of this at risk so easily?

"You know, the Russians are already in this little cozy piece of shit town and it's not a whole fucking continent to hide in. If you are tied in any way to Mr. James's daughter, we're up shit creek. Christ!" He paced around the tiny room, the sweat pouring down his forehead. His cotton dress shirt soaked through, racing down the center of his back and under his armpits.

"Okay, now that I've given you the big picture, I'm going to try and calm down. My doctor said my blood pressure was getting too high. I needed to adjust the stress in my life." A sinister laugh blasted from his throat. "I'll take a few deep breaths and calm myself. Fuck. Forget calm. Tell me exactly what they have I should know about if I'm to get our sorry asses out of this jam and out of here in one piece as quietly as possible?" he stared at Browning, biting on his upper lip. He waited for Browning's report and his plan of extraction.

The Board members sat around the conference table with mixed expressions on their faces. At their last meeting a vote was taken and it passed by a majority. The contract had been awarded from that vote and put into motion. Only one member voted against killing Jennica James once and for all. The latest news reported that she was showing progress and was expected to recover.

During Board discussion, the members agreed that if she survived, it wouldn't be long before she was well enough to talk, and point the finger at them. Their secret vigilante group would be exposed and every prominent businessman in town would be imprisoned in a Federal penitentiary when the dust settled, if it became known exactly who and what they were all about. It was agreed that her death was the only way they could guarantee and protect the Sons of the Pioneers anonymity. No one was going to screw with their one-hundred year existence in the county, no one.

They held the underlying power of the local government, keeping a tight rein over the court systems, its judges, lawyers, and juries to maintain justifiable justice, according to the doctrines set forth by their founding fathers in 1896. They were some of the richest men in the state with controlling interests in the locally owned banks, and major landowners, holding a majority of the real estate in the county.

At today's meeting another vote was taken. It named a member of the Board to kill the hired killer of Jennica James. No one could be kept alive with the knowledge the contract killer would have gained after he did the job.

Mr. Babcock had voted no at the previous meeting, and now heard his name being nominated for completing their mission. He heard a second. The Board called for the vote. His heart plunged when he heard the unanimous vote cast by the Board members. His punishment for going against them. His hands shook beneath the table.

The Chairman slid a handgun to him from across the thick mahogany table. Their eyes met. He felt the ice and read the message clearly. Sweat glistened from the corners of his eyeglasses as he placed his hand over the gun. His mind felt the cold metal burn into his palm. He was marked for life. He knew he had better not fail or the next vote would be to extinguish him.

It was Thursday evening. A full moon hovered above the hospital, giving the hospital parking lot an omniscient glow. The weatherman had predicted storm clouds with severe lightning and thundershowers for later in the evening. Tonight, the weatherman's prediction came right on time. A thundercloud rolled in and clapped above, while rain pelted down on the town.

A beat up Ford pickup truck crossed over the line into oncoming traffic and swerved back in time to miss a passenger car. He swore as the passenger car's horn blasted him from inside the cab of his truck. Pulling over, he jumped out in the downpour and gave his windshield wipers a push. He was just a half a mile or so from the hospital. He could see it off to his left. The windshield wiper motor gave out. "Fuck." He'd make it the rest of the way or be killed trying.

The policeman assigned to Jennica's room asked a hospital security guard to relieve him for a few minutes and cover his watch while he took a quick break. Nicotine ruled his life. He leaned against the brick building under the awning and lit a cigarette and watched the lightning streak across the black sky. He wondered if by the end of his shift the rain would turn to snow.

He heard a horn blaring off in the distance and watched as a pickup barely missed a passenger vehicle. The truck pulled over, then came back out and turned into the hospital parking lot. He watched the beat up truck lurch to a stop and decided the driver must have an emergency on his hands. The man slammed the door and jogged inside of the building.

The night shift at the hospital progressed slowly until after the dinner hour. As the hours moved ahead the beds filled to capacity. Tonight, the doctors predicted a full house with the full moon overhead. The OB GYN floor always had a run on it on nights like this. Every pregnant woman close to her delivery date managed to go into labor and give birth during a full moon. Not only did the delivery rooms fill, but the emergency rooms as well. The emergencies were stranger than the average cases normally seen on any other night. During a full moon, the hospital psychiatrist always claimed to have their busiest nights.

The doctors, nurses, and staff who worked the night shift always knew to be prepared for the unexpected. It was not just a superstition or an old wife's tale to those who worked in the health care industry; it was a known fact. If you were new, and didn't believe it, you soon found out the rumors were all true.

The police mulled around the room, waiting for their assignments. The last shift punched out. Just a few minutes went by before their radios went off. The hospital had another shooting. The officers scrambled to get to their cars and to the scene.

"Christ." The Captain shook his head, sitting at his desk as he hung up his phone. Dylan stood in the doorway, waiting to hear the news. "A man just went into the hospital, shot and killed the man guarding Jennica, then continued shooting the rest of the place up. A Bozeman Police officer happened to be coming back, heard the first shot, and returned fire. He was able to stop him, but the man's dead."

"Jennica? What's her status? How many other casualties?" Dylan said.

"A team is on their way. Looks like he missed Jennica, but a nurse is in critical condition." The Captain mopped his brow with his handkerchief and pushed back his chair.

"It confirms somebody is desperate to get her out of the picture, but why? First Browning, now this man. Who is he?" Dylan wanted to head to the scene, but Browning waited. He wanted to really get his hands on him now.

"We'll know just as soon as they do," the Captain said, rising from his chair. "Speaking of Browning, I'd better get back to our visitors."

Chapter 45

Thursday, the 12th day of September

Entering the conference room where the meeting with Rob Browning was to take place, Dylan found a seat. Della followed, reading the notices posted on the walls. The room was sullen with them holding onto their silence. Dylan scribbled on a pad in front of him, making notes to himself. Captain Mitchell appeared, looking at the two detectives, their faces as glum as the walls covering the room.

"You're not going to like this. You two are off this case as of right now."

Both detectives jerked their heads towards the Captain. The surprise of his statement overwhelmed them.

"The case is closed." The Captain turned towards the door.

"Wait a minute, that's it? You're not going to give us an explanation for this?" Dylan said. "Captain, this can't be, Detective Bishop and I have worked on this shooting from the moment it happened. It's not finished."

"It is as of now. You won't pursue this any further, and that's an order."

"Captain Mitchell, with all do respect, this isn't like you. What happened in there? Can't you at least tell us why?"

"As I said, the case is closed. We have our confession and other cases to solve. Now get out of here. I'm giving you both a two-week vacation. You both deserve one."

"But, Captain?" Della said.

Captain Mitchell quickly turned and started walking out of the room, ignoring Della. Slamming his fist against the wall, he left cursing under his breath.

"This is unbelievable," Dylan said. "I can't believe he backed down. What on earth could this be about? I don't like this one bit. Rob

Browning is guilty. He may not be guilty of shooting Jennica James, but I know he's guilty of something. My gut tells me we've just scratched the surface. He's going to walk away from this whole deal like it never happened. I can't just sit here and let this happen. There are too many questions I still have in my mind. This just isn't making any sense, and the Captain is letting it happen."

"He probably doesn't have any choice. They probably threatened him and this department to stay out of it. When the Feds are involved, you can bet this is something extreme. They don't want us getting in their way."

"I don't like it." Dylan stood and walked towards the door.

"You don't have to like it, but it's an order. Where are you going?" She followed him as he kept walking.

"I'm following an order. I'm punching out and going on vacation. I thought the wilderness would be a good place to get away from it all."

Grabbing him by the sleeve, she pleaded, staring into his eyes. "No, please. Don't involve yourself any further. You'll jeopardize your job, and I know that's one thing you love more than anything else in this world."

"You don't know me, Della. Yes, I love my job, but only because it allows me to pursue the truth and bring justice through the system. If they won't allow me do that, I have a hard time still believing in it. I didn't think we would be so easy to walk over, but I can see we are. It reeks like garbage."

"You don't really believe that do you?" Della said.

"I don't know. I'm feeling confused, but my mind is clearer than it's ever been on this one. I've been stopped from pursuing an investigation that's not complete. It all feels wrong to me. I need closure on it, even if no one agrees with me. Just because Father Murphy said he shot Jennica, doesn't mean we can just ignore everything else and close the case at the Fed's orders." He pulled two quarters out of his pant pocket. He flipped her one. She caught it before it bounced off of the table. "I'll bet you right now, that the Captain feels the same way."

"Of course he does. He wouldn't have smashed his fist against the wall and left us with his parting words if he liked it."

"Well, here. Heads I go follow my heart, tails I'll stay and follow orders."

"This isn't a game. This is your job."

"Don't worry. I can always start my own private investigation service after I'm fired. Isn't that what all ex-cops do?"

"You're serious, aren't you? Dylan, think about this for a little while longer. Don't go being a cowboy here. You might not come back at all."

Dylan flipped his coin in the air and caught it, keeping it covered. "Come on, Della."

She flipped her coin. He walked over. They both lifted their hands away at the same time, so they could see.

"Heads. I'm going camping in the wilderness. Come on, you need a ride home." He motioned her towards the door.

"I do. I thought you'd try and pawn me off on one of the other officers, like you did Dr. Greene. Don't get me wrong, I'm glad you didn't. This will give me a little time to talk you out of your insanity."

"I guess, I still could. I saw Will, sitting over at the city desk on the other side. He looked like he could use something to do. Officer Wainwright already informed me he'd like to get to know you better. He said you asked him to think about joining the county when the next job opened up. He would enjoy taking over for me. You might prefer his company over mine too."

"Don't even try to get rid of me. You're not getting out of your promise." She started to walk ahead of him towards the door. Glancing back at him, she smiled. "Well, just don't sit there, give me that ride."

He opened the door for her. "Wait here. I'll pull the car around and pick you up. You've walked enough on that foot already today. The doctor would crucify the two of us if he knew what we've been up to."

She watched him bound to his car at the end of the parking lot under the dim light. In a flash, he returned and jumped out to open the door for her.

"Thanks. You amaze me, Dylan." She slipped into the car.

"Why's that?"

"Because you can be such a gentleman sometimes, it makes me forget the other side to you."

"Hey, what can I say that I haven't already said before? You bring out the best and the worst in me." He slammed the door and ran around back to the drivers's side. Spinning out of the lot like a kid with his first set of wheels, he smiled.

"Dylan."

"Don't try and talk me out of this. I need to go. I promise you, I'll be back tomorrow."

"Stop this time and think this whole thing through."

"I don't need to. Nothing has changed."

"Are you still calling in Colton, and bringing the right gear along this time?"

"No. I can't risk using him now. I'm going alone. Asking him to help out will only put his job in jeopardy. He's too good a friend to do that to."

"He'd do it."

"I have no doubts about that, but I don't want anyone to do me any favors."

"Please call him. You can't do this alone. If you won't ask him, then take me. I can be some sort of help, if it's only for another set of eyes."

"No, Della. We've been through all of this before. You're going home to rest. Don't worry, nothing is going to happen to me."

"I can't help, but worry. You don't know what you're up against. Even the wildlife is unfriendly. The bears would just as soon eat you than waste their time looking at you."

"Funny, Della."

They reached her house. Opening the door again, he reached his hand out to help Della get out of his car. She opened the gate, expecting Kiki to attack. The dog was gone.

"Kiki, where is she?" Della's voice turned to a fevered pitch. "Something's not right here." Turning around in her yard, she looked for any sign of him.

"Stay here," Dylan said. He slipped his gun out, creeping along the front of the house towards the back. Peering in the windows, he followed along the fence looking for clues of what might have happened to her dog. Reaching the back of the house by the screen door, he noticed a faint glow reflecting in the glass. A lamp was on in her living room.

Reaching for the sliding glass door, he yanked and slid it open, so he could slip in quietly. Hearing a low growl coming from the other room, Kiki met him as he stepped into the living room. Kiki jumped and almost knocked the gun out of his hand as a bewildered Matt sat up, rubbing his eyes on the couch. A book fell from his chest, hitting the floor.

"What the hell?" Matt said.

"What the hell is right. What the hell are you doing in here? I could've shot you."

"I heard Della was out of the hospital, so I came to see if I could help her out."

"How did you get in?" Dylan said.

"What's the third degree all about? Where's Della? Is she all right?"

"I'm fine," Della said. She was standing in the entryway staring at Matt. "What are you doing here?"

Kiki jumped on her, licking her face.

"I came to help you out," Matt said.

"I didn't ask for your help. How did you get in my house? I keep it locked."

"I used your hidden key."

"And you just let yourself in?"

"That's right. I thought I'd wait for you. I started reading, and must've fallen asleep." He glanced at his watch. "I didn't plan on staying this long."

"Well, it looks as if you have someone to take care of you now. I'll be leaving," Dylan said, turning to go.

"Not so fast," Della said. "Can I talk with you for a minute before you go?"

"I think we've covered about everything there is to cover. I'll just borrow your bathroom before I leave." Dylan turned towards the stairs. Della reached out and touched his arm.

"I'm sorry. I should be going. I can see I'm intruding here. I just wanted to see if you needed help or anything." Matt placed the book on the coffee table.

"No. I'm sorry Matt. I didn't mean to sound ungrateful. It's just a surprise to find you here inside of my house. Now that you're here, please stay. I don't want to be alone tonight." Della turned towards Dylan. He pulled away from her touch, a hurt expression apparent on his face. Jogging up the steep stairs, he disappeared.

"Excuse me." Limping up the stairs, she met Dylan coming out of the bathroom.

"This isn't what it looks like," she said. "I never gave him my key or told him where it was hidden. I'm as shocked about this as you are."

"I'm not shocked. It's also none of my business. I'm sure he'll take good care of you."

"That's not what I want and you know it."

"Do I?"

"You do. Admit something to me for once, before you leave." She reached for his hand and pulled him gently inside of her bedroom. Willingly, he followed her. "If I was just an ordinary woman who didn't work with you, would you let yourself be with me?"

"That's just it. You aren't an ordinary woman and I do work with you."

"You're avoiding my question. Would you fall for me?"

"I already have."

"You have?" Then when can we really share that bed over there?"

Following her hand as she pointed, he remembered the morning he woke up next to her in it, wishing he'd remembered it. "When I open my private investigation firm."

"Shit, Dylan. Be serious."

"I am." Reaching out he placed his hand under her chin and turned it up to him. Bending over, he grazed her lips softly with his, then pulled her into him, kissing her totally and taking her by surprise. Holding her tightly against him in his arms, he felt her body clinging to his. He felt the heat radiating and the fusion of sparks beneath them. He pulled gently away before he lost his strength to do what he had to do. "I promise we'll finish this, but I've got to go."

Her face flushed, her lips still parted slightly, she stared at him dumbfounded. Turning back to her as he reached the door, he formed the words he wanted to say, but decided to leave them for now, safely tucked inside.

Without speaking his final thoughts, he reached the stairs, hesitating again before descending them. Feeling deliriously happy and totally confused at the same time, he shook his wild mane of black hair as he ran for the door. His body pulled him towards her and his heart held hers, but his mind kept flashing warnings. Hurrying out the door, he breathed in the crisp mountain air, hoping to keep his head clear for the stakeout he planned.

Chapter 46

Friday, the 13th day of September

Dylan collected his supplies and carried them into the garage. He opened the back to his 1966 Willys Jeep he had inherited from his father, putting everything inside. He kept it parked in the garage covered by a tarp. He never drove it anywhere, preferring to keep it in the condition he received it in, as if that would keep the memory of his father intact. His dad kept everything immaculate, leaving it in vintage condition.

Knowing he needed four wheel drive up there tonight, he felt confident using the Jeep. If he'd used his brain before, things wouldn't have turned sour the first time. Della would be with him now, not at home with Matt watching over her. Shaking his head and shrugging those last thoughts from his mind, he finished and closed the back door.

Uncovering the vehicle the rest of the way, he walked around admiring it. Checking fluids under the hood, then the tires, he got in and turned the key. It started right up as if it had been yesterday that he had taken it out and driven it. Backing it out, he parked it in the driveway and left to finish packing.

Entering his house, he thought about his mother in the hospital. When he came home at night, the lights were always on, and the place always had a delicious smell from her constant baking. Now the place seemed dark and empty without her in it. She'd be furious with him for not checking in, like he told her he would. It was too late to call her. He'd check in with the nurse. Dialing quickly, he spoke to the night nurse. He felt relieved at her report that she slept soundly in her room, and everything was fine.

Leaving home, he filled Willy up on his way out of town and grabbed a couple sandwiches. Before he had a chance to rehash the week thoroughly in his mind, he found himself at the turnoff to Teepee Creek. The night sky cleared even at that altitude to an array of stars shimmering above him after the quick rainstorm. He peered at his watch that glowed faintly, realizing it was now Friday. Then he thought, Friday the 13th. His spine stiffened. Turning and driving across the rough graveled road up the hill, further toward the wilderness area, he crept along carefully because of the assortment of ruts and holes. He imagined a regular car would have been swallowed up in one of the deep holes.

He backed into a turnoff area, until his vehicle was out of sight of the winding road into a stand of trees and down another drop. Pulling out his equipment, he loaded it on his back and started the hike. Scouting a spot above the warehouse where he could camp out and watch from above, he struggled in the darkness. The thick forest and the deadfall made it hard to make good time.

He came upon a spot up the mountain a few hundred yards north of the area. A solid rock wall jutted out of the mountain and trees grew out the sides above and beside it, making a good cover from all sides. Locating a narrow opening between the mountain and the rock, he stepped into a small cave. Deciding it would provide him with a place to hide and protection from the unexpected weather that erupted out of the skies, he unloaded some of his equipment.

Taking off his backpack, he reached for his night vision equipment. He squatted, taking a surveillance of the area. Not detecting anything moving in the woods or around the perimeters of the area, he sat back keeping his goggles on and just listened. Hearing a cacophony of sounds coming from the nocturnal animals conversing across to one another in the lonely night, he felt a rejuvenation of his spirit taking place.

After an hour of peacefulness, he stretched and decided to hike in the direction of Browning's cabin. Making a full circle around the area of the warehouse, he'd search for any signs of recent activity. Carefully he chose his path, not wanting to disturb anything. Watching the best he could, he kept his feet solidly underneath him and avoided the holes and the slick boulders as he descended back down the mountain side.

Viewing the cabin from a half-mile away, he saw a light. Stopping in his tracks, he took out his goggles and tried to see. Sneaking down the hill before it flattened out again, he inched his way closer.

The cabin sat on top of a flat area. At the back of it, the land ended, and it looked out over a valley and the mountain range looked as if it reached to heaven. Thick pine trees covered the front of the cabin. A path wound up from the valley and stopped at the side of the house.

Through the protection of the woods, he kept cover as he crept closer. Crawling over fallen trees, he waded through the snow and partially muddy terrain. Hearing a snap behind him, he froze.

A whirring sound approached off in the distance and echoed across the valley disrupting the still of the night. It became louder as he lay against the earth listening. Feeling a vibration beneath him, he looked up and saw a helicopter flying over. It spun back towards the area of the cabin. It landed on the flat area at the back of it. Hearing the blades wind down as the engine stopped, it brought back memories of his days as a Navy SEAL. He watched closely as six men jumped from the chopper.

Hearing another snap, he lifted his body up slightly to turn and scout behind him. At the same moment, a thud made contact with his back. Flinching as another thud hit him, a crack sounded from his skull, making his eyes blur. A horrendous pain racked his entire body sending him crumpling back flat to the ground. The blackness engulfed him.

When he came to, he felt like a semi-truck had hit him. The pain pierced through him, shooting up his back as he tried to sit up. His eyes felt swollen. It was totally dark. His eyelash felt the blindfold, and a gag was stuck in his mouth. Finding that his hands and feet were tied, he wiggled, trying to loosen them. His feet were bare.

Focusing, his mind fuzzy, he tried to make sense of where he was. Hearing the sounds of heavy trucks, he stopped his vain attempt to free himself for a moment. The ground rumbled below him, vibrating under him like an earthquake.

A while later, he heard voices shouting orders. It sounded like an officer commanding an army. The words were not in English. He listened carefully, concentrating on the language. It sounded as if it were Russian.

Voices approached, speaking rapidly. They were coming for him, and he had no idea where he was, where the door was, or what his next move was going to be. With no time to decide, a heavy boot kicked the door and it crashed in. He knew it had landed close beside him as a rush of air moved as he heard the thud.

Large hands grabbed him by his feet and dragged him outside into the chill of the night. One of the men pulled the gag out of his mouth. Taking in a quick breath of fresh air, he laid still.

He could smell a heavy diesel fuel and grease odor. Smelly hands jerked the blindfold away from his face. He knew he was a dead man by the look on the face of the man that faced him. A scar ran down the right side of his face, making him look hideous. The skin on the left side of his face was also scarred, but scarring that looked like he had been seriously burned.

Two men dressed in camouflage uniforms stood to the side of him. The man wearing an evil grin pulled out a knife the size of a machete. He brought it up quickly in front of him. Dylan noticed his hands also were badly scarred from burns. His knife swooped down, cutting away the ropes binding his ankles.

The men yanked him up and stood him on his feet. They faced him towards the man wielding the knife. Dylan swallowed.

"Who are you?" the man said in broken English. The Russian accent he could not hide.

Dylan faced the group, knowing his end wasn't going to be pretty. "I'm a cop."

Repeating in Russian something, they all laughed. The man gave another order to the two men.

One of the men swung his rifle, stock first, directly into Dylan's stomach knocking the wind out of him. The man kept hitting again and again, wielding the heavy stock against his ribs. Doubling over, he fell to his knees. The other man pulled him back up and held him to face the burned man again.

"A cop." He laughed again, giving another order to the other two men. One man came up behind Dylan. Grabbing a hold of his hair, he jerked his head back. He ripped the stud from his ear and flung it. As he came around pulling his hair to face him, Dylan spat in his face.

The man grabbed his rifle and slammed it across Dylan's kneecaps. The force sent him reeling forward. His hands tied in front of him couldn't catch his fall. His face hit the wet earth. Managing to turn his face sideways, a boot kicked his face in. He heard the sound of cartilage busting inside his head at the same time blood spurt from his nose, splashing into his eyes. Tasting the blood, he spit. A bloody tooth hit the ground in front of him.

The burned man shouted another order. Dylan gritted his teeth and almost choked on another tooth. He sputtered, spitting it out. Waiting for the next assault, he prayed he'd pass out. Faintly, he heard another whirring sound off in the distance. Moving closer, he could hear it. Voices were yelling from behind him as the three stopped their assault and turned towards the sounds. Gunfire and a loud explosion echoed off of the walls of the valley and back to them. Rolling onto his back, he watched as the skies filled with bright lights.

The burned man noticed Dylan had rolled onto his back. Slicing the ropes off of his hands with another swoop, he nicked Dylan's wrist. Blood spurted and started soaking his shirt.

The other two men pulled him up and tried to keep him standing. They ripped the clothing away from his upper body while trying to keep Dylan from slipping out of their grip. His knees screamed with pain each time he put his weight on them. He couldn't stand by himself. From the side view, he caught a glimpse of the burned man holding his giant knife. Turning his head slightly, he saw him replace it with a machine gun.

Holding it under his right arm, he pointed it at Dylan's chest. "Run," he yelled at Dylan over and over again. Gathering his remaining strength, he fought the pain. He wasn't going to let this bastard shoot him in the back. He would not run away from him, so he could tell his superiors that he was shot trying to escape. Wanting them to know he wasn't a coward and that he was not afraid to die, he stared straight ahead. He wanted the burned man to have to look him directly in his eyes when he killed him.

The two men released him and he started sinking slowly to the ground. Biting his tongue, he held himself up, willing the pain, so he could stand facing him eye to eye. Shots broke out from above their location, and one grazed past his head. Dylan dropped to the ground. The three men fell simultaneously, arms splaying wildly as they hit the ground with a loud thud.

Staring at the men's dead eyes, he pivoted in the mud, looking for some cover from the gunfire. He realized three clean shots to the head had killed them all. He recognized the work of a professional sniper. He'd been one in the Navy.

Rolling across the open space to the building to take cover, he heard the gunfire rocking the silence out of the night. Hearing crunching in the grass to his right, then left, he knew he was surrounded and looked up.

Rob Browning held a gun an inch from his chest. "What the hell?" He let the gun swing loose at his side. "Detective Drake?"

Looking up, he could only shake his head and nod.

"I got word one of my men had been spotted and captured. What the hell are you doing up here?"

Dylan tried forming the words in his mind. He felt lightheaded. "Looking for you."

"You went against direct orders from your commanding officer. I was afraid of that. You just made a big mistake."

"It doesn't matter now, does it? Just kill me, finish me off." Dylan's voice weakened. "Go ahead."

Rob Browning knelt beside him and checked him over. Dylan shivered against the cold, his top half bloody and exposed. His feet were blue. Browning took off his down jacket and placed it around him.

"Let's get him to safety. Take him to base camp to the doctor. He's in bad shape." He looked back at Dylan,"You're going to wish you were dead tomorrow. You're one crazy son of a bitch to come up here. What were you thinking?"

Dylan strained his neck, trying to lift his head. "Who the hell are you?" he said.

"That doesn't matter right now. You need immediate medical attention, or all of this hero stuff is in vain." He reached and gently touched his shoulder. "Don't worry, we have everything under control." He stood. "Take him."

Dylan heard them speaking into their radios, their voices sounded slurred, like listening to a recording low on batteries. He felt like the world and everything in it moved in slow motion, he knew he had to be dreaming. Watching, he tried to keep his mind from coming to a complete halt and with it the last light left in his mind from being snuffed out. Through the dimming light, he thought he saw a military chopper touch down and several men jumping out carrying a stretcher. Dylan blacked out.

Chapter 47

Sunday, the 15th day of September

Dylan woke with a start, thinking he was falling from a cliff after being sprayed by machine gun fire. He blinked his eyes open, finding himself in a small room the color of eggshells. He turned his head, observing the space, finding no paintings or personal items in the room. The only things he saw were a small metal stand next to the bed, a lamp sitting on it and the hospital bed he lay in. The floor appeared to be smooth gray cement.

A pole sat next to the bed with a bag attached to it. He followed the line with his eyes. It led to his arm. Lifting his arm to rip the tube out as his anxiety heightened, he found his arm restrained.

Having no concept of where he was or how long he had been there, he searched his memory to no avail. The door opened a crack. Diana Edwards walked in.

"Glad to see you're awake. You've been asleep for a couple of days."

Relief swept over him after hearing she quoted days not weeks.

She came in closer and stood over his bed. "Don't look so surprised." She pressed a button on her watch and noticed his confusion. "Don't worry, you'll know everything in just a sec." She glanced over at the door at the exact time it opened. Rob Browning strolled through, sporting a huge smile.

"Detective Drake. Glad to have you back among the living." He turned to Diana. "You may leave us now."

She left the room and closed the door quietly behind her.

Dylan tried sitting up in bed, so he could face the man eye to eye. He fell back. A yelp escaped his lips. Sweat drenched his forehead from the effort. He slowly and agonizingly reached for his side with his free hand, feeling tape wrapped around the top half of his chest. Inching the sheet down with just two fingers he craned his neck forward and tried looking at the rest of his body. All he saw was white.

"Easy there. Don't try that again. You've been through a war. You've broken ribs, broke your nose, a few teeth were knocked out of your mouth, and you have a hairline skull fracture that will be the cause of some severe headaches for quite a while, the doctor tells me. You have a few stitches here and there. I hate to be the one to inform you of this, but you also won't be taking any romantic strolls under the starry skies for awhile. Your kneecaps have been badly damaged. Luckily for you, they aren't broken, just severely bruised. The tape is to keep your ribs in place while you're healing. You're very lucky."

"How's that? I'm a prisoner. I'd rather be dead than taken alive."

Rob Browning started to laugh.

"You bastard. I wish I could get up. I'd kill you with my bare hands," Dylan said.

"Whoa, cowboy. I know you're very capable of doing just that after learning you were once a Navy SEAL, but you have this all wrong. I want you to know right now, I'm on your side. I really am. I'm a good guy."

"Eat shit and die."

"That's no way to speak to someone who just saved your sorry ass."

"Save it for someone who cares."

"No. I'm going to set you straight right here and right now. My name is not Rob Browning."

"No shit. And I suppose that wasn't Diana Edwards either."

"Please, save your remarks until you've heard me out. If you don't want to hear it, then just say so. I'll be out of here." He studied Dylan's face. "Okay, have it your way. I'll leave. Have a good night." He stood up and faced the door.

"Wait. Tell me. I do want to know what the hell's going on before I die, so fill me in."

"I knew you'd finally see the light."

"I don't have much of a choice now, do I?" He tried smirking, but found it too painful.

Browning sat back down and pulled his chair closer to his bed. "My first cover was a US Marshal. The Marshal's service, as I'm sure you know, is a Federal agency. They gave me a badge and sent me here to Gallatin County. Of course, the local law didn't know there was another US Marshal living in the area. It was my cover to keep my other mission and identity secret.

"The US Forest service land the cabin sits on is owned by the Federal government. The lease of that cabin is under Federal jurisdiction. They took it over three years ago when they decided to put me in here officially. It was easy enough to do. No one would question it. Hell, not too many people know that cabin sits up there. The land the warehouse sits on borders US Forest Service land and is next to the wilderness area. It is two sections up there that is held in private ownership.

"Guess who owns it? TransAmerica Telecommunications Corporation. They design, manufacture, and market commercial satellites. I'll get to that company in a minute. That's why my base was strategically placed where it was. The cabin's lease with the Federal government sat closest to the action. The company bought up the lands during the slump in the economy back in the 80's.

"The Federal government also used me to keep a watch on a small military movement growing in your state over the past few years. The so called private militia and the copycat groups that are multiplying at a phenomenal rate because they don't like living within the boundaries of the law. They started gaining attention, catching the Federal government's eye when they started coming out of the woodwork and banding together with other states and their militias. So, I could serve two purposes for them. Your tax dollars at last well spent." He chuckled.

"My employer is the Federal government. It's not the US Marshal's service, although I am deputized. My second job, so to speak. I work for an unknown agency inside the CIA. It's part of our government that only a select few know about. It's not part of the Secret Service or the Federal Bureau of Investigation. All of us do work together, as much as rumor has it to the contrary. We're all separate entities of the Federal government.

"It's an agency most crucial to our national security. Now that you're here, you're among, one of the few who'll have knowledge of our operation. It's a secret that I expect you to keep, or I'll have to kill you." He stared back at Dylan giving him a cynical laugh. "That's a government joke that I know you've heard before. I've studied your background thoroughly. A seriously funny joke that could be deadly if one doesn't understand?"

Dylan fixed his eyes straight ahead, staring at the walls, trying to focus on the whiteness in them, hoping it would help him concentrate through his doped up mind. He didn't want to look at the man sitting across from him. The very person who made him boil with hatred from the depth of his bowels with a vengeance like he'd never felt before. Rotating his face a little, he stared directly into the eyes of his devil, hoping he could read his mind.

"It's been the best kept secret in the history of the government. We keep a watch on all the military activity in other countries and around the world by powerful spy satellites hovering above us out in space. We have a team that constantly keeps surveillance, alerting us to any covert activities our government isn't privy to.

"It keeps us on top. Nuclear power made this agency what it is, and continues to keep it as our number one priority. With the collapse of the Soviet Union and the Berlin Wall coming down, people stopped worrying and just kicked back. Nuclear disarmament is only played up for the media and the rest of the people living out of reality that think we can have an ideal world and peace is possible. We know that's bullshit. It doesn't even make good fiction. Believe me, it's going on in every country in the world. Even the third world countries are being brought into the larger deals. It's a magic act."

"What's this agency called? It must have a name?"

He stood walking around the stark room. He came back looking at Dylan lying in the bed; Dylan's eyes followed him like a hawk. The rest of his body remained motionless.

"I know you know what agency I'm referring to, and you are well aware of their activities Detective Drake," he maintained direct eye contact.

"We became involved in this town of yours when Mr. James arrived in it. We have been monitoring him for ten years. He runs the company TransAmerica Telecommunications. It's a research company specializing in the cutting edge of technology in the communications world. It's a nice cover to blanket yourself in when you're delving in espionage.

"Mr. James travels around the world gathering information, then he sells it. His company has worldwide assets amounting to billions. He sells spy satellites to other countries, among other things. His latest deal, the one we have under surveillance here, is with Russia. And you thought the cold war was over. It is, but the nature of the beast still remains. History is always being made.

"Mr. James was one of the top scientists recruited after the NRO's pilot project succeeded and we brought home the goods on all of our neighbors to Washington. They had Japan, Germany, Russia, Iran, Iraq, Africa, and Cuba. Everything was covered. No one could hide anything from their view. As the technology in the field expanded and became more complex, so did the agency.

"They brought in Mr. James, even though he was much too young and had not been tested for his loyalty to the project and to his country. At the time, the agency needed his brilliant mind. He was one of the best scientists on the team. I'd say now, he is by far, the best. He lost his commission when he was caught red handed trying to slip top secret plans out of a classified area. It contained some highly detailed drawings of one of our newer systems back then that was scheduled to be tested in the field within weeks. Of course, it was his design, but he signed his rights to it away when he was recruited and joined.

"He's been on our list ever since. We let him roam freely around the country, but we have kept our spies above and below on him. We've learned volumes from his activities since his departure. It might sound odd, since he's on the opposing team. He leads us to our weakest spots, the enemies that hate us and are willing to do anything to gain an edge over us.

"His biggest scheme of this decade is the reason we're here in your lovely state of Montana. We needed to infiltrate and annihilate his current plans. He started formulating his plan with other rogue countries, and eventually caught the attention of the Russians. Designing and manufacturing the cutting edge systems our government continually upgrades; he cut the deal and arranged shipment after he'd secured the financial arrangements. In the business, it takes time to develop and test. Then they're launched into space. The cost of these projects is astronomical.

"Russia is not a wealthy country anymore, but it is a major player that still holds power and is a force to be reckoned with if they start building up their nuclear arms, and dealing through rogue countries that are full of international terrorists. James promised several state of the art models in the next few years.

"He has been manufacturing and testing them right under our noses, but our eyes were wide open. The shipment became viable as promised this week, and they planned to take possession of the spy satellite quietly and unobtrusively high up in the mountains in Montana where no one would be the wiser, or so they thought.

"You know, it's a perfect state for operating anything illegal. Dope dealers, mobsters, thieves, all the unsavory have a large state in which to hide, where the law is few and far between. I bet you didn't know international spies were lurking here also?"

"Mr. James was ready to ship on schedule. The last installment of the financial arrangement had to take place at the same time the satellite was being exchanged. The last installment is the largest payoff of them all. The deal went according to plan, or so they thought. Russia sent a small army to accompany the shipment back home in planes that were bought illegally from U.S. privateers, the communist bloodsuckers. They can enter our country easily with their false flight plans and with the help from whom else, but TransAmerica's worldwide web. The arrangements were coordinated like a military strategic command with all sides keeping a close eye on each other. Trust isn't a word they're familiar with.

"So what's the big deal? Russia has spy satellites. Yes, you're right. I do know about reconnaissance satellites." Dylan coughed from the smoke seeping into his damaged lungs.

"You know everything about the National Reconnaissance Office. I told you, I have read your whole military background, even the red files. I might add, it is all quite interesting reading. As a Navy SEAL, you had one hell of a record, Detective." he said.

Dylan scowled in light of Browning's last statement. He did not like where the conversation was heading. "Okay, so, get to your fucking point."

"No one has seen the likes of this satellite, no one, not even us. That's the scary part. It had been our hope that the US would be the ones to bring the technology this far forward, but he beat us to it. The design, the entire package of this satellite, is one of the most advanced models that has surpassed what was hoped for in the future, even by the NRO in the next ten years. If Russia had gotten a hold of it, we'd have our final fucking. So, that's why we had to step in on this one. We intercepted their bank exchanges via computer. We wired back to Mr. James's headquarters that the money was successfully transferred and sitting in his various bank accounts, which set the final stage in motion. Interception of the satellite that was on its way to a private airstrip in the wilderness area. It was to be flown to Russia with Mr. James's ordinary company cargo plane across the ocean. The Russian planes right there with them. Russia is a democracy now. It's easy to land in Moscow."

"That's the war you ended up in." He slipped a cigarette from his shirt pocket, offering one to Dylan. When Dylan didn't respond, he put the pack away and lit one. He blew rings into the air, inhaling deeply. "I'm sorry you ended up in the middle of it. You were warned."

"Some warning. I didn't know I was walking into the middle of a fucking James Bond flick. What did you say your real name was? Is it James? James Bond?"

"You might think this is a joke, but I can assure you, it isn't. Let me make myself perfectly clear here. This is real. And now, you're involved in it. I'm going to finish what I came here to tell you, unless you tell me you don't want to hear anymore. I can't guarantee what will happen after tonight. It's up to you. All I can tell you now is why. Do you want to hear the rest?"

"By all means. You have me sitting on the very edge of my fucking seat."

Chapter 48

Sunday, the 15th day of September

Browning paced around nervously, smoking another cigarette before he continued his story. "Of course, you've figured out by now that Jennica James is Mr. John James's daughter. The shooting, during her concert debut, sent all of us in the agency Helter-Skelter for awhile. We didn't know who was responsible for it. We all had our theories.

"I thought my cover had been blown. I had actually worked my way into the Bozeman society, met Jennica in church, and moved in on her for the kill. It was a plan my superiors thought necessary, in case we needed an edge later on. She could be used as a hostage, a bargaining chip, if it came down to that. I didn't like the plan, but I had to go along with it. I follow my orders." He emphasized the word orders.

"I ended up actually falling in love with her, although I tried like hell to deny it. Three years is a long time to play a ruse without getting personally involved. That's why I thought her shooting was a direct message to me, that I had been compromised in some way in this elaborate set up. By whom? I was only theorizing.

"At one point, I actually thought her father's own team had a rogue who found out and was warning me to back off. If the deal didn't go down, all his team members had a lot to lose. Then I figured it must be another group he pissed off in some other country, retaliating against him for selling out to the Russians by hitting him where it would really hurt, his family.

"Jennica was the light of his life. He was proud of her success. I'm speculating that Mr. James thought an opposing player decided to shake him up right before the biggest deal of his life. The man has many enemies. Russian backers worried they would be blamed, one of their disenchanted own who wanted to create havoc. Everyone was put under the microscope. You never know in this line of work, who can be trusted and who can't be. There's always a hair-trigger waiting to go off. Sometimes it happens unexpectedly, but then, you already know that, don't you?"

He leaned back, stretching his arms in front of him, dropping the cigarette to the floor and crushing it under his foot. He looked over at Dylan, his eyes scanning Dylan's face. "Have you heard everything so far?"

"Yes, every word. Now I'd like to ask you a question?"

"Go ahead, I'll answer it if I can. There's not too much more you won't know about me after today. We're going to become quite chummy."

"Did you secretly marry Jennica?" Dylan said.

"No. She brought it up a time or two. She agreed the timing was off. She just started touring as their album started reaching the top of the charts. She was gone more than she was in town, making it easy for me. I could carry on with my own agenda without her being too close to detect anything out of the ordinary.

"I told Dr. Greene we were secretly married to get her to respond to my wishes to let me in to see her. I just needed to see her one last time and see for myself that she was going to be okay. I wanted to hear that she would make a complete recovery. I was on my way to end this project, therefore, severing our tie. I would be moving on to wherever they sent me next. I felt responsible for her life and for her laying in the hospital fighting for her life. I blamed myself, even though I didn't know who the guilty party really was at the time. I still blame myself.

"That's why I refrain from getting involved in relationships of any kind. It usually turns ugly in the end. That was a set up and I fell hard for her. That part of the job is difficult to swallow sometimes, but you get use to it. I don't like using innocent victims as pawns in government games. To them everyone is fair game. They don't give a rat's ass if someone innocent gets in their way. They just knock them out of the field.

"I worried that they had done just that. They detected my apprehension about using her, sensing that I was too personally involved with her to remain completely objective. They couldn't have me compromise the mission. At that point, they could have stepped in and taken her out. I realized though, the job would have been done right. Nice people I work for don't you think? But then again, you know this too."

"Choice." Dylan nodded his head and cleared his scratchy throat, feeling the gapes with his tongue his teeth use to occupy. He was glad it wasn't his two front teeth. "Why did you risk your cover by threatening Dr. Greene with a gun, just to see Jennica, if you knew that action could bring the local law down on you?"

"I'm not use to being told no. Dr. Greene didn't give in. I knew I could make her let me see Jennica by adding a dimension of fear to the situation. So, I acted out my absolute desperation. I was pissed off at the world and I really didn't care anymore. I didn't trust anyone at that point, and I wasn't even sure about the people I worked for. I would've been out of the country before you local cowboys found me anyhow.

"I also knew that if I was caught, I'd be exempt from your laws. They would've pulled me out of your grip. I did have a plan. I just didn't plan on Father Murphy hitting me on the head and taking my gun away from me."

"So, it's true. Did you see him hand the gun to Dr. Greene?"

"Yes. He asked her to shoot him. I was trying to get the gun out of his control by motioning to her to accept his offer and take it. She saw me sneaking up on him. I wanted her to take the gun. She hesitated, then started to grab it as he handed it to her. He heard the floor creak when I stepped in the room from the hall. He freaked. He pulled the gun back towards him and it went off. The barrel was pointed at his chest.

"I didn't know what kind of crazy she was dealing with at the time, but I knew she treated the mentally ill. I figured it was one of her patients that had lost it and she needed my help. I could've left her to him at this point, you know, but I couldn't let her get hurt. I'm not as cold hearted as you think. I didn't know it was Father Murphy until he was on the floor, dead. The whole thing left a bad taste in my mouth. I'm sorry, I couldn't stay around and answer your questions to clear Dr. Greene. It was an accident."

"You expect me to believe all of this?" Dylan raised his eyebrows. Just the motion of rolling his eyes left an excruciating pain shooting through his head. His head started throbbing in the first few minutes he started listening to Browning's story

"I don't care what you believe. I'm not here to try and convince you of anything. I'm just trying to fill you in on the missing pieces to your investigation that went bad."

"It didn't go bad."

"It did. You missed following up on some very important leads." He stood raising his watch. He pushed a button.

A woman he didn't recognize entered carrying a plastic bottle full of fluid. She took the one that was almost empty from the pole and replaced it with a new one in her hand. She left without saying a word.

"What are you shooting in me?" Dylan said.

"Morphine. It's for the pain. You'll thank me later."

"I can't see that ever happening. I have another question I'd like for you to answer. Was it your gun that Father Murphy shot Jennica with?" The pain killers in his IV drip started to kick in. He felt a surge of heat rush through his entire body, making him melt into a kind of euphoria. His tongue felt heavy and thick moving across the holes where teeth use to be. It didn't seem to bother him much now.

"Yes, it was. That sent the first alarm into our whole operation. The first thought at the round table was that someone set me up because of my relationship with Jennica linking me to her father's operation.

"When Father Murphy called and told me how he found the gun missing from my cabin and how it ended up with him at the church, I felt a small sense of relief. I wanted to believe it was a coincidence that some kids stole it from the house and took it with them when they went to the concert.

"I imagined they consumed some mind altering drugs that kids are so fond of these days and it blew their little minds. I could see how some kid probably took out the gun and started playing with it. It went off, hitting Jennica up on stage. They ditched it and ran. Another kid decided he wanted it and picked it up without thinking. That sent him to confession. I really needed to make myself believe that, that was all there was to it, an accident, plain and simple. Nothing made sense at that point. I just wished he hadn't taken it down and turned it in to you.

"The other scenarios I found myself playing with only led to bigger problems from that point on in our operation that might have compromised it. We couldn't lose that satellite. It wasn't an option.

"Where am I?" Dylan said.

"You're in a safe place. No one's going to hurt you. We know that your commanding officer put you on a two week vacation. He doesn't expect you back. He knows you're pissed off at him anyway, so he doesn't expect to hear from you until you return. You're in the Naval Reserves. You'll be called away, since you're the one officer in your unit who is specialized. We need you. You know there's a real war going on, don't you?" Browning smirked. "They'll be informed of your departure for active duty when your vacation is up. That should give you plenty of time to heal, no questions asked.

"Those knees might take awhile to get back in shape. Physical therapy will start after you've rested another few days. We have the best doctors here in the world.

"The Russians aren't pleased about the outcome here in Montana. They probably left a few of their own men behind to retaliate. You don't want anything to lead back to you and of course, nothing will lead back to the agency."

"Where am I? You can at least tell me that."

"We've flown to a top secret installation. We'll all remain here until we receive further orders."

"Goddamn it. Tell me where here is?"

"Cheyenne Mountain. You might be familiar with it."

Dylan rolled his eyes, waiting for more details.

"The rest is on a need to know basis. You know what that means," Browning said.

"Mr. James. Where is he?"

"He's dead, along with all the men in his operation. The warehouse is empty. There isn't a trace of anything out there to be found. We've gone over it with a microscope. The official report says Mr. James died after his plane went down in the ocean on a business trip. He did file a flight plan."

"Right. You kill the most brilliant mind of our time. I don't think so, but if it makes you feel better thinking I believe what you're telling me here, so be it. Diana Edwards. I don't understand her being here. That was a set up?"

"No. She's Jennica's best friend. She was the only one in the band who knew about me. She contacted me, because she was scared of the militia after she'd been picked up by them. She thought Mr. Tate wanted her to vanish, because she would blow their plans to transfer arms and expose the operation she walked into that night. She wasn't aware of his own agenda in the movement. She really believed they were trying to shoot her, not Jennica that night.

"You had left when the identity of the second shooter at the hospital became available. He was on one of our lists.

A list I built while I worked undercover and infiltrated the local militia. It was a board member of the Sons of the Pioneers. We'd uncovered the organization while investigating the militia's activities in the county. Interesting history.

"If Diana was the original target and the job was botched, then they could have decided to finish her off to keep the dogs from sniffing closer to the trail leading to them. If they'd known Father Murphy confessed, they probably would have let it go. They'd never be linked to Jennica's shooting since Father Murphy confessed and was no longer around to take his confession back or for more evidence to surface. Diana's life would have still been in danger. They'd still want her out of the picture completely to guarantee that their identity was still kept a secret.

"You don't think Father Murphy really shot Jennica?"

"No, I don't. My infiltration of the local militia gave me information that supports Diana was the one that was to be hit during the concert, hired indirectly by the Sons of the Pioneers. It was a mistake in identity that cost that man his life also. One of the ones who buried him had too much sauce and spilled his guts to one of my men on the inside."

"Christ. Father Murphy's confession sticks in light of that?"

"Yes, it has to for now. We can't risk unveiling what we've found. Father Murphy was my close friend and confidante. I don't like it, but knowing him and now the private hell he suffered, his soul will be redeemed for being the fall guy in this one. I have to believe he would be a Saint now."

"Cut the redemption speeches. It doesn't suit you," Dylan said.

"No, it certainly doesn't. One day, though, we will be able to clear his name officially. The militia is still under our eye." He continued, "Jennica was privy to my cover of being a US Marshal a couple years into our relationship. It started by her finding my badge one night. I became comfortable and got careless. I had too much to drink one night and let her talk me into bringing her to the cabin for the weekend. That was my first mistake. She found my Marshal's badge. She demanded an explanation. I gave her my cover story and convinced her why I was there. She swallowed it hook line and sinker after a very heated discussion.

"She actually thought I was spying on her and the band, looking for a drug connection. I convinced her I wasn't. Of course, the agency checks everyone out. She was clean and so were the members of her band. Her dossier reads like a contestant for the Miss America pageant.

"I played my part as a cop real well, asking her if she and her band were involved in a drug cartel. I told her she acted paranoid, like she was trying to hide something from me. She became violent. It became ugly for awhile, until I brought her back under my control. She told me she never even experimented with drugs. They had ruined her older sister's life. She wasn't a fool. I found that was true.

"She made up to me then, pouring on her charms. She'd discovered my weakness early on in our relationship. She used it against me. I gave in to her. We made up. I made her swear during that episode to keep my identity a secret or both of our lives would be in danger. That seemed to thrill her. I meant it to scare her. She promised and I thought she kept my secret until Diana called and asked for my help.

"We had a serious discussion, then I had her taken out of the picture with her consent. I didn't want her killed because of me. Anyone tied to Jennica with a link to me could have been in danger. Jennica told her about the militia movement and that was why I was here. She didn't trust anybody at this point. I was her only hope."

"And the Sons of the Pioneers?" Dylan said.

"Yes. I fed her that story to feed to you. I wanted you to lead your investigation in that direction, while we finished our mission up in the canyon. Let the local law expose them. Diana thinks we're all here because of the militia's activities, which isn't entirely made up. She never was in Billings with a sick grandmother. She was under my protection the whole time.

"How did you know I would get that story?"

"She told me of your first meeting. How you had to leave. The arrangement she cancelled after her fears caught up to her. I knew you would get her to tell you the rest of the story. I added to it, before you could arrange another meeting with her. It was very clever of you to set her up with Dr. Greene. I thought it was a genuine appointment. We had the lines monitored. It was after that she told me about you intercepting her in Dr. Greene's office. I was glad I had supplied her with that information so quickly. If you would have checked out a few of these things for yourself, you might have gotten closer to the truth. You assumed too much. You just fell into all of this by accident."

"Truth?" Dylan barked out a laugh that hurt like hell. "That's a misnomer if I've ever heard one. And, I think, I moved in closer to your little undercover mission than you'd care to admit. I didn't believe that cock and bull story about the Sons of the Pioneers, but I could tell she believed it and that her fears were genuine."

"Scott and Josh Tate's father's great-grandfather was one of the original founding fathers of the Sons of the Pioneers when it formed in 1898." Browning said. "The current members watched as the local militia group gained notoriety and became a threat to their county. When they started forming alliances with other counties and militias in the surrounding states, they knew they had to infiltrate and stop them before they ruined the town's good name. The militia were aligning with Washington, Idaho, Utah, Wyoming, North and South Dakota. They spread out and were multiplying at a phenomenal rate with lots of help by the World Wide Web and various other resources too available today. You knew about the Freemen that holed up in Jordan in Justice Township. They even linked themselves to the head of the militia movement in Montana until they had a falling out.

"Scott and Josh aren't active members of their father's group. However, they know the group exists historically and of their father's place in it. Their father expects them to join. They are heir to it. So, if I were you, I wouldn't have just decided it's a cock and bull story. That's your problem. You kept jumping without completing a thorough investigation.

"The FBI was focusing on Fergus County then, and they've had a plan of action in place for a lot longer than just the time the Freemen pulled there little standoff off up here. They had a plan that included every arm of law enforcement available. That kind of plan doesn't have any jurisdiction. All the agencies banded together to fight them. The FBI couldn't afford another Ruby Ridge or another Waco incident. Help had been asked for so they gave it. They just had to be careful in their methods this time. We fed them coverage from our satellites. We informed them of their activities. We could see things as small as a postage stamp. That's how the first two were bagged in Jordon. The government can't afford to have all these lunatics coming together and creating a new world by their law.

"I told Diana that after the Oklahoma City bombing the government increased surveillance on all militia type activities in the country. That's the reason they put me, an extra US Marshal in Montana to do some undercover work, just as I had told Jennica and she in turn had told Diana.

"I told her our plan to infiltrate their operations, a spy on the inside. We have people on the inside all over. Oklahoma City resulted from a hair-trigger theory. We wanted to make sure that if they planned anything for each anniversary of Waco and the Oklahoma City bombing or anything else they felt offended by, that we shut them down first. So, you see, I haven't been just sitting up in the majestic mountains of Montana enjoying the view and collecting my paychecks."

"Christ. This is shit. I'm still wondering who the real you is," Dylan said.

"No one knows, you never will either. In my line of work, you change identities like you change your pants. Only a few good men are cut out for this line of work."

"You must've been a Marine."

"Don't let your tongue get sliced by those razor blade remarks. They won't phase me in the least. I've grown thick skin."

"Like a chameleon. I'm waiting for your next skin shedding."

"You must be tired. I've given you a lot to swallow."

"I'm fine. I have more questions for you."

"Shoot."

"Believe me, I'd like to. Where's my gun?"

"I suppose, buried with all the other evidence burnt beyond recognition and trucked to a hazardous dump site in Nevada. You didn't have many clothes on, let alone a gun when we found you. Whatever was collected in the field was destroyed."

"My Jeep?"

"Your Jeep? Yes. We found it parked down on the road with another vehicle parked next to it. They both were destroyed."

In an instant, red blanketed his mind. He tried lunging at Browning. The pain stopped him. "Tell me what the other vehicle was?" he said, grimacing and wishing he could get out of bed to strangle him.

"A brand new four-wheel drive Ford Ranger. One of the Sheriff's new vehicles."

Dylan knew immediately that Colton had driven up to look for him. He had called, telling him his plans had changed and he wouldn't be needing him. "Where's the driver?"

"Relax. He's here. Colton is it? A deputy in the Sheriff's Department and one of your good friends. Don't worry, we don't make a habit of making honest people disappear permanently. He's here under the same assumption that everyone else is. An undercover operation that's monitoring the militia activities in the state. We pulled him out, convincing him you were okay. He's as cocky as you are, but he listens to reason. He's demanding to see you. I can arrange it now, if you think you're up to it. Got the whole picture now?"

"Sure. What did you do, hire a bunch of people to go out there and play army for you to make this convincing to them?"

"Hell, no. We have an army here. It's up to you to make it all convincing when you talk to them. Now, I want to tell you about Detective Bishop. She's a whole different story.

Chapter 49

Sunday, the 15th day of September

Dylan's eyes popped out of his head with the mention of Della. His heart skidded to a stop. He felt the sweat start to roll off of his body, soaking the sheets.

"You look as if you've seen a ghost, detective?" Browning said. "What's the matter? Is the pain getting worse?"

"No. Tell me about Della. What's happened to her? If something has happened to her, I'll kill you if it's the last thing I do in this life." He tried to sit up and move his legs across the side of the bed. He moaned and fell back.

"I'm sorry to cause you such distress, but you're quick to jump the gun. It's unfortunate for Detective Bishop that she's the feistiest female I've ever come across. She fought my men like it was her last fight. She had to be put out."

"No," Dylan screamed, his head pounding from the sound of his own voice.

"See, there you go again. I wouldn't kill someone as beautiful as her. My men had to tranquilize her to get her here. She was hysterical. Biting, kicking, using some of that fancy kickboxing with a cast on her damn foot. Fortunately for me, she was way out of her league. It was for her own good that we gave her that shot. She would have been seriously hurt if she kept it up. I was shocked to discover this was your partner when you took me down to the station that night after Father Murphy 's shooting. The first time I saw her, the two of you were out in the parking lot of the hospital fighting. I thought she was someone you were trying to arrest. She let you have it. At first, I thought she needed help, but then I realized that you were the one who could have used the help." He chuckled. "I enjoyed watching her. She's a hellcat that's for damn sure. Ms. Bishop is awake now. She slept almost as long as you did."

"You are enjoying the hell out of this aren't you? You like playing fucking games. Well, I don't. She'd better be in here standing in front of me in five minutes or this game will get serious."

"I'm not playing a fucking game, this is your new life. You're threatening me? What are you going to do, hot shot? You can barely wiggle your toes. Come and get me? I know you want to kill me, but I'm not the enemy. I haven't done anything to deserve this vile wrath of yours.

"Look at you. You're an invalid right now, but you're alive and eventually your body will recover. However, nothing will be back to the way it was and that is your fault. I saved you and your two friends from being killed. Like it or not, all three of you are involved in this now. That's your reward for living. You hold the safety of your two friends in your hands. You're the only one outside of the circle who knows the whole story. It stays here. As long as you play the part, no harm will ever come to them. You're their guardian angel. You go along with our orders from now on and everyone will come out of this just fine. We'll operate as we always have, unless you screw up."

Browning stood up from the chair and picked it up, turned it around in his hands then slammed it back down on the concrete. He straddled the steel chair, leaning forward closer to Dylan's face. "Do I make myself perfectly clear here? If you don't think you can do it, then here," He reached inside of his blazer and pulled out his gun and held it high above his head so Dylan could see it clearly. "Shoot yourself right now, because these are the only two options that I can offer you."

Dylan's eyes remained steady as he made a decision he knew would alter the rest of his life. He knew he had no chance of getting the gun away from him and killing the son of a bitch. He had no strength to carry it through. "Bring her in."

"First, I want to ask you a question," Browning said.

Dylan nodded. He felt himself weakening. His body felt like a lead weight.

"You would do anything to protect Detective Bishop, even if it meant killing yourself to keep her alive?"

"Yes." His mind clouded in a haze of memories of Della.

"That's because you love her. Admit it, then I'll let you see her."

"I've loved her for a very long time." He heard his own voice whisper it to him because he wanted to live long enough to see her face one more time. He felt his life draining away.

"I know the symptoms. I'm a victim myself. That's why I'm letting you both be together right now. I'm a romantic at heart. I convinced my superiors that it would work better this way."

Dylan's eyes blurred. Browning's face faded into the white background.

Pressing his watch, Browning turned to leave. He picked the chair back up and placed it against the wall. The door opened as he reached it.

Della was wheeled in past him, and placed next to Dylan's bed. She took in Dylan, laying in front of her and stifled her cry. It came out a gasp that Dylan heard. His eyes fluttered open. "You're the best thing I've ever seen," he managed to say.

"Don't ever do that to me again. I thought you were dead."

"I might feel better if I were." He turned his head more to get a better look at her. "I'm sorry."

"Dylan. You promised you would never tell me that again. God, you look bad."

"Thanks," he gave her a weak smile, "I have to break my promise."

"Under the circumstances, I'm letting you. I'm going to take care of you. I can't return to work for a while myself. I kind of messed my foot up again. I can't have a walking cast this time, just crutches." She tried giving him her best smile.

"I may not be such a great patient," Dylan said.

"I already know that for a fact, but I'm willing to take the risk."

"How are you going to take care of me, when you should be having someone take care of you?"

"We'll manage. Besides, we have some unfinished business to take care of, remember? I have a feeling it'll take up a lot of our time."

"I'm counting on it." He shut his eyes, trying to keep the smile on his face. Intense pain started shooting through his body.

"Can I get anything for you? Do anything?" Della said.

"Just shut up and kiss me." He opened one eye and caught the worry behind her eyes.

Della leaned over and pushed herself up in her wheel chair, gently touching her lips to his cheek. Then she lifted the sheet to look under it.

"I saw that." He opened both eyes noticing the surprise on her face as she blushed. The fuzziness around the edges cleared long enough to see a small smile form around her mouth.

"I just wanted to see if any part of you wasn't covered in bandages."

"And?"

"I'm happy to report that parts of you have been spared."

"That's reassuring." He grinned back at her. Della placed her hand on his and he grasped it and squeezed tightly through his pain. "You should go now," he said.

"No. I'm not leaving you."

"Please. I need Browning. Get him for me, will you?" His words were short and broken, his breathing labored. "Tell him about my mother. He'll know what to do." Della rushed to the door calling for Mr. Browning, confused by his request.

Browning came immediately. Upon entering the room, he observed Dylan for a while, then called the nurse. More pain medication through his IV was ordered. He waited to speak to Dylan, until he knew the pain medicine was working once again.

Della wheeled herself back to Dylan's side. "I hope you have another one of these steel beds for me to sleep in, because I'm not leaving here until he does."

"I assumed that. Arrangements have been made for the two of you. Detective Drake?" Mr. Browning called loudly. Dylan's eyes opened slowly. "Your Mother is fine. I took the liberty of handling the situation for you. Rest assured, everyone has been notified."

Mr. Browning left the room quietly.

"Dylan, don't worry. Everything's going to be just fine. I'm not leaving you. I don't care what you say. Do you hear me?"

He nodded his head slowly. His eyes opened and stared at the blank wall. He knew now that this was not some crazy dream. It was time. He turned his head slowly to Della, trying to move his arm and reach her. Managing to move an inch at a time before he stopped to rest, he searched in her eyes to give him the strength he needed right now. It would be the hardest thing he had to ever do in his life and it would be his biggest regret.

She watched as his arm moved slowly up off of the sheet and to her face. "I just want to touch you."

She placed her hand on his, caressing it against her cheek. A tear escaped, landing on his hand.

"Don't cry. I'm going to make it," he said.

"I know. I just wanted to tell you something before you fell back to sleep. I—"

"No. I need to tell you something first," his fingers searched out her lips, trying to feel them, wishing he could kiss her and feel the spark behind them once again. His mind fought the drugs, his words feeling heavy on his tongue. He needed to say this before he gave in to the pain that was killing him, much more than any physical pain his body felt at this moment. So many things he needed to say, so many things he should have told her long ago. It would be his last chance to tell her, he was sure. "I love you, Della, with all of my heart." His eyes flickered, catching one more glimpse of the most beautiful woman he had ever known before having to say goodbye. His hand slid away slowly as he struggled to save her image, forever in his mind.

Epilogue

The 30th day of September

Captain Mitchell cleared his deep voice, interrupting the chatter of the officers gathered for a special joint meeting, including all the arms of law enforcement agencies throughout Gallatin County.

"Good morning. I wanted to thank all of you for coming in this morning and for your dedication and hard work the past two weeks. Two shootings within a week in our county brought a hell of a lot of work down on all of us. Just handling the media took on a life of it's own for Public Relations Director, Officer Bradley. Both cases have been officially closed after receiving two statements that were eyewitness accounts to Father Murphy's confession and his fatal accidental shooting. Jennica James is in rehabilitation and is reported to be doing well. Her doctors expect her to recover completely. She's one tough lady. So, to everyone of you that lent a hand to solve this one, good work." Captain Mitchell turned, watching Chief Bishop talking to one of his officers.

"I have some good news and some bad news to leave you with this morning." He hesitated, looking the room over.

The room fell quiet. All eyes became alert and faced the front, waiting.

"Most of you know Detective Dylan Drake. He's not with us today, as you all can see. The bad new is and I'm sure most of you already knew, Dylan is an officer in the Naval Reserves. The Navy has sent him orders, returning him to active duty until further notice. This will be a hardship on the department. His dedication, loyalty and hard work will be missed. I want you all to know that his job will be here when he returns.

Detective Bishop will be returning after a medical leave in two weeks. The good news is that Detective William Wainwright of the Bozeman

Police Department will be joining our team at that time. He will fill Detective Drake's position temporarily until he returns.

We elected to put him in Dylan's position until the position he applied and was accepted for begins January 1 with the retirement of Officer Perty. Officer Wainwright was the top candidate for that position. Chief Bishop has consented to let him leave early, even though he isn't too happy with me for stealing another one of his men. Detective Drake transferred from the city, six years ago. He didn't talk to me for a month then," he chuckled, grinning at Chief Bishop. The room filled with laughter, watching Chief Bishop nod in agreement with the Captain.

"Officer Wainwright will assume the permanent position after the first of the year. Let's all hope Detective Drake will be back with us by then. This is a sudden move, but the strain on the department in Detective Drake's absence would be severe. We're already bogged down with some of our biggest caseloads in our history. Detective Wainwright was able to fill our needs with his impeccable record in law enforcement. I'm sure you'll all find him an asset to the department." The Captain solemnly turned away. His voice started to break up. Glancing back into the faces of his officers, they appeared shocked by his news. The room turned into a hum, changing to a low roar.

"Another thing, before you all get back to work. In the budget this year, a request was made to create a position for a staff psychiatrist. It would be funded jointly by the Bozeman PD and the Gallatin County Sheriff's Department. The Commissioners finally okayed our half. We have filled the position. Dr. Caitlin Greene put in a transfer for that position and has been selected. The County will be advertising to fill the vacant position her transfer created at the hospital. She also closed her private practice to work with us. Any questions?"

The buzz caught a hold like a whirlwind. "That's all I had for today. Thank you all for coming." Captain Mitchell joined Chief Bishop. They walked out together speaking in hushed tones, ending the special meeting.